FINCH MERLIN AND THE DJINN'S CURSE

Harley Merlin 12

BELLA FORREST

ONE

Finch

———

The cold seeped into my skin like I'd downed liquid nitrogen. Everything felt numb. A vast, white landscape of ice and snow stretched before me, interrupted by fractures that revealed a dark, impossibly deep ocean beneath. I floated above it all, half dreaming, half awake. The lines of reality blurred through the bluish haze that burned my eyes and seared into the backs of my retinas.

My body—my real body, not this *Casper* reboot—was somewhere else. I couldn't remember where I'd put it. It evaded my mind, just out of reach. Wherever it was, my body sketched these sights and put names to important landmarks. If I really concentrated, I could sense a hand trembling over a page, way off in the ether of… that other place. *My* hand. Though it felt like it belonged to someone else.

I hung in limbo, detached from my physical body yet still faintly linked. The terrain below was starkly beautiful but felt dangerous. Like I could tumble out of the sky and fall into that frigid water, never to be found.

I need a break before my eyeballs blow.

I plunged into my mind and reached for the blue-tinged strands that formed a direct line to my body. I tugged on them, as if I were a caver in trouble, which wasn't too far from the truth. A moment later, the icy world disappeared and I landed back where I'd started with a painful thump. I blinked a few times to get rid of the lingering blue haze and weird sensation of spectral floating.

"Is all well, Mr. Merlin?" A voice behind me made me jump.

"Mary, you've got to stop doing that!" I yelped, turning to face a familiar presence. "You might not have to worry about having a coronary anymore, but I'm still fair game." *Speaking of spectral floating...*

Mary Foster hovered nearby in all her translucent glory, dressed in a high-collared gown complete with a cameo brooch at her throat and about five strings of pearls. The whole nineteenth-century shebang. She had been shot by a Winchester rifle and sought sanctuary in this house after her death, as allowed by the woman who'd built the place —Sarah Winchester. Mary wouldn't admit it, but I got the feeling she liked to scare the living daylights out of me. I'd only been here a day, and she'd already made a habit of it.

Mary smiled. "You were gone for a long while. I started to worry."

"I just needed a break. No worrying required. Look at me—I'm the picture of A-OK." It made me uneasy, leaving my body in this study room with the likes of Mary and the rest of her spooky pals, who could all come and go as they pleased. They had walking through walls down to a fine art, and it made for some tense trips to the bathroom.

"Why do your eyes glow when you go into that peculiar trance?" She swooped in, coming right up to my face and stealing the breath from my lungs. Another activity these spooks just *loved* to indulge in. I'd stopped outwardly screaming about twenty-four hours ago—aka, within the first thirty minutes of arriving—but the inward screams were still in full force. Staring into the dead eyes of a ghost would never be comfortable.

I shrugged. "It's just part of the map-drawing."

"Is it coming along as you desire?" She stared down at the paper in front of me. Half of it was covered in the same lines, markings, and names as before—a partial road to Atlantis. The rest lay frustratingly blank. Etienne had underplayed the whole "it'll be more difficult without the oranges" thing. *Way* underplayed it. He'd described it as trying to write an essay, when tired, without caffeine. But this was like trying to write an essay while comatose, or, at the very least, with half my brain leaking out of my head.

So, why not regrow some more of those screamy orange willow shrubs, right? Well, as it turned out, they were hard to get hold of. The chemist team from San Francisco had swiped the last rare cutting of one to help me out, via Ryann. But they'd destroyed theirs, as per Ryann's insistence, in case they dabbled in some orange tasting and started wigging out. And Etienne wasn't about to hand more over to me, or he'd have done that before I left.

"I'm getting there. Slow and steady wins the race, right?" I broke out of my cramped headspace.

She frowned. "I am not sure that can be correct. The swiftest has always been the victor, from the races I have witnessed. Slow and steady would only win if you were racing against someone who was slower and less coordinated than you are."

"Well, lucky for me this is a one-man race, then."

I sat back in my chair and looked around the room. It always took a few minutes to readjust after delving deep into that altered state. Melody had given me a study room for privacy, though privacy was a pretty loose term with a mansion full of spirits who didn't give a damn about locked doors or "alone time." The sickly green walls, with a thick border of mahogany, hadn't gotten any prettier since the last time I took a break. If Sarah Winchester had been aiming for haunted vibes, she'd hit the bullseye.

"How long have you been watching me, anyway?" I jolted again as Mary's face loomed over my shoulder. Every time she did that, she took a good ten years off my life.

"I have decided to be your sentinel during these times. One can never be too careful in a house such as this. Not all spirits herein are as amiable as myself," Mary replied, in her clipped, old-timey British-American hybrid accent that would've put Cary Grant to shame.

I nodded. "I guess it's only natural to have a few angry souls hanging around, considering the nature of this place."

"Oh, more than a few." Mary floated off to the far side of the room. "The majority of us have softened over the decades, with a sanctuary to call home, but there are some who, I fear, will never relinquish their grudges upon the family whose rifle stole their lives."

"You never did tell me exactly how you ended up here," I said. She couldn't have been older than twenty-five, not unless she'd been using a dynamite skin cream before she died. She drifted to the hefty desk where I'd been working. Or the "escritoire," as she liked to call it.

"A man hurt me, Mr. Merlin. Well, he did more than hurt me."

Her voice sounded sad, and it made the hairs on the back of my neck prickle. I stared down into my lap, feeling guilty for bringing up the subject.

"Ah… Was it your husband?" I wasn't sure why I'd jumped to that conclusion. Given the time she'd come from, I just assumed she'd have been married.

"No, the wretch robbed me of any hope of marriage. He was a jealous suitor who did not like that I cast his affections aside for another. I went out walking with the man who might have been my husband, when he shot us both in cold blood. The man with me survived, but I... well, you can see that I did not." She hovered back and forth—the spirit version of fidgeting.

"How come you haven't crossed over?" If that had happened to me, I'd have been off like a shot on a one-way ride to the afterlife.

She laughed softly. "I suppose I am not ready to depart this world. I had so much life left to live when I was murdered, and I cannot quite surrender this existence, even if I no longer walk in the real world. Being here is a... compromise of sorts."

"It's not a curse, then, to stay here?"

"Goodness, no. It is a gift," she replied, with a faraway smile. "It is a place to appease the angrier souls, who might otherwise have turned into poltergeists. Sarah Winchester did us a great service when she built this mansion. A prime example of feminine grace and dignity. She did not have to make amends for those who died by her husband's creation, but she did. And it gives us an echo of life, though our hearts no longer beat."

I'd learned a lot about the Winchester Mystery House from Mary Foster. Sarah Winchester had hired a Kolduny to place a spell on the foundation of the house, and that spell held strong to this day. From what I'd gathered, the Kolduny magic in the very bones of this place acted as a vortex—though Mary had used the term "specter funnel"—drawing deceased victims of the rifle into the house if they didn't pass on, giving them a choice as to whether they wanted sanctuary here or not. A sort of primary intervention to prevent potential poltergeists. A lot of Ps. If they stayed, the spell made the ghosts visible and able to speak to the breathing residents, as a constant reminder of the history of the Winchester name. The main part of the house was open to tourists, but an interdimensional bubble provided the secret hiding place for the ghosts and the Winchesters.

"What wonders did you discover on your latest voyage of the mind? Did it reveal that rogue you mentioned?" Mary broke me out of my thoughts.

"Davin? No." I'd soared over Antarctica a few times now and found no sign of him. I took that as an indication that Davin was nowhere near done deciphering the map. We were still in the running.

"That is excellent news, is it not?"

I sighed. "I hope so, or Erebus will have his panties in a twist."

"Mr. Merlin! You should not speak of undergarments in a lady's presence!" She gaped in horror.

"Sorry. I mean, he'll have my guts for garters."

Mary shook her head. "Mr. Merlin, please—you will turn my cheeks quite scarlet!"

I doubt it... I didn't say so, since I didn't want to be mean. She was dead, after all. That required a softer touch.

"Erebus is that chaotic fellow you told me about? The one on whose behalf you are doing all of this map business?" Mary recovered from her mortification pretty quickly.

I nodded. "Yep, that's the one."

"You speak so very peculiarly, Mr. Merlin, if you do not mind me saying. I confess, I hardly comprehend half of what you say."

"I wish I could say you're the only one." I grinned at her.

"Will you continue in your endeavors, now that you have had a moment to collect yourself?"

I stretched out my arms. "I might go talk to Melody." I only had two more days to finish this map, but if I didn't take a breather, my brain would splatter all over these nasty green walls, which would only add to the horror-movie aesthetic.

"Oh no, you should not do that," Mary replied. "She is busy in the family library, poring over the many tomes within. I believe she seeks a way to relieve you of this exchange you have with Erebus."

"I wouldn't call it an exchange." I sighed.

She chuckled. "This burden upon you, then?"

"Does this mean you spy on everyone?" I squinted at her. "Way to make a guy feel special."

"Oh my, I did not mean to offend you! You are very special, Mr. Merlin. But you are not so interesting when you are away in that other place, with your eyes glowing. I must entertain myself, so I drift from room to room until I feel compelled to return to you."

I laughed. "You know, getting bored and flitting off doesn't make you a particularly good guard."

"I was always rather scatterbrained. My beloved mama always scolded me for having the concentration of a magpie—the moment I saw something bright and shiny, I would be off."

"Was the future husband the bright and shiny thing?"

She nodded slowly. "The brightest and shiniest."

"I'm sorry, Mary." It became clearer every hour that I had no idea how to behave around dead people. I'd even tested Melody's patience with an ill-timed joke about the difference between *The Sixth Sense* and *Titanic*—one is "I see dead people," the other is "icy dead people." She'd tutted and told me to have a little more respect. And she was probably right. But, in my defense, I always made jokes when nervous, and there was nothing more nerve-wracking than spirits coming out of nowhere and making me wish I'd worn my brown pants.

"Call me Miss Foster, if you please," Mary replied sternly.

"Of course. Miss Foster. Sorry, I keep forgetting."

She mustered a smile. "You have a face that one cannot help but forgive."

"And only a mother could love." I smirked, but she didn't get that one, either. My comedy prowess was wasted on these folks.

"I thought your mother did not love you? That is what the other spirits whispered when they discovered that Finch Merlin had arrived in this house. I suppose it is better for you, not to have been loved by such a woman, considering the monster she revealed herself to be."

Wow... let's just air out all my dirty laundry, shall we?

"You make a great point. Forget I said anything." I hurried to change the subject.

"Not that it is your fault, of course," she continued, not getting the hint. "I imagine you are very easy to love."

"Try telling Ryann that," I mumbled.

"Pardon?"

I smiled up at her. "Nothing." I hadn't been able to stop thinking about Ryann since Melody spilled the beans regarding her emotions right in front of me. There'd been love in there, among other things. Or something like love. But I was determined to consider it the real deal, even with Ted Bundy in the picture. Unfortunately, she hadn't come with us to the Winchester House, choosing to stay behind and help Kenzie out with her mom and sister instead. So, I hadn't had the chance to delve deeper into the revelation.

"You really are strange." Mary tilted her head at me. "So, will you stay a while longer and continue drawing? You seem to have made progress. I do not know what any of it means, but it is rather pretty to behold."

I glanced down at the map. The city of Atlantis, from my memory of the old one, was right in the middle of that ocean—between the big landmass of Antarctica and the smaller island of South Georgia. But I hadn't gotten to that part yet, to iron out the specifics.

"I suppose I should put in another shift." I sagged back against the chair, looking for any excuse not to dive back into it. Procrastination at its finest.

"Is Atlantis really there?" Mary drifted closer. "I heard about it in stories, as a child. I never once believed it could be a real place."

"Yep, the old girl is hiding somewhere on this page. Though you have to go through a gateway to reach it." Yet another obstacle in our search for the lost city of Atlantis. Erebus had told us about it, and I vaguely remembered writing something about a gateway in the last iteration of this map. But the details were hazy and probably wouldn't return until I redrew the entire thing.

"When I heard of Atlantis, the legend said it was underwater. Surely, no one could survive such an environment. Are we to believe there are mermaid inhabitants?"

I chuckled. "You know what, I've never seen a mermaid. Selkies and sea serpents, sure, but never a mermaid. No seashell bras or singing crabs, either." She stared at me blankly, so I continued before the ground swallowed me up. "We don't know what's actually down there… wherever 'there' is. We don't have much to go on, aside from stories. It's likely ruins by now."

"Why would this Erebus fellow want you to search ruins?"

"Another question I don't have the answer to." I put my elbows on the desk and held my head in my hands. "My guess is, it's filled with treasures and ancient, powerful artifacts. Erebus *loves* his rare toys."

Mary frowned. "Is Miss Winchester unable to answer these questions, despite her knowledge repository?"

"I wish she could." Melody was still a fledgling Librarian, and since any scrap of intel on Atlantis was as scarce as a hippo in the Mojave Desert, she had no idea what Erebus might be after. Whatever it was, it had to be pretty important if he'd gone to the trouble of getting himself a human body. He wouldn't have gotten all dressed up if he had no place to go.

"Is that an artifact?" Mary came so close, a chill shivered up my spine as her spiritual form brushed my arm.

"What?"

"That." She caressed the pendant resting against my chest. *Getting a little too handsy there, Miss Foster.*

I tugged it away from her translucent fingers. "This? Yeah, but it doesn't do anything. Not at the moment, anyway." Erebus had let me keep the Eye I'd stolen from the monastery, but he yakked on about needing rare ingredients to resurrect the dead eye inside. I got the feeling he wanted me to track down said rare ingredients, but I already had a lot on my plate. I wasn't about to go schlepping after some fancy herbs or whatever just to revive an item we might not need.

"You used it to uncover Davin's spy, did you not?" Mary drifted away from me.

I raised my eyebrows. "These walls must be very thin."

"I told you, I frequently grow bored. And when bored, I listen. There is not much else spirits can do to amuse themselves, and the fleshies within this mansion do not care for it when we use them for sport. One weak heart and a poorly timed scare in the water closet, and it ruins the pastime for the rest of us."

I had to snort. "And you wonder why we're all terrified to use the toilet?" I paused. "Wait, did you just call us 'fleshies'?"

"A colloquial term, yes. It is no worse than the names we have heard—ghouls, spooks, frighteners, wispies, and I will not repeat the curse words hurled at us when we appear unexpectedly." She sniffed. "I prefer 'specter.' It sounds dignified."

"All right, 'specter' it is. And, yeah, we used this thing to uncover

Davin's spy. Not that it did us any good, in the end," I replied. "Davin got everything he needed. He's been a step ahead of us this whole time, and it's worse now that he has my map. I wouldn't be here if he hadn't stolen it."

"Well, I am rather glad you are here. But that is by the by. Why did he take your map? What use could he have for it?"

I grimaced. "He's looking for Atlantis, same as Erebus."

"But why? What is it about some sodden ruins that has these two fellows in such haste to get to it first?"

"Yet another excellent question that I can't answer," I replied, shaking my head. I was just a teensy bit sick of those.

TWO

Finch

Time and space had become abstract concepts. I might've been floating over Antarctica for a week or a few hours. I couldn't tell. Though I supposed someone would've come to snap me back to reality if I'd been out for a week, Erebus being at the top of the list to chuck a bucket of cold water at my face, if not worse.

On Mary's insistence, I'd returned to drawing the map. Surprisingly, she'd turned out to be just the kind of cheerleader I needed. Since she knew, more or less, where everyone was in the Winchester House at any given time, she'd nipped any further attempts at procrastination in the bud before I'd even risen out of my chair.

The cold grew worse. I might've been a floating specter in this icy domain, but the bitter chill was very, very real. And the colder I got, the less I sensed my physical body. It had turned into a vague memory —a solid hand holding a quill, scratching the nib across paper. I knew it was happening, in a way, but it was far removed from my mind.

Is this what it's like for Kenzie? Not being a Morph, I had no experience as a Mighty Morphin' Power Ranger like her. But when she'd come to Greece, she'd had to throw her mind over a hell of a distance. This must be a similar sensation, though maybe without the burning eyes and numb extremities.

I thought of her for a moment and felt my hand twitch back in the study room. It was like an electrical charge passed through the blue tendrils that held me here, sent from the real world. We hadn't had much time for goodbyes, with her mom and sister emerging from the bottle—the end result of Erebus actually upholding his end of a bargain with no small print for once. She'd gone straight into nurse mode to take care of them, and we'd chalk-doored to San Jose. I regretted not hugging her, at least, but I knew I'd see her again soon.

Focus! The cold served as a sharp reminder of the task at hand. Thoughts of Kenzie faded away, and the chill bit deep with freshly sharpened jaws of ice. I wasn't sure how much longer I could stay here. Then again, I still wasn't sure how long I'd been here in the first place.

My spectral form drifted over the smaller island of South Georgia, right up to an even tinier island on the far-left side. "Island" might have been too generous. This was the Pluto of islands—a cluster of rocks with a few bits of flat ground thrown in so it wouldn't have an inferiority complex. As I inspected this island, my eyes burned brighter, and a dagger of icy pain stabbed my heart. Somehow, I could feel the burn, despite being separated from my body.

The Gateway between Life and Death... It wasn't so much a voice in my head as a thought bursting into my skull.

Casper-Finch wheeled around, fleeing the tiny speck of an island. I soared lower than before, but still stomach-churningly high. Finally, I stopped between the main continent of Antarctica and South Georgia, right in the middle of that dark ocean. A spout of water erupted, breaking the near-black surface and startling me so badly I almost spiraled back to my physical body. A pod of whales had joined my scouting session, their silky bodies moving effortlessly through the water before they disappeared again.

Beautiful... I didn't get much time to enjoy the sight. A second later, my eyes stung with blue light, blinding me. The brutal sparks filtered down to my chest and sent barbs of white-hot pain into my heart. I had no doubt that real-Finch was screaming, but I didn't have the mouth for it.

Atlantis... A new thought burst into my head without my say-so.

The pain became unbearable. It splintered through every part of me. But I dug in my figurative heels. Davin was out there in the world somewhere, racing against us. He wouldn't have given in to a little overwhelming torture, and neither could I.

Casper-Finch stopped floating. I hovered for a split second before plummeting toward the black water below. I had no way to stop my fall, especially as I had no idea what had changed. Was someone trying to snap me out of the trance? Had I done something wrong?

I braced myself for impact. Casper-Finch hit the water and disintegrated into a million blue sparks. Pain surged through me like never before—worse than Blanche's ice wall, worse than anything Katherine had ever done to me, worse than Kenneth's murder attempt.

Everything turned white.

I rocketed out of the blinding light, fighting my way to the surface. Dragging air into my lungs, I forced my eyes open. I was back in the study room, panting, my hands gripping the edge of the desk. Sweat drenched my clothes and plastered my hair to my forehead. I could taste the salt of it in my mouth, mixed with the metallic tang of blood. I must've bitten my tongue.

"Mr. Merlin?" Mary swept forward. "Mr. Merlin, are you well? My goodness, you look an absolute fright!"

"Thirsty…" I croaked. "So thirsty."

"I am not surprised. You are perspiring profusely!"

I managed a pained smile. "You don't say."

"Do you require assistance? May I fetch someone for you? Oh dear, you look rather unwell."

I shook my head. "I'll be fine in a minute."

"Are you certain? I would hate for you to… die unexpectedly."

"Don't start sizing me up for a coffin just yet." I let go of the desk, my knuckles darkening from bone-white to a less ghoulish pink. "How long was I out?"

Mary shrugged. "Ten hours or so."

"What?" I gaped at her.

"Should I not have allowed you to stay away so long?" She wrung her hands nervously.

"No… I just… didn't expect you to say that. I thought it might've been a couple of hours, tops." No wonder I felt exhausted. To be honest, I was a little put out that nobody had come to check whether I was alive. Maybe Mary had given Melody updates. I had no idea. I'd been floating across Antarctica for the last *ten hours*.

"Mr. Merlin!" Her gaze flitted toward the paper in front of me. "Mr. Merlin, you filled the page!"

I mopped my brow with the back of my forearm. "Huh?"

"The map, Mr. Merlin! You finished it!"

My gaze darted to the paper. Sure enough, all the lines and images and names were there, from corner to shining corner, just like the first one. The names were written in that same unfamiliar language. Atlantean, according to Erebus. Even though I couldn't pronounce the symbols, I knew what the words meant:

Black Rock, South Dawn, Land of the Green Lights, The Sapphire Sea, Where the Dancing of the Spirits Takes Place, and the Gateway between Life and Death. The glowing stars were there again, as well—two of them pulsated with blue light. One shone above the Gateway between Life and Death, and the other above the spot where Atlantis itself lay.

"Son of a Nutcracker!" I pounded the desk with my fists. Startled, Mary flew right back to the far wall and disappeared through it.

Aha, not so fun now that the shoe is on the other foot! She pulled herself together and floated over, clasping at her brooch.

"Congratulations, Mr. Merlin," she said, her tone oddly sad.

"You don't sound too happy."

She smiled. "I am, but it means my watch over you is done."

"I couldn't have done it without you." I reached for her hand, momentarily forgetting what she was. My fingers passed straight through, and an odd sensation made me shiver. "Seriously, you got my ass in gear. I'd still be looking for an excuse not to finish if it hadn't been for you."

"I would prefer if you did not use such coarse language, but I thank you for the sentiment. At least, I think I do—I am still not entirely sure of your meaning, most of the time." That seemed to cheer her up.

I laughed. "It's just my way of saying thanks. Now, I've got to scoot. I have good news for everyone!" I jumped up on shaky legs, taking a second to walk off the residual effects of the map-making. I'd probably ache all over in the morning, but that would be Tomorrow Finch's problem. Right now, I had adrenaline coursing through me, and I wasn't going to waste it.

Rolling the map into a scroll, I headed for the door. I was about to pull the handle when Mary emerged through it, making me stagger back.

"Mary! Dammit!"

"My apologies." She looked embarrassed. "I want to give you a warning before you go."

My heart rate slowed. "A warning?"

"I know you are already aware of the angry souls within this mansion, but I feel it my duty, as your sometimes-sentinel, to tell you to be careful in your travels around these hallways. Not all the souls here are angry, but not all of them are friendly, either." She lowered her gaze. "I would hate for anything bad to befall you. I know that you and I have only known one another for a day or so, but I feel we have become friends. I do not get to make friends very often here."

"Likewise." I felt bad for yelling at her. "And thanks for the warning. I'll be careful."

"Do not be a stranger, Mr. Merlin. I will endeavor not to frighten you next time," she said, though I didn't believe her. She had to get her kicks somewhere, and who was I to deny her some spiritual joy? Even if it was at my expense.

"Catch you later, Miss Foster." I grinned. "That means 'I'll see you soon.'"

"Ah! Very good." She stepped aside so I didn't have to put my hand through her to get to the door handle.

I opened the door and walked into the hallway, my hand wrapped snugly around the map. All I could think about was how amazing it would feel to slap this success in Erebus's face like a wet fish.

"Suck it, Ereb—" My self-congratulation turned into a shriek as I rounded the corner and collided with an oncoming figure. I almost cussed Mary out but quickly realized it couldn't be her, or any ghost for that matter. I'd bumped into something solid. Looking down, I saw Melody in a heap on the floor.

She grinned up at me. "Don't worry, it happens all the time. There are three kinds of people in this place: the ones who practically run in the hopes of avoiding any ghostly encounters, the ones who creep around for the same reason, and the ones who are so used to seeing specters that it no longer frightens them."

I stuck out my hand to help her up and hauled her to her feet. "I'm guessing you're the last kind?"

"I've seen these ghosts since I was a child. They don't frighten me any more than the living do."

I chuckled. "I don't know, the living can be pretty scary when they want to be."

"Sometimes even more so than ghosts." She linked her arm through mine, taking me by surprise. "But speaking of non-scary living people, I have two that I want you to meet!"

I arched an eyebrow. "Who?"

"My mom and dad." She squeezed my arm excitedly. "They've just come back from their business trip, and they're dying to meet you."

"You should be careful saying that sort of thing in this house," I teased.

"You're so funny, Finch. For some people, like you, it comes naturally. For others, they try so hard and never manage it." She giggled.

I cast her a sly smile. "Like Luke, you mean?"

"Finch!" She nudged me in the ribs. "He has his moments."

"I haven't witnessed any."

She dragged me down the hallway. "Did you know that laughter lowers cortisol, making us feel relaxed and comforted? It has long been theorized that laughter began as a way of connecting humans to one another and forming a community through the good feelings it creates. Crying shows distress, while laughter shows unity and bonds people together. Fascinating, isn't it?"

"They should call you the Encyclopedia, not the Librarian."

She smiled. "What would that make you? The Jester?"

"Oof, low blow."

"I didn't mean any offense. See what I mean about being naturally funny? I can never land the punchline properly." She looked genuinely guilty, switching from laughter to distress in a heartbeat. Ironic, considering what she'd just told me about human nature.

I gave her arm a squeeze. "I was just teasing—no offense taken. You keep coming at me with quips like that, you'll take my comedy crown in no time."

Her smile returned. "Phew! For an Empath, I'm pretty bad at reading people whose emotions I can't sense. I get so worried about offending folks without meaning to."

"You and the rest of the world. Nowadays, people think 'I'm offended' means 'I'm right.'"

"That's very philosophical of you, Finch."

I shrugged. "I can wax philosophical when I want to."

"Although, maybe keep it neutral with my parents? No inappropriate jokes." She flashed me a serious look. "I don't want them to get the wrong idea."

I gave a mock salute. "I'll be on my very best behavior. Besides, parents love me—my mother being the sole exception."

We walked in comfortable silence for a few minutes through the creepy labyrinth of corridors. The Winchester Mystery House was a mystery for a reason. Its hallways led nowhere, its staircases ended in ceiling, and its doors opened to blank walls. Some doorways were visible from the outside and looked like they opened to nothing but empty air. That wasn't exactly true. Most led into the interdimensional pocket, but the non-magical public didn't know that.

The house itself looked like an elaborate Disney World exhibit or a huge Swiss chalet. The red roof tiles gave the impression of castle spires, and the yellowish exterior featured Tudor-esque paneling and colorful stained-glass windows. Palm trees and landscaped gardens covered the front of the property, and two statues stood guard over the entry. Magicals could touch the stone dish of the right-hand statue and whisper *Aperi Portam* to enter the interdimensional part. A fountain stood between the two statues, too, which looked like... well, it wouldn't be polite to say. Fortunately, magicals didn't have to touch *that* to gain entry.

Rounding the corner of a hallway that actually went somewhere, we met up with my favorite person in the world—Luke. He stood anxiously by the corner, his gaze darting around like he was in the front row at Wimbledon. I guessed he wasn't quite used to the spooks yet.

"There you are!" he said, evidently relieved. Then, he saw Melody's arm through mine and scowled. The ol' green-eyed monster at play.

"I was told to look for a man with a rose in his buttonhole," I shot back, untangling my arm from Melody's.

Luke narrowed his eyes. "How about you shut your buttonhole?"

"Ooh, that was quick for you." I grinned at him. We still weren't exactly pals, but we tolerated each other. Mostly. Melody had to mediate a lot, but I liked to think of this as friendly banter.

"How come you're so sweaty?" Luke frowned. "I know it's not because you've been to the gym."

"Actually, I've been freezing my ass off in Antarctica," I replied.

He smirked. "Then shouldn't you be shivering instead of dripping?"

"I don't make the rules."

"Is that map finished yet?" Luke was giving it full sass. "You've been taking your sweet time. I don't get it—the first one didn't seem like such a big deal."

That one hit a little too close to home. "I had the oranges then. Need I remind you of the caffeine metaphor?"

He groaned. "Please don't."

"Well, the oranges made it easier, magnet-boy. Without them, it's been… tough. Like trudging through a swimming pool of mud to get to the other side, only it's my mind that's filled with mud, and the mud is on fire, and now creatures are coming out of it and trying to pull me under, and, oh, there's Satan and his pitchfork trying to jab me in the ass."

Luke snorted. "Okay, okay, so it's been a little difficult."

"But…" I brandished the rolled-up map. "Satan didn't jab me in the ass, the creatures didn't drag me down, I put out all the fires, and I trudged through that damn swimming pool to the other side!"

Melody gasped. "You did it?! Why didn't you tell me?"

"I wanted to tell you together so I could enjoy double the admiration." I grinned at her.

"Oh… but my parents. They're really eager to meet you. It's not often we get a celebrity in San Jose." Melody floundered. "You don't want to go straight to Erebus, do you? Please, it won't take long. They just want to have dinner with you, and then we can go."

"Dinner sounds good to me. I've been in my head for at least fourteen hours today. I could use some grub." I didn't want to disappoint her. She was impossible to say no to, with that adorable cherub face. "Which brings me to my next point: Why didn't someone check on me? Anyone would think you didn't care." I pretended to pout.

Melody frowned. "Mary kept me informed. Didn't she tell you?"

"No, she didn't. Then again, I didn't ask."

"She's a good egg." Melody smiled. "She would've told me if something bad had happened. Especially as she seems rather taken with you."

"Wouldn't that be a reason *not* to tell you if something bad had happened?" I replied.

"No! She's not like that. She'd never wish death on someone, after what she's been through," Melody scolded. "Besides, she's fond of a few of the men here, and they're all still alive. My dad is one of them. My mom has taken Mary aside a few times, to tell her to stop flirting with him. And it's not easy to take a ghost aside when they disappear through walls whenever they want."

I grinned. "See, you're perfect at landing punchlines."

Melody beamed. "Come on, we shouldn't keep my parents waiting —and we shouldn't keep you from eating after what you've achieved today, Finch. I'd say you definitely deserve a little celebration."

She led the way, since I was clueless about navigating this place. We headed downstairs to a country-style kitchen with a big wooden table. Two people were already sitting with half-empty glasses of wine. They looked up as we entered, before rising to greet us.

"The famous Finch Merlin!" The woman came right over and pulled me into a hug. I froze, unsure what to do with my hands. So I just let them hang limp at my sides.

"Most folks go with 'infamous,'" I joked as she pulled away.

"Nonsense. We've heard all about you, and I'd say you've done more good than bad recently. Isn't that right, darling?" She glanced at her husband.

He nodded. "Oh yes."

"This is my mom, Cecily, and this is my dad, Richard." Melody gestured to them in turn.

Cecily was a striking woman of almost six feet, with a willowy frame and silky black hair coiled in an elegant bun. Melody looked a lot like her. She had the same big eyes, though she wasn't tall like her mother. Richard was a well-groomed man in his mid-forties, with a full head of brown hair and a stocky build that couldn't have been more opposite to his wife's.

"Pleased to meet you," I said. Richard had a firm handshake, which reminded me of my first meeting with Melody. She'd told me her dad always said you could tell a lot by a person's handshake, so I made it the firmest damn handshake I'd ever given in my life.

"Let's have a toast, shall we?" Cecily declared.

"Be rude not to, after we hauled six boxes of wine all the way back from Germany," Richard replied, with a weary roll of his eyes. "Melody's mother can't resist a Riesling."

"I really can't." Cecily ushered us to the table and poured wine for Luke and me, while Richard poured something fruity and fizzy for Melody.

I took a tentative sip, letting it slip down my throat to warm my empty stomach. A surefire recipe for disaster. "You've been in Germany?"

"Mmm, yes. We had business in Berlin," Cecily replied. "There's a German ghost here who wants to cross over, but he can't until he finds out what happened to his family. Seeing as he died such a long time ago, it took some digging."

"I had my spade out and everythin'." Richard chuckled, sipping his wine. His Southern accent made me want to instantly warm to him, but I couldn't. Maybe it was because of Blanche, maybe it was something else, but I felt oddly detached from the situation. Even the wine didn't help to loosen me up.

"You'll make Finch think we're body-snatchers, talking like that," Cecily chided, giving him a despairing look.

He waggled his eyebrows at her. "Who says we aren't?"

"Do you do that a lot, then?" I thought of Mary, who couldn't give up this existence just yet.

"It keeps things interestin'. Be no good just sittin' here, twiddlin' our thumbs," Richard replied. "The business takes care of itself, so we do what we can to keep the specters happy. Wouldn't do, being the only Winchester to abandon the family promise."

I frowned. "The business?"

"This here house is the business." Richard waved a hand around. "It was my Cecily's idea to monetize the haunted house thing. I'd never have thought of it, and I wasn't too keen on the idea at first. It seemed like too much risk. But she convinced me—she always does. I guess that's why she's the brains and I'm the brawn. Ain't that right, sweetheart?"

"Someone had to bring some life into this place, if you'll pardon the pun." Cecily smiled at her husband, a hint of exasperation in her voice. A thread of friction existed between them—what I'd expect from a long-married couple who weren't the idyllic Smiths, existing in a romantic fairytale of their own creation. But they looked at each other like they loved each other, instead of wanting to wring each other's necks. Mostly. Maybe a tiny bit of neck-wringing.

"Don't let the specters hear ya." Richard put his hand over Cecily's and stroked it gently, diffusing the minor tension, before nodding toward a few ghosts I hadn't noticed. They floated around, one sweeping without a broom and the other making the motions of dusting off the mantelpiece. As if they were stuck on servitude loops from their previous lives.

"Oh, they never pay me any attention anyway. I'm not the one with Winchester blood." Cecily rolled her eyes. "That Mary Foster never listens, at any rate."

I attempted a smirk. "I've been hearing about her."

"Don't tell me she's gooey-eyed over you, too." Cecily swirled her wine like a pro.

"I wouldn't say gooey-eyed, but it's hard to tell with ghosts."

"Would you like me to have a word?" she offered.

I shook my head. "No, that's okay. She's been pretty helpful."

"I will, if you want me to. She's scared enough young men out of this house." Cecily tapped her elegant fingernails on the stem of her glass. Clearly, Mary had pissed her off one too many times.

"Easy, tiger," Richard soothed. "You know I never entertain her flirtations."

Cecily arched a perfect eyebrow. "You say that, but I've seen you blush when she tells you she likes your suit."

"Compliments are embarrassin'!" he protested.

"And when I compliment you, where are your blushes then?" she replied.

"When do you ever give me a compliment?" His eyes twinkled with mischief.

Cecily shrugged. "On special occasions."

"You'll have to refresh my memory. There was Christmas in 1998, but that was a long time ago," Richard said.

"Don't give our guest the wrong idea. I compliment you plenty," Cecily muttered. I guessed they did this a lot, judging by Melody's face. She looked like she wanted to crawl under a rock and stay there.

"What's it like, Richard, being non-magical in a place like this?" I felt antsy and needed to change the subject.

"I'm used to it. It's all I've ever known, so it's not too shockin' to the old system."

"So, you must be a magical, Cecily. Is that right?" I stared into my drink, trying to center myself. I didn't feel right. *I'm tired, that's all.*

Cecily nodded. "That's right."

"Is that how Melody ended up magical?" My hand trembled on the stem of my glass, and I couldn't get it to stop. I'd been fine until a few minutes ago, but it was like someone had flipped a switch and now I struggled to act normal. I hoped that if I kept talking, I'd be okay. This was probably just the residual effects of the map-making kicking me in the caboose. I'd been out for ten hours—that was bound to leave an impression.

"Actually, that came as a surprise," Cecily explained, casting a warm glance at her daughter. "The Winchester line has been without magic for generations. It may have been caused by the Kolduny spell put on this house; we don't know for sure. Anyway, the Winchesters only had sons until our Melody was born. None of those sons had magical abilities. And then, along came Melody, complete with Chaos—a true cause for celebration. I was convinced she'd be a boy, but Richard kept saying we'd have a girl. I suppose he won that one."

Richard smiled. "Yup, that I did. And I haven't let her forget I was right, just that once. Got to take my wins where I can get 'em."

"You must be proud of her." I took a deep gulp from my glass, praying it'd help.

"Very proud," they chorused in unison.

"Light of our lives, ain't that right?" Richard blew an air kiss at Melody, who blushed furiously.

"Dad!"

He chuckled. "What? I can't tell my little girl I'm proud of her?"

My hand tremors eased slightly. I wasn't sure if it was the wine kicking in, but I could breathe again, and the weird feeling dissipated. *See, it was just the map-making messing with you.* Every time my brain gave its input, I thought of Puffball—that cute yet terrifying manifestation of my mind gremlins.

I should've been grinning like an idiot right now, joining in the fun, but I'd been double-crossed and stabbed in the back one too many times. I had a hard time trusting anyone these days, even Melody's parents. But I made an effort to be charming, nonetheless. I wouldn't ruin our little get-together.

THREE

Finch

_____

I sat in the shower, my knees tucked up to my chin, my eyes closed. The hot water cascaded over me, and I liked the way it drowned out everything else.

I hadn't slept a wink last night, and my stomach gnawed with hunger. I'd thought the wine had helped for a short time, but it only ended up making me vomit. So, after that little trip to the bathroom, I cut out early from dinner with Melody's parents, claiming illness before I even touched a bite. But it wasn't the food I had no stomach for. It made me sound bitter and twisted, but I couldn't stand to sit there and watch all that fluffy love and happiness. They had nothing to worry about. They had each other.

But me? I had a horrible, growing fear that this wouldn't end well for me. I couldn't trust anybody, not even myself. Erebus had eyes and ears everywhere, even in his human form. And my paranoia led to darker questions. Would he leave me alive at the end of all this? Why wouldn't he just tie up that loose end? But it wasn't as if I could just throw in the towel on Atlantis, because that'd end the same way, only sooner.

You're tired. You haven't slept. Your mind has been working overtime for two days.

But given how Erebus had found his way to Kenzie, and how he'd fooled me into getting him a body, and how he'd strung me along with his friggin' breadcrumbs… the paranoia might not have been in my head. And now Ryann was involved, which just added a truckload of terror to my overextended brain. What if Kenzie couldn't wipe her mind? What if Erebus didn't let her? Or… what if something happened, and she couldn't get her memories back from wherever Kenzie wanted to store them?

She'll forget about you. Ah, those were the mind gremlins I knew, kicking me when I was down. Or maybe they were giving me the best solution when it came to Ryann. A true escape from all of the danger and trouble she was mixed up in because of me.

Stop wallowing and get your ass out of this shower. I had places to be, and none of this would fix itself by staying here. Erebus had sent me a message. No mirrors, no blood-smeared windows, just a good, old-fashioned text message. No one was more shocked than me. I didn't know if it was because of his human body, or if it had something to do with the Winchester House, but he seemed to have entered the digital age. And badly, at that. It was less of a text, more of a letter, and he'd clearly had a few issues with autocorrect.

Dear Flinch,

Meet me at the Clearist Industrial Pork at 11 o'clock in the morning. Bay 4, near the refuse collection. Do not disappoint me. You have had apple time. Three days, as agreed. If you do not have the mop by now, then you know the prize you will have to pay. I will be waiting.

Best regards,
Error bus.

Reluctantly, I clambered out of the shower and dressed. It'd probably take me an hour to find an exit, and then I'd have to figure out how to get to the Clearist Industrial Park. At least I knew Erebus wouldn't have reason to kill me today. I had his map, and he still needed me to find his gateway. So, that bought me a little more time, even if it just delayed the inevitable.

Man, I'm laying it on thick, aren't I? I had to snap out of this funk, fast.

I pulled up to the industrial park, stopping just shy of a building with a big number "4" emblazoned on the side. I'd gone for a cab in the end, and I hadn't had much trouble getting out of the Winchester House. Mary had helped me find the front door after swooping in on my aimless wandering.

"Can you circle the block for a bit?" I asked the cabbie.

He nodded. "Sure, though it'll cost you."

"That's fine." I'd rather shell out some cash instead of trying to hail another cab out here. And I really didn't want to walk back. I got out and watched the cab move off before heading for the warehouse. It took a couple of minutes to find the dumpsters, but Erebus was nowhere to be seen.

"Finch! Over here!" a deep voice hissed. I whipped around to find my old pal Erebus poking his head out of a nearby alleyway.

"What, this wasn't clandestine enough for you?" I asked as I headed toward him.

Erebus raised an eyebrow. "Pardon?"

"Nothing. I just didn't think you'd call me into some back alley in the middle of nowhere. You know this is the beginning of every *True Crime* documentary I've ever seen, right?" I sensed Erebus had a penchant for playing gangster. Even the weather had decided to cooperate, with gray clouds rolling in overhead and the first spits of rain starting to fall.

"Never mind that. Do you have what I require, or not?" Erebus ignored me and held out his hand.

"You think I'd be here if I didn't?"

He smirked. "I honestly couldn't say. Perhaps you would be foolish enough to come empty-handed. It's not as if you could hide from me. I may not have my usual skills, but I have my ways, and I am excellent at improvisation."

Why did you have to say that? The creeping paranoia set in and bristled up the back of my neck.

"Well, I've got it, so I guess we'll never know," I managed to reply, swallowing my fear. Delving into my jacket pocket, I removed the folded map and handed it to him. His eyes lit with excitement as he took it from me.

"Excellent work, Finch. I knew you had it in you." He smoothed his fingertips across the paper. "However, you look rather weak. You should rest. I would hate for your heart to give out from fatigue before you finish my work."

I shook my head. "My heart's fine, and I'd sleep better if I didn't have you and your tasks looming over me at all hours."

Erebus laughed coldly. "At least I know you're giving these matters all your attention. Now, speaking of tasks, your next will be to find the key to the Gateway to Atlantis. But, before you start complaining and despairing, you will be pleased to know that I'm giving you a few days' respite."

"What's the catch?" Benevolence wasn't one of his usual qualities.

"No catch—there are simply a few wrinkles that must be ironed out before you can start that endeavor."

I frowned. "Wrinkles?"

"This body has kept me very busy, now that I no longer have my cosmic form. My various tasks take much longer than I'm accustomed to."

"Sounds like you're the one despairing and complaining," I observed. "You wanted this, remember?" The smell of the dumpsters stung my nostrils—the sweet, sickly, foul scent of decay. Erebus didn't seem to notice.

"Watch yourself, Finch," he snapped. "Or do you need reminding of how powerful I am, even in this form?"

I sighed. "No, you've proven that. I think I've still got a lump on the back of my head from where you knocked me flat."

"Good, then let that be a lesson you actually learn."

I eyed Erebus closely. "Can I ask a question?"

"If you must."

"What happens if you lose your human body? Do you go right back to being cooped up in Tartarus? Or would something else happen?" I'd been wondering for a while, after finding out that he wasn't quite as powerful in human form.

"Mind your own business," he replied coolly.

"Can I ask another question?"

Erebus rolled his eyes. "What now?"

"You seem pretty chipper, considering Davin already has the map and now we've got to figure out this gateway key. Well, *I've* got to figure it out, once you've ironed out your wrinkles. We had an edge before, but that advantage seems to be getting smaller—or do you know something I don't?" I folded my arms across my chest. "I mean, this probably brings him level with us again, right?"

Erebus laughed, his black eyes glinting. "All this fretting you do must be exhausting."

"You think I get these bags under my eyes from kicking back and relaxing? You could send a family of six to Japan for a month with these bags—they took a lot of time and effort." That just made him laugh harder.

"There is no need to worry about Davin."

"Are you kidding? That's all you've had me doing for the past three days—freaking out over getting this map redrawn before he deciphers his copy!" I couldn't hold my anger back.

Erebus brushed his fingertips across his lapel. "I had to find some way to make you work quickly. Nevertheless, Davin does not possess the skills that I do. Thus, you needn't worry yourself over him, now that I no longer need to use that impetus to spur you on with the map-drawing."

"And threatening everyone wasn't enough? Jiminy H. Christmas, Erebus! A little transparency wouldn't kill you, you know!" I heard police sirens wail in the distance, cutting through me and ramping up my irritation.

"There is reason in everything I do. Did mentioning Davin work in speeding your progress? Yes. Therefore, transparency served no purpose. Now, let us move on to far more pressing matters… all in the name of your beloved transparency." He smirked, before continuing. "As I said, Davin lacks the skills that I possess for my current endeavor in seizing the key to Atlantis. Even so, with regards to that, the key's retrieval is more complicated than mere fetching, otherwise I would not be handing the task to you. With it being of vital importance, I would do it myself, if I could." He sounded frustrated, his confident bluster fading for a moment. I couldn't help but poke the bear a bit.

"More body troubles, or is it something else?" An alarm went off inside one of the nearby warehouses, splintering my skull like the police sirens.

Erebus's jaw twitched. "Another matter that is none of your business."

"How about telling me why you want to get to Atlantis? Or is that none of my business, too?"

"Ah, I'm pleased to see you're starting to understand. Very little of what I do is your business. I am not indulging in any exploits that will endanger or enslave the mortal world—magical and human alike—so it is of no concern to you."

Frustration rippled through me. "It involves me, so it concerns me."

"That is your problem, not mine. Just be grateful my schemes are nothing like your mother's and leave it at that." Erebus raised his palms, ending this conversation. "I will call for you again in a few days, as I said. Be ready. Do not turn off your phone. I hate to resort to such measures, but necessity compels."

He twisted his hands and vanished in a rush of hot air faintly scented with sulfur. Maybe I'd asked too many questions, but I needed answers. If he just gave me more of them, I wouldn't keep asking. But that wasn't getting through that thick skull of his.

And now I had this key to worry about, once Erebus came a-calling again. What would await me behind chalk door number one? A brand-new sports car? A teddy bear? An all-expenses-paid trip to Hawaii? No… a boatload of trouble. I'd bet my life on it.

FOUR

Finch

The cab dropped me off outside the Winchester House, leaving my pockets a lot lighter. Fortunately, with the mansion closed this afternoon, there weren't any tourists wandering around. Cecily and Richard were performing a goodbye ceremony for the German ghost. He'd filled in the gaps in his family tree so he could cross over without unfinished business. Apparently, things could get weird during these farewells, so they figured it was best to close up rather than have to deal with a bunch of screaming tourists.

I approached the right-hand statue by the front door. She was one of two sculpted women, supposedly carved in the image of Sarah Winchester, who held a shallow dish. Sometimes, people put flower petals into it, to pay their respects. Today, however, it was empty.

I put my hand on the dish and said the *Aperi Portam* spell, just the way Melody had shown me. A bronze shimmer flickered across the gap between the statues, and I walked through it, passing the slightly obscene fountain and striding up to the door.

"Finch!" Melody came running at me the minute I stepped through the door.

"Last time I checked." I patted myself down, trying to be funny. But she looked worried.

"Mary told me you'd gone out. I tried calling your phone, but you didn't answer. Is everything okay?" She scuffed the floor with the toe of her shoe. "You weren't acting like yourself last night, so I wanted to make sure. Don't get me wrong, I totally understand that dinner was probably too much too soon, after all that map-making, but you had me worried."

I forced a smile. "I made the handover with Erebus. He chose somewhere suitably cloak and dagger, and I didn't want to drag anyone else along. I should've sent you a message or something. And sorry about last night—I felt completely out of it and I didn't want to babble nonsense all night. Your parents probably think I'm a weirdo now, right?"

Melody looked instantly relieved. She chuckled. "They're used to weirdos here. Do you feel better now? Did everything go smoothly with Erebus? You don't look hurt, so I'm guessing it did. Did he tell you anything else about Atlantis, or what he wants next? Did he know anything about—"

"Whoa, whoa, whoa there!" I lifted my hands in mock surrender. "Go easy on me, Sarge. It's too early in the day for the Gestapo."

"Sorry." Her cheeks flushed. "I got carried away again, huh?"

"Hey, I'm a big fan of your enthusiasm, but I've got a 'handle with care' label slapped on me today." I didn't want her to ever apologize for who she was, but my head couldn't withstand a Melody barrage right now. Baby steps and eggshell tiptoeing were required.

"There you are, Melody." Luke appeared from the nearside corridor, looking pale. "I went to the library to find you, but you weren't there. Then Mary leapt out of the wall and told me you came this way."

I smirked. "She gave you the willies, huh?"

"Excuse me?" he shot back. If I'd been in my right mind, I'd have died laughing.

"I mean, she scared you?"

"I didn't expect her, that's all," he countered sheepishly.

Melody smiled. "I saw Finch from the window and came down as quickly as I could."

"Where were you?" Luke frowned at me. "Do you know how worried Melody has been?"

"Go easy on him, Luke. He just came back from Erebus," Melody told him.

"Oh." Luke visibly relaxed, then stood next to Melody. I noticed he stopped as close to her as possible without being creepy. He and I weren't so different, pining after girls who were either oblivious to our feelings or couldn't feel the same. A pair of poor, lovesick chumps.

"So, the next stage is to find some key that'll get us through the Gateway between Life and Death and into Atlantis," I began. "Erebus is still working out some wrinkles—he'll call in a few days when we're ready to rumble."

Melody rubbed her earlobe, a nervous tic. "But how did Erebus order you to go and meet him?"

I snorted. "By text."

"Ah, that makes sense," she replied.

"It does?"

She nodded. "Well, he wouldn't have been able to breach the house defenses to send you a message."

"He wouldn't?" I was starting to sound like a dumbass.

"No, he wouldn't," Luke cut in. "The mansion is sort of like the monastery, in that sense. The interdimensional bubble is reinforced with Kolduny protection spells that keep unauthorized personnel out, and the spirits here are on constant watch to defend it."

Melody gazed up at him in admiration. "Exactly. This is their safe haven, so they have a vested interest in protecting it from miscreants—including communication spells, transportation spells, and any other unwelcome spell that tries to slip past the outer defenses. That's why, when we chalk-doored here, we showed up outside."

"Seriously?" That certainly answered my question about why Erebus had turned to digital communication. Although, what human could resist the pull of a shiny new cellphone? He'd probably be snapping pics for Instagram before he was done. *#Atlantis #Childof-Chaosvibes #humanbodygoals*

"Super serious." She gave me a reassuring look. "So, if you're worried about Davin getting in or Erebus making the statues move, don't. You're safe. We're all safe here. It's the perfect place to work on this Atlantis project; that's why I suggested it." Other folks would've been smug about the vast expanse of a home she'd brought us to, but Melody didn't have a smug bone in her body.

I sighed. "Can I just stay here for the rest of my life, then? It's not exactly Vegas, but I'd get used to it. I could even learn to like the jump scares, after a while."

"I wish I could say yes, but Erebus is still a Child of Chaos. If he had to get in here to find you, I'm sure he would use everything in his arsenal to break down its defenses." She lowered her gaze. "I'm just saying, you're safe from Davin in here, and from Erebus's less-human avenues of communication."

"Just when I thought I'd cracked it." I sighed. "Have you made any headway on my Erebus problem?"

Melody's eyes lit up. "Actually, yes. Well, yes and no. It's more of a maybe, but it's a fairly good maybe."

"Color me intrigued." I pretended to scratch my arm with an imaginary pen.

"You're an idiot." Luke scoffed.

Melody flashed him a look. "Be nice. You know he makes jokes when he's nervous. Speaking of which, do you know the effects anxiety can have on a person? It affects the brain, yes, but then the brain sends all sorts of messages to the rest of the body. It can have an impact on physical health, putting a strain on the heart and lungs as well as causing muscle tension, shortness of breath, shaky hands, palpitations, pins and needles, and insomnia. There can also be fatigue, dizziness, dry mouth, excessive sweating, and all sorts of other symptoms."

"Aren't I the lucky son of a gun? So many symptoms, so little time." I thought back to last night's weirdness. Melody had pretty much described all the symptoms that hit me out of nowhere. Was I just anxious? Somehow, that comforted me. Giving that strange attack a name made it easier to deal with. I'd already discovered that old chestnut when I'd had my delusional disorder diagnosis. Although, my trusty pills had been the biggest help with that one.

"So, what's the fairly good maybe?" I returned my attention to Melody.

"I'm looking into a connection to the djinn," she replied. "I was delving into my mind palace to find as much information as possible, and I came across the name of a book—it's called *The Dark Souls of the Magical World*."

I smirked. "Nice and ominous."

"Now, I'm still figuring out how to pluck information from books mentally without having the actual book in front of me, which means we may have to find it and read it normally," Melody continued. "But it's got detailed intel about the djinn and their connection to Erebus's power, and I think that might be our key—not the Atlantis gateway key. I have no idea about that. I mean, the key to getting you out of your deal."

"My favorite kind," I replied, with none of my usual sarcasm. Melody's research meant we might have a lead. And I'd waited so long for a shred of hope.

"Did you find somewhere that sells this book?" Luke smiled at her like an adoring puppy. He might as well have licked her face.

Melody nodded. "I found three locations. It's a rare book, but it's not the sort that's impossible to find, or buried under a temple somewhere. There's actually one in your neck of the woods, Finch."

My heart leapt. "There is?"

"Yes, in a bookshop called 'Buy Its Cover,' located in Waterfront Park. Does that ring any bells?"

I tapped my temple. "Oh yeah, they're all clanging."

"And you think the solution might be in this book?" Luke prompted. He clearly just wanted to hear her rattle on some more… and to be honest, on this topic, so did I.

"I think it might give us more information about Erebus and how he liaises with his underlings. You mentioned he has eyes and ears all over, and that got me thinking—what if he's able to do that through a network of djinn? What if they make up the bulk of his minions?" Melody said excitedly. "I've learned that djinn are connected to one another, and they, in turn, are connected to Erebus, so it makes perfect sense. That would give him a certain level of omniscience, or at least be enough to fake it."

"I thought he *was* omniscient. Aren't all the Children of Chaos?" I frowned. Had that thorn in my side duped me?

Melody shook her head. "Not in the way you might think. They must all have similar networks that allow them to give that impression. Take Gaia, for example. As she controls where Chaos goes, she can probably use all magicals with that gift to see and hear through. As for the others… I don't know what their networks are, but they must have them. I imagine they wanted to keep an eye on the mortal world after they were shipped off to their otherworlds for being meddlesome."

I frowned. "But how does that relate to me?"

"You and the djinn have something in common where Erebus is concerned. You're technically one of his minions, too. So, if anything, or anyone, knows how to detach someone from Erebus's 'network,' it'll be the djinn." She shot me a hopeful grin. "And the book should be filled with general information about Erebus, as well, since it's very old and is aimed almost exclusively at djinn lore, and ergo, Erebus lore. From what I've found, it was written before the Bestiary was even founded."

I gave a low whistle. "She's going to be dusty. I'll pack my antihistamines."

"Then don't go operating any heavy machinery." Luke snickered, pleased with himself.

"I'll try to keep away from the combine harvesters and cherry-pickers, just so you don't worry yourself over little old me." I gave him my best butter-wouldn't-melt smile.

"I don't worry about you," Luke replied stiffly.

I made a show of wiping my eyes. "Ouch, that hurt. You wound me, Luke. You wound me deeply."

"With skin as thick as yours? I doubt it," he huffed.

"I might look like an elephant, after all that goat cheese in Greece, but I've got quite a thin skin, really." It was only half a lie.

"Did you know that elephants, when they see humans, have the same mental reaction that we have to puppies?" Melody chimed in.

I mustered a lackluster chuckle. "I imagine it's similar to the reaction Luke has to you whenever you enter a room. Although, that might give him too much credit—he's probably just the puppy."

"That's not true!" Luke protested. "I'm not some puppy."

"Could've fooled me. All you're missing is the wagging tail," I shot back, but I wasn't really feeling it. Usually, landing a comedy jab gave me a rush of satisfaction. But this one just left me... hollow. Maybe another symptom of anxiety. Or maybe I needed to take another dose of my pills. I was supposed to take two a day, but I'd upped it since leaving the monastery. The mind gremlins had grown rowdier than usual after my first orange-poison trip, and the only thing that kept them vaguely at bay were those pills. Truthfully, it hadn't been this bad since I'd first met Harley and messed with the gargoyles back at the SDC. My condition, and my gremlins, hated being ignored. Soon, I'd be taking half a bottle to stop them fighting their way through.

Luke opened his mouth to retaliate, but Melody put her hand on his arm, and he closed it instead. He eyed me curiously, making me feel as if I were under a big, glaring spotlight. Why was he looking at me like that? Did he know something was wrong with me? Could he sense it? I hadn't told them about my delusional disorder, but that didn't mean they couldn't see it in me.

"So, I guess this means I'm going back to the SDC for a while?" I didn't want to banter anymore. And I didn't want them to start asking questions. "I can go and get the book, and I'll drop in on my sister at the same time. You know what, this could be good timing—I've kind of missed the place."

"Aww, you miss her!" Melody clasped her hands together. "I've actually wanted to meet the famous Harley for a long time. Why don't

Luke and I come with you, to keep you company? I'm very interested in learning more about the SDC and in putting faces to the names of all these people you've been telling us about. The Rag Team—that's what you call yourselves, isn't it?"

"Muppet Babies, and I'm only an honorary member," I corrected her, using my preferred term. "But I don't think it's a good idea for you to come along. Another time, maybe. I should scope out the security first before I bring the new Librarian over. We wouldn't want you causing a ruckus, now, would we?"

Luke nodded. "I agree. I'll need a full security report before we can even think about going."

"I'll be fine. No one will know who I am," Melody replied desperately.

"Even so, we can't take the risk." Luke offered her an apologetic smile. "You said it yourself, Melody—we're safe here, with the spirits protecting the house. The SDC is unknown territory. I'm sorry. I know you're eager to meet Harley and the rest of Finch's... uh, Muppet Babies, but it'll have to wait."

She sighed sadly. "Being the Librarian sucks sometimes."

"But it comes with some damn good perks." I flashed her a wink.

Honestly, my reasons for keeping Melody away weren't entirely selfless. I wanted to keep her safe, sure, but I had no clue how my mental state would play out. Even if it was just a case of severe anxiety layering itself on top of my gremlins, I needed to be around people who understood my condition in case it got worse. Which I had a horrible feeling it might. I'd already had four pills today, and I may as well have been taking Tic Tacs.

FIVE

Finch

There wasn't much more to say after that. Luke wouldn't let Melody run wild in San Diego, and I had a book to find and a sister to hug. So, I'd said "See you later" to them and popped my head in to say thanks to Cecily and Richard before heading back to the closest thing I had to a home. I'd have preferred a glitzy set of ruby slippers to get me there, but a chalk door to the Science Center and using the front door worked just as well.

It felt weird to walk these hallways again after everything I'd been through at the Fountain and the monastery. I kept expecting a monk to suddenly appear and usher me into a pottery studio or something. Instead, I got some curious looks and whispers from the other members of the coven.

That's right, lads and lasses, get a good eyeful—the boy is back in town. I checked my phone and saw a message banner. I'd texted Harley the moment I landed, so to speak.

You're back?! Meet me in the Alton Waterhouse Room! I promise I won't strangle you.

Not exactly the fanfare I'd been after, but at least I'd get to see her. Man, I really had missed her. Being the Count of Compartmentalization, I hadn't let myself linger on it, but all that delayed emotion crashed into me at once. Having to keep secrets from her, and not letting her help me, hadn't been easy.

Fifteen minutes later, I stood nervously outside the Alton Waterhouse Room—formerly the Luis Paoletti Room. A fitting tribute to our fallen director. I'd want something way bigger if it were getting called the Finch Merlin Room, but hopefully there'd be no homages to me anytime soon.

I stepped in. Immediately, a Harley-shaped bulldozer hurtled into me, almost sending me flying back into the corridor.

"I missed you so much!" She flung her arms around me and squeezed tight. This time, I knew exactly what to do. No limp-arm syndrome here. I pulled her close and hugged her hard, stopping just short of crushing her.

"I missed you, too," I murmured into her shoulder. "So friggin' much."

She pulled away. "It's so good to see you, Finch. Seriously, after you disappeared from the Jubilee mine, I almost lost my mind. Everyone was pretty glad when I finally got word from Ryann that you were okay. I went a bit militant for a while."

I chuckled. "What's new? I blame the special-agent uniform."

"Hey, I like this uniform." She stared at me like she couldn't quite believe I was real.

"That's part of the problem. You'll have everyone saluting next."

Her eyes turned suddenly sad. "You look like crap, bro. Haven't you been sleeping?"

"Not really." I'd popped two more pills before I came back, to keep the gremlins behind enemy lines. But I could still feel them nagging away, trying to wiggle through. Like mental fruit flies that I couldn't get rid of, no matter what I did.

She looked concerned. "You're not doing well, are you?"

I shrugged. "You know me. I'll be fine, I've just got a lot on my plate."

"Are you going to tell me *what* exactly is on your plate?" She ushered me over to the stools by the main workbench. I sank down, letting out the kind of weary groan you'd expect from an octogenarian trying to get out of an armchair.

I hesitated. "Didn't Ryann tell you?"

"She told me you were on a job for Erebus, that's it. I tried to get her to say more, but she said you'd explain when you were ready." Harley put her hand on mine and curled her fingers around it. "What's going on with you, huh? You can tell me. Whatever it is, I'm here for you."

"I know…" The "but" hovered in the air between us.

"Actually, I've done some research into Erebus myself. I know you told me not to get involved, but he's got you by the balls, Finch, and I couldn't just sit here and do nothing. I wanted to try and find something, anything, to… well, get your balls free, if that's not super-weird of me to say."

I gaped at her. "You haven't. Tell me you haven't."

"I'm your sister and you're in trouble. Of course I wasn't going to listen to you." She squeezed my hand tighter.

Panic rushed through my veins, piggybacking on my twitchy anxiety. She'd been researching Erebus? Why hadn't she listened? I'd more or less begged her not to do anything about it, and she'd gone ahead and investigated anyway. Then again, I'd have been a class-A hypocrite if I laid into her about it. If she were in my position, I'd have done exactly the same thing, swooping in to try and save her. In fact, I'd already done that.

I'd snapped at Erebus just this morning about being transparent, when I was leaving my own trail of frustrating breadcrumbs for my sister. Knowledge had power. And, maybe, the best way to keep Harley safe was to give her the bigger picture. Then, she might understand the danger everyone I cared about was in. And that might be enough to stop her from digging deeper and traveling into even more treacherous waters.

"You need to stop looking into Erebus," I said. "I'll tell you what's been going on, but you have to promise not to keep investigating on your own."

She peered at me cautiously. "How can I promise that if I don't know what you're going to tell me?"

"You just have to." I sighed. "Please, sis. Trust me on this."

"I can give you a conditional promise." *Why do you always have to be so stubborn?*

"Unconditional, or I can't tell you the truth," I insisted. "Lives are at stake if you don't. Namely, yours."

Her gaze darkened. "Okay… then, I guess I promise."

"Unconditionally?"

She bit the inside of her cheek. "Fine. Unconditionally."

"Here's the short version." I took a breath. "Erebus is planning something huge. I don't know what—I really don't—but it's big. I don't know what Garrett and Saskia told you about the Jubilee mine, but Erebus got himself a nifty little meat suit from the Fountain of Youth hidden there, which is now drained and buried under all that rock. Now, he's looking for Atlantis."

"Atlantis?" she gasped. "Why Atlantis?"

"Oh, you have no idea how many times I've asked that question. It's literally on repeat in my head, like I've been Atlantis rick-rolled."

She gave a nervous smile. "Erebus isn't spilling the beans?"

"Erebus *never* spills the beans. So, I have no idea why he's looking for Atlantis, but I *do* know he's not on the same psychotic trail as my mother. A shred of good news in a mountain of crap. He says none of this has anything to do with enslaving humanity, and, I can't believe I'm saying this, but I believe him. It seems... personal, somehow."

"How can you be sure?" She leaned forward on her stool, no doubt having Elysium flashbacks. I could almost see the memories of Katherine's cracking face flitting across her eyes, oozing black goop.

"The human body gives it away," I replied. "It took him a lot of scheming to get it, and it's giving him a few glitches. Glitches he'd already prepared for by sending me across the globe, picking up Ephemeras. If he wanted to lord it over humans, he'd have done it already. He's still powerful enough to make it happen, so we're not dealing with Katherine Mark 2."

Harley's mouth gaped like a beached fish. "So, Erebus is... human now?"

"Well, human hybrid is more accurate," I replied. "He's got most of the Child of Chaos juice, but he's run into some limitations now that he's all fleshy."

"Is that what the Ephemeras were for?" That was the beauty of Harley—she always asked the right things.

I nodded. "I didn't know why I was collecting them at the time, but most of the trips I took for him involved finding rare Ephemeras from ancient magicals. They're basically like his premium unleaded, to fuel his human body and make the limitations less of a problem for him."

"Is that where you've been? Searching for more Ephemeras?" She kicked her foot anxiously against the workbench.

"No, Erebus tasked me with finding Atlantis. That's what I've been doing."

She took a shaky breath. "Did you find it?"

"Yeah, I did."

"You *found* it?! It's real?" Her eyes bugged. "I mean… how did you find it? How do you even go about finding a mythical place like that? Atlantis is the biggie, right—up there with El Dorado and Shangri La, and all that legendary stuff?"

"Oh yeah, and that, my sweet sis, is a pretty long story. Let's just say I had to go into an altered state of mind for it. A bit like Euphoria." I wasn't deliberately keeping the monastery from her; I just didn't have the energy to go into detail. My body felt like lead, and the more I spoke, the more I sensed the uprising of the gremlins. Besides, the specifics didn't matter.

She nodded in understanding. "Then we need to research Atlantis. Maybe there's a clue somewhere."

"No, you can't go searching for intel on Atlantis, or Erebus. He's already threatened the lives of everyone I love, which is why you need to listen this time and keep away from the missions he's got me on," I urged, my heart sinking. "It's bad enough that Ryann is involved, and I didn't know about that until it was too late. But as long as I keep toeing the line and everyone keeps their heads down, Erebus won't have a reason to hurt her. I'm not planning on giving him one. However, if Erebus found out that you—the Great and Powerful Oz— were looking into him and his plans, and he thought you were trying to thwart him, he'd kill Ryann without batting an eyelid. That *would* give him a reason to get trigger-happy."

"Let me get this straight—if Erebus thought I was trying to ruin his plans, and thought you were somehow involved in it because you're my brother, he'd kill Ryann to punish you?"

"Got it in one, sis."

Her expression shifted toward the curious. "Because she means a lot to you?"

"We're not getting into this again," I replied, with a subtle warning in my voice. "But that's what he thinks, and he's not going to change his mind about it. Right now, she's leverage, and I don't want her getting used against me for any reason."

Harley's shoulders sagged. "I'm guessing he's not bluffing?"

"When has a Child of Chaos ever bluffed? Like I said, this job feels personal, and he'll take it personally if he thinks someone is trying to get in his way. It's safer for everyone if you stay out of it." I shifted uncomfortably in my seat. "I wish you could help. But you can't. All I can offer you is the truth so you can see the danger we're all in."

"We know what the wrath of a Child of Chaos feels like better than anyone, right?" She gave a wry laugh, but her face hardened with worry.

"Oh yeah, and I doubt either of us wants a repeat."

She held my gaze. "You're sure it's not going to affect humanity?"

"As sure as I can be, but I promise you, you'll be the first to know if that changes. The first whiff of global domination, and I'll be speed-dialing you."

Her eyes glistened. "You've really been through the wringer, haven't you?"

"About a hundred times, yeah." I choked out a laugh. "I should be flat as a pancake by now."

"For what it's worth, I'm glad you told me everything. Even if I can't help, at least I can understand why." She chuckled sadly. "Let's face it, if I were in your shoes, I'd run off trying to do it all solo too."

"You *did* try to do that, remember?" I managed a smirk, but it felt off. All of me felt off. This tall glass of milk had soured. It made me glad that Harley couldn't use her Empath mojo on me, or she'd have been able to tell that I was on the edge and struggling to keep up appearances.

"Yes, and now I'm getting major déjà vu. I'll be honest, I don't like it one bit, but you've made a heck of a case." She sighed and shook her head. "I hate that you're going through this. Erebus should've let you go by now, but he was always a snake. And I'm worried about you, still tied to him like this. I'm worried about Ryann, I'm worried about the rest of us, but you're the one with the ax hanging over your head. I hate it. And I hate it even more because it should've been me."

"Then we'd be having this conversation on opposite stools," I reminded her. "And I'm friggin' thrilled you're not sitting where I am. I don't have the willpower that you do. I'd have wound up dead a long time ago by sticking my nose in, if you'd been tied to Erebus instead."

"Still…"

"Or I'd have offed myself for having to deal with a mopey Wade. He'd have had all this separation anxiety and jealousy, wondering if you were having a wild fling with some Polynesian beefcake while picking up an Ephemera for the Prince of Darkness." I forced myself to lighten the mood, and it seemed to work.

She chuckled. "I suppose I wouldn't have been able to tell him, would I?"

"Not unless you wanted Erebus dangling him over a sea of Purge beasts or threatening his life at *literally* every possible opportunity. He just loves to whip that one out. I think it might be his party trick."

"Why Polynesian?" She raised an eyebrow.

"Why not Polynesian?" I shot back, with a grin. "They are some beautiful people. I nearly got a tattoo during my stay, but it wouldn't have had the same impact as the guys out there. No one wants to see me roaming around with my top off."

She flashed a genuine smile. "You didn't nearly get a tattoo!"

"You're right, I've already got two I don't want. If only they were drunken mistakes I could laser away."

"You know, I used to hate this thing." She pulled up her sleeve to reveal her golden Apple of Discord. "But now, I look at it and I remember everything we did. I remember that we finally killed Katherine. And it doesn't feel like her symbol anymore—it feels like ours. Yours and mine, bonding us together."

"Has Wade been reading self-help books to you again? How to turn a negative into a positive—that sort of fluff?"

She gave me a despairing look. "He doesn't read self-help books."

"He does. I've heard him rattle off philosophical garbage like he's center stage at his very own TED Talk."

She stifled a snort. "I've missed having you around."

"I've missed being around." I lowered my gaze. "And I like what you said about the apples. You know me, I struggle with the warm and fuzzies, so I say something snarky instead."

"I love you, bro." She put her hand over my tattoo.

"I love you, too, sis."

"You're going to get through this. You know that, don't you?"

I shrugged. "Some days, yes. Some days, no."

"If Erebus tries to screw you over, or he hurts you, then I'm sorry, but I'll break my promise not to get involved. He'll learn what human wrath can feel like if he does anything to you."

"Hell hath no fury, right?"

She nodded. "Exactly."

"Let's hope it doesn't come to that."

A tense silence stretched between us, both of us waiting for the other to break it. In the end, Harley took the leap.

"We should probably go see O'Halloran. He'll know you're here by now, since you came through the front door, and he'll be eager to see you." Harley got up, and I had no choice but to follow. Even if every step felt like trudging through that proverbial mud pool. Only it wasn't Satan and his pitchfork waiting to jab at me—it was my mind gremlins.

We hadn't gotten too far through the coven, when the man himself appeared around a corner. Diarmuid the leprechaun sat on his shoulder, the two of them dressed in identical black suits. *Ugh... I'd forgotten about you.* The angriest, scariest creature under ten inches.

"Finch, there you are. I hoped to catch you before you left." O'Halloran put out his hand. I gave him a handshake, as firm as I could muster.

"We were just coming to find you," Harley replied.

"Ach, so ye've brought me on a wasted trip, ya great, daft mushroom." Diarmuid threw up his tiny arms. "I told ye, they'll come te ye. Ain't that what being director is all about?"

O'Halloran laughed. "I think he's pleased to see you, as well."

Diarmuid shot him a dirty look. "Stuff that up yer arse. I ain't pleased to see no one."

"It's good to be back, Director O'Halloran," I said, trying to keep my distance from the leprechaun.

"Where's yer red hair? Ginger ain't good enough for ye no more?" Diarmuid peered at me.

"Just trying not to look like a Shipton," I replied.

"Aye, that'll do it." Diarmuid barked a laugh, somehow more terrifying than his perpetual anger.

"Now then, I hear you've been on a mission for Erebus. How's that going?" O'Halloran took me by surprise.

"Uh... fine. The usual." I stumbled over my reply. How did he know that? I'd forgotten O'Halloran's knack for gathering intel.

Harley shifted awkwardly. "I may have told him what Ryann told me."

"Ah, right." So that was how he knew. "Yeah, it's all… uh… going smoothly. Nothing I can't handle."

"Aye, and I'm a soddin' unicorn," Diarmuid muttered. "Ye couldn't handle a donkey."

"Is it anything I should worry about? If I need to rally forces, I have to know as quickly as possible." O'Halloran ignored him and focused on me.

I shook my head. "Nope, no cavalry required. It's more of a self-serving thing for Erebus, from what I can tell."

"Would you mind coming to my office so we can talk more about it?" O'Halloran said.

"Ach, yer pullin' me leg!" Diarmuid complained. "Ye drag us all the way out here, now yer wantin' te go all the way back? I bet if I looked in yer ear, I'd see right through te the other side."

How do you get through a meeting with THAT chirping at you all the time? I would've said it out loud if I wasn't certain Diarmuid was hiding his mighty shillelagh somewhere. And he'd give me a few choice whacks if I insulted him.

"Actually, we're in a rush," Harley cut in, ever the good sister. "Can we catch up another time?" Now that she knew the stakes, it seemed to be working in my favor.

O'Halloran frowned. "Yes, I suppose it can wait. But didn't you say you were coming to find me?"

"We were just going to stick our heads in and say hello on our way to see the others," Harley replied without missing a beat. Oh, she was good. I'd forgotten how good.

I missed you, sis. I really did.

O'Halloran nodded. "Right, you must be looking forward to seeing them after being away so long."

"Very much so," I said.

"Then, I won't keep you. But I do want us to continue this talk later," O'Halloran insisted.

I smiled sweetly. "Sure thing, Director."

Leaving a curious O'Halloran and a nagging Diarmuid behind, Harley and I pressed on.

"Thanks for that," I whispered. I expected a "no problem" or a "don't mention it." Instead, Harley turned to me with a furrowed brow.

"I just hope you know what you're doing," she said firmly. "And, please, remember your promise. As soon as this starts to sour, you tell me so we can figure something out together. Just because I can't help you now doesn't mean I'm not ready to dive in at a moment's notice."

"Hey, I'll stick to my promise, you stick to yours."

"Fair exchange." Her lips turned up in a slight smile. "On one condition."

I squinted at her. "What condition?"

"You come to Ignatius's Restaurant tonight at eight o'clock."

I groaned. "I'm not in the mood for dinners and stuff. Anything that requires more than a T-shirt and jeans, I'm out."

"Not taking no for an answer, Finch. You're hauling your ass to Ignatius's tonight, or I will flay you."

"Maybe I'll flay myself and make you stare at my sinews over spaghetti Bolognese. I bet that'd put you off. Is it mincemeat, is it Finch, who knows?" I managed my first real laugh. What could I say? I was hilarious, even in a deteriorating mental state. Maybe more so.

She shot me a withering look. "Eight o'clock. Be there. I mean it."

"All right, all right, I'll be there. I'd rather sit through a meal than have you chasing me around, guilt-tripping me for the rest of my life."

"Good." She smiled, evidently satisfied.

My phone pinged. I took it out and hardly dared to look at the screen, in case it was another autocorrect minefield from Erebus. Instead, Melody's name flashed. Puzzled, I swiped the banner and read the message:

Hi Finch! Hope you don't mind, but we had a change of plans. I'm outside the Fleet Science Center. Luke's here, too. I managed to badger him into submission! Yayyyy! Come let us in.

I rolled my eyes. Of course she'd badgered Luke into bringing her here. That man just couldn't say no to her big eyes. The moment I'd indulged in a bit of showboating and mentioned knowing Tobe back at the monastery, I should've known it'd spell trouble. Melody had a weakness for all things knowledgeable, including the Bestiary, and she wouldn't leave until she'd seen it herself and spoken to its big pussycat of a guardian.

"Who is it?" Harley asked, like a paranoid girlfriend.

I put the phone away. "Come with me. There's someone I'd like you to meet."

SIX

Finch

———————

"Should I be worried about who we're meeting?" Harley asked as we exited the coven and headed through Kid City. A few rug rats ran around making a nuisance of themselves. Tommy Pickles had Chucky in a headlock while their moms chattered amongst themselves, talking about their plans for next weekend.

"Nope. She's all cotton candy and fairy dust."

Harley pulled on my arm. "Are you being sarcastic?"

"For once, no." A few minutes later, we made it through the glass doors of the Fleet Science Center and out into the warm sunlight. I drank it in and enjoyed the gentle breeze drying the sheen of sweat that had beaded on my forehead. *Here comes the excessive sweating Melody warned me about... The laundromat better be ready.* My hands trembled slightly, but I shoved them in my pockets to hide it. It would pass, like it had at the table with the Winchesters.

Melody being here had amped up my nerves and set the gremlins jittering. I mean, she hadn't really given me time to scope out the security measures. Then again, the SDC had security up to the eyeballs after the Katherine-Imogene fiasco. O'Halloran had implemented every protocol around. After a lifetime in covert military operations, he was practically the maestro of all things security. Without him, Harley and Wade wouldn't have had their shiny new uniforms. Even so, having the Librarian here just stank of a bad idea. It brought a different kind of danger—one that O'Halloran might not have prepped for.

"Finch!" Melody waved from a short way up the road. Luke stood beside her, as ever.

"I've got to say, this is an unexpected surprise," I said dryly.

Luke grimaced. "For you and me both."

"Did she take all your toys away, until you promised to bring her?" I arched a knowing eyebrow.

"I tried to sit and wait for you to come back, I really did, but it seemed more useful if we were close by. I realized you might not know what you... uh... needed, so I thought we could drop in and make sure everything was clear as crystal," Melody replied, blinking innocently up at Luke. "I also convinced him it would be an invaluable learning opportunity, and you know me—I love a learning opportunity."

I gave a weary smile. "Queen of the bibliophiles."

"I like that!" She beamed, making it difficult to hold a grudge. She absolutely shouldn't have been here, but how could anyone say no to that enthusiasm? It radiated out of her, like a perpetual kid on Christmas.

"Sorry, my brother is terrible at social etiquette," Harley interjected. "I'm Harley Merlin."

"Oh, I know!" Melody chirped. "Everyone knows who you are. I've heard all about you from the papers, and the news, and from Finch, of course. The way he speaks about you is so beautiful. I can tell you mean a lot to him. You know, I always wanted a sibling, and I used to beg my mom and dad for a little brother or a sister, but they said they were happy with just me. And I suppose you can't force them, can you?"

"You might consider taking a breath there, Melody," I teased.

Her mouth fell open. "I'm so sorry, Harley. I've been rabbiting on without letting you get a word in edgewise. I guess I'm the one who's forgotten my social graces." She put out her hand. "I'm Melody Winchester, and this is Luke Prescott. He goes everywhere with me."

I cast him an amused look. "He really does. Stuck to her like glue."

"Well, it's nice to meet you, Melody." Harley shook her hand, then moved on to Luke. "Are the two of you together, then?"

Melody giggled nervously. "No, nothing like that. He takes care of me. A bodyguard of sorts… not that I need a bodyguard! There's nothing special about me, unless you count being a Winchester as special. My parents are just overly protective, so he goes where I go."

Oh, Melody. That mouth of yours will get you in trouble one of these days. She'd babbled a little too much. Harley could sniff a rat from twenty feet away, and we were a lot closer than twenty feet. I hoped she'd chalk it up to youthful exuberance and Melody's tangible elation at meeting the famous Harley Merlin. Meanwhile, Luke tried not to look crushed. I had to hand it to the guy: he had perseverance by the bucketload.

"A Winchester? As in the—" Harley started to speak, but I cut her off.

"Yep, the rifle guy and the creepy house. It's got spooks coming out of every outlet."

Harley frowned at me. "How do you know?"

"That's where I've been the last couple days," I whispered. "I met these guys on my latest mission for the E-man. They were supposed to wait in San Jose, but I guess they just couldn't stay away."

"I really did try," Melody said, her tone apologetic. She couldn't fool me. She was itching to get inside the SDC and pick Tobe's brain.

"How did you even get here?" I eyed her curiously.

She flushed. "Chalk door. I picked up a thing or two from you."

"Of course you did," I mumbled.

"So, you've told your sister?" Luke came in, the voice of solemnity.

I sighed. "Turns out, honesty is the best policy. Who knew?"

"Doesn't that put her in the same predicament as the rest of us? You, me, Melody, Kenzie, and that human girl?" I knew he'd deliberately pretended to forget Ryann's name, and I didn't bite.

"Harley knows what we're up against, better than most. She's not going to put herself in the firing line—isn't that right, sis?" I put my arm around her shoulder and gave her a jolt of a hug.

Harley gave me a sharp hug back. "That's right, bro."

"Look at the two of you!" Melody cooed. "It's everything I imagined. You must be the most formidable pair of siblings on Earth."

"Don't forget the Basani twins," I retorted. "Their ears are probably burning."

Melody pulled a sour face. "They're nothing but a couple of fakers compared to you two. I don't see either of you plastered over the front cover of glossy magazines, selling photos to add a few zeroes to your bank accounts."

I swept back my hair theatrically. "I'm camera shy."

"And the press doesn't want any photos of me besides the candid, unflattering ones of me crossing the street without makeup and my hair all over the place," Harley added. "I swear, they know when it's laundry day."

"Once, they took one of her trying to get her mouth around a double cheeseburger. Funniest thing I've ever seen, like a demon trying to devour someone's soul. I've got it framed." I shot Harley an evil grin, feeling slightly more like myself. She'd had that calming effect on me ever since our cult experience. Either that, or the six pills I'd taken were finally kicking in.

"Well, let's not leave our guests out in the cold with that image stuck in their heads," Harley announced. "Let's get you inside."

"Can we see the Bestiary?!" Melody blurted.

Harley straightened in surprise, a flicker of caution in her eyes. "The Bestiary?"

"Nothing to worry about. She's got a thing for Tobe, that's all," I explained. "There'll be posters on her walls after this."

"Finch!" Melody protested. "Don't make it sound weird. I'm simply interested in hearing what life is like for a thousand-year-old Beast Master, and I'd love to see the creatures he cares for. I know a lot about them, but I haven't had the chance to actually see Purge beasts, so I'm very curious."

"It's a heck of a place." Harley's shoulders relaxed. "And I'm sure Tobe would be happy to talk with you for a while. He's good like that. Honestly, I think everyone who meets him falls in love a little bit."

I wrinkled my nose. "Gross."

"You're no exception, Finch. I've seen you go in for a hug when you think nobody's watching," she replied, grinning. Luke smirked, no doubt stowing that knowledge away for a rainy day.

"Hey, sometimes a man just needs to be held by a six-foot-something lion-eagle hybrid!" Tobe really did give damn good hugs. A living teddy bear, exactly what a person needed.

We headed back inside the Fleet Science Center, past the warring brats and through the fire exit behind Kid City. Melody and Luke waited behind us as Harley did the honors. She placed her hands on the door, said the *Aperi Portam* spell… and nothing happened.

"Having problems?" I poked my head over her shoulder. "Does it need a gentler touch?"

"No, I've got it." She tried again, but the door didn't open.

"Is everything okay?" Melody fidgeted. Could the coven sense what she was?

Harley pushed her hand firmly against the door. "It's fine, it's just stubborn. After everything that happened last year, it's got a vendetta against newcomers."

"Ah, yes, the sentience of a coven." Melody's eyes twinkled, and I sensed another incoming encyclopedia entry. "It's fascinating how they have a life of their own, in a way. They are living, breathing entities, the same way we are. Magicals often forget that. Some aren't even aware of it."

"I said, *APERI PORTAM!*" Harley boomed at the poor door. The words thundered out of her like she was about to wrangle a horde of gargoyles. The interdimensional bubble fizzed in fright, and the door popped open a second later.

As head tour guide, minus the flag and name badge, Harley took us straight to the Bestiary. It looked like she couldn't resist Melody's passion for knowledge, either. The entire trek, Melody prattled on about covens, Purge beasts, the former directors of the SDC, and a million other things. I let her voice wash over me, not because she bored me, but because I just didn't have the stamina to listen.

Harley shoved the heavy double doors that opened out onto the majesty of the Bestiary. I doubted the novelty would ever wear off. Melody's eyes transformed into saucers.

"Oh my," she gasped.

I flashed her a smile. "Lions, and tigers, and bears."

Speaking of lions, Tobe stood before the huge atrium, its silvery veins sparking and glinting as it sent power to all the covens of the world. Another figure stood with him, the two of them in deep conversation.

"Is that Leonidas Levi?" Melody whispered, her voice filled with awe.

I puffed out a breath. "Unfortunately, yeah."

He didn't look good. Sweat drenched his white shirt, which made for uncomfortable viewing—I could see more of Levi's chesticles than I'd ever wanted to. Dark circles ringed his eyes, and he looked to be panting despite standing still. Every couple seconds, he mopped his forehead and neck with a dirty-looking handkerchief. *Ugh...*

"Tobe, we've got someone here to—" I started to introduce Melody, but she beat me to the punch.

"It's an honor, Mr. Beast Master!" She actually bowed. "My name is Melody Winchester, and I've been looking forward to meeting you for such a long time. And, may I say, you have a beautiful Bestiary. Honestly, my mind is blown. This is all so… amazing."

Tobe flashed his fangs in a surprised smile. "It is a pleasure to make your acquaintance, Miss Winchester. I would be delighted to show you more of the Bestiary, once I finish this discussion with Mr. Levi."

"Forget it. We were done anyway," Levi muttered. *Who peed in his cornflakes?*

Harley tilted her head. "Are you okay, Levi?"

"I'm fine. Why wouldn't I be fine when it is about a hundred degrees in here and my head is pounding?" He smeared the handkerchief over his brow. "You go and show them around, Tobe. I need to sit for a minute and catch my breath. Must you keep it so warm in here?" He fanned himself with his hand.

"It is not so warm, Levi." Tobe put his paw on Levi's shoulder. "Are you sure you are quite well? Perhaps you should visit Dr. Krieger."

"I've got too much to do to bother with doctors," Levi huffed and sat on the nearest glass box. "Go on, what are you all gawping at? Pay no attention to me while I slowly melt. If you find a puddle when you return, pour me in a jar and bury me."

Tobe ushered us away. "I think it may be best to leave him to his own devices."

I glanced over my shoulder as Tobe led us to a different part of the Bestiary. Levi hunched over, dabbing his face and taking deep breaths. He definitely needed to see Krieger, even if it was only a case of man-flu.

"If anything specific tickles your fancy, Miss Winchester, you must tell me, and I will ensure you get ample viewing time." Tobe paused beside a large box with swirling black smoke inside. He sang softly, and unexpected tears sprang to my eyes. His voice urged the black smoke to solidify. Four creatures appeared, with the legs of goats and the upper halves of men. They trotted up to the pane and peered out.

"What's that song?" Melody sniffled, wiping her eyes. Even Luke seemed to be having trouble.

"It is the Song of the Satyrs," Tobe replied. The song lingered in the air, choking me up.

Melody approached the glass. "These are satyrs?"

"They are, Miss Winchester." Tobe stood beside her, his arms tucked behind his back underneath his folded wings. "I thought we could begin with the most familiar Purge beasts before moving on to the more obscure creatures."

"They're beautiful," Melody whispered. "I knew they would be."

Tobe smiled. "I am pleased you think so."

"So, where are the others?" I sidled up to Harley while Melody admired the satyrs.

"You'll see them soon enough," she replied distractedly. "Right now, I'm more interested in your new friend. Who is she? And don't tell me she's just a Winchester, because I won't believe you. There's something… odd about her. Not a bad odd, but something's not quite right."

Smelling that rat, are we?

"She's just a friend helping me out." I wanted to see if Harley could figure this out on her own. As far as I knew, she had never encountered another Empath. And I was dying to find out what happened when Empaths collided. Could they read each other?

"Bullcrap," she hissed. "What's the deal with her?"

I shrugged. "You tell me, Mademoiselle Empath."

"You're infuriating."

I knocked into her gently. "I love you, too."

"I'm already using my Empath abilities, dumbass. That's how I know something's off," Harley explained. "I can sense something special about her."

"Like what?" I probed.

"I don't know. It's hard to tell. It's not like I can read her mind—it's a sensation I feel." Harley scrunched her face up, deep in thought. "It's like a pulse, under layers of excitement, and awe, and curiosity."

"Ooh, that's weird." Melody stepped away from the satyrs and twisted to stare at Harley.

"Is something the matter, Miss Winchester?" Tobe stooped toward her. "Did they alarm you? We can look at more agreeable creatures, if you prefer."

"No, it's not the satyrs." Melody kept staring at Harley. "Is that you? Are you doing that?"

Harley raised her eyebrows. "Doing what?"

"Sensing me out." Melody began to vibrate excitedly. "Oh, I can feel it! I feel what you're feeling, like it's right inside my brain! You're curious about me, aren't you? And... what's that? Ah, you're wary, which I suppose is natural considering what you've been through. But you don't need to worry about me, I promise."

Harley gaped. "You're an Empath?"

"Same as you." She nodded eagerly. "That's a very strange sensation, isn't it? Can you feel my emotions in your head, too? As if they're yours?"

"I can." Harley squealed in a very un-Harley-like fashion. "You're so excited to be here. It's making me excited, and I've seen all this a thousand times. This is so cool!"

"It's hard to separate, isn't it?" Melody giggled.

"It is, but I kind of like it." Harley rushed to Melody, and they clasped hands and began jumping around like madwomen. "I could use enthusiasm like this when I'm trying to get through a shift."

Melody danced a jig that Harley copied. "You can have it, whenever you want. I'll feed it to you. I can be your Energizer bunny."

"I definitely need one of those." Harley laughed as they spun. Tobe looked on, baffled. He wasn't the only one. Luke and I stepped back and exchanged a look that said, *What the hell is happening?*

"You're nervous, too. What's that for?" Melody stumbled to a halt. "Is it me? You don't have to be scared of me. Finch will vouch for me. I'm here to help him—nothing to worry about."

Harley shook her head. "No, that's not what I'm nervous about."

"And... wait... you're in love. That's wonderful!" Melody chirruped, flitting through emotions like a rolodex. "Who's the lucky guy?"

"His name is Wade. I'll introduce you to him. He'd like you; I know he would." Harley looked at me. "Finch, why can't you make more friends like this?"

I stared at her. "I'm not exactly in the market."

"Well, you should be!"

Luke went into protective mode, narrowing his eyes at Tobe. "Did the satyrs do something to them?"

"This has nothing to do with the satyrs, I am afraid," he replied. "This is entirely their own doing. I have a wide breadth of understanding about Purge beasts, but mortal beings are more mysterious to me."

"Should we see more creatures?" Harley suggested to her new best pal.

Melody squeaked. "Yes, please!"

"Tobe, show us what you've got," Harley instructed.

"As you wish, Harley." A throaty chuckle escaped his jaws. He led the way, giving the girls a brief history of all the critters we passed: sylphs, sprites, wraiths, will o' the wisps, goblins, hobgoblins, every kind of goblin. Harley and Melody gazed into each box like schoolkids on a zoo trip. All Luke and I could do was steer into the skid and follow from a safe distance.

Melody was beside herself, adding tidbits to Tobe's knowledge. "Sylphs can be manipulated by magicals with Air abilities. They are one of the only Purge beasts linked directly to an Element. Isn't that right, Tobe?"

"It is, Miss Winchester. Very impressive. You have a keen interest in Purge beasts."

"I love them," she agreed. "It's mind-boggling that these beings are created by us, but we can't predict which ones we might Purge."

I smirked. "I mean, some of us go all out and Purge a Child of Chaos. Putting everyone else's efforts to shame."

Harley rolled her eyes. "I'm sure it was a fluke."

"I've got a question for you, Tobe." I returned my attention to the Beast Master.

"Of course. Ask away."

"How many of the Purge beasts here were captured by the Basani twins?" I couldn't resist.

Tobe ruffled his feathers. "The Basani twins sent perhaps one or two percent of these creatures."

"Ha! I knew they were bluffing." I punched the air in satisfaction.

"I doubt anything honest has ever left their mouths, except what the gas made them say," Luke chimed in.

Harley raised a hand. "Am I missing something?"

"We've met them. Nothing important, just glad to confirm they were a pair of liars." I smiled smugly.

Only when Tobe led us to a familiar hall with one solitary box did Harley's giddiness ebb. This box should've been frosted over, but it wasn't. Black smoke twisted and turned inside, slamming against the glass. Harley went right up to it with Melody in tow and placed her nose to the pane. Immediately, the smoke stretched into the slithery form of Leviathan.

"Harley, Harley, Harley. Long time no see," he purred. "Anyone would think you've been avoiding me."

Harley shot a grim look at Tobe. "Who took him off ice? And how the hell is he talking to me? Aren't these boxes meant to be soundproof?"

"I am owed, Harley." Leviathan swept up to the glass. "Do not keep me waiting too long. I grow impatient."

I hurried to my sister. Tobe wouldn't have taken him off ice if there was a chance in hell of him escaping, but that didn't mean Harley was safe from Leviathan. They had a deal, passed down from Echidna to her son—Leviathan would name Harley's firstborn. It didn't sound like a huge issue, but names were powerful. And Harley clearly didn't appreciate the reminder.

"My apologies, Harley. I should have warned you before entering. I had to release him for a short while in order to take Chaos samples. Dr. Krieger needed them for a personal project, and the samples could not be taken while he was frozen," Tobe explained.

"Taken without my permission, I might add," Leviathan muttered.

"You know that is untrue, Leviathan. Your permission was sought, so do not lie. Which brings me to the matter of you being able to hear him," Tobe continued, with a sharp look at Leviathan. "Unfortunately, I had to implement an auditory spell to allow him to speak through the glass. It was Leviathan's one condition, in return for behaving himself with the sample extraction. He likes to have himself heard."

Leviathan snorted against the glass, leaving two streaks of condensation. "So would you, after long stretches of being frozen into silence."

Harley paled. "I think I've had enough of Purge beasts for one day. Why don't I show you around the SDC, Melody?"

Clearly sensing Harley's distress, Melody squeezed her hand. "I'd love to see what else you've got here."

"Come back soon, won't you?" Leviathan called, as we made our way from the room.

We'd just reached the atrium to find Levi long gone, when Remington Knightshade barreled in. He had Krieger with him, evidently to collect those Chaos samples.

"Are we early, Tobe?" Remington stopped in front of our merry band of misfits and eyed Melody and Luke. "I thought you said to meet you at two o'clock to take more samples."

Remington had spent more time at the SDC this past year after finding his nephew, Dylan. The news that Remington was his uncle hadn't gone down well with Dylan at first, but he'd warmed to him over time. Fighting a war together could do that.

"No, you are precisely on time. I have just finished giving a brief tour to Finch and his new friends," Tobe replied.

"New friends?" Remington frowned.

Melody put out her hand. "Melody Winchester. And this is Luke."

Remington shook her hand hesitantly. A moment later, he made a strained sound, his face pained. His fingers gripped Melody's, refusing to let go even when she tried to pull away. "No… that's not possible."

"Please let go," Melody said, alarmed. Luke strode in and pried Remington's hand away.

"Touch her like that again, and you'll regret it," he snapped.

"I'm sorry." Remington blinked in confusion, his eyes sad. "It's just… I… you're like her. You're like my Odette. I can feel it, coming out of you."

Oh, crap. I had a nasty feeling that Melody's secret was about to tear wide open.

Melody stepped closer to him. "You're Remington, aren't you?"

"I am."

"You can sense what I am?" She sounded dumbfounded.

He flinched. "Yes."

"How?"

"I'm not sure. I touched your hand, and I… felt it. And in your voice and your eyes—it's hard to put my finger on, but it's there. I knew Odette for so long. I memorized her every nuance. She had an atmosphere about her, after she inherited the Librarian's knowledge. You have it, too."

Harley turned her focus on me. "She's the new Librarian?"

"It wasn't my secret to share," I replied stiffly. Melody lifted her hand to Remington's face, and I watched with interest while Luke actually turned green from envy.

"She loved you so much," Melody said. "There are so many memories of you. I've often thought I already knew you because of them."

"Memories?" Remington choked.

Melody took her hand away. "I inherited more than Chaos knowledge from Odette when she passed. I have fragments of her memories, too. Some, toward the end, are terrible. I don't like to dwell on them, though they creep in from time to time. But there are good moments —so many—and you're in every one of them. They have this sort of rosy aura. It lets me feel what she was feeling when the memory was made. My goodness, she loved you. Even at the very end, in her worst memories… you were the last thing she thought of. A faint, rosy hint of you, embedded inside the terror."

Someone hand me the tissues... I didn't know what to do with myself. It seemed wrong of us to listen in on this. Any hope for a normal life had been stolen from Odette when she'd become the Librarian. Librarians weren't allowed to have relationships, per Chaos rules, but it hadn't stopped her heart from loving Remington all the same.

Yeah, and she'd still be alive if it wasn't for your mother. Guilt twisted my stomach. Guilt by association of the blood running in my veins. Bitter tears trickled down my cheeks, and I wasn't alone. Even Tobe dabbed his eyes with his paws. Remington completely broke down.

"I miss her so much." He gasped for air, clinging to Melody's hands.

Melody clung right back. "She misses you, too. During my transition into being the Librarian, I was able to communicate with her spirit for a short time—a spiritual handover of sorts. And she spoke of you often. Your love helped her face what came for her. It gave her the strength to stare into the eyes of her killers, and know she'd be at peace when it ended."

"I should've been there for her." He sobbed, his shoulders shaking.

"Nothing could've saved her. She wouldn't want you to think like that," Melody urged. "She knew you'd have given your own life for hers, and she was glad it wasn't you in her place. She's not burdened anymore. She's at peace, I promise you."

Melody put her arms around Remington, and he sank into her shoulder, gripping her tight as the tears flowed. I tried not to watch, but I couldn't help it. Looking at Remington, and hearing him, my thoughts drifted toward Ryann. What would I do to save her?

I thought about the book I needed with a renewed sense of fear. All this time, I'd been looking to escape my deal with Erebus, when maybe the way to keep everyone safe was to do what I was told. It sucked the life out of me, sure, but maybe it was supposed to, since I doubted Erebus planned to let me survive this. But the others… they didn't need to have that death sentence.

Coward. My gremlins swooped in. My mother had ripped Odette's mind out of her head, and she'd still found a way to help Harley and the others. If I just bowed my head and accepted my fate, then I *would* be a coward. She'd faced her killers because there'd been no escape. But I still had a shot. If I got out of my deal, maybe it'd get everyone off the hook. Erebus wouldn't be able to use them against me anymore.

Sometimes, love meant sacrificing everything. Sometimes, it meant taking a leap of faith. I just had to be ready to jump, and hope I was flying toward safety.

SEVEN

Finch

Between them, Tobe and Krieger managed to put Remington back together again, like a regular Humpty Dumpty. They all had work to do—the perfect distraction for Remington after having all those old wounds reopened.

"Will you have coffee with me tonight, Melody? I'd like to talk to you again," Remington said while Tobe held him steady.

"Of course," she replied.

Luke stepped up behind her. "I'll be coming with you."

"What?" Remington looked over at Luke as if seeing him for the first time. "Yes, that's fine. Whatever makes Melody comfortable. You must be her protector. Or are you more? Like Odette and me?"

"He is my protector, yes, but we're not like you and Odette," Melody answered. "If you know Librarians, then you know the rules. I'm not allowed to have... more."

Luke's brows lowered in disappointment, though she didn't see it with him standing behind her. Remington, however, caught it. A flicker of understanding crossed his face, and it must've broken his heart all over again. There was only one thing worse than what he'd suffered—watching someone else go through the same thing.

"You're right. I know the rules all too well." Remington sighed. "Tonight, then? You'll come for coffee?"

"We'll be there," Melody replied.

As Remington, Tobe, and Krieger walked away, I let out a sharp whistle. "Well, that was depressing. Anyone got spare Kleenex?"

"Poor guy," Harley said quietly. Knowing her, she'd be thinking about her relationship with Wade and going through the same mental motions I had. Wade could be a royal pain in the ass, but I hoped they'd never be separated. He'd sort of grown on me this past year, like a nasty rash.

"Maybe we should lighten things up?" I suggested. "How about the Aquarium? Cool monsters, but less hassle. I mean, none of *them* are vying to name your firstborn."

Harley shot me one of her best withering looks. "That's not a bad idea, actually."

"Sounds good to me," Melody chirped. It sounded forced, like her mind was elsewhere. On Odette and Remington, probably.

We set off, leaving the Bestiary for the main body of the coven. Harley caught Luke in conversation while Melody lagged behind with me.

"So, when did you start watching over Melody?" Harley asked.

"About a year ago," Luke replied.

"Did the Winchesters employ you?"

He nodded. "They'd heard about Odette on the news, during the posthumous medal ceremony. It got them worried, so they called me in."

With them distracted, I took the opportunity to have a word with

Melody. "I'm heading to Waterfront Park tonight, so I'll try and find the book while I'm there."

"I was about to mention that," she whispered back. "I've done more research into it, which is part of the reason I insisted on coming. You're looking for a book with a red cover and a ruby on the spine, written by Jabir ibn Hayyan. I say that, because if you go in, you'll need to know your onions. It's not a book many people know, so it might pique some suspicions if you don't know much about what you're looking for."

"Good to know."

"Say you're a collector of rare pieces if they press you, and you should be covered," she continued. "Don't mention that you know what's inside, and maybe throw in the name of a well-known rich person. Someone notable, so they don't think you're messing around."

Here's looking at you, Daggerston. If I could get some use out of that weasel, I would.

"What else did you find?" I pressed.

She tucked herself right into my side and lowered her voice. "There's definitely a connection between the djinn and the servants of Erebus. I managed to pluck a footnote of sorts from my head—so, you know, progress on the Librarian thing—and it implied a collaboration between the two. Not much detail, but the servants of Erebus from previous decades and centuries were known to work with djinn in order to complete specific tasks. They also helped the servants find certain people or artifacts earlier in history, since many of the spells we rely on today didn't exist back then."

I dragged my arm across my forehead. The sweats had returned after Remington's breakdown. Not the same feverish sweats Levi was going through—mine were cold and beading with anxiety, coming from the mind, not a physical illness. "So, it sounds like the djinn *are*

Erebus's eyes and ears? They watched his servants and helped them accomplish things that they couldn't have done alone."

"That seems to be the case, yes."

"But we're talking magical servants as well as djinn?" Erebus had rattled on about having other slaves, but I'd never crossed paths with another, so I had no clue who they might be or what they might look like.

Melody nodded. "He has both, yes. And you're in the former category."

"No djinn has ever helped me." I sighed.

"That's the weird thing. Erebus seems to have kept you isolated for some reason. I have no doubt he's had some of them watch you and pass on his messages, but they haven't made contact." She'd gone into sleuth mode. A modern-day Sherlock in a fluffy jacket.

"But this book might shed some light on it?"

"If my guess is right, and I'm pretty good at that sort of thing, the djinn should know the history of Erebus's former servants. It'll be in their collective memory. The book won't have an exhaustive list, as it's so old, but it might give you a way to research some of his past servants so you can see if any managed to find a loophole in the servitude bargain." She pulled her jacket tighter, like she'd felt a sudden chill. "It's a starting point, anyway."

Curiosity was the order of the day. I wanted to know everything about these past servants and their supposed collaboration with the djinn. This book might have some useful information on my particular category of slave, and maybe even a way to escape said slavedom.

After I read the book, I knew my next port of call. Kadar, Raffe's djinn, was a small fry. He hadn't racked up enough years to be connected to the mainframe and collective memory, but Zalaam was plenty old.

Let's hope Levi's man-flu hasn't affected his djinn.

Later that evening, I coerced myself into wearing a button-up shirt and dragging a comb through my hair. After all, I didn't want Harley to flay me. It was the only button-up shirt I owned—the one Saskia had bought for me at Bandersnatch's Boutique of Haute-Nonsense. I'd thought about going whole-hog and putting on the entire overpriced getup, if only to peeve Wade by being the best-dressed guy in the room. In the end, I settled for an old pair of black trousers and the silky shirt. And, not to toot my own trumpet, but I didn't look too shabby.

I set out solo to the Waterfront, not wanting a gaggle of Muppet Babies in tow when I had a bookshop to scour. Melody would be at her coffee date with Remington by now, with Luke third-wheeling. I'd bumped into Krieger on my way back from the Aquarium, where Melody had gone gaga over selkies and sea sprites and Kraken. He'd commented on how crappy I looked, though in a more polite way, but I'd shrugged it off and switched the topic to Remington. Apparently, the poor guy hadn't been in any state to collect samples, and neither had Leviathan, so they'd agreed to work on Fish-face tomorrow instead. Leviathan had been pretty agitated after seeing Harley; the power inside her had an impact on most monsters she ran across.

He'd make a great pet, sis. Stick him on a leash and walk him around, but make sure you've got heavy-duty poop-bags.

For a brief moment, I'd thought about asking Krieger for an evaluation, to see if my pills needed switching up. But then I'd remembered the hassle of it all when I'd first gotten my prescription. Too many questions, too many trials, too many experiments with this pill and that pill, some of which left me like the walking dead, others which knocked me out completely, and others which made me feel like... someone else entirely. So, I'd decided against it and headed off. I was coping with what I had, for now.

I entered the interdimensional shopping mall and found Buy Its Cover pretty quickly. There were a bunch of bookshops, but none had a name that tickled my funny bone quite the same way. Whoever ran this place was a pun master after my own heart.

A bell tinkled above the door as I stepped into the store, and that musty old-book smell bombarded my nostrils. A few tables had "New Arrivals" written on stands, but the shelves belonged to the ancient and the yellowed. The kind of books where you could sense how many thumbs had gone before yours, flicking the aged pages.

"Can I be of assistance, young man?" A smiling old woman appeared behind the counter and shuffled over to me. She evidently didn't recognize me, though I was something of a big deal in these parts. If I did say so myself.

"I'm looking for a book called *The Dark Souls of the Magical World*, by Jabir ibn Hayyan." I hoped I'd said that right. "Red cover, ruby on the spine. I'd look through all these shelves myself, but I'm in something of a hurry." I gestured to the myriad tomes. It wasn't like the book I needed would come whizzing out of its own accord.

The old lady's eyes widened. "Goodness, now that *is* a book." She shuffled off and ran her fingertip along the books before stopping in front of one, exactly as Melody had described. Holding it reverently, she brought it to me.

"Is this it?" I asked. It looked the part.

"Oh yes, it certainly is." She smiled eagerly. "Will you be making a purchase?"

"How much are we talking?" I had my credit card with me, but it wouldn't take much to max the thing out.

"Ten thousand dollars." She practically squealed the words. Now her excitement made sense. Buying this book probably would've paid the rent on this place for a year. And left me in debt for the rest of my life.

I tried not to choke. "A bargain, but I'll have to check with my buyer first."

"Would you like me to put it on hold for you, dear?"

"No, that isn't necessary. I just need to make a phone call." I scampered outside, leaving the bell ringing.

Crap! What was I supposed to do now? Melody hadn't mentioned such a massive price tag, and I sure as hell couldn't afford it. *Oh, you know what you have to do,* the gremlins whispered in my head. They weren't usually the best with ideas, but I had to agree with them this time.

The only way to get that book was to steal it. Buying it wasn't a possibility. I didn't have that kind of dough, and I didn't have time to rustle it up.

It didn't sit well with me, to swipe it from under that kind old lady's nose, but I was fresh out of choices. Maybe I could've called Saskia, but that'd bring flirtations and protestations of "You only want me for my money," which I didn't have the patience for right now.

Ah, screw it. If that book could free me before I wound up dead in Atlantis, then drastic measures called for drastic action.

I found a darkened alleyway between stores and Shifted into O'Halloran before heading back to the shop. I pretended I'd been running, panting for breath as I burst in, badge-flashing like my life depended on it.

"I'm sorry to bother you, ma'am, but we have it on good authority that one of Davin Doncaster's minions has targeted your shop, using the form of one of my people. We have been watching your shop, in case they struck, and he was just spotted a moment ago, leaving here," I wheezed. "Security personnel are chasing the Shapeshifter as we speak, but the book they were sent to steal is no longer safe here. Unless... they took it? Did they take it, ma'am? This is of vital importance."

The old lady trembled. "N-no, they didn't. I've just put it away."

"That is good news, ma'am. I thought I might've come too late. May I take it from you, temporarily, and put it in lock-up at the SDC? It will be returned to you as soon as we know the threat has passed." O'Halloran would kill me for this, but hopefully he'd never find out.

"It's a v-very valuable book."

"Which is precisely why we must keep it out of the hands of those who'd use it for ill, ma'am," I insisted, O'Halloran's voice coming out perfectly. The beauty of Mimicry. "You'll have it back soon enough, I promise. I will personally ensure nothing happens to it. Please, ma'am, this is a matter of life and death."

"Life and death?" she shrieked, hurrying to the shelf and removing the book.

"I'm afraid so, ma'am." That wasn't entirely a lie.

She pressed the book into my hands. "I wouldn't want anyone getting hurt."

"Thank you, ma'am. Truly, you've helped the SDC a great deal today. I'm only glad I arrived in time. Doncaster's minions are slippery creatures—they can't be trusted."

"I had no idea. He was so convincing." She wrung her hands, which made me feel awful. I *was* convincing. One of the perks of Mimicry was the ability to Shift my Esprit, as well as the rest of myself. And I'd

Shifted it into O'Halloran's badge—an item unique to him. No one else had it.

"They always are, ma'am," I replied. "It would be best if you didn't mention this to anyone. We're still watching Waterfront Park closely for any strange activity, and I'd hate for these troublemakers to be tipped off."

She nodded effusively. "Of course. I won't say a word. I hope you can catch them before they make any mischief."

"As do I, ma'am. As do I." I held the book to my chest. "Now, I won't take up any more of your time. Thank you again for your service."

"Thank you for *your* service," she said. "It's a comfort to know that we're being protected by the likes of you."

"Good day to you, ma'am." I tilted my head at her before exiting the shop with the book safely in my arms. Yeah, I felt bad, but she'd get it back. I planned on returning it… at some point. Hopefully before O'Halloran found out that a Shapeshifter had used his identity to steal from a local shop. Then, there really would be a manhunt.

EIGHT

Finch

W alking like John Wayne with the dusty book wedged in the back of my pants, I made it early to Ignatius's Restaurant—a chintzy Italian joint with waxy gingham tablecloths and candles shoved mercilessly into wine bottles. Still, I'd heard the food was better than the décor. And my tummy growled like a rabid wolf on the hunt for calzone.

To be honest, I'd rather spend my evening finding Melody and having a little alone time with this here book, but the prospect of Harley hounding me for the next decade held me to my promise. Besides, I'd been away for a while, and I'd kept her in the dark even longer. Now that the truth was more or less out, I owed her a family dinner. Even if cozy get-togethers weren't really my jam.

"Good evening, sir." The host picked up a solitary menu. *Wow, do I really look like that much of a sad sack?*

"Hi there. I'm meeting people here, but I'm early."

The host made an "ah" of understanding. "What name is it?"

"It'll be under Merlin."

He ran his hand down the list. "Yes, here it is. Merlin. I believe another guest has already arrived. She must be as eager as you, but with gnocchi like ours, it's only natural. If you'll follow me?"

I stifled a laugh. "Lead the way to the gnocchi."

My good humor died as we rounded a corner and arrived at a big wooden booth with shiny, red vinyl upholstery. Very much in keeping with the rest of the restaurant's chintz. I'd expected the guest to be Harley, as the hostess with the mostest. And she was a stickler for punctuality. But Ryann sat there instead, alone at the table. She had her head bowed over her cellphone, tapping frantically.

Oh boy... I'd have preferred Santana and that scaly biter of hers over trying to make small talk with the girl I was madly in love with. Emphasis on madly. I was a couple missed pills from going around with a top hat and a March hare, and maybe a dormouse in my teacup.

"Can I get you a drink, sir?" The host interrupted my trip down the rabbit hole.

"Uh... lime and soda, please." Something boozy would only feed the gremlins. Cecily's beloved Riesling had taught me that. It might have stopped my hand from trembling, but I didn't want it to become a crutch.

"Very good, sir." The host scuttled off, leaving me stranded at Awkward Central.

Ryann still hadn't looked up. A small smile curved the corners of her lips as she typed. A "sick smile," Mrs. Anker had called it. I was ten, trying to woo my first girlfriend. We'd used MSN Messenger back then. I'd changed my username to "Finch<3Jenny" and everything. It'd lasted a month and gave me my first taste of heartbreak, and I'd never forgotten Mrs. Anker's relentless teasing. But Ryann didn't have to worry about heartbreak. Dr. Feelgood adored her. I mean, who wouldn't?

"Good game of Angry Birds?" I slid onto the bench opposite her.

She gasped. "Finch! I didn't see you there."

"Ouch." I pressed a hand to my chest.

"Just let me finish this and I'll be all yours," Ryann said, returning to the glow of her screen. *If only that were true...*

"The Boston Strangler giving you the details on his latest victim?"

She arched a disapproving eyebrow. "I'm texting Adam, if that's what you mean. I'm meeting him after dinner, and we're trying to decide whether to catch a late-night movie or drive along the coast. What do you think—a movie or a drive?"

"A movie, every time, as long as it's not some crap blockbuster. Well, unless it's Marvel. Then always go for the Marvel movie." I stayed casual. Clearly, her having a vague idea of how I felt about her, and knowing she'd had some conflicted emotions about me, hadn't changed a thing. *Hello, friendzone, my old pal.*

"Adam's not really into movies. He always whispers about how they're doing the medical stuff wrong." She chuckled to herself as she typed back. "I think we'll go for a drive."

Then why did you ask?! The constant reminder of Psycho Killer irked my gremlins. And me. It was getting harder to figure out where I ended and they began. I tapped my fingernails on the table, agitated. The cold, anxious sweats came on again, making this stupid silk shirt stick to every part of me. I wanted to rip it off, Hulk out, and scare a few servers to boot. Maybe then Ryann would notice me sitting here. I wasn't asking her to bare her soul—I just wanted her to acknowledge my existence instead of staring at her phone.

I'm losing it... I closed my eyes and dug my fingernails into the palms of my hands, fighting to keep it together. This wasn't her fault. She loved Adam. Loving her didn't give me the right to get pissed off about that. I mean, there was a reason why genies didn't grant wishes to make people fall in love with other people. The heart wanted what it wanted, and Ryann's didn't want me. So, I had to keep calm and not be an asshat. *Slap THAT on a T-shirt!* It beat "Keep Calm and Carry On," any day.

The only trouble was, my gremlins wanted what they wanted, too. And they wanted me to topple over the edge of self-control and give in to every impulse, no matter how bad. They'd wanted it from day one, and these pills weren't doing their job anymore. I had no idea why, but since my orange-poison Magical Mystery Ride, they'd stopped being effective. Taking more had helped a little, but that wasn't exactly sustainable.

"Hey, are you okay over there?" Ryann's hand touched mine. Her phone was gone, stuffed in her bag.

I blinked slowly. "Me? I'm fine."

"You don't look fine. You're all… twitchy." She peered at me intently. "Is it Erebus?"

"Can we not talk about him?" I asked softly.

She gave my hand a squeeze. "Sure, no problem. I just want to make sure you're all right. I haven't seen you since Kenzie's apartment. I didn't even know you'd come back."

"Ta-da." I rallied a weak laugh.

"Did you get everything done?" She slapped herself lightly on the forehead. "Ah, sorry—I can't help talking shop. I won't say the E-word, but I'd like to know what we're up against, if you can manage it? I know you must be having a hard time."

"Understatement of the century." I sighed, feeling calmer with her hand on mine. "But yeah, I got everything done. For now, anyway. Have you heard from Kenzie since you left her apartment?"

Ryann tilted her head from side to side. "Yes and no. She's been busy with her mom and sister, so she hasn't been replying. But they're awake and okay, and Krieger looked over them and gave them the all clear."

"That's the kind of news I like to hear." Thinking of Kenzie, at home with her mom and sister, pushed my gremlins farther back. Erebus had screwed me over plenty, but he wasn't a total douchebag—not to other people, anyway. He'd stuck to his end of the deal with Kenzie, and he'd saved Saskia and Garrett from the Jubilee mine, as well as the miners who'd have been crushed otherwise. The two of them had told me about that in an influx of texts that my phone picked up post-monastery, once I was free of its communication embargo.

"Have you talked to Harley?" Ryann gently let go of my hand. "I haven't said anything, aside from you being on E-word business. But I keep expecting her to whip out a spotlight and use Wade to play good cop, bad cop."

"Well, you don't have to worry anymore," I replied. "I told her everything today—mostly everything. I left out the monastery, but only because I didn't have the energy. She knows I've been tasked with finding Atlantis, so she's up to speed."

Ryann's smile widened. "I'm proud of you, Finch."

"Nothing to be proud about. It was just easier if she knew. Turns out, making someone aware of danger is a good way to stop said someone from doing stupid things," I replied.

"Did you just come back to see her, then? So you could tell her the truth?"

I took the book out of my waistband. "Actually, no. Melody ransacked her mind palace and found out that this existed. According to her, it's got a bunch of stuff in it about djinn and Erebus's former servants. She thinks it might be my way out."

"Where did you get it?" She stared at the tome. On closer inspection, it proved to be an impressive piece of craftsmanship. Black vines swirled across the bright red leather, twisting up toward the letters in the center that spelled out the book's title. Tiny rubies were embedded on the cover in addition to the larger ruby on the spine, and they all glinted in the ambient lighting of the restaurant.

"A bookshop."

She narrowed her eyes. "Which bookshop? This doesn't look cheap, Finch."

"You'd be surprised. It was very cheap. Free, in fact." I grinned.

"You stole it?" She gaped at me in horror.

"Why would you jump to that conclusion?"

"Finch, did you steal it or not?" she hissed.

I sighed. "Fine, I stole it, but only because it was ten thousand dollars. Do you have that kind of dough lying around? Didn't think so. Nobody does, except Saskia, and I wasn't about to ask *her*. Can you imagine? She'd be all, 'What will you give me in return?' and make me feel like I needed twenty showers."

Ryann shook her head. "You can't just take things, Finch."

"I *borrowed* it. I fully intend to give it back."

"Do I want to know how you 'borrowed' it?" She sounded disappointed. Well, she could go on being disappointed, because I had a damn good reason to swipe it. Honestly, I was a little disappointed myself—that she'd fixated on the theft and not the fact that this book could get me free from Erebus.

"I Shifted into O'Halloran, told the old lady I needed it on important business, and that I'd bring it back soon," I replied stiffly. "Done and dusted. Nobody got hurt; nobody's upset. It's all good."

"All good? Are you kidding? This could get you into deep trouble!"

I shrugged. "Pfft, add it to the pile. Anyway, no trouble compares to the E-man. I'll repeat myself, since it seems you didn't hear me the first time: this book might help me free myself from that monster before it's too late for me."

"Melody really said that?"

I sucked air through my teeth. "Why else would I have pinched it? I'm not reckless, Ryann, though everyone gets pretty free with that tarring brush when they talk about me."

"Sorry, Finch. I guess I tend to get on my high horse when it comes to legal stuff." Her expression softened.

"I'll be glad to yank you down if you start climbing into the saddle again." I relaxed, focusing on her face to keep me centered.

She smiled and reached for the book. "Can I?"

"I don't know, can you?" I replied, aiming for endearing.

"You sound like my dad." She chuckled, not realizing that was the last thing I wanted to hear from her. "Fine. *May* I?"

I pushed the book toward her. "You may."

She flipped through, skimming the pages. My gremlins started jangling in my head, possessive of the book, but they could stay in their lane. Erebus had made Ryann part of this. Breaking the deal had as much to do with her as it did with me. And she looked insanely hot, sitting there all bookish and focused.

"Have you read this?" Ryann pointed to one of the pages.

I shook my head. "I haven't had a chance."

"It's got a whole chapter on djinn and their special relationship with Erebus. Did you know they were linked?"

"I knew djinn were linked to Erebus somehow. It's why Zalaam couldn't tell everyone that Imogene was Katherine initially, because my dear old mother made a deal with Erebus, too—that promise that she wouldn't challenge him in the last ritual in exchange for the djinn staying quiet about her. Zalaam was bound to silence because Katherine was loosely tied to Erebus, and he couldn't cross Erebus's wishes. Then he made his own deal with her, in order to spare Raffe, but I imagine that was because he couldn't rat her out earlier because of that whole 'sworn to silence' thing. Complicated, I know." I offered a wry smile. "Melody thinks there's a link between the djinn and the servants of Erebus, too. It's why she asked me to get the book, since there's probably more detailed info in there."

"Incoming," Ryann whispered, thrusting the book at me. I hastily tucked it back into my pants under my shirt, right in the nick of time. Two more guests had arrived, though they swerved toward the bar, occupied by a tense conversation.

"Can't we just have a nice evening?" Raffe muttered.

Santana furiously pushed a strand of hair from her face. "You're the one who brought it up."

"I know, but... I don't want to talk about it now. Come on, let's just forget I ever mentioned it," Raffe pleaded.

"How can I forget you mentioned it? It's pretty freaking important," Santana replied sharply.

Raffe hung his head. "Please, Santana."

"Fine, but we're going to have to talk about it later." Santana moved away from the bar and strode over to the table, with Raffe following. The poor dude looked drained, like he'd had an unexpected run-in with Mary Foster. His usual olive tone appeared ghoulishly pale and haggard.

"Long time no see, Finch." Santana sank beside Ryann while Raffe took a seat next to me. "Did you get tired of that rock you'd crawled back under?"

"Aww, did you worry about me?" I smiled sweetly.

"No way, *pendejo*. I was just wondering if we'd have to put you in a coffin or a jar. You know, since you made us all think you'd been crushed by a load of rocks, when really you were fine."

I wouldn't say "fine." But I wasn't going to give her the satisfaction.

I made a show of lifting the tablecloth to search under the table. "Speaking of *pendejos*, where's the ankle-biter? I wore my shin pads, just in case."

"*Slinky* is back at the SDC. I told him you were coming, and he decided he wanted to stay home and sharpen his fangs for next time," Santana retorted. Man, she was on fire tonight.

"Oh, don't tease me." I sat back in my seat. "Next time I see that slithery worm, I'll be in full body armor. He's not getting so much as a nip, unless he wants to end up as a fancy wallet."

Santana glowered at me. "I'd say I'm pleased to see you haven't changed."

"But?" I prompted.

"But what? That's the whole sentence. Make of it what you will," she replied.

I grinned. "I've missed you too, Santana."

"Oh yeah, and I'm Salma Hayek." A ghost of a smile tugged her lips.

"Alas not, or this would be a much more interesting dinner, and Raffe's eyes would pop out of his head." I knew she'd worried about me. But she and I were like oil and water—we'd never quite gel. And we'd never admit to being friends, though in a fight, I knew she'd have my back and she knew I'd have hers.

"We all missed you, Finch," Raffe said. "And my eyes already pop out of my head whenever Santana's around. She's all the Salma Hayek I'll ever need."

Santana gazed at him as he reached out and took her hand, all their former irritation gone. At least for now.

"Excuse me, waiter? Could I have a barf bucket with a side of cheese?" I pretended to click my fingers, even though I hated when people did that. Fortunately, no waiter came by, or that would've been embarrassing.

Ryann tutted at me. "I think it's sweet."

"You would. I bet the Zodiac Killer wakes you up with GIFs of otters holding hands and says things like, 'You're my otter half,' and you get all gooey." I pushed back the wave of gremlins, trying to keep it Finch. I couldn't let anyone at this table know I was struggling. They had to believe the façade, or I would fall apart, like Mother Dearest and her oozing cracks.

Ryann gasped. "How did you know that?"

"Waiter, can I have your sharpest knife from the kitchen, too, so I can end it all here?" I joked.

"You need a little romance in your life—that's your problem," Santana cut in, fully aware that the woman I wanted to romance had a boyfriend.

I shrugged. "No, my problem is nobody appreciates my comic genius."

"You'll have to let us know when you start being funny, then," Santana fired back.

Raffe rubbed his eyes wearily. "Guys."

"What? He knows I don't mean it." Santana hit me with a disarming smile. It was the friendliest I'd ever gotten from her. Maybe Harley had told her to go easy.

Soon enough, the rest of the Couples Brigade filtered in. Tatyana and Dylan arrived giggling like high school sweethearts, his arm draped over her shoulder in true jock style. Astrid and Garrett came next, holding hands and being a little less in-your-face. I guessed Garrett's brush with death at the mine had bridged the gap between them, at last. Garrett put a hand on the small of Astrid's back as he helped her into the large booth.

"You've got no idea how good it is to see you, man." Garrett shuffled past Raffe and Dylan, who let him through, and grabbed me in a hug.

"Likewise," I replied, with a pointed nod at Astrid. "Looks like the two of you managed to get your act together?"

He beamed at her, radiating happiness. "Yeah, we did."

"At least one good thing came out of that debacle, then." I hugged him back, wishing I could feel the happiness I deserved to feel, seeing my friends alive and well. This constant hollow sensation was worse than sadness. At least that would've sparked some emotion. But this was just... emptiness, plain and simple. And it hurt.

"I can't believe you're actually here." Garrett squeezed me harder.

I mustered a laugh. "You trying to crack a rib?"

"Sorry, man. We thought we lost you. It didn't look good, and O'Halloran said we should prepare for the worst-case scenario. Harley didn't take too kindly to that—she amped up the search parties, determined to find you."

"Then I'm the one who's sorry, for scaring you all like that," I said quietly. For a horrifying moment, I thought I might cry. The tears brimmed, ready to rumble, but I battled to keep them at bay. Flipping between moods like this made my head spin. From hollow, to weepy, to happy, to lost, to angry... it'd drive anyone nuts.

"It wasn't like you had a choice. Anyone who says different will have to deal with me," Garrett assured me.

I raised an eyebrow at Santana. "You hear that, Santana?"

For once, she had no comeback. She just sat there, looking at me weirdly. That concerned me. Could she tell how close I was to the edge? Did they all know? Was paranoia on Melody's list of symptoms? I couldn't remember. My chest gripped in a vise and panic bristled through me. As Garrett released me, I clung to the red vinyl of the booth and prayed for the wave to pass.

Saskia and Jacob appeared a moment later, giving me something new to focus on.

"Anything you want to tell us?" I asked, covering my inner turmoil with a snappy bit of teasing. "Are you the newest recruits in the SDC's not-so-covert mating project?"

Saskia shrieked. "Finch! No one told me you'd be here! Aren't you a sight for sore eyes!"

"It seems I'm the main event." I smiled.

"And no, Jacob and I aren't together. It's purely platonic," Saskia went on. "The boy needs advice on women, and I've accepted the challenge. I'm trying to change his status from 'lonely loser' to 'charming lothario,' since you men have been woefully inadequate in helping Jacob get a date."

"Hey, there's nothing wrong with Jakey's charm. He just had bad luck, that's all," I retorted. Of all women, he'd gone for the human minion of my mother. That hadn't had a rosy ending. Not unless you counted all the blood on the floor. Dark, but true.

Saskia readjusted the straps of her daringly cut dress. "Well, I'm here to change his luck. Isn't that right, Jacob?"

Jacob ran a nervous hand through his hair, his mouth set in a sad line. "So I've been told."

Poor guy. Having a first girlfriend like Suri would put anyone off for life. Or they'd end up going for unattainable women, to lessen the risk of getting hurt again. Unrequited love would always be easier to bear than getting in deep with someone and having them torn away.

Harley and Wade arrived, completing the chain of couples. Wade wore a slick blue suit, and Harley matched him in blue pants and a silky blue shirt. Ordinarily, I'd have commented on it, calling them out as one of *those* couples, but they looked too damn happy for me to rain on their parade. Giddiness exuded from them, and they both looked flushed.

"It's not like you to be fashionably late," I said with a wry smile.

"We wanted to make sure everyone arrived before we came in," Harley explained, the words tumbling out of her mouth a mile a minute.

Wade chuckled. "Seriously, we've been sitting in Daisy for the last half hour."

"I told you that was Harley's car." Dylan nudged Tatyana playfully.

"But there was no one in it when we passed," Tatyana replied, confused.

Harley chuckled. "Yeah, we may have ducked down in case you saw us."

"Is that what the kids are calling it these days?" Santana flashed her friend a wink.

"Brother, sitting right here!" I protested.

"So, what's the occasion?" Saskia leaned her chin on her hand. "Someone getting married?"

I snorted. "Yeah, good one. You think I'd just be finding out now, if my only sister was getting hitched?"

"Actually…" Harley lifted her hand, where an enormous diamond glinted. "Wade and I have something to tell you all."

NINE

Finch

"Bet you feel a little stupid now, huh?" Saskia folded her arms, giving me the full Cheshire Cat treatment.

I ignored her and gaped at Harley. "You're... engaged?"

"Wade asked me yesterday, and I accepted." Harley flushed with delight, intertwining her fingers with Wade's. He gazed at her like he'd won the jackpot, leaning to kiss her. A whoop went up from the table, Santana leading the riot of congratulations. Everyone else followed suit. I resisted asking where Wade had gotten the ring; Mr. Abara had given me a whole new perspective on diamonds.

"Mi hermana! You pinned the sucker down!" Santana hollered, clapping loudly.

Raffe stared into his drink. "Yeah, congratulations, both of you."

You fancy mustering a little more oomph there? His odd brooding didn't give off congratulatory vibes. Then again, I couldn't talk. I was still wrangling my gremlins into submission so I could actually get on board with the celebrations.

"My dudes! Major congratulations!" Dylan joined in, his applause splintering through my skull.

"I knew you wouldn't have scheduled dinner for nothing." Saskia smiled smugly. "I don't wear the glitz and glam for just any occasion."

Tatyana left her seat to hug the affianced. "This is amazing news, guys! I'm so happy for you both."

"We're pretty happy, too." Wade lifted Harley's hand and kissed it.

"*Very* happy. Seriously, I can't remember being this happy before," Harley agreed, her smile so wide I worried her cheeks would crack.

"Congratulations." Garrett stole a glance at Astrid, whose eyes swam with joy. *Ah man, this is going to start a chain reaction of weddings, isn't it?*

"That's just... so... wonderful!" Astrid stumbled over her words, clearly overwhelmed. Someone had caught the love bug while I'd been away. I shifted awkwardly, unsure what to do with myself. I looked at Ryann, who seemed ready to explode.

"Aaaaaaah! I can't believe it—I could kiss you both! Mom and Dad are going to be over the moon," she gushed. "You better brace yourselves for wedding magazines and a million texts about flower arrangements and cake tastings and menu choices. You know Mom will want to be involved in everything."

Harley grinned. "I hope she'll want to help out. Give me monsters and evil minions; I know what to do with those. Wedding planning stumps me. Naturally, I'll bug you about it, too."

"Bug away!" Ryann raised her glass. "Let's toast the happy couple."

Everyone clamored for their glasses. I did the same, not wanting to be the odd one out. I hoped nobody had noticed that I hadn't actually said congratulations yet. Don't get me wrong, I was happy for them, but I didn't know how I fit in this picture. Everyone's lives had moved on without me while I'd been away. I hadn't expected them to wait around or anything, but I felt like I was playing a losing game of catch-up.

"Three cheers for Wade and Harley!" Santana hollered, drawing amused glances from other tables as everyone unleashed a trio of mighty cheers. The other diners applauded, feeling the love. You just had to look at the couple to see how much they adored each other. They'd survived so much and come out of it more in love than ever. And... I admired them. So much that I decided not to bother with self-pity. They deserved this, probably more than anyone.

As everyone settled down, Tatyana leaned over the table. "Don't keep us in suspense. How did he propose? Was it insanely romantic? Candlelight, roses, the whole nine yards?"

Saskia wrinkled up her nose. "That's tacky."

"You're high-maintenance," Tatyana retorted. "You wouldn't be happy unless the entire room dripped diamonds and you got a rock as big as your head. I pity the poor guy who wants to marry you."

"Who says I want to get married? It's not the be-all and end-all," Saskia huffed. "Not that this isn't great news. I just mean, it might not be for me. Divorce seems like a lot of hassle, and I see myself as the divorcing sort."

"Saskia!" Tatyana complained. "Let Harley tell the proposal story!"

Harley gave a teasing glance to Wade, who'd already turned beet red. "Well, he took me to the Aquarium at midnight last night. He'd arranged the entire thing with Tobe, who was there when we arrived."

Tobe knew before me?! I forced myself to smile and listen. That stung a tad, but this was my sister's moment. I had no place being all mopey. Harley would soon marry the love of her life—the man who'd been by her side through all of her troubles. If I couldn't be happy for them, then I might as well have stayed at the Winchester House.

"Wade and Tobe had lit the entire place with candles, and these glowing white snails from the Bestiary—Clusterwink snails, I think they're called. Anyway, Tobe started to sing. All the sea sprites and firefly squid came out, with the selkies and the sirens joining them, holding glowing orbs and singing the most haunting, bittersweet song I've ever heard. All about love and loss and hope. It was like staring into a whole undiscovered universe, all the stars twinkling just for us."

She put her hand on Wade's shoulder. "I turned to him to tell him how amazing it was, but he was down on one knee, with the ring box open. And he said, 'I wanted to create a galaxy just for us, because I can't give you the stars, but you're the center of my universe.' With the music, and all the glowing lights, and his face peering up at me with so much love... I burst into tears and said yes." She laughed and pulled Wade closer while he cringed. "I wish I'd said something more profound, but I'll save that for the wedding."

"'Yes' was profound enough for me," Wade replied with an embarrassed grin. "You could've left some of the details out. I'm burning up, here."

"No, she couldn't!" Santana protested. "We wanted to hear everything."

Dylan nodded. "Yeah, man, thanks for setting the bar so high."

"I wanted it to be perfect," Wade said.

"It was. It really was." Harley kissed him, not caring that everyone was watching. Another explosive whoop of cheers erupted from the table, startling the server who'd come to take our orders. He quickly scurried away, probably realizing it wasn't the best time to give the specials.

Jacob toyed with his shirt sleeves, looking as uncomfortable as I felt. "But... aren't you a bit young? No offense, I think it's cool, and I'm mega-pleased for you both, but I couldn't imagine getting married at your age."

Wade smiled. "After all we've been through, I think it's added about a decade to our real ages."

Harley kissed his cheek. "And we're already partners in work and in life and in love, so it just felt... natural to take the next step. You know, make it official. Believe me, I didn't think I'd get married this young either, but when you find the right person, and it feels right, then it doesn't make sense to wait."

"Precisely." Wade gazed at her as if he held his entire world in his arms.

"Personally, it makes me want to gouge my eyes out, and maybe rip out my ear canals while I'm at it. Or your tongues, to cease this sickening sweetness." Raffe's eyes snapped up from his drink, glowing red. "We are at dinner, after all, and I could use a little tongue *hors d'oeuvre* to start me off. I'm ravenous."

What the—! Raffe had vacated the building, and Kadar had seized control.

"You think this is the time for an engagement? You think anyone cares about your pathetic human rituals?" Kadar slammed his fists on the table, smoke billowing from his shoulders. "If you used your eyes for something other than gawping at each other, maybe you'd see that one of your own is in pain! I ought to rip you all to shreds and use your entrails as a veil."

"Kadar!" Santana put her hand on his arm. "Take it easy. Focus on me. Just look at me and listen to me and try to calm down. I know you're in pain. I know Raffe hasn't been sleeping, and you're both tired."

Kadar glared at the table. "And what have you done about it? Nothing! Your voice is like razorblades."

"Kadar, stop." Santana grasped his face and forced him to look at her. "You don't get to speak to my friends like that. I know you're hurting, and I *have* been helping you. So calm your ass down. I'll use my Orishas—you know I will."

Kadar twisted his mouth into a scowl. "And I'll send them running."

"What's going on?" Harley peered at the raging djinn, his billowing smoke thickening as his skin flushed scarlet. Realization hit me like a bitch-slap: Raffe's sullenness and Kadar's apparent pain had something to do with Erebus. I just knew it.

Santana cast her a strained look. "He's been like this for a while. I don't know why, and neither Raffe nor Kadar can tell me. Honestly, I don't think they know what's happening."

"Not that you care about me," Kadar spat. "You only think about your precious Raffe, but he and I are a package deal, sweetheart. He hurts, I hurt. He doesn't sleep, I don't sleep. He loses it, I lose it."

"Yeah, well, don't go losing it, pal." Dylan gripped Kadar's wrist.

Ah, you shouldn't have done that.

"Unhand me!" Kadar roared. Heads turned throughout the restaurant.

"Kadar, listen to Santana," Wade cut in, hands raised.

Kadar sneered. "She's about as useful as the rest of you measly flesh-bags. She can't help me. If this could be fixed, I would've done it myself. I have more power in my left eyeball than you all have in your entire bodies."

"It's Erebus, isn't it?" I found my voice.

Kadar's eyes flashed. "Don't speak to me of that wretch!"

"I'll take that as a yes," I replied. "Since the djinn draw their power from Erebus, there's only one person to blame." And Erebus had a jazzy new human body, which restricted his power. I hadn't realized until now that his limitations would affect the djinn.

Garrett, Ryann, and Saskia gasped in unison. They knew about

Erebus and his human body. Harley did too, now, but she seemed to be a little slower to slot the pieces together.

"When did this start, Kadar?" I asked.

"None of your business," Kadar rasped.

Santana looked at me desperately. "It started a few weeks ago."

"Right after the Jubilee mine collapse?"

"Y-yes… around then," she stammered, keeping a firm hold on Kadar. The timelines fit. Erebus got his body, and the djinn went nuts. Cause and effect. But I couldn't tell the others about the Erebus part—not yet. Enough people knew, and I wouldn't drag the rest in. I'd owed Harley answers, but I didn't owe the rest of the Muppet Babies. They were out of it, and I planned to keep it that way.

"Enough of your incessant chattering! Every word you speak pains me! If I have to listen to another sound, I will kill you all and strip your bones bare!" Kadar slammed his fists into the table again, harder this time. The wood split on impact, and fire surged from the cracks, sending up licking flames. Everyone ducked for cover. The other diners screamed as the waiters rushed to find fire extinguishers and yelled for anyone with Water abilities to come and help out, since this was a magical restaurant.

In the mayhem, Kadar leapt onto the table and ran through the blaze. Wade tried to trap him behind the flame wall with a burst of Fire, while Dylan dove for Kadar's ankles. Wade got a swift punch in the jaw, and Dylan took a sharp kick to the face for their trouble. Kadar darted out the door.

So much for a happy engagement.

TEN

Finch

———

"R yann, stay with Saskia and Jacob." I jumped up to tear after the Hellboy wannabe. Erebus had Kadar's panties in a bunch, and he needed to be stopped before he did any more damage. I hated to think of the size of the bill for this table, and we hadn't even ordered entrées.

"But—" Ryann started to object, until Harley cut her off.

"It's safer if you stay here."

Tatyana nodded. "You too, Saskia."

"It's your funeral," Saskia said sullenly, but we had no time for teenage sulking.

The Muppet Babies and I sprinted from the restaurant. Kadar's trail proved easy to follow. Huddles of frightened magicals littered the walkways of Waterfront Park, staring in the direction the grumpy little fireball had gone. We raced through and burst into the warm night air. If any humans saw him, we'd be up crap creek without a paddle. Laws surrounding mind-wiping without permission had gotten a little hazy, and calling in a cleanup crew would mean reams of red tape.

"Where is he?" I stopped on the edge of the street and glanced up and down the road.

A roar pierced the night, sending a shiver up my spine. My eyes lifted skyward, and I spotted a figure on the rooftop opposite. I ran across the road and made for the fire escape. Using a lasso of Telekinesis, I wrapped the tendril around the first metal platform and hoisted myself up. Harley was close behind, though she briefly paused to help the others while I pressed on.

By the time I reached the roof, my throat burned and my lungs were gasping for air. I'd mostly recovered from Marlene's ice wall, but I still had a few bruises that made breathing trickier than it should have been.

Kadar stood on the roof's edge, hunched over like a gargoyle. He roared again, his growl filled with pain. I didn't need to be an Empath to sense the guy's agony.

"Kadar." I lifted my hands, appeasing.

His head twisted toward me. "It hurts! I want to rip out my insides. Anything to make it stop. I have to make it stop!"

"And throwing yourself over the roof won't do that. It'll end up with Raffe splattered and you slowly decaying inside a dead body," I reasoned. "You'll have to suffer through all of that, and what comes after."

"You don't understand," Kadar snarled. "I can't take it anymore!"

"Then make me understand." I stepped closer. From this distance, I'd have a split second, maybe less, to throw a lasso of Telekinesis if he decided to jump.

"As if you could." He buckled over, wrapping his arms around his stomach.

I edged closer, trying to up my chances of a successful catch. "I'm a servant of Erebus, too. I might understand more than you think."

"Not the way I am." He unleashed another roar that shook the building. "He's killing me."

Santana reached my side. "Tell us what's going on, Kadar, so we can help."

"There's nothing you can do." He turned to her, red eyes glinting. "Only death or Erebus can end this torture. And Erebus no longer listens."

Everything happened in a blur. One moment, Kadar stood on the edge of the roof. The next—he'd hurled himself off.

My hands reacted instinctively, tendrils of Telekinesis rocketing over the edge. They touched something solid, and I yanked back hard. Kadar flew upward, landing on his back.

"NO!" he bellowed, fighting the tendrils. I gripped tighter, using them to hold him down. Santana and Tatyana rushed past and skidded to their knees beside him. Santana's Orishas exploded out of her, while Tatyana's eyes glowed white, calling on the nearby spirits. Blue and white sparks collided, the Orishas working with the spirits to immobilize Kadar. They sank into his body, taking temporary control.

Still gripping the Telekinesis strands, I walked up to him. He'd stilled, though his ruby eyes stared upward, scarlet tears trickling down his face. They flitted toward me as I neared.

"Why did you do that?" he hissed. "I don't want to live anymore. I can't live with this. The pain, the emptiness, the dread. It's like slowly dying and not being able to stop it. I'd rather make it quick, for both our sakes—Raffe's and mine."

My gremlins jostled inside my head. He and I were in similar positions, for different reasons. "Because you have people who care—people who want to see you fight this. People who'll stop at nothing to make sure you see another day. If you'd ended your life tonight, you'd have broken Santana's heart, and everyone else's."

"They don't care for me." The blood-red tears stained his cheeks. "They only care about Raffe. And I was doing this for *both* of us. He's in as much pain as I am. He doesn't want to go on, either."

"No. We know you, Kadar. We know you as well as Raffe. And we don't want to bury you," I said. Santana took hold of his hands, visibly fighting to keep herself together.

"It's true," she whispered. "I love Raffe, but you're part of him. A part he can't live without, and a part I can't live without. Why do you think I've stayed up with you all night when Raffe passed out cold and you've been at your worst? Why do you think I've had Slinky wrap himself around you to keep you safe? It's not just for Raffe... it's for you, too. So don't do that again. Please."

"All you've done is prolong our torture." Kadar shook violently as the Orishas and the spirits tried to calm him. His djinn energy was clearly having a bad reaction to the spiritual influx. "All you've done is bring... more... pain."

"Then tell us how to fix you," Santana begged.

Kadar gazed at her with a sad smile. "That's just it, *señorita*. We don't... know how."

His eyes rolled back as the red glow faded, along with the scarlet sheen of his skin. The smoke stopped billowing, and his body went limp. He'd passed out, taking Raffe with him into oblivion.

"That was a close shave." I exhaled, keeping the tendrils around him just in case.

Santana leaned forward and buried her face in his chest, while Tatyana released the spirits and returned to her usual, non-glowing self. The rest of the Muppet Babies approached, taking in the mayhem with solemn expressions. This probably hadn't been the night Harley and Wade expected. I hated that Kadar had ruined their evening, but I hated his agony more.

Erebus's signature was scrawled all over this mess. That level of suffering... I couldn't comprehend it. Through all my mental struggles, there'd only been a handful of times when I'd thought about... well, what Kadar had almost done. It took a mind that had reached complete hopelessness to take that jump. A total belief that there was nothing left to live for, that death beat any pain you were going through.

"Don't you dare do that again. Don't you dare leave me." Santana grasped Raffe's shirt, her tears leaving damp spots on the fabric. "I don't want to be without either of you."

Make a joke. Lighten the mood. Do something! I banished the impulse. Even in my fractured state of mind, I knew this was no time for humor. Kadar really had meant to kill himself. All because of Erebus. Erebus or death; he'd said so himself. And that understanding took a weird toll on my brain. Paranoia gave a roundhouse to the old gray matter, out of nowhere. What if Erebus was watching me through the djinn's eyes, at this very moment? What if he suspected I was up to something? I subtly touched the book hidden under my shirt.

"He'll be all right, Santana." With a shaky hand, I touched her back in attempted reassurance.

She jolted. "What if he's not?"

"We'll find a way to help him." I kept my hand on her back. "Let's take him to the infirmary and have Krieger give him a onceover. When he wakes up, I'll find out exactly what's going on with Erebus."

"Why? It's not like you're great *amigos*. Why would you help him?" Santana didn't even look at me—she just smoothed Raffe's ruffled shirt.

Because I'm not a selfish assclown, like everyone seems to think. I resisted the urge to snark. Santana was suffering, and she needed an outlet for her grief. It hurt, sure, but I could be her emotional punching bag if she needed one, for now.

"Because I understand the pain he's in, to some extent," I replied. *And helping him might help me.* That might've been backtracking on the non-selfish thing, but Raffe and Kadar might have intel on Erebus. Intel that might supplement the book I'd stolen and whatever Melody had gathered from her mind palace. One way or another, I was ending my servitude to Erebus.

Santana eyed me strangely. "Really?"

"Is that so hard to believe?" I said quietly.

"No… I suppose not."

"Come on. Let's get your smoldering *señor* back to the SDC." I took a step back and crouched nearby, sketching a doorway with my trusty charmed chalk.

I whispered the *Aperi Si Ostium* spell and opened the door.

"How do we get him through?" Santana asked.

Dylan appeared beside Tatyana. "I'll help. What else are muscles for?" He scooped up Raffe like he weighed nothing and jumped through the chalk door to the infirmary, visible below. Tatyana and Santana followed him down, and I prepared to do the same. Before I could, someone tapped my shoulder.

"Where are you running off to?" Harley furrowed her brow.

"I need to talk to Raffe when he wakes up," I replied.

She nodded slowly. "E-man stuff?"

"What else?" I rolled my eyes. "Apparently, I've got an unhealthy obsession with him. But you guys should stay and salvage your evening. Or at least pay the restaurant for singeing their table. Ryann and the others will be worrying about whether they'll have to foot the bill."

"I've been meaning to talk to you about that, actually." Her tone turned even more serious.

"About what?"

"Ryann." Harley fiddled with her shiny new ring. "Is there something going on between you two? I've noticed the looks between you, and she stayed tight-lipped about where you were. Keeping secrets like a... a girlfriend might. And you seem protective, which I'm super-grateful for, of course, but it feels... like there might be something going on. You'd tell me if there was, right?"

I cleared my throat. "You'd be the first to know, but there's nothing to tell. She loves Adam, and I'm a lone wolf. That's all there is to it."

"You just called him Adam!"

"Did I?" I fumbled for words. "Maybe I'm running out of serial killers. Anyway, there's nothing going on, and I need to leave before this doorway shuts. You go deal with the fallout and stop worrying. It's your engagement night; you're not allowed to worry."

She gave a bitter laugh. "Hard not to, when a djinn sets fire to everything."

"You know what they say—the worse the engagement, the better the marriage."

"I thought that was the wedding."

I shrugged. "How should I know? I'm hardly an expert."

"Well, do you need any help? Do you want me to come with you? I'm sure Wade can—"

"Nope, it's all good," I interjected. "You go back to the restaurant, take Ryann and the kids home, and I'll let you know if I need anything. Love you, sis."

Before she could object, I jumped through the door and slammed it behind me. The engagement party might've ended, but my night had just begun.

ELEVEN

Finch

I'd had to hold my horses on questioning. Half an hour went by in the infirmary, and Tatyana and Dylan had finally left. Krieger busied himself around the place, collecting vials and medicine bags to string up for Raffe. He was still unconscious, passed out on a narrow hospital bed. Slinky coiled around him like living rope, no doubt to stop him from escaping if Kadar woke first. It rested its scaly head on Raffe's chest, tongue flicking.

Gross...

"How'd you get it here so fast?" I perched on the opposite bed, observing the feathered snake in case it lunged for me.

Santana sighed. "He comes when I call now. I can summon him, as long as I'm in the SDC."

"Suitably creepy."

"He keeps Raffe calm," Santana replied tersely. "If Kadar tries to do anything rash, he tightens his coils. Slinky's stopped a few outbursts so far, so he stays. Don't even think about having him thrown out."

I raised my hands in mock surrender. "Whatever works, as long as it keeps its fangs to itself."

"Damn straight," she shot back.

"So, what *has* been happening to Raffe?" I segued smoothly into my interrogation. My concern for Raffe was genuine, though my motivations might have been slightly selfish. If the djinn were suffering, that didn't spell good news for me. I needed the djinn.

"He hasn't been sleeping or eating. I bring him food and he pushes it away, like seeing it makes him feel sick," she replied. "When he's weak, Kadar takes over, and that's when the pain comes."

I nodded. "That must be hard on you, dealing with all of that by yourself."

"I've got Slinky's help." She sagged against the bed. "Thank you for helping him, by the way. I know I'm bitchy with you sometimes, but he'd be... I can't even say it. He'd be... gone if you hadn't stepped in. So thank you. I mean it—thank you."

"Don't mention it." I processed that for a moment. How often did Santana give me sincere appreciation? I wanted to absorb it, just this once. "Has either of them mentioned anything to you about where this pain and sickness is coming from?" I knew by now that it was Erebus, but I wanted to find out if Kadar had mentioned anything about the Child of Chaos to Santana.

She shot me a cold stare, her mood switching faster than lightning. "Why are you so interested? Is this some Erebus bullcrap? If it is, and you're involved, you best believe I'll strangle you into next year."

"I just wanted to make sure he was okay!" I replied. It wasn't exactly a lie.

"Again, why? What does this have to do with you? I know you're not telling me something, and I want to know what it is." Her tone hardened. "Is this some Erebus stuff?"

I shifted to face her. "Look, I'm concerned about Raffe and Kadar because the djinn are linked to Erebus. So, yes, in that sense, but there's nothing seedy to me staying here with them. I want to help if I can. So, why don't you tell me everything that you've seen and heard, and let's see if we can work this out together?"

Santana glanced back at Raffe, and her shoulders relaxed. "It came out of nowhere. One day, he was fine, and then... it took hold of him, like a fast-working fever."

"Has he spoken about Erebus before?" I pressed.

"No, that was news to me," she said. "Maybe we should talk outside. I want to speak to you properly, but all I can think about is Raffe when I'm in here."

I smiled. "You read my mind." If we left the infirmary, maybe Erebus wouldn't be able to hear what I said. Unless he had another djinn hiding in the shadows. Either way, I'd be more comfortable away from *this* djinn.

Together, we left and walked a fair way up the hallway before Santana halted. Her expression shifted. Gone was the quiet suspicion and sad gratitude, replaced by a firecracker's sparking anger.

"Seriously, what's with the secrecy, Finch? Why won't you let anyone help you? You clearly need it—I mean, look at you! You don't look much better than Raffe."

"I've been running around—"

She put her hands on her hips. "Do you have any idea how freaked we all were when you vanished without a trace and didn't tell anyone where you were? We thought you were dead, Finch! Harley went to pieces. She was ready to call the president and send every Earth magical and Geode in the United States to Russia to dig out your body."

I winced. Harley hadn't mentioned that.

Santana shook her head. "Over and over, Harley said, 'We have to bring him home. Even if he's dead, we have to bring him home. I have to say goodbye.' Tobe sat with her in his arms for hours, singing to her. Nothing else calmed her down. Why do you think she got so overwhelmed by Wade's proposal? Tobe singing probably brought it all back. She had Tatyana on standby to speak to your spirit."

I stared at her, gobsmacked. What could anyone say to that? And she wasn't done tearing me a new one.

"You saw what I was like tonight, when I thought I might lose Raffe. Well, Harley was exactly the same," Santana continued furiously. "And, *dios mio*, why are you getting Ryann—a freaking human—involved? She was almost as bad as Harley. In fact, I think she only tried to hold it together for Harley's sake. And Saskia, while I'm at it. She's Tatyana's baby sister, for crying out loud. Are you insane?"

Guilt, shame, anger, sadness—it all rushed through me in a torrent. It hurt more than I could describe. Just thinking about Harley sobbing into Tobe's arms, saying she wanted to say goodbye to me, made me sick to my stomach. I'd done that to her.

This is what they really think about you, Finch. They think you're only out for yourself. And you're not exactly proving them wrong. If I could've reached into my skull and ripped out every last dark thought, I would've. Even if it killed me. This was the pain Kadar meant. This was unbearable hopelessness, live and in vivid Technicolor. No matter how many Katherines I killed, or what I gave up, it didn't matter. Everyone's first assumption was selfishness. Nobody expected me to do anything for their sake instead of mine.

"Do you really think I wouldn't have phoned, or walked through a chalk door, or done *something* to let her know I was okay, if I could've?" I fired back, my friendliness gone. "Do you think I wanted Ryann involved? Or Saskia, for that matter? I care about them all. If I could have, I'd have kept right on doing things solo, but I reached a point where it wasn't possible anymore. I tried... but I couldn't do it alone. I *would* be dead if I had, though maybe you'd prefer that? Seriously, Santana, do you think so little of me that you believe I'd willingly bring them into this disaster?"

It was her turn to look dumbfounded. In fairness, I wasn't entirely shocked to get an earful. Both Harley and Tatyana must have mentioned their issues with me before, while I'd been gone. And Santana had obviously been their go-to. But I was in no mood to explain myself and have my character smeared by Santana. Not now.

"I... I don't think badly of you at all. I just want to understand what's going on. You weren't here. You didn't see what everyone was like, and it truly sucked, Finch." She managed to find an answer, her tone softening slightly.

"And I'm telling you, I wish I had been here. I didn't ask for any of this." I balled my hands into fists, knowing if I went too far, I wouldn't be able to take it back. "I've done my damnedest to keep everyone safe. And you and I might not always see eye to eye, but you're included. I'd fight tooth and nail to make sure you, and everyone else in this place, don't have to go through what I'm going through."

Santana sighed heavily. "I'd like to believe that's true, but Ryann, Saskia, and Garrett are already involved."

"I didn't want them to be!" I barked. "I love her. Why would I want her in danger? That's why I'm not curling into a ball and giving up, even though I want to every second of every damn day."

"What did you say?" Santana's eyes widened.

"What?"

"You said you love her. Who? Ryann?"

My mouth fell open. "I meant as a friend. I love them all as friends. I love all of you as friends." The words rattled out like gunfire.

"That's not what it sounded like," Santana replied, her eyes fixed on mine.

"Well, apparently nothing is what it sounds like to you." I couldn't believe I'd said that out loud. "You think I'm some dumb, reckless prick who only cares about himself."

She shook her head. "I never said that. You saved Raffe. That's not the action of someone just out for himself."

Oh, way to make it worse! After all, my motivations weren't entirely selfless.

"And I don't think that about you," she continued. "I said things I shouldn't have, and I'm sorry for that. I'm majorly stressed over everything with Raffe, and I let my frustration get the best of me. You're not a bad guy, Finch. But all this secrecy and trouble you're in… it's really freaking upsetting for someone on the outside looking in, with no idea what's happening."

"It's not much better for those on the inside looking out, either," I said, hastily trying to rebuild those walls. "And I don't know much more than you, about what's going on. If I did, it would be easier."

Santana lowered her gaze. "You won't put Raffe in danger by being here, will you?"

"I want to talk to him, that's it. No harm, no foul."

"If he gets hurt, I swear—"

"He's not going to get hurt! Not by me, anyway," I cut her off. "Although, if you don't let me speak to him, that'll be out of my control."

She frowned. "You really think you can help?"

"I wouldn't be here if I didn't."

She toyed with the keyring on her belt loop. Her Esprit. "Then we should head back in."

"You're done ranting at me?"

Her cheeks reddened. "For now."

"Good. Lead the way while I scoop up what's left of my *cajones*."

I waited until she'd walked a few steps ahead before taking two pills out of my pocket. I'd stowed them there before leaving for the restaurant, an 'in case of emergency, shove these down your throat' scenario. I did just that, swallowing them and praying they'd take the edge off the monsters in my mind.

The trouble was, if the pills really had stopped working, then I was at the top of a slippery slope with only one way to go.

TWELVE

Raffe

I blinked awake. Bright lights stabbed my eyes. In the distance, I heard Santana. Had that brought me out of the darkness? Her voice had that effect on me. I glanced around but couldn't see her. But I did see the familiar landscape of the infirmary. The sterile white walls and rough blue sheets. A drip snaked out of my arm. And a feathered snake rested on my chest.

Hi, Slink. My mouth couldn't quite form words. Not yet. My throat had dried, and the scent of smoke rested in my nostrils. Memories flooded my mind: the restaurant, the fire, the rooftop. Not my memories, per se. These belonged to Kadar. I could always tell the difference. His memories had a spikier edge to them.

The serpent raised his head and flicked his tongue, slithering closer. I tried to lift my arm to stroke him, but there seemed to be a delay between my brain and my limbs. It wasn't the first time this had happened. Since getting sick, every time I switched with Kadar, it took time for my body to readjust.

So, I lay there with only my thoughts for company. I thought of Santana, mostly. She was always on my mind, especially recently. Even before the strange sickness took hold, which Kadar and I couldn't explain to anyone, least of all ourselves.

The simple truth was that I loved Santana. I'd probably been in love with her from the moment we met. Back then, I'd thought a relationship would be impossible, but she'd changed my mindset. She'd embraced me and the beast—both of us—though Kadar could be terrifying when he wanted to be. He still scared *me* sometimes, but we had to coexist.

I'd believed, perhaps foolishly, that I could manage a relationship. When Kadar warmed to her, it had bolstered that hope. In fact, he loved her almost as much as I did. I didn't always like that, but at least we were on the same page. And he knew not to tread on my toes. He'd seen what had happened with my father and Zalaam, and he likely hadn't wanted to give me a reason to suppress him the way my father had suppressed his djinn for so long.

Everything had gone smoothly... until it hadn't. I couldn't say when the change had occurred. I suppose it was the first time we spoke about a future, a month or so ago. Our relationship had grown serious, and that sort of talk was a natural progression. It should've been fun—discussing children, a house, a family. But it had filled me with a sense of dread. Not because I didn't love her enough, or because I didn't want those things. I did. But I realized as we talked that I couldn't give them to her.

Since then, I'd slowly tried to push her away. Not very successfully, I might add. I had no idea how to begin. Santana was my one weakness, more a part of me than the djinn, in many ways. I loved her too much. *Kadar* loved her too much. I knew I had to, but I couldn't bring myself to sever ties. It would've destroyed me as much as cutting Kadar loose.

And that brought confusion and frustration. I was an only child raised by a bitter father. The curse of the Levi family took my mother —his wife. It was the punishment of my ancestor, who crossed a powerful sorcerer, and it had plagued us ever since. It didn't always happen that way, with death, but my mother had been unlucky. And Santana came from a big, happy family, a world away from the life I'd led. She'd told me she wanted a houseful of children, and it pained me to know that every child would risk Santana's life—more than the ordinary risks associated with childbirth. We might not even make it past one kid before the curse claimed her. How could I chance that? I couldn't play Russian roulette with the woman I loved more than life.

The sickness with Kadar had only added to the strain. Santana had been incredible, sitting up all night with me. I wouldn't have eaten or drunk anything if it hadn't been for her care. I'd fallen in love with her even more, experiencing that. Kadar had, too. She had maternal instincts already. Who was I to say she couldn't use them on her own children? Who was I to take that from her? People always said love knew no boundaries, but sometimes they had to be set, for the happiness of the person you loved most.

I hated feeling so weak. My djinn's strength had generally faded, though it came back in violent spurts of Chaos that I couldn't control. When he wasn't lashing out like tonight, he'd become much easier to placate. Rising to the surface took a lot out of him. But what he felt, I felt. I may not have felt the pains he endured, but I suffered the aftermath—the tiredness, the feebleness, the need to sleep for a year.

You almost killed us tonight. Kadar didn't answer. He was buried deep. As much as I wanted to free Santana from our relationship, so

she could find the happiness she deserved and live without limitations, I didn't want it like that. I didn't want her to grieve my death.
Kadar's outbursts had grown unpredictable. And I feared what he
might try next while he held our body's reins.

"Ah, you're awake!" Krieger's voice distracted me. "I wondered how
long you might be out."

"How long *was* I out?" I croaked. Slinky slithered up my chest and
draped himself around my throat, warming my stiff muscles. Not
usually what you'd expect from a reptile, but he was no ordinary
reptile.

Krieger came over to check my drip. "Less than an hour."

"Good, I thought it might've been longer." I struggled to sit up. "Is
Santana here? I heard her voice."

"She stepped outside with Finch," Krieger explained.

"Finch?" I pictured the rooftop and recalled something pulling me
back. Finch had saved me, I remembered.

As if summoned, Finch and Santana entered the infirmary. They
both looked awkward. Considering I'd heard her from all the way in
here while unconscious, I imagined they'd had a heated conversation.
Santana had wanted a word with him ever since Harley told her Finch
would be at dinner. I'd urged her to leave it alone, but I guessed a
moment had presented itself. It was hard to gauge who the victor was.
Neither looked particularly satisfied.

"Raffe! *Dios mio,* you're awake." Santana ran over and sat on the
bed. She dropped kisses on my face, prompting Slinky to join in with
reptilian licks.

"I'm sorry I scared you," I said, kissing her back.

She clutched my face in her hands and pressed her forehead to
mine. "You didn't scare me. Kadar scared me. But you're okay, and
awake, and that's all that matters."

"I couldn't control him. He took over, and I… vanished." I kissed her again, more passionately. When I was near her, that was all I wanted to do. My weakness, my reason, my love. A magnetic pull I couldn't resist, despite knowing our relationship had a shelf life.

Finch coughed. "If you could keep the romantics to a minimum? I don't want to end up spewing on Krieger's polished floors."

"Don't mind my floors. They've seen worse. And a kiss is often the best medicine," Krieger chided.

Finch groaned and sat down on the opposite bed. "What do you remember about tonight?"

"All of it," I replied. "They're Kadar's memories, but I have access to them."

"I bet that's a barrel of laughs." He shook his head.

I smiled. "It would be worse if I didn't know what happened during Kadar's outbursts. Thank you for saving me, by the way. I owe you."

"So you weren't up for offing yourself?" he asked, serious and curious.

"Not at all. If I'd known what he'd planned, I would've fought harder for control."

Finch ran an anxious hand through his hair. "Is it just Kadar dealing with that unbearable pain, then? Or do you experience it, too?"

"I feel the aftereffects, not the pain itself. I ache after an outburst, and I tire quickly, but when I try to sleep, I can't. It's like a migraine, where you know you have to rest, but the pain keeps you from falling asleep. Only, I don't feel the actual pain. I just sense Kadar dealing with it, and it keeps me awake." I hoped that made sense. The situation was difficult to explain to someone with no idea what it was like to share a body.

"Kadar mentioned, pre-jump, that only Erebus or death could end the pain. And he said Erebus wasn't listening anymore. Has he said anything like that to you? Can you access his thoughts on that kind of thing?" Finch leaned forward.

I wracked my brain. "He isn't connected to the djinn mainframe, but he has mentioned that he can't feel anything anymore. I thought he meant he felt numb, but that doesn't make sense, given how many nights he's been up, howling in agony."

"Interesting," Finch said softly.

"Do you know something about it?" He seemed overly inquisitive for someone with just a casual concern for my wellbeing.

He shook his head. "Not exactly, no. But I'll help however I can, to get to the bottom of it."

Santana twisted to shoot him a scowl. "Bullcrap. You know something. You said you wanted to speak to Raffe, and that if you didn't speak to him, something bad might happen—you had a specific reason for that, I know you did. You saved him, and I'm grateful, like I said, but there's something off here. So start talking."

"I just want to help," Finch fired back.

"There's more to it. Why won't you tell us?" Santana urged angrily. "Would it kill you to be honest with us, for once?"

He gave a bitter smile. "It might not kill *me*."

"What the hell is that supposed to mean?" I felt Santana tense in my arms. She was ready to lunge at Finch. I tightened my arms around her.

"Both of you, stop," I said. "You're arguing like little kids. I heard you from in here. It's bad enough dealing with a suicidal djinn without wrangling the two of you."

"You heard us?" Finch's entire demeanor altered, and his voice sounded strangled.

"I heard Santana and figured you were arguing." I looked back at my love. "If he's here to help, then let him help. If he has any other reason on top of that, it's his business. If it affected us, he'd tell us. Just leave it, okay? For the sake of my sanity."

Finch opened his mouth, but the doors of the infirmary burst wide open, silencing him. Two security magicals carried a limp figure between them. One with a face I recognized like my own.

"Father?" I gasped.

Krieger rushed over, gesturing for the security personnel to lay my father in the next bed.

"Is he okay?" I craned my neck for a better look. He appeared to be out cold, and I saw dark purple circles beneath his eyes. His skin had taken on a waxy sheen, and he was visibly exhausted. "Father? Father, can you hear me?"

He lay still, his eyes closed. I tried to get up, but Santana pushed me down.

Krieger gathered a tray of vials. "I will do what I can. It may be the same condition you've been suffering."

"What?" I murmured, my heart pounding. If anything happened to my father, I didn't know what I would do. We may not have the best example of a father-son bond, but our relationship had improved this past year. We'd started having dinner together—voluntarily. Albeit, not recently. My father had been keeping to himself of late, and now I understood why. He hadn't wanted me to see him like this.

"I'll let you know what I find as soon as I've evaluated him," Krieger promised, getting to work.

Santana sat back and gazed into my eyes, panicked. "What the actual heck is going on?"

"I don't know, my *ciela*," I replied.

Santana rocked slightly. "Someone has to know something. If this happened to Levi, too, it's not some random sickness—it's a pattern."

Her face scrunched. "You and Kadar are calm now, sure, but how long until this thing breaks you? Kadar said it himself: he can't bear it anymore. What if nobody saves you next time?"

"He's asleep now. I've got the reins." I tried to comfort her, but she was way past that.

Her gaze darted to Finch. "You said you wanted to help, so help us. Please."

"What do you want me to do?" Finch replied, entirely sincere. No name-brand sarcasm.

"Talk to Erebus and find out what's going on. Please, Finch. You know him better than anyone. He might speak to you," she begged.

Finch gripped the edge of the mattress until his knuckles whitened. "I'll try."

Santana had been right. There *was* something off with Finch. His whole manner seemed odd. I might've attributed it to his disorder, but this didn't feel delusional. I hadn't seen him have any episodes, but I'd read up. This didn't fit the bill. No, something else was afoot here. Finch wasn't telling us everything, just as Santana suspected. However, I knew Finch. If he was staying quiet, he had a reason. Likely, one that involved sparing us from Erebus's unpleasantness. Unfortunately, he didn't get to stay silent if it affected me and my father.

He had a good soul, deep down, and he had certainly shown he was no longer driven by selfish motivation. He'd done his mother's bidding because she'd brainwashed him. Since meeting Harley, he'd been on a steady path to redemption. So his silence couldn't be selfish. That wasn't who he was anymore.

"I'll speak to Finch alone, later," I said to Santana, attempting to calm her down. She opened her mouth to protest but changed her mind.

When I *did* speak to Finch alone, I'd get to the bottom of this. With my father lying unconscious next to me, and the djinn inside me trying to kill us both, finding out what Finch knew had skyrocketed to my second-highest priority. A tiny step behind Santana, who would always have the top spot.

THIRTEEN

Finch

M eet me at the infirmary as soon as you get this.
The buzz of Raffe's text interrupted the precious few hours of sleep I'd managed. My cheek lay squashed against the opening chapters of the pilfered book, and a streak of drool was drying on the page.

You'll have to wait, my pretty. I closed the book and slid it under my pillow for safekeeping. Rubbing the gunk from my eyes, my hair sticking up at all angles, I slipped out of my threadbare PJs and headed back to Krieger's lair. Not nude, of course. I put clothes on first. Raffe had endured enough horrors.

"Morning sunshine," I crowed, entering the infirmary with a spring in my step. My gremlins seemed to be enjoying a well-earned lie-in. Either that or my pills were finally working again. *Or it's the calm before a big storm...* I shrugged off the last possibility.

Raffe was sitting up in bed, sipping coffee. "That was quick."

"You thought I'd just lay around?" I smiled, and it came easily for the first time in days.

"No, you looked insanely tired last night. I thought you'd be out of it for longer," he replied.

"The early bird gets the worm and all that." I plonked down on the seventies-esque vinyl chair beside his bed. It still felt warm, like someone had recently vacated it. Santana, probably. Raffe had likely waited until she'd reluctantly gone to bed before calling in the big bad wolf.

"For what it's worth, you look better today." He poured a second cup of coffee from a pot on his side table, using a clean mug that'd probably been put there for Santana, and handed it to me.

I smirked. "I can't look that good if you're offering me the strong stuff."

"That's because we've got a lot to talk about." He flicked some internal switch, turning serious on me. "I want to know what's really going on. You didn't want to say anything in front of Santana last night, and I figure you've got your reasons. But if this affects me and Kadar, I need the details."

"Can't a guy just help out without everyone leaping to conclusions?" I focused on my mug, taken aback by his bluntness.

"Not when you go all pale and awkward at the mention of talking to Erebus," Raffe replied. Dammit, he definitely had my number.

I raised an eyebrow. "I always get twitchy over talking to Erebus. It's not good for my health."

"You're withholding information. I can see it in your eyes." Raffe wasn't backing down.

"I didn't realize you were gazing into them. If I'd known, I'd have given you my most seductive stare." I realized I'd entered a losing battle. Would it really be so bad if Raffe knew? He had a djinn inside him. Maybe that made him immune to any dastardly deeds Erebus might rustle up, if Raffe ended up on the ever-growing hit list...

"If this was just about you, I wouldn't pry. And I won't spread it around. I need to know for Kadar's sake. I don't want him to throw us off the nearest roof again." Raffe's voice faltered, slamming me right in the feels.

I took a deep gulp of coffee. "You asked for this."

"I did, and I'm ready to hear it," Raffe replied firmly.

I glanced at Krieger's office. Through the glass, I saw him at his workbench, poring over blood samples. He wouldn't interrupt us anytime soon. And Levi, who lay in the next bed, was out cold. Though him overhearing wasn't really a problem, since this concerned him, too. Without further delay, the story slipped out easily, as I'd had quite a bit of practice telling it by now. Like a well-rehearsed monologue on opening night, I told him about my missions for Erebus and painted the horrifying picture of Erebus emerging from the Fountain of Youth like a male supermodel, now able to walk in the real world. I stopped there, steering clear of Atlantis. I figured it was best not to mention it, in case it did get them an honorary spot on the hit list.

"Anyway, his 'emergence,' as I like to call it, coincides with Kadar's sickness." I wrapped the facts up with a neat bow before moving on to my assumptions. "I wouldn't be surprised if this is happening to djinn across the world. Erebus is a go-big-or-go-home guy."

Raffe's gaze flitted to his father, still in deep sleep beside us. "You think having a human body might have blocked his link to the djinn?"

"If it looks like a dog and barks like a dog… yeah, that's my current hypothesis." I took another long sip of coffee. "The timeline fits too perfectly for it to be a coincidence."

"*No manches!* I knew you were holding out on me, you scheming sack of *pelotas!*" Santana appeared out of thin air, jabbing her finger at me. I glared at Raffe, thinking he'd set this up. But he looked as shocked as me, if not more so.

"Have you been eavesdropping this whole time?" Raffe gaped.

"You bet I have. I knew he was lying! You let me pour my heart out, and you didn't say a damn thing, even though you had all that tucked up in your head!" She raised her hands to unleash a hailstorm of Orisha at me. I put my arms up in defense, hoping a wall of Chaos would protect me from the buzzing, spiritual onslaught.

"Hear me out before you set your sparky balls of peeved spirit at me!" I yelled. "I had no choice. I did it to protect you! Erebus is dangerous. You know that, Santana. I'll ask Erebus about the djinn, but I'm at that bastard's beck and call, in case it escaped your notice?"

She shook her head angrily. "You don't get to play victim. I don't buy this protection thing. We've dealt with danger before. How's this different?" The Orishas spiraled around her head in a mesmerizing belt of blue-and-white light.

"I *am* a victim. Maybe not the only one, but that doesn't mean I'm not one. I'm a servant of Erebus, same as the djinn—we're linked, in a sense, because of that." I let Air spill out of my palms, creating a wall between me and Santana. "And this is a new level of weird and dangerous."

The Orishas spun faster, in time with her swelling anger. "Then you should tell us all. If it affects us, then—"

"It doesn't affect you all!" I shot back. "That's just it. I'm trying to keep as many of you away as possible, because this isn't a Katherine situation. It's a... pet project, I don't know. He hasn't been chatty, but it's not like last time."

The Orishas turned into a blur, and I knew they'd lash out soon. "How can you know that?"

"I just do!" I sounded desperate and I didn't care.

"Even if that's true, this *does* affect Raffe. You kept that from me. You knew my heart was breaking, and you still didn't tell me. I gave you every opportunity." Her fingers folded inward.

Frustration bristled through my body. "I don't want Erebus gunning for every friggin' person close to me!"

An almighty roar split the air.

"Would you stop your flaccid human mouths from flapping!" Kadar bellowed, silencing everyone. The Orishas abruptly halted, arcing over Santana's head and hiding behind her shoulders. Their edges quivered in fear.

"Good morning to you, too." I sighed. Kadar's ruby eyes burned into me.

Santana chewed nervously on her bottom lip. "How are you feeling?"

"I'm not planning on driving one of Krieger's hypodermic needles into Raffe's heart, if that's what you're asking," he replied.

"Better, then?" She sounded worried.

"I'm fine for now, so you can put those insipid fireflies away. I have much to discuss with Finch, so I prefer him breathing." Kadar heaved an exhale that seemed to ripple across his skin, turning it a deeper shade of red. "And Raffe says *I'm* the one with anger-management issues."

Santana twisted her hands, and the Orishas retreated. "I don't like being lied to," she said defensively.

"Maybe not, but you don't have to assail everyone who keeps a secret, and, between us, we are quite capable of fighting our own battles." Kadar smiled dryly. "After all, Raffe kept me secret for a long time, yet you don't hold him to the same level of condemnation."

"What do you want to talk to me about?" I brought the subject back around, to spare Santana. Love made folks crazy. And she'd dealt with enough to warrant an outburst or two.

Kadar relaxed slightly. "You mentioned servants of Erebus and djinn being linked. I realize it must be a topic of great interest to you, given your situation. You likely hope to gain some breakthrough from me, which is why you came with Raffe last night."

I opened my mouth to protest, but I couldn't exactly deny it.

Kadar chuckled. "Don't worry, I have no qualms with a sliver of selfish motivation. I rather admire personal determination, at any cost. If you aid Raffe, you will aid yourself. A bargain, in anyone's book."

I nodded awkwardly. "That's right."

"Unfortunately for you, I do not know much about the relationship between djinn and the servants of Erebus, as I am not connected to the collective consciousness. But I listened to your assumptions about my predicament, and I'm inclined to agree." Kadar's smoke thickened. "Have you spoken to Erebus lately?"

"No. I'm still... waiting for a sign," I replied stiffly. "A text" would've sounded anticlimactic.

Kadar scraped his nails against the coffee mug, and the sound cut through me. He was clearly nervous but holding it together, djinn-style. "At least there is comfort in understanding my separation from Erebus. And I believe you're correct in thinking it affects all djinn. I may not be connected to the network, which is perhaps why I am not suffering as much as Zalaam, but my connection to Erebus has always existed. Ergo, him gaining a human body has severed the tie with me, too."

"Is there *anything* you can tell me?" I urged.

"If I had reached the required age to connect to the network, I might be able to locate information for you regarding servants of

Erebus and the djinn's relationship to them. But I have not. And even if Zalaam were awake, the network has likely gone dark."

"Not giving me much silver lining, Kadar."

"I am getting to that, ingrate. Patience is a virtue—learn it."

I cleared my throat. "Sorry. Go on."

"I might not have your answers, but I may know someone who does," he continued, surprisingly solution-oriented despite his obvious anxiety and pain. His face looked strained, his smoke billowing wildly. A dead giveaway that he was struggling.

I gulped. "Who?" *Please be someone easy to find, please be someone easy to find, please be someone easy to find...* I crossed every extremity.

"The oldest djinn in the known world. The Storyteller. She may be able to help."

Santana took a step forward. "And where's she?"

"In the country now called the United Arab Emirates, the last I heard," Kadar replied. "She'll have far more information than, say, a stolen book."

My jaw hit the deck. "How did you know about the book?"

Kadar leered. "I'm a djinn, you idiotic spawn of a clurichaun. Even inside Raffe's dense skull, I can do things, see things… and I can sense that book you've got tucked away a mile off. It holds a djinn ruby, if I'm not mistaken; the kind used to signify ancient djinn literature."

"My bad. I didn't know you could 'sense' this stuff." *What else can you sense?* I fought the paranoia, those thoughts rising again like scum in a stew pan. The gremlins had been so quiet. I didn't want to wake them now. My bickering with Santana had woken one beast today, and that was enough for me.

"Hmm… very well, I'll resist stripping off the skin of your forearm and frying it for breakfast. Tempting, but you may need your flesh intact." Kadar flashed sharp teeth. "And I wouldn't want to be a hypocrite."

Santana grimaced. "I wasn't going to do *that*."

"More's the pity. We could have shared breakfast in bed." Kadar's eyes glinted.

An idea came to me, through the horror of becoming human bacon. "I'd like my flesh intact, if it's all the same to you, but you and Raffe might have to be the ones who find this Storyteller."

"And why's that?" Kadar purred. "Feeling lazy, are we?"

"I just don't want to wind up in a conflict of interests," I explained. "I'm expecting Erebus to contact me. If I vanish, he'll track me down, and that'll open a can of worms. But you and Raffe can do this, and you'll have a better shot at finding the Storyteller, since you know who you're looking for."

Kadar tapped his nails against his lip. "It would cut out the middleman."

"As long as you're not *cutting* the middleman." I smirked.

"Very amusing." He chuckled darkly. "It does seem like the better path to success. And, as there are many djinn in the UAE, I can see firsthand if our assumptions are true."

I took a breath. "So, that's settled, then?"

"It appears so," Kadar replied.

"Then I only have one more favor to ask." I chanced a look at Santana. "Please—and this includes Raffe, too—don't tell anyone what I've said regarding Erebus. It honestly is the only way to keep people safe. Everyone who doesn't already know, anyway."

Kadar inclined his head. "I will not say anything, knowing Erebus as I do. You shouldn't either, Santana. Your silence may be the difference between life and death."

She hesitated, rubbing the back of her neck. "Fine. If it freaks Kadar out, then... maybe you're right about the silence stuff, Finch."

I didn't get the chance to make a dig about her being wrong, though it teetered on the tip of my tongue. At that moment, Levi woke up. Well, Zalaam did. The ruby-red eyes gave it away.

"You must do this... Kadar," he rasped, those telltale eyes unfocused. "Go to... the homeland. Find... the Storyteller. She may be our only... hope to remedy... this. Finch's problem... is of lesser... importance."

Pfft. To you, maybe.

"Though... they may be... intertwined." He coughed violently, his scarlet skin phasing in and out like a Rorschach test on steroids. "You must... stop this before... the djinn lose... control."

Santana strode up to Kadar and grasped his hand. "I'm coming with you."

"I don't think Raffe will like that," Kadar replied. I got the feeling Kadar wasn't crazy about the idea, either.

She shot him a cold glare. "Tough."

Zalaam wheezed a laugh. "Oh, I wouldn't... mess with this... *bruja* if I were you, my son."

I had to smile. *Nope, neither would I.*

FOURTEEN

Raffe

A couple hours later, Krieger discharged me from the infirmary and Kadar retreated. The doctor gave me a pouch of magical herbs to help me cope with the stress of my sleepless djinn. A pungent blend of Lullaby Weeds, to smell or ingest depending on the severity of Kadar's potential outbursts—sniffing them would put us to sleep while taking them would knock us out for days. My father needed more attention, and I didn't mind resorting to self-care if it meant Krieger could focus on him.

"I'm sorry about last night." I sat on the edge of my bed, glad to be back in my own room. Home had a way of easing pain in a way the infirmary never could. I could've sworn they designed medical facilities specifically to freak people out, with brutal strip-lighting and muted colors.

Santana flicked through channels on the TV as Slinky twisted across the floor and up onto the bed beside me. "It wasn't your fault, *mi amor.*"

"That doesn't mean I'm not sorry." I rubbed my hands down my thighs, attempting to release the tension in my muscles. Slinky rested his head on my leg, staring up expectantly until I ruffled his feathers. "You told Finch your heart broke. I can't ignore something like that."

"You're alive, that's all that matters." She kept her back to me, forgetting that I could see her profile in the wall mirror. Her face contorted in a mask of anguish as she bit her bottom lip to hide her pain. I'd seen her do the same thing countless times before when she had to deal with something she didn't want to confront.

"I won't let it happen again." I had no idea if I could keep that promise. I hoped that now that we had a chance of fixing this by finding the Storyteller, Kadar might be less inclined to do us permanent harm.

Santana's shoulders sagged. "You didn't see him, Raffe. He looked so... done with the world. It wasn't a bluff. He really did throw himself off that building intending to kill you both."

"Is that why you're insisting on coming to the UAE?" I didn't mean it unkindly.

"Yeah, it is. From now on, you and Kadar don't leave my sight. If I had to sit and twiddle my thumbs waiting for you to return, I think I'd end up with my own bag of herbs." She tried to laugh, but it echoed false.

I tucked my legs underneath me, absently petting the feathered serpent. "You don't have to put us on suicide watch, Santana. We have hope now that we didn't before, and that's enough to keep Kadar going. He won't toss that aside until he's investigated our options fully."

"I'm not putting you on suicide watch. I'm here, and I'm coming with you, because I love you." She finally turned to look at me. "I almost lost you. I never want to be in that position again."

And if we reach a crossroads, where you want something I can't give?

What if we have to let each other go? To my mind, that would be more painful. To know it was nothing either of us had done, yet we couldn't overcome it. To come so far only to lose each other anyway. She deserved the world. She deserved that galaxy—the one Wade wanted to give Harley.

"What's going on with you lately?" She sat on the chair by my desk. "I say, 'I love you,' and you don't say anything back. It's happened more times than I can count, all this blowing hot and cold on me. And you know I hate the cold. I keep trying to convince myself it's just Kadar's sickness, but it started before that. Have I done something? Do you not want this anymore? If that's the case, all you have to do is—"

"I love you, Santana," I cut in. I didn't want to hear the rest of that sentence. "I love you so much. You haven't done anything, and I'm sorry I made you think that. It has nothing to do with me not wanting this anymore."

She lifted her head. "Then what is it? If you still love me, why have you pushed me away? At first, I thought I was imagining things. You know, not holding my hand, or telling me you were busy only for me to find out you'd gone to the pool. I'm not crazy, I know people need their own space, and I've got no issue with that. But then there were other things, like you leaving the Banquet Hall when I arrived, not replying to messages for hours even though I could see you'd read them, not answering the door when I knocked, and not saying 'I love you' back."

Slinky looked up at me with the same sad eyes as his Purger. I looked away. "I'm sorry, Santana. I know I've been acting like a jerk."

"I just want to know why, because it feels like you don't care anymore." Her voice hitched. I hated seeing her so vulnerable and hurt. I hated it more, knowing I'd caused her to feel this.

"I *do* care. I really do." I paused, trying to put my words in order. "I don't want to see you in pain. That isn't my intention at all."

An exasperated sigh escaped her lips. "I'm confused, Raffe. Nothing you're saying makes sense. If you love me and you still care, why are you trying to put a wedge between us? Is it Kadar? Does he not want you to be with me anymore?"

"That couldn't be further from the truth," I assured her. "I know I've been an ass. It's just... we have to figure some things out, Kadar and me. And those things hinge on the possibility that the Storyteller can cure us."

It was a huge *if*, but maybe the Storyteller could solve more than just our present djinn problem. Maybe she'd know a way to reduce the risk of harm to Santana if we decided to build a life together. If that were possible, I wouldn't have to keep pushing Santana away. Trying to be blunt with her now and telling her I couldn't be with her because I couldn't give her what she wanted would only result in her telling me not to be an idiot.

We'd been through the rigmarole before. We'd started discussing the future, I'd told her my fears of her dying in childbirth from a djinn Purge, and she'd shrugged it off. It was as predictable as clockwork. That was the trouble with falling for a fearless Santeria. Nothing frightened her. Not even the Levi curse.

"My symbiotic friend has a point." Kadar rose to the surface for a moment, though still mostly zonked out from the Lullaby Weeds. "We need to focus on the UAE and the Storyteller now. No time for mortal paranoia. He loves you. You love him. Give it a rest."

I shoved him down. The Lullaby Weeds affected him more than me. I'd already metabolized them while he remained drowsy, which made him easier to push to the bottom of my consciousness.

"Sorry about that," I said. "He's eager to head out on this mission, and, honestly, so am I. This could solve all our problems."

"All of them?" She raised an eyebrow.

I offered her a loving smile. "I hope so."

"Then why are we waiting?" She went to my closet and pulled down a bag. "We can use one of the mirrors to get to the Dubai Coven, find some leads on this Storyteller, and work our way forward from there. It's the biggest coven in the UAE, so it's a decent place to start."

"Dubai it is," I replied, praying this trip would help salvage my relationships with the two people I held dearest: the one I'd been "cursed" to spend my life with, and the one I hoped I'd get the chance to spend my life with. If I lost either, it'd kill me.

FIFTEEN

Finch

W hile Raffe and Kadar prepped for their *Arabian Nights* adventure, I had other fish to fry. A big, ugly trout by the name of Erebus. Or was I the trout, dangling on his hook? Either way, he'd texted and given me another unexpected reason to get suited and booted. I hated to say it, but it almost sounded like a date. A pushy one, at that:

> *Dear Flinch,*
>
> *Your presence is required at Gatsby's Speakeasy at two o'clock. I assume you can locate the a dress with your cellular device's mop function? Dress well, or as well as you are capable. I would prefer it if you did not look out of place. Do not be late. I will be waiting under the name Mr. Erebus.*
>
> *Best regards,*
>
> *Erebus.*

I didn't want him to think I was *too* obedient, so I'd gone for the same silky monstrosity I'd worn at Ignatius's and my trusty pair of black jeans. Gatsby's Speakeasy was a snazzy joint on the pricey side of San Diego, famed for its fishbowl-sized gin cocktails and wealthy clientele. They'd no doubt sniff out my measly bank account from a mile away. But at least this shirt screamed money, and plenty of it.

Weirdly, Gatsby's was as human and magicless as Astrid, not exactly the vibe I'd expect Erebus to go for. Maybe he had developed a taste for the finer things in human life, though I imagined he'd had to use a blanket spell on the staff and clientele to draw any unwanted attention away from his distinctly unnatural appearance. Even in 'human' form, he didn't exactly look human. But at least this wasn't a shady alleyway in some eerie industrial park. Small mercies.

I pulled up in a cab and stepped out, letting the cabbie go, since it'd be easy to get another from here. If Erebus kept calling me like this, he'd end up with a hefty invoice for all my travel expenses.

The exterior didn't look like much—a drab brick building with a tiny sign above the door spelling out the name. If you didn't know it was here, you'd walk right past it. Very in-keeping with the speakeasy aesthetic. Well, if you ignored the burly bouncers on standby. I broadened my shoulders, puffed out my chest, and strode right up to the door. I'd prepared a speech and everything, but the bouncers nodded and let me through.

Your loss. It would've been Oscar-winning.

My jaw dropped as I entered the bar. The interior was a world away from the unassuming outside. Red velvet curtains, dark wood paneling, crystal chandeliers, and circular tables with hooded lampshades casting a saucy glow on everything. I pictured old-timey chaps wooing their chapettes over sidecars or whispering furtively about their next heist. Even in my fancy shirt, I felt woefully underdressed. The bartenders were in tuxedos while the hostesses sauntered about in sparkling flapper dresses. A little sexist, sure, but I didn't run the place.

"Good afternoon, sir." One of the penguin-suited hosts greeted me. "Do you have a reservation?"

I started to answer when a figure at the main bar caught my attention. She sat directly in the center, her legs crossed elegantly over a twisting barstool, her body turning slightly to the side as though offering a better look. Long blonde hair cascaded past her shoulders in loose curls while a white, sequined dress pooled downward. "Mesmerizing" didn't cut the mustard. And she clearly knew I was watching.

She glanced over her shoulder in a majestic display of choreography, and a pair of twinkling, pale yellow eyes stared into mine. This bar might not have been magical, but those eyes were unlike anything I'd ever seen before. And that shrieked magical.

No... it can't be. I physically flinched at the sight of her. Probably not the effect she wanted. But her movements, fluid and dancer-like, and the glitzy white dress, reminded me so much of Katherine in Imogene's guise. Panic struck me like a thunderbolt of bad memories, and it brought a storm of paranoia with it. What if Katherine was still alive? I'd used her image to trick Davin in the Jubilee mine, but what if that had been a sick irony? What if she'd tricked us into believing she was gone, while she'd bided her time? What if Erebus had doublecrossed me in Elysium and somehow spared Katherine? What if this woman was her? And what if I'd walked right into her trap?

"Sir?" the host prompted, but I barely heard him.

Snap out of it, idiot! She's dead. You killed her. You watched her die. Common sense kicked in. Erebus had hated my mother as much as anyone. He'd been chomping at the bit to end her when he took over my body to make it happen. I'd felt his excitement. There was no way he'd given her a hall pass out of her demise.

"Sir? Do you have a reservation?" The host sounded impatient.

The mesmerizing stranger smiled and raised a champagne glass to me before stepping from her barstool and heading for a doorway in the back wall. She paused for a moment and sipped from her glass, beckoning for me to follow.

"I'm... with her." I gestured to the beautiful woman. It was as though someone had taken over my voice-box. I felt compelled to say it. A magnetism drew me to her. I knew it was magic of some kind, but I was helpless to do anything but obey her call.

The host's mouth fell open. *"You?"*

"Yes, me," I replied coolly. *Way to give a guy a complex.*

"Very good, sir." The host stepped aside, giving me free rein to go after the curious minx. I mean, where was the harm in following a mysterious, insanely hot woman through unknown territory? Thinking of it that way didn't make it sound wise, but wise could take a long walk off a short pier. Common sense had vacated the building. My mind demanded I forget my apprehension. Not my gremlins... something else. It wasn't all that often a pretty woman wanted my attention, and it wasn't like I had reason not to give it. Ryann had a boyfriend. I could do what I liked. And maybe a drink with a siren would get my mind off Ryann Smith.

Curiouser and curiouser... A white rabbit, or, rather, a white-dressed beauty, leading me astray. It certainly piqued my interest. And I still had fifteen minutes before my meeting with Erebus.

Aware of the host watching enviously, I strode through the tables and up to the doorway where the stranger had disappeared. A strange unease grew at the thought of losing her. The door led to a hallway with multiple doors branching off. The woman paused beside the very last one and went inside. I followed her footsteps, edging into the room beyond—a private suite, with velveteen sofas and a table set with dinner service resting beside a small pool of water, with a flowing fountain in the center. She stood looking into it, her dress sparkling in the ambient light.

"Did you want me to follow you?" I found my voice. I felt pretty sure this was what she'd intended.

She turned, a satisfied smile on her perfectly red lips. "Oh yes, very much so."

"Why did—" I didn't get to finish. She lifted her hand and snapped, and the door slammed shut behind me. *If it looks too good to be true...* I darted back toward the door and tried it, but it held fast.

"Look, I don't want any trouble." I pressed against the doorway, the magnetic allure evaporating. Fear replaced it. Yeah, this woman had definitely done something to me to get me in here.

"Neither do I." She laughed softly. "Come closer, Finch. I promise I won't bite."

I shook my head. "I'm fine here." My eyes narrowed. "How do you know my name?"

"You don't recognize me?" She sipped her drink delicately. "Disappointing. But then, I don't look the way I normally do, and you deal mostly with my husband."

Lux.

I relaxed slightly. "But... how can it be you? Last I checked, you weren't wandering around Earth, free as you pleased." *Although, I can't say the same for your hubby.*

"I borrowed this form from one of my priestesses. She was only too grateful to be permitted this gift," Lux replied. "Apologies for the subterfuge that led you here. A simple spell, which will have no lasting effects. I did not know how you might respond if I demanded you come with me."

Yeah, I'd have run like a bat out of hell. Meatloaf-style. I skimmed over that and focused on the weird part. Children of Chaos bending me to their will was nothing new, after all.

"You have priestesses?" Man, I could fill a book with things I didn't know about the Children of Chaos and their idiosyncrasies.

She sat on the fountain wall. "A select handful of beautiful young women worship me. They are devoted to the name of Lux, or the Light, as they sometimes prefer to call me."

"So you can just hop into a meatsuit whenever you feel like a jaunt through the real world?" I gaped at her.

"You find that difficult to believe?" Lux set down her champagne flute and leaned back, a little too seductively for my liking. "Unlike other Children, Light has always found a way in the world. I suppose that is because Light is sought by so many, to see them through Dark-ness. Unfortunately, I can only maintain this presence for a very short time."

I gave a low whistle. "You held that card close."

"Out of necessity," she replied. "Children are envious creatures, by nature, and they would seek the same for themselves if they knew it could be done."

Except your darling husband, who resorted to draining the Fountain of Youth for a more permanent fix. I didn't say it. After all, I didn't know how much she knew. She had to be keeping an eye on her pesky beloved, but I had no clue how much spying a Child of Chaos could do on another Child of Chaos.

My insides turned to jelly. Lux exuded calm, but her voice held a cold note that made the hairs on the back of my neck stick up. Being the so-called Light didn't make her Miss Goody Two-Shoes. She'd been on my side whenever she caught Erebus hounding me about my missions, but there'd always been something… off about her. Once again, if something looked too good to be true, it probably was. And it wasn't as if I could leave. She'd locked the door.

What did she want from me?

"I'm guessing you didn't bring me here to flaunt your human form. It's a good 'un, I'll give you that, but you wouldn't be locking doors unless you wanted something from me or you were in the mood to break marriage vows. I'd like to flatter myself, but I don't think the latter is what's on your mind."

She chuckled. "Very astute, Finch. Dallying with mortals does nothing for me, I'm afraid." Her laughter suddenly faded, replaced by a cold stare. "No, I brought you here to ask for Erebus's plans."

"You don't have him on Child-of-Chaos GPS?" My voice shook slightly, betraying my fear.

"Unfortunately not. Now, I know you are worrying about what he may do to you, so I'll make this easier," she continued. "I know about the human body he has acquired, but I do not know why. It came as quite a surprise, and he will not speak to me about it. I have tried to apprehend him in Tartarus, but… he does not often return there."

I frowned. "Is he locked out?"

"He is not 'locked out,' as you say, but it has changed. It is difficult to explain, and I have no means to show you, but our otherworlds adapt to our states. As his matter altered to a human state, his other-world adapted in kind," she explained. "That is not important. Since he will not tell me what he is doing, I have resorted to borrowing this body to speak with you, in hopes you may be more forthcoming."

You're going to force me to be more forthcoming, you mean.

"I'd love to spill the beans, but if Erebus finds out, he'll—" I started to protest, but she rose sharply with her glass in hand, cutting me off.

"He will not do anything. I will see to it myself. I simply desire to know what my husband is up to, as any worried wife might. I will not interfere in his business, so there is no need for him to know about this conversation. He has a nasty habit of keeping secrets from me, and it irks me in ways I cannot begin to describe."

I sighed. "And I'm not leaving here until I tell you?"

"You have always been quick on the uptake, Finch. That is one of the things I admire about you." She walked over to me, hips swaying.

"You're not giving me much choice here."

She adjusted her strap. "No, I suppose not. But I mean it: I will protect you from his wrath if he discovers you spoke with me. You will not be harmed."

I had to tell her, or I'd be late for my meeting with Erebus and he'd come looking for me. The chance of him finding out I'd talked to Lux would go up considerably if he appeared and caught me with her. I had a gift for weaseling my way out of sticky corners, but trying to get out of that scenario would require an expertise I lacked.

Reluctantly, I filled in the gaps between Erebus getting his body and him depositing me at the Mapmakers' Monastery. I hadn't even gotten through the first trial when the champagne flute clutched in her hand exploded in a shower of shards. Blood trickled down her palm, dripping onto the plush carpet.

"The bastard wants to go to Atlantis," she said in a low voice.

I eyed her bleeding hand. Well, her priestess's bleeding hand. "You don't want a refill, then?"

"I could murder him." She balled her hands into fists. "I could literally murder him." The ground shook slightly, and steam rose from the fountain.

That didn't exactly put me at ease. From what I could gather, Erebus and Lux were eternally bound, but they bickered and argued like any couple who'd been together for millennia. Sometimes I got the feeling they hated each other more than they cared for one another. Maybe it hadn't always been like that. Who knew? The trouble was, their lovers' spats had a more cosmic effect than ordinary couples arguing. Erebus had told me once, in one of his chattier moments, that their anger had caused global catastrophes and star implosions, among other things. The last thing this world needed was Light and Darkness literally fighting.

"You skipped a step, Lux," I said with forced cheer. "Erebus needs me to find the *key* to Atlantis first. Do you know why he wants to go there?"

But Lux wasn't listening. The door behind me burst open, and I sailed through it at breakneck speed. The last thing I saw before I hit the ground was the glare of strange yellow eyes.

"Tell anyone you met me, and I will flay you," she warned.

Anyone ever tell you that you sound like my sister? Seriously, what was everyone's sudden obsession with flaying me? I liked my skin covering my muscle. No human bacon for anyone, thank you.

From my heap on the floor, I struggled to sit up. The doorway stood open, but the woman in white had vanished. I sat alone in the empty hallway, the sound of jazz filtering from the main bar area. Refreshed panic hit me, and I fumbled for my phone. The time read five past two. I was late for my meeting with Erebus.

Ah, for the love of Chaos...

SIXTEEN

Finch

———————

I sprinted to the main bar, thrown by what just happened. Two Children of Chaos in one afternoon—my lucky day. Why did they have this irritating habit of leaving me with more questions than I started with? It was plain rude.

The host in the tux made a show of flicking through menus as I ground to a halt next to him, panting.

"Done already?" The man grinned, evidently thrilled my "date" with the hot blonde hadn't lasted long.

"I've got another reservation with Mr. Erebus. Where is he?" I wheezed. Being hurled through a doorway tended to tire a person out.

The man's face clouded. "Upstairs, sir. First door on the right."

"Thanks." Time to face my doom. Erebus would be sharpening his proverbial blade, ready to run me through for being late.

I raced for the winding staircase, taking the steps two at a time until I reached the landing. I went to the described door and knocked, my hand shaking.

"Enter!" my overlord's grim voice thundered.

Gird your loins, people. Gird your loins. I drew a tense breath and entered. For a second, I blinked rapidly, doing a hell of a double take. This room looked identical to his wife's, down to the cascading fountain and the oh-so-romantic table set with dinner service. My brain déjà vu-ed all over the place, my heart lodged firmly in my throat.

Erebus sat in one of the dining chairs. "You are late."

"'A wizard is never late; he arrives exactly—'"

Tolkien couldn't save me. A bomb of pain detonated in my chest, and clawing vines of agony shot through my limbs. I crashed to the floor, the plush carpet doing little to break my fall. My hands grasped my throat, my windpipe replaced with raw fire. Clearly, Erebus didn't like being stood up. And he definitely didn't like his tardy date making jokes.

Erebus loomed over me. "You know I abhor lateness. I have a cellular device now—if you thought you would be delayed, why did you not send a message?"

Oh, yeah, 'cause that would've gone over well.

He leered down at me, enjoying my torment. Erebus and his sadistic kicks. I could probably write a book about those, too. Maybe I would, just to spite the prick. But right now, I needed to beg forgiveness or end up with flames for a tongue.

"I'm... sorry!" I rasped. "Traffic... was terrible. I didn't... want to chalk-door... here, since it's... a human... joint. Please, forgive... me!"

"Pardon? I can't understand through all the straining." Erebus laughed coldly. His human body might limit him, but he couldn't resist showing off how much power he had left. This was nothing but a flex. A reminder to keep me in my place.

"I'm sorry!" I bent double, sputtering. "Forgive... me."

He twisted his hand, and the pain disappeared. I coughed violently, my hands braced on the carpet, my body shaking from the aftermath.

The agony had gone, sure, but my throat felt like I'd swallowed a prime slice of razorblade pie. My chest spasmed, my lungs unsure they were allowed to take full breaths again.

"Get up. You look pathetic." Erebus stalked to the table. "Although, you remind me of my precious Purge beasts when they disobey me."

I compelled myself to get to my feet. I gripped the door handle and leaned there for a moment, waiting for the nausea to pass. "You treat your Purge beasts like that?"

"Naturally."

"I guess to you, I'm no better than they are." I knew I shouldn't poke the bear, but had he really needed to do that, for the sake of a few minutes?

He gestured to the opposite seat. "That's correct. Though you have opposable thumbs, so you can hold a fork and knife."

I'll give you a forking knife. Right to your heart, if you're not careful. I staggered to the table and sat, sweat dripping down my face. "You're done with dumpsters and shady alleyways, then?"

"I have grown partial to human food," Erebus replied. "And after all, we have cause for celebration."

I leaned back in surprise. "We do?"

"Yes. I have an approximate location for Calvert." He sipped champagne, his behavior eerily similar to his wife's. That probably caused most of their conflicts—they were more alike than they'd ever care to admit. Two stubborn asses with too much power.

"Calvert? Is that a wine you've taken a liking to, or some place you want me to find?" I toyed with the stem of my glass but didn't drink. My gremlins hadn't been vocal recently, and I needed them to stay that way. No distractions.

He smirked. "*Nash* Calvert. He is a person."

"Ah, so it's a dude you've taken a liking to. Erebus, you surprise me. Playing away from home, are you?" Teasing helped me focus.

Erebus elegantly swept his champagne up to his face again before bothering to reply. "Even if I were, that would be none of your business. So I thank you to keep your smart comments to yourself."

"Who is he, then?" I decided to behave, in case he triggered another pain bomb to underscore his point.

"Nash Calvert is the key to the Gateway of Atlantis."

I faltered. "Huh? When you said we needed a key, I figured it would be more of a... metal object. What makes this guy special?"

Erebus swirled his glass. "Nash is a relatively rare Sanguine."

"A blood magical?"

He nodded. "Precisely."

"You say 'relatively' rare. That doesn't sound special." I watched the bubbles in my own glass rise to the surface.

"It is the nature of his blood that makes him special," Erebus went on. "He is a direct descendant of two Atlantean Primus Anglicus—a pureblooded child of those who took refuge in that mythical city."

My eyes widened. "He's a *child*?"

"It is a turn of phrase, you imbecile." Erebus groaned. "He is a descendant, as I said, and the blood in his veins is unmarred by lesser lineages. Those who emerged from Atlantis many moons ago painstakingly kept their heritage intact."

"He's inbred, you mean?"

Erebus's eyes glinted darkly. "He is pure."

"Potato, pot-ah-to." I cast him a sly glance. "And what do you want to find in Atlantis, again? You know, after you get this key? Refresh my memory." *Or, you know, give me a straight answer.*

"Nash Calvert's blood can replace the rare and extinct ingredients of the ancient spell required to open the Gateway." Erebus didn't bite.

But at least he gave me something to go on regarding this Nash dude. That was a rarity in and of itself.

"Okay… but why can't you collect him yourself? If he's important to you, surely you don't want to put him in my slippery mitts?"

Erebus sighed and gazed at the fountain. "A djinn-made curse was placed on Nash long ago, which makes his blood useless, and even poisonous, to other magicals. I have very few weaknesses, as you well know, but my inability to break djinn-made curses is one of them."

"Don't you, like, *own* the djinn?" I thought of Kadar and Zalaam and the royal mess he'd made of them.

"I created them, and they are bound to me, but that grants them certain advantages. They can't intervene in my deals or curses, and I can't intervene in their deals or curses," he replied bitterly.

I wiped the sweat off the back of my neck. "That's why Zalaam couldn't tell us Katherine was Imogene?"

"Exactly. Because she had entered an exchange with me—giving me the soul of Shinsuke Nomura in place of hers—she was off limits to the djinn. They could not even mention her, as her exchange with me protected her." His lips curled up. "Not from *me*, of course, in the end."

"Wait, so Children of Chaos can create Purge beasts?" I flitted back to his previous comment, the words only now tickling my curiosity. "I thought they just came from… well, Purges."

Erebus laughed. "There is much you do not know, Finch."

"Fair point." I sucked air through my teeth. "I'd still like to know how that's possible, though."

"In my early days, I enjoyed experimenting with raw Chaos. Beastly manifestations resulted. In fact, all beastly manifestations are the result of a Child of Chaos playing with Chaos."

"Have you got a 'Chaos' quota to fill there?" I joked. How many times did he want to say that word?

He gave me a hard stare. "Do you want to know where the djinn come from or not?"

"I do. Sorry. Go on." I pretended to zip my lips.

"The djinn, among other Purge monsters, came from my Chaos matrix."

Yes, Mr. Anderson... I fought the urge to say it. He wouldn't get the reference, and he'd seal my mouth shut if he thought I was being clever.

"The magicals call it a Purge Plague," he continued. "In reality, I had fiddled with Chaos and pushed it through many magicals at once; hundreds expelled djinn at the same time, though this was a very long time ago. And, as most experiments do, it backfired somewhat. They are bound to me, as they take their magical abilities from me, but I can't break their magic. A punishment from Chaos, for treating it lightly."

It served him right, but it was about to be a gigantic pain in my ass. His inability to break the curse meant the monkey had to do it, instead of the organ grinder. And here I was, with my opposable thumbs and my tail between my legs.

"You want *me* to break this curse? I'm not sure I have the expertise for that," I said, a token protest.

"I can always splatter Ryann across the city if you don't feel like it." His tone sizzled with menace. "Blood sprays far if you strike carefully."

I sank into my chair. Yet again, Erebus had me wedged between a rock and a hard place. I had to do this. He wouldn't have brought me here if I could defy him. Frankly, it had already gotten tedious having to go through the same thoughts over and over.

"No need to get feisty. You know I'll do it," I replied sourly.

"It never hurts to add a bit of encouragement." Erebus sipped his champagne, satisfied. I wished him a healthy dose of botulism to go with it.

I held back my awaking gremlins. "Where am I going to find this Calvert guy? Let me guess, you won't tell me?"

"Of course I'm going to tell you. How else would you find him?" Erebus smirked. "His last known location is an off-grid interdimensional pocket, much like that one Kenzie's uncle made for himself—in the carcass of a crashed airplane in Churchill, Manitoba. I do not know if he is still there, as he moves often, but it gives your search a starting place."

"Manitoba? I'm going to Canada?" I rolled my eyes so hard my eyeballs almost popped out.

"Problem, Finch?"

I flashed a fake smile. "Not at all, just let me grab my thermals and a bottle of polar bear deterrent."

"I suggest you do. I hear they're hungry, thanks to the mess you humans made of this planet."

"Hey, you're human now, remember? Our mess is your mess." I could already picture the icy tundra, and my extremities panicking that they might not all make it.

He smiled. "I am not human, Finch. *You* would do well to remember that."

How could I forget?

"Before I head out, there's one thing I need to ask." I recalled my promise to Santana. And now that I knew a touch more about djinn, this meeting had transformed into the perfect opportunity.

"You want to know where to acquire polar bear repellent?" Erebus chuckled.

I shook my head. "I want to know about the djinn."

"I told you about them."

"Not that. I want to know if you're responsible for what's happening to them. They're going crazy, and nobody knows why. Not even them."

Erebus's eyes glittered with amusement. "Oh… that. It is simple, really. Their access to Darkness is restricted because my form is compressed inside this body, meaning my power must be channeled differently. I suppose it's like cutting off their air supply, very slowly."

Annoyance splintered through me. "You made them, Erebus. Don't you feel responsible? They're suffering!"

"And they will continue to, until I resume my Child form."

"So, you *are* planning to return to your original form?" That didn't surprise me. In his body, he had limits. Erebus didn't like limits.

He swirled his drink again. "Naturally, at some point. I cannot say when that will be. I am hoping to find a happy medium of flitting between forms, but I am in no rush to figure out the details of that just yet."

"And you'll just let the djinn suffer until then?" The gall of him made me sick.

"In simple terms that you will understand… yes. I imagine my other creations in Tartarus are struggling, too." He shrugged. "Oh, well."

"'Oh, well'? That's all you have to say?"

He tilted his head. "What would you like me to say? They are expendable. I do not trouble myself over insignificant beings that would not exist had I not experimented with Chaos in the first place. They ought to be grateful for the time they've had."

"Unbelievable," I said, not attempting to hide my disgust.

He smiled coldly. "Is it?"

When did Erebus plan on getting back into his smoky skin again, exactly? His desire to stay like this had everything to do with Atlantis. That didn't take a genius to figure out.

My mind flitted to Lux, and I wished she hadn't gotten so angry. She might've been able to tell me more about Atlantis. It had taken her all of two seconds to realize Erebus's goal, which meant she probably knew more about it than I did.

"Something the matter, Finch?" Erebus's eyes bored into my soul. I must've been quieter for longer than I'd thought.

"Nothing aside from you not giving a crap about the creatures you created," I answered, a beat too quickly.

His glare intensified. "You aren't hiding anything, are you?"

"Of course not." I squirmed in my chair and avoided his gaze. Could he see Lux written all over my face?

I made the mistake of taking his silence as a good sign and dared to glance at him. An eerie smile stretched across his mouth. A blast imploded in my ribcage.

I lurched forward and grasped the table as a howl tore out of my throat, scraping trails of fire up my esophagus. Thundering rounds of white-hot pain discharged inside my skull, ricocheting between my temples and using my brain as a bouncy castle.

You knew this would happen! Lux can't protect you—she can't even keep an eye on her own husband! Erebus's curse had jolted the gremlins awake, and now they swarmed my head. They'd gone ape, screaming at the tops of their lungs until I didn't know the difference between them and the blood rushing in my ears.

I'm not getting out of this alive, am I? Unless Melody found an escape, it'd be torment after torment, task after task, pain on pain, until I died of exhaustion or Erebus offed me when I'd served my purpose. Until then, he'd use the same threats, and I'd keep bowing my head and obeying from terror.

"I can make this stop, Finch, if you tell me what you're hiding. I can sense your deceit. For a former cultist, you do not excel at lying," Erebus scolded, his hand clenched. A direct reflection of what he was doing to my insides.

Telling him would only make it worse. I dug deep, pushing past my limits and using fumes to hang on.

"I'm… not hiding… anything. I don't… have anything… to tell you!" I roared, scraping my nails across the tablecloth. It yanked most of the plates and cutlery and glasses to the ground, but the shattering eruption gave me something to focus on.

He flicked his fingers, and I flew, then slammed into the back wall. The air choked out of my lungs, leaving me winded. "Are you sure about that?"

If I told him, I'd have them both vying to kill me. Where was Lux's promised protection? I didn't see her riding in on her white steed.

"I'm not… keeping secrets!" I rasped, dangling from the wall.

Erebus literally harrumphed and released me. I fell to the floor with a hefty thud, since he hadn't bothered lowering me first.

"Very well." He picked up his glass and sipped casually. "If you remain honest with me, you have a better chance of surviving what comes next. Now get on with your task."

"Will you give me more information first?" I stood on wobbly legs. "How do I break the curse?"

Erebus sighed irritably. "You misunderstand, as ever. You cannot break the curse."

"But you said—"

"Nash Calvert must break the djinn curse himself," Erebus interjected. "You will convince him to break it, then retrieve his blood. I need at least five vials."

I stayed put until I had my strength back. "You make it sound like a walk in the park. How am I supposed to convince Nash to do that? I'm guessing he knows he has this curse, right? Or am I the bearer of bad news?"

"He knows," Erebus replied.

"Do you know what curse the djinn put on this guy? Do you know how to break it?" I pressed.

Erebus gave that irksome shrug that made me want to rip his head off. "Nash knows. It is your job to find these answers and plan from there. I can't micromanage you, Finch. I am much too busy."

"I'm not asking for micromanagement. I'm asking for details. Useful details. Details that will get you what you want." I groaned in exasperation.

"Uncover the details yourself." Erebus's face shifted to a blank canvas. "And don't return from Canada unsuccessfully. I will not repeat myself. You understand what is at stake by now."

"Yeah, I know." *You're a vindictive asshole, and proud of it, too.* The thing was, I got the sense he didn't actually know the details, which was why he couldn't give them to me. A lot of showboating to cover the fact that he was in the dark about the specifics.

Regardless, it looked like I was going to Canada to find Nash Calvert, our key to Atlantis.

SEVENTEEN

Raffe

Before you start jet-setting, don't forget to take that book!

I reread Finch's message. Santana and I had our bags packed, and I'd texted Finch to let him know we'd be leaving in a moment. This was as much his mission as ours.

Are you at the SDC? Can you bring it? I replied, tapping the screen while Santana sat nearby, watching curiously. Kadar knew about the thieved book, and it rested in our shared memory. Finch evidently wanted the Storyteller to look at it, since she had the expertise in books.

A flurry of pings erupted a moment later, each sentence a separate text:

Nope, I'm not there. E-man business.

It's under my pillow in my room.

Don't give me the third degree on security.

It's secure because it's simple.

No need to break my bedroom door down though!

There's a spare key on top of the door—feel around and you'll find it.

I have pristine figurines in there that'll be worth hundreds someday.
I'll know if you've touched anything.

I chuckled as I typed back. *I won't touch anything. Pinkie swear. Hope*
everything's okay?

The phone pinged again:

The usual. Travel safe, Raffster.

Will do, I sent, before putting the phone away.

"What does he want?" Santana asked coolly.

"He wants us to take a book with us," I replied.

She frowned. "Book?"

"Yeah, he… uh… picked it up at a bookstore and wants the Storyteller to look at it. Apparently, it's got information on Erebus and the
djinn, so it could have something that'll help us."

Santana shifted her bag onto her opposite shoulder. "Where is he?
Do we have to wait for him?"

"No, he gave us the all clear to get it from his room."

Santana's eyes glinted with mischief. "Do I get to break down his
door?"

"You could, but he left us a key and strict instructions *not* to do
that. Apparently, he's got boxed figurines in there that will make him a
fortune one day." I smiled at her, trying not to let my apprehension
show about our trip to Dubai.

I knew she couldn't be dissuaded from coming with me, but I'd
have felt better if she stayed here. We'd be stepping into the homeland
of the djinn. Not a safe place for a magical who wasn't in my unique
situation. Djinn were known tricksters and manipulators, eager to get
their hands on powerful magicals. But the decision had been made,
and with the djinn weakened and preoccupied, she would likely be
fine. That's what I kept telling myself, anyway.

"What do you think he'd do if I opened one?" Santana grinned.

I laughed nervously. "Make Slinky into a feather boa?"

"Pfft, he could try." Santana nodded down the hallway. "Shall we? Time's a-wasting."

"After you, my love." I made to move, but her face stopped me. Her eyes had gone wide and were swimming with bittersweet happiness. A moment later, she started walking, her head down. I followed, wanting to pull her back and wrap my arms around her so she'd know I still loved every fiber of her being. But I didn't. I couldn't... until I found a way to live a normal life with her. At least I could offer her small affections, though, instead of being a jerk and pushing her away.

I found Finch's key easily and entered his private domain. I hadn't been here often. People always said not to judge a book by its cover, but you could gain a lot of information about a person by looking at their room. Finch's gave off an air of a mother's-basement-dwelling geek, with a hint of cinema aficionado: posters of old movies like *Captain Blood, Spartacus,* and *From Here to Eternity* and shelves neatly stacked with his beloved figurines and framed first-edition comic books. His covers were ruffled, his pajamas a pool on the floor.

Santana lingered on the threshold. "He's an odd one, isn't he?"

I reached under his pillow and found the book. "How so?"

"You wouldn't think he was a nerd, then you step in here and—bam!—you get smacked with a torrent of geek." She crossed the room to a framed photo on the desk. It had all of us in it, smiling at the camera. I couldn't remember when it was taken. Santana picked it up and smoothed her thumb across my image, a sad smile tugging her lips.

"People like what they like," I replied, stowing the book in my bag. "Everyone needs a hobby."

"You mean, like your photography, and your newfound love of swimming alone?" Santana set the photo back down.

I shrugged. "The swimming cools and calms me down, like playing with Slinky calms you down." I slung the straps of my backpack onto both shoulders. "We should go. O'Halloran will be wondering where we are."

He'd agreed to let us use the mirrors to get to the Dubai Coven. We'd told him, given the problems with me and my father, we wanted to visit the UAE to find a solution from one of the oldest djinn in existence, and O'Halloran had wholeheartedly supported our decision.

Santana took one last look at the photo. "Come on then, slowpoke. Wouldn't want to keep the boss man waiting."

After locking up and replacing the key, leaving Finch's treasure untouched, we arrived at the Assembly Hall ten minutes later. O'Halloran paced the mirror platform, Diarmuid emulating him in miniature steps, though they both stopped at the sight of us. A wash of relief drifted across O'Halloran's strong features.

"Janey Mac, man! What time de ye call this?" Diarmuid grumbled. His usual cantankerous self. "Yez are takin' the pish, lads."

"Sorry, we had trouble packing. It's going to be hot over there," Santana replied.

"Aye, an' what? Are ye a Mexican or a Mexi-can't? Ye should be used te hot." Diarmuid folded his miniature arms across his miniature chest.

Santana glared at him. "Yes, but it's been a while since I've dealt with 104-degree temps."

"Enough, Diarmuid. They're not that late." O'Halloran moved to the mirror and pressed his palm to the pane. A courtesy, to send us on our way, even though we were perfectly capable of using it ourselves. The mirror shimmered liquidly as it opened to show Dubai.

"And yer soft as a cowpat, O'Halloran," Diarmuid mumbled.

O'Halloran stepped back. "I hope you find what you're looking for,

Raffe. It's been a long time since anyone's visited the Middle Eastern covens from the SDC, but they've always been warm and welcoming folks, so I'm sure you'll have no trouble."

"Thanks, O'Halloran." I tucked my thumbs under my backpack straps and stepped onto the platform with Santana.

"Let me know when you find something," O'Halloran instructed.

I smiled at him. "Of course, sir."

"And if you need help, you know who to call." He seemed agitated.

"Aye, bloody someone else." Diarmuid scuffed his shoes on the floor.

O'Halloran rolled his eyes. "You call me if you need me."

"We will."

I went through first, Santana behind me. When we crossed the threshold to the Dubai Coven, my jaw hit the floor. A dome of curved metal arched over our heads, like the belly of a spaceship. However, the walls were made entirely of glass, giving the most incredible view over the night landscape of Dubai. Or, rather, the skyscape. By the looks of it, we towered over the city.

Ordinarily, me and heights didn't get along, but the neighboring skyscrapers were so vast that they made the scale of this building seem less terrifying. The huge towers surrounding us were lit up, sparkling in the darkness. In the distance, boats glowed on the sea, and the famous manmade fronds of the Palm Islands cast a bright haze outward. To the other side lay a dark, empty desert, with a few building projects under construction.

"Whoa." Santana clung to my arm. "This place is giving me vertigo."

"Good evening to you." A man walked from the reception desk with a tray containing two glasses of bright green liquid. Impeccably dressed in a stone-gray, silk kandura, his black hair neatly slicked, he had a regality about him. It'd been a long time since I'd seen anyone in a kandura, though it was a distant part of my heritage. While it was cool in this building, I wouldn't mind an outfit like that if we went outside in the searing daytime.

I put out my hand and shook his. "Good evening to you, too. My name is Raffe Levi, and this is Santana Catemaco. I believe our director, O'Halloran, sent word that we'd be coming?"

"We expected you. Please, take these beverages to refresh yourselves." He spoke in a velvety tone with a hint of an accent. "I am Hussain Al Gaz, and I am the preceptor of Physical Magic. I have been tasked with welcoming you, to make your time here as pleasant as possible."

Santana took a glass and sipped suspiciously, only for her face to morph into a mask of contentment. "This is delicious. But where are we, if you don't mind my asking?" Santana's gaze fixed on the flashing towers below.

"You are at the pinnacle of the Burj Khalifa. The majority of the coven is below ground, but this is where we welcome guests. I am sure you understand why, with such a magnificent view?" He gestured to the windows, smiling proudly.

Santana kept on gaping. "Yeah, it's really something."

"You are of Iranian descent, Mr. Levi?" Hussain asked.

"That's right. Iranian-American," I replied, taking the second glass. I took a large gulp, my mouth filling with the citrus tang of lime and a hint of clove, with a background of something I couldn't identify, maybe apple or kiwi. Whatever it was, it really hit the spot and thoroughly refreshed my dry mouth.

"I suspected. You have the heritage in your features." He gave a small bow. "You are here regarding the djinn problem, I understand? Your director did not say much, but he mentioned that a djinn symbiotically entwined with one of his staff had been rendered incapacitated, and he would send individuals seeking a cure."

"That's right." It was hard not to get drawn in by the expanse of lights, or the elegant vocabulary of Mr. Al Gaz. He spoke English better than I did. "Are your djinn affected, too?"

Hussain grimaced. "Unfortunately, which is why we are all too happy to help you. Most of the Emirati djinn are suffering, and we have heard that the djinn of neighboring countries have fallen ill from the same affliction. We hope that any party who finds a solution will share it."

"Are you the man we're here to speak with?" Santana dragged her eyes from the windows.

He paled. "No, I am only your introduction to the Dubai Coven. You need to converse with the coven director, Ms. Nayla Al Kaabi. She will be aware of your arrival by now, so I suggest we make our way to her office immediately."

His formal friendliness carried a note of agitation, as if we were already running late. Ms. Al Kaabi clearly ran a tight ship. Which meant we shouldn't keep her waiting any longer.

EIGHTEEN

Raffe

———————

We found ourselves in an elevator, plummeting at mind-blowing speed from the top of the Burj Khalifa to the main body of the Dubai Coven. My ears popped on the way down, while Santana steadied herself on the handrail along the walls of the elevator. A film played on screens embedded in the walls, showing the history of the Dubai Coven, from its birth in the arid desert to the complex interdimensional bubble it had become over the years, rising to superiority at the same rate as the impressive city.

A few minutes later, the elevator doors opened and left me breathless with awe once more. A myriad of cultures and mythologies adorned the walls, figures from Egyptian, Arabic, and Indian legends, and everywhere in between. Up ahead, a pair of looming, dog-headed Anubis statues held their hands out, guiding guests down the ensuing hallway. Gold shone from every arch, wall, and furnishing. It even existed in snaking threads that glistened in the marble floors. Paneled partitions enclosed various statues and historical paintings, with patterns that gave an almost Moroccan vibe. Ambient light shone through them, casting shadows and shafts of illumination that seemed to follow me.

"This way," Hussain instructed, hurrying down the main hallway. We followed, though I felt a little disappointed I couldn't take the time to absorb more of the beauty of this place. Everywhere I looked, I found another feast for the eyes. And the entire place felt powerful and ancient, like the air itself was imbued with Chaos.

He stopped in front of gargantuan white doors with golden handles shaped like a crescent moon and a star. He took a deep breath before knocking, shuffling back a step or two as he waited for a reply.

"*Adhal*," a rich, musical voice replied. I knew enough Arabic to know the director had told us to enter.

Hussain pushed the doors open and let us through. Nayla Al Kaabi's office was more impressive than the rest of the coven. It looked like a courtyard, with running, icy blue water that created a square island in the middle of the room. A set of stairs led to a balcony that overlooked the island from all four walls, where bookshelves overflowed with books and doors led to who-knew-where. Overhead, a glass roof showed the twinkling stars outside. It had to be nearly one in the morning here, yet nobody seemed tired.

A desk sat in the center of the island, and a woman behind it. She wore glasses, which she pushed down to the point of her nose as she surveyed us. Her dark hair lay half-hidden by a loose *shayla*. The silken headscarf was cobalt blue, to match the *abaya* she wore—a long, flowing outfit to keep her cool in the heat. Not that she had anything to worry about here—it felt blissfully cold. A breeze drifted in from somewhere.

"Our American guests, I presume?" She rose slowly.

Santana gazed around in wonder, taking it all in. "I'm Mexican, actually."

"My apologies," she replied, her English once again putting mine to shame. "I am Nayla Al Kaabi, the director of this coven. You are very welcome here, as your objective aligns with ours."

"Mr. Al Gaz told us the sickness has reached here." I struggled to say something that made me look like I knew what I was doing. Her presence radiated power and imposing strength, the same way her coven did. The last thing I wanted to do was look like an idiot in front of her.

"Yes, it has, which is cause for great concern." Nayla beckoned us closer. "It is heartening to have more minds on the problem. Perhaps we will help each other."

I swallowed and passed over a stone bridge to the central island. "My father is currently suffering, and we're eager for a cure."

"Your father? Leonidas Levi, if I am not mistaken?" She rested her hand on her desk.

"That's right."

She pushed her glasses back up onto the bridge of her nose. "You do not seem to be suffering, though if your father is experiencing the complications of this djinn sickness, I would expect it to affect you."

"You know about me?" I looked to Santana, who gave me a worried glance.

"Of course." She smiled serenely. "I am well-versed in the Levi family's unusual relationship with the djinn. Perhaps I didn't phrase it correctly—how are you still standing while your father is in the infirmary, in the grip of this pestilence?"

I folded my arms to look more casual. "My djinn is very young and isn't connected to the wider djinn network. I think that's why I'm not having the same problems as my father. His djinn is much older than mine."

"Ah yes, so very few people understand the intricacies of djinn lineage," Nayla said thoughtfully. "There are many categories of djinn, and their variances are so much more complex than outsiders realize. Even magicals struggle to distinguish between types of djinn, though they walk through a world with countless kinds of magicals and have little trouble understanding that concept."

"There are different types of djinn?" Santana found her voice.

Nayla smiled sympathetically. "There are. This one, for example." She took an old, dusty brass lamp from a concealed pocket in her *abaya* and whispered into it. *"Anst elie. Tadhar. Hanak haja lek."*

Listen to me. Appear. You are needed. My Arabic wasn't as rusty as I thought. As soon as she spoke, the symbols etched into the lamp began to glow, casting the shapes onto the wall like a candle carousel. Black smoke poured from the spout, and limbs and a body extended until they were almost solid. I hadn't seen a djinn without a human host before, but it didn't look too different from Kadar's red-fleshed form when he took the reins. Aside from the fact that it stood over seven feet with shoulders three times broader than Nayla's and ruby-red eyes that burned with flames.

"This is Al-Abdhi. His name means 'everlasting,' though you may refer to him as simply 'Abdhi.' He has been in the service of the Dubai Coven for centuries," Nayla explained.

"I'd prefer 'indestructible,' but it's a mouthful." The djinn chuckled, his voice high-pitched. Not what I'd expected from someone so terrifying.

"Everlasting, indestructible—they are almost synonyms," Nayla retorted with a hint of a smile.

"Fine and majestic are almost synonyms, but I know which I'd rather be called." He gave her a nudge in the arm, his demeanor taking me aback.

Santana eyed him. "Does looking scary come as part of the deal, but *you* make up for it by acting like a pussycat?"

"I find no reason to be threatening unless I am threatened," Abdhi replied. "Do you intend to threaten me?"

Santana shook her head. "No."

"Then I have no reason to put on the fire and brimstone. It's exhausting, in truth. I find it so much easier to be peaceful and enjoy my existence. Perhaps because I've been here so long—youngsters are *all* fire and brimstone." He grinned, flashing sharpened teeth. "Hot-tempered and always ready for a fight. Usually, it ends with them being knocked down and humiliated, though it never deters them from acting out when the next opportunity presents itself." He sighed. "It is the gift of age to see the futility of violence and learn the art of calm. These days, I'm a connoisseur of tranquility."

Santana mustered a curious smile. "If it's not a rude question, how come you speak English? If you've been here so long, shouldn't you speak Arabic?"

"Are you Arabic?" he replied.

"No."

"Then what use would it be for me to speak Arabic?" He had a bit of sass to him, as well as being a connoisseur of tranquility. "I adapt to those in my care. I don't find the English tongue nearly so musical or satisfying, but we have to understand one another. Otherwise, I'd be playing an endless, infuriating game of charades with you, and that's something neither of us wants."

I frowned. "Those in your care? What do you mean?"

Nayla looked up at Abdhi. "I am assigning him to you. He will take you where you wish."

"To the oldest djinn in the world?" I needed clarification. I hadn't mentioned the Storyteller to O'Halloran, so I doubted the message had been passed on.

"The Storyteller, yes. Let's not beat around the bush," Abdhi replied. "It is my firm hope that she will be able to resolve this issue, and I am pleasantly surprised that you newcomers have just suggested it. I enjoy it when the West takes an intellectual interest in the East."

Santana pointed at him. "How come you're not all pale and sickly?"

"Why, thank you, I'll take that as a compliment." Abdhi snickered. "Alas, I have also been suffering this recent malady, though I am not quite full djinn, so I am less affected. My lamp gives me a steady flow of additional energy, dulling the effects of this sickness somewhat."

Nayla made a noise of agreement. "Yes, that is what I meant to tell you. Thank you for the reminder, Abdhi. He is a genie rather than a full-blooded djinn. It means his power is less than an ordinary djinn's."

"Being shoehorned into a lamp will do that to a creature," Abdhi said with a dramatic sigh. "The binding of a djinn to a physical vessel restricts their abilities. In this instance, it has served me well, though I cannot sleep. And I feel so ugly these days. I am not the beauty I ought to be."

"I think you look pretty good, considering." Santana flashed him a grin. I could tell immediately that they would get along like a house on fire. Or, a djinn on fire.

"You flatter me." Abdhi wafted his hand at her. "But you don't need to lavish compliments on me—I have already vowed to lead you to the Storyteller, so I'm a safe bet. If I do this, I might have a good night's sleep at last."

"Where do we find her? The Storyteller, I mean?" I returned to the task before he got carried away. However, Nayla was the one who answered.

"Only a djinn can find the Storyteller. Abdhi knows where to take you, fear not, but he can't announce the location aloud. It is, by all accounts, of utmost secrecy, and I would not wish to break djinn legislation."

Abdhi nodded. "I couldn't have said it better myself, though I wish you'd come in daylight. I hate traveling in the dark. Weird, I know, considering my kind are tied to Darkness, but we all have our quirks."

"Yeah, we might've forgotten about the time difference," Santana said apologetically.

"At least you won't be dealing with jet lag. I might have changed my mind if I had to haul two zombies around." Abdhi's wisps of smoke rolled over his body, as if amused.

I was glad we had found a path to the Storyteller, but I had my doubts about this assigned djinn. I had enough trouble with the one inside my body. Abdhi sounded like either a lot of fun or one hell of a headache. Nevertheless, he could take us to the one person who might be able to help Kadar, and my future with Santana. That was more than worth the headache.

NINETEEN

Raffe

A fter we'd said a polite farewell to Nayla, who had a handshake of steel to match her fierce exterior, she'd plucked an emerald from the indoor stream in her office. I hadn't noticed the emeralds at first glance, which made me wonder if they had been concealed somehow. Regardless, she gave the gem to Abdhi so we could travel quickly through a djinn portal to where we needed to go. Given that the Arabian Peninsula was the djinn's homeland, it made sense they'd have easy access to the emeralds that allowed the djinn to form their unique portals. I supposed Nayla controlled the emeralds so the djinn in her employ couldn't just flit off whenever they pleased.

Abdhi gripped the gem in his palm and beckoned us close. "Santana, if you'd care to take Raffe's hand?"

She smiled and put her hand in mine while Abdhi seized my wrist. His fingers burned against my skin, though it would've been worse for Santana. He closed his eyes, and the emerald enveloped us in a blinding flash of green light. My stomach lurched as my body started to disintegrate and twist up through Abdhi's portal. Beside me,

Santana flowed from solid to wispy matter and spiraled up into nothingness.

The portal spat us out in the heart of the Arabian desert. The bitter cold hit me, and harsh grit stung my face like a thousand tiny hornets as the icy winds swept the sand off the dunes. A clear night stretched above, with no light pollution to mar its majesty. There were more stars than sky, and I could almost see the blend of shadow and light that made up the Milky Way.

"I bet you wish you'd brought your jackets now." Abdhi's black smoke rippled, creating two solid legs. He wasn't the sort of genie from human stories. No harem pants here, only a golden loincloth to hide his dignity, if he even had dignity to hide. Djinn in their natural form were brand new to me, and I didn't know how things worked without a human host.

Santana swung her backpack to the ground and pulled out a thick sweater. "I came prepared."

"Oh, I like you. You can stay." Abdhi flashed his sharpened teeth in a grin. Apparently, Santana was a djinn magnet. Even Zalaam showed her a healthy respect.

"So, is the Storyteller nearby?" I took a sweater from my own bag and slipped it on. It took the edge off the biting cold, while Kadar warmed the rest of me. After all these years, he'd gotten used to sharing a bit of heat when the weather turned cold. He sensed me shivering and went into radiator autopilot.

Abdhi started to walk. "We have a long trek ahead of us, so brace your quads. You'll need them in these dunes."

"You can't just portal us to the Storyteller?" I glanced at the undulating desert, some of the dunes towering hundreds of feet. With Kadar and me weakened, I didn't fancy my chances of surviving a long journey.

"Where's the fun in that?" Abdhi replied jovially. "And no, I can't. The Storyteller never stays in one position and has fortifications preventing other djinn from popping in unannounced. But I have her location, so get those legs moving."

"I'm here, Raffe. You'll be fine." Santana looped her arm through mine and set off, tugging me along.

We'd barely walked ten minutes before I ran into my first bout of trouble. The sand might as well have been a quagmire of mud. Every step made my thighs burn and my lungs strain, my feet slipping as we ascended a vast dune. My body craned forward until I was almost horizontal to try to keep going, my balance totally out of whack. Kadar's illness made physical exertion that much harder for me, too. Santana helped me along as best she could while fighting the sand herself. Abdhi had no issues. His didn't make a single imprint in the tumbling grains.

"Abdhi, could you tell us about other kinds of djinn? Director Al Kaabi would have told us more, I think, but we got off track. Actually, I guess we got on track, but still, I'd like to know more," Santana said. A distraction tactic if ever I'd seen one. I breathed an internal sigh of relief. If we had something else to focus on, the trek might not feel so dire.

He glanced back, smiling. "I'd be delighted. In my heyday, I was a Marid: a giant being of immense power. Though, if you'd seen me then, your heads wouldn't even reach my knees and I could have squished you underfoot. Now, my power has been diminished, and I am not nearly as large as I was. A shame, for I was truly magnificent."

"You were bigger than this?" Santana gaped.

"Oh yes, though, like the regal elephant, it made us a target for hunters, to be forced into servitude as a genie. Then again, that may have something to do with our propensity for wish-granting, rather than our mighty size." He waved a dramatic hand. "The greed of mortals."

"You grant wishes?" An idea formed in my head.

"Yes, but don't think about wishing to be delivered to the Story-teller. That is beyond my capabilities, now that my power has been reduced by decades in that lamp." He flashed me a knowing look.

Santana paused for breath. "Don't you want to break free? Ulti-mate cosmic power, itty-bitty living space and all that?"

"Once upon a time, I would've given anything to free myself. In Nayla's care, I don't mind so much," he replied. "Besides, if this coven hadn't trapped me in a lamp, it would've been another. We were constantly on the wrong side of things, sought by magicals and crea-tures working on behalf of Children of Chaos. One Child's minions, in particular."

"What do you mean?" I prompted. Despite sharing a body with a djinn, it occurred to me how little I knew about them. I guessed that was partially due to Kadar's comparative youth, meaning he lacked access to djinn history, but it felt wrong that I didn't know more.

Abdhi's smoke rolled across him in excitable waves. "We try to anticipate creatures called Sylphs. They intervene in the fates of mortals more than most, so Erebus tasks us with getting ahead of them, to make other deals to mortals' benefit—and to Erebus's—but we always get shooed away by the Sylphs' fiery missiles. If you ever see a shooting star, that is a Marid getting a stern telling off at the business end of their artillery."

Santana tilted her head in curiosity. "Sylphs?"

"You've never heard of them?" he replied, as if she were a moron.

"I thought they were floaty Air fairies," Santana responded in kind.

"A common misconception. There are many varieties of Sylph, similar to magicals and djinn. Certain types are mistaken for angels.

But they are all creatures of the Light, as we are creatures of Darkness. The result of a Child of Chaos meddling in matters they shouldn't."

"You mean Lux?" I chimed in.

"Yes, that old wench." He smirked coldly. I sensed a divide between the beings of Light and Dark. "We get tarred with the brush of evil because of our maker, and they flutter about in the fairy-like glow of Light, and everyone thinks the sun shines out of their backsides. Not entirely true, in case you're wondering. They have a nefarious streak in them, just like *their* maker."

I hadn't realized the Children of Chaos had creatures of their own making. I'd obviously known the djinn were bound to Erebus, but the fact that they were actually made by him was news to me. Lux had these Sylphs; Erebus had djinn. Plus, Gaia had the four Elements at her beck and call. I had to wonder what the other Children happened to create during their lengthy spell as watchers of Earth. And what Abdhi meant about Lux's nefarious streak.

"What kind of djinn is Kadar?" I asked, curious. Remembering Finch's book, I paused to take it out of my backpack and flipped to the section on djinn varieties.

"He is likely a Qareen," Abdhi replied, after a moment of thought, "the most common type of djinn. They are companions to mortals, like shadows who follow you through life. Many people are in possession of a Qareen and don't know it. In your case, yours is actually entwined with you, thanks to your family curse, so you had no choice but to know of him."

Santana pressed on up the dune. "Do I have a Qareen?"

"Not that I sense. Don't be disheartened—not everyone has one, and those with immense power of their own are often avoided by the Qareen. You should take it as a compliment to your prowess as a Santeria." His flaming eyes sparked with humor. "Very few magicals have them, for that reason. They are more inclined to follow Mediocres and the magicless."

"This is fascinating," Santana declared, looking happier. "What other types are there?" I kept pace with her as Abdhi talked, his voice acting like an energy drink that kept me trudging forward.

"There are Ifrits," I said, following Abdhi's words and finding the corresponding ones in the book.

Abdhi nodded. "Oh yes. If you ever come across one, I'd urge you to run in the opposite direction, though they'll likely catch you anyway." He chuckled to himself—a djinn inside joke we didn't get.

"Why, because they're winged?" I scanned through the brief notes about the Ifrits.

"Exactly so, and they move very fast because of it." Abdhi pointed to the dunes in the distance. "In fact, a few linger in this very desert, though you're safe from them while you are with me."

I frowned. "Are you sure about that?"

"I have existed for centuries. Even with my limitations, they have the sense to fear me." His flaming eyes burned brighter, emphasizing his point. "Ifrits are civilized, for the most part, frequenting ruins and living in tribal societies with kings and titles and that sort of thing. But they shapeshift at will and cause sudden sandstorms. Tricksy as individuals, but fairly inert when they are in their civilized groups— they don't want to enrage their overlords by doing something that might get them in trouble. Getting on my bad side would qualify."

I looked toward the dunes, half expecting to see a sandstorm rising in the distance. Fortunately, we only had natural wind to deal with, and the spiky grains of sand flying in our faces.

"I've heard of djinn who haunt cemeteries. Is that true?" Santana asked, her dark hair whipping back in shadowed tendrils. A tremor went up my spine. She'd been spending too much time with Tatyana.

Then again, what was she supposed to do when I made excuses not to see her? Sit alone in her room? Not likely, and not what I wanted for her.

Abdhi clasped his hands. "Beastly creatures. As a whole, the djinn like to pretend the Ghul don't belong to us."

"You mean ghouls?" Eerie beings that devoured people who happened to be in cemeteries at the wrong time.

"A Western bastardization of a perfectly good word. I mean what I say—Ghul." Abdhi shot me a disapproving look. "Although, the meaning is more or less the same: flesh-eating creatures who feast on the living and the dead."

Santana nodded eagerly. "A friend told me they encountered a few."

"Is your friend of the female or male persuasion?" Abdhi asked, interested.

"Female."

He made a noise of understanding. "Then she was likely at less risk, unless it was a Qutub."

"The things you clean your ears with?" Santana squinted, putting her hand across her eyes to protect them from the sand hissing across the dunes—hopefully not the sign of an Ifrit on the rise.

Abdhi chuckled. "You're amusing, for a mortal."

"A Qutub is the animal form of a Ghul, right?" I found the section in the book.

"I'd be impressed if you hadn't just read it." Abdhi snickered. "But you are correct, and they are the lowest of the low."

"What's the other, non-animal kind? It doesn't say in here; it just says Ghul and Qutub," I interjected, closing my eyes against the sand.

"That's because the 'other kind' are just called Ghuls," Abdhi replied bluntly.

"And they appear as beautiful women who lure men to their deaths?" This book had everything a person could want to know about djinn.

Abdhi gave a belly laugh and performed a charade of walking on hooves, though it gave off more of a T-Rex appearance. "In theory, but you'd have to be fairly stupid to fall for it, as they can never get rid of the donkey legs of their natural form."

I frowned. "According to this, there are several djinn who like to trick mortal beings."

"Mm-hmm, especially men—being the more foolish of the sexes," Abdhi retorted.

"Hey!" I protested.

He shrugged. "Where beautiful ladies are concerned, men often lose their minds completely."

Does he know? His words nagged at my insecurities surrounding Santana, and the wall between us that was part of the reason for us trekking through this freezing cold desert in the small hours of the morning. Had I lost my mind for Santana and the future we might never have? I supposed trying to let go of the most incredible thing in my life would qualify as being borderline insane.

"What about Si'lat?" I moved to the next description on the page, changing the subject.

"They also take the form of beautiful women to trick men into... you know, *laying* with them." He gave a mischievous wink. "Think succubus. There are Qarinah and Shiqq who behave similarly, though the former is associated with sleep paralysis, where they suck the dreams and nightmares from their immobilized victims and feed on them."

To my surprise, we'd covered a lot of ground while talking. Then again, most of the landscape looked the same, and sand dunes seemed to have an impish way of shifting when you weren't watching.

"And the Hatif, who mimic the voices of loved ones." Abdhi continued on our whistle-stop tour of djinn classification. "They don't possess solid form, but if you're ever alone and hear the voice of someone you know, dead or alive, when they have no reason for being there, you can bet that it's a Hatif."

"Yeesh, who knew there were so many types? It's like a pick 'n' mix of djinn." Santana chuckled, rubbing her arms briskly.

"Oh, sweet girl, I'm not even finished yet." Abdhi grinned, effortlessly climbing the next dune. As distracting as he was, my thighs weren't listening to his information. They were on fire, and Kadar stirred inside me, aggravated by the effort. He hadn't chimed in with his own intel, or smart comments, so I took that as a sign that the Lullaby Weeds still had him under their spell.

"Lastly, we have the Hinn—not technically djinn, more of a rival species. We say subclass, they say separate. It caused a war many years ago, the sparks of which exist even to this day, though we mostly avoid each other for the sake of peace." Abdhi gestured to the sky. "So, as you can see, djinn come in all shapes and sizes. A pick 'n' mix, as you said. We have varying abilities—some appear as weather phenomena, others play tricks, some toy with mortals and drive them mad or cause sickness, and others are so dangerous you would have to have a death wish to go near them."

"Let's not meet any of those, okay?" Santana shivered. I didn't know if it was from the cold or from Abdhi's sharp, warning tone.

"No, indeed," Abdhi agreed.

He went on to tell us about how each of the planets was associated with a djinn, but I'd tuned out, the book no longer drawing me in. Kadar made himself known, with spiky pains stabbing my abdomen.

My limbs dragged like they'd had the life drained from them. Another side effect of Kadar's illness.

"Who cares about other djinn?" Kadar rose up, stamping me down. "While you're waffling on, some of us are dying here. And I don't see those cretins coming to our aid, do you? Every branch of djinn is out for themselves, and I would wage another war against every single one of them, to teach them a lesson."

"Kadar?" Santana whispered.

I felt him leer. "Who else?"

"Maybe you should sleep some more," she suggested.

"And maybe you should mind your own business," he retorted. "This is your fault, anyway."

Santana's expression shifted to anger. "Excuse me?"

"You wouldn't stay behind, and you being here is messing with Raffe's mind—distracting him. Why do you think he's pushed you away? Honestly, for someone who acts like an intellectual, you can be dense." I fought to wrangle Kadar, but he wouldn't budge. "And he won't say it, so I will. His greatest fear is his inability to give you children—well, without potentially killing you, anyway."

"What?" Santana grazed her bottom lip with her teeth. "I told him we didn't need to worry about that."

"Then you really are stupid," Kadar shot back. "Of course you should worry. You're not exempt because you're powerful in your own right. His mother was, too, and it didn't do her any good."

Kadar, stop! I tried to take back control.

No. Why should I? She needs to hear it, and she needs to hear it from someone with more punch to them, Kadar replied inside my head.

"That's why he's been trying to push me away?" Santana looked heartbroken.

"Did you think he'd just gone cold? You—the one he's been pathetically in love with from day one?" Kadar scoffed against my wishes. "You think *señoritas* like you come along every day for a guy like him? Pfft, as if. They might for me, but Raffe's a sap."

Santana rallied. "Then why didn't he just say so? I bet you had something to do with it, didn't you?"

"He did say so, but you wouldn't listen!" Kadar snapped.

Her eyes widened. "Not being able to have children with him doesn't mean he has to push me away. There are ways around it, Kadar."

"Not satisfactory ones." He grabbed her arm and pulled her around to face us. "He wants your kiddos, Santana. He wants the shiny, happy family he never had, the one you constantly harp on about. You think he'll give that up? You think it doesn't hurt us when you say you want a billion children, knowing each could be a death sentence for you?"

"I—"

Before Santana finished, Abdhi swiped Kadar across the face with a slap that sounded like a lightning crack. Instantly, Kadar disappeared inside me, and I came back to the surface, feeling the almighty sting from that smack.

"Djinn. Such drama queens. Am I right?" Abdhi shook his head. "They should all spend some time stuffed in a lamp. That'd teach them."

"Sorry about that." I peered at Santana, but she'd turned away. Evidently, Kadar had given her food for thought at the worst possible moment. Did he want *both* of us distracted during this mission? At least it had brought my mind back to the task at hand, as mortified and angry as I was with him for bringing up that sensitive—and secret—subject. I'd been trying my best to keep it from her, and he'd gone and blurted it out. Impulsive idiot. I glanced at the book to skirt past my embarrassment, ignoring the throb in my cheek and moving on to the specifics of the collective djinn world. "Are all of these djinn connected to Erebus?"

"They are indeed," Abdhi answered. "All of us born of his Chaos mutations."

Santana turned her attention on Abdhi. "So he's like your dad?"

"Alas, he lacks paternal instincts. With that in mind, he is more the scientist who botched us into being. If he were truly our father, he wouldn't leave us to suffer like this." Abdhi's tone held a bitter note as he gazed over the shadowed dunes where a strange, goat-like creature grazed on sparse shrubs. It had spiraled horns, bent backward. An oryx, if memory served.

"'Botched into being.' It doesn't sound like you're all that glad to exist," I cut in.

He shrugged. "I make the best of my situation. But let me ask you—what is the use of existing if you are destined to be a slave?"

"There aren't free djinn?" Santana asked. We made quite the tag team of questioners, but I wished she'd look at me. Kadar really gave it to her straight, and I knew I had to clean up his mess.

"'Free' is a subjective term." Abdhi huffed a sigh. "There are djinn who consider themselves free, but they can be called on any moment to do their overlord's bidding. So how free can they truly be? At least in my lamp, I am relieved of that duty. The lamp protects me from the call of Erebus, as it is imbued with djinn magic that shields me from him, as per the instruction of the spell of the one who placed me in my lamp. Again, it spares me the worst of this illness because it has an energy source of its own. Lamp or no lamp, however, the fabric of my being is linked to Erebus."

I was about to ask another question regarding Erebus's servants who weren't djinn, but Abdhi stopped abruptly at the top of the dune. A second later, I understood why. Below us, in a deep valley between the dunes, lay a massive city of rocks and ruins, literally sitting in the middle of nowhere. It must have once been an incredible feat of architecture, with towers and spires and walls of white and gold, but it had crumbled, leaving the shell of its former glory. Flames flickered within and shadows darted between buildings, letting me know we'd reached true djinn territory.

"What the—!" Santana gasped.

"Welcome to Salameh," Abdhi replied. "The city of sanctuary for the supposedly free djinn. You cannot see them all, but hundreds of djinn reside here."

"Hundreds?" My throat clenched.

Abdhi smiled. "There are many here like your djinn, born inside magicals but freed by their magical's death. Consider it… a retirement home for djinn."

"They're crusty old folks?" Santana looked down at the city with worried eyes. I shared her apprehension. Even from here, the ruined city gave me the creeps. Shadows swirled, with bursts of fiery light scattered throughout, and whispering voices drifted up on the wind. Not the kind of place non-djinn would want to find themselves.

I really wish you hadn't come, Santana. It would have done no good to flog that dead horse. She *was* here, and she wouldn't go anywhere. I just had to hope that, between Kadar and Abdhi, we could keep her safe from errant Ifrits and Ghuls.

"I wouldn't say that in their presence." Abdhi's eyes glowed like beacons in the darkness. "And no, they aren't. These beings have a thousand or so years left to live. The Storyteller is the only djinn I know who has lived so long, though you wouldn't know it from what I've heard of her."

I turned the book to its final pages. "Older than two thousand years? It says here that djinn only live that long, which makes sense if you're similar to Purge beasts."

"There is some leeway, if the Storyteller is anything to go by— perhaps because we are far superior to the everyday Purge beast. Some say she may be over ten thousand years old, though none know her true age." Abdhi's voice filled with quiet reverence.

"Ten thousand years old?" I jabbed at the book. "It says here, in black and white, that djinn only exist for up to two thousand years. Is she like an exception to the rule or something?" I may have been retreading old ground, but I wanted proper clarification.

"The Storyteller is unique in many ways. Not everything must be black and white, Raffe... and there are always exceptions." Abdhi gave me a pointed look, making me wonder if he was talking about more than the Storyteller. "Come, we mustn't linger, in case they decide we are a threat."

Abdhi descended the slope to the broken gates of the city, and we had no choice but to follow. He was our guide and defender here, on djinn turf. I stayed close to Santana and took her hand. I braced for her to pull away, but she didn't. Instead, she gripped my hand tight and cast me a sideways glance, filled with sorrow and a million things she didn't say.

As we reached the gateway, my instincts screamed to run in the opposite direction. Out of the darkness, smoky forms swept up to block our entry. Innumerable burning eyes flickered to life, red and wrathful and trained on us.

TWENTY

Raffe

No one said a word, a stalemate stretching between us—the outsiders—and the resident djinn. Even Abdhi stood in silence. Nayla had put us in his care, but he hadn't made any assurances as to how this might turn out. And the longer we stood here, the more djinn materialized to stare, each more menacing than the last. I felt their anger surging from their fiery eyes and slamming me in the chest, sending roots of terror deep into my heart.

We're not welcome here... I didn't know if that was me or Kadar, but the fact remained.

Emphasizing my fears, a howling wind tore through the ruined city, screeching between the broken gaps in walls and shattered windows. It extended toward the sand dunes into the night, conjuring black storm clouds that masked the starry sky overhead. Thunder growled in the near distance, and my nose stung with the metallic scent of oncoming rain. When I looked over my shoulder, my stomach churned at the sight of a wall of sand rising and rushing toward us like a tidal wave. Abdhi had informed us of the djinn's abilities, and it seemed every power had come out to play in defense of their refuge.

"Calm yourselves, before you draw attention to our location. These are my guests, and you will treat them with due courtesy!" Abdhi finally spoke, his voice booming across the horde of ruby-eyed hostiles.

The djinn jostled nervously, giving hints of their true forms as they phased between wispy smoke and solid appearances. Some monstrous individuals stood toward the back of the gathered army. At first, I'd thought they were shadows cast by the city's remaining towers, but they moved fluidly and were clearly sentient. I understood then that Abdhi's description of un-subjugated Marid was no exaggeration.

That wasn't the only thing I came to understand through being closer to the city. Thanks to the incendiary glow sizzling from the djinn, I could see more of Salameh. Bioluminescent pools glowed inside the fortifications, with palm trees swaying and lush greenery growing at the water's edge. From within dilapidated structures, delicate tulle drapes billowed from windows. A secret paradise in the middle of the Arabian desert—an oasis, quite literally. Their sanctuary.

And we'd shown up unannounced.

"*Abeq fe al-khalaf!*" Abdhi bellowed, switching to Arabic as a few shadows slithered forward. It meant "Stay back," which didn't exactly fill me with confidence, considering they paid no attention.

I decided to attempt some Arabic of my own, in hopes of extending an olive branch. "*Nahin la naani ei darar lek.*" Basically, I told them we meant no harm. Whether they'd listen or not was another matter.

The encroaching djinn paused in surprise. The winds died slowly as the sandstorm sank into the desert, and the clouds rolled away to reveal the clear night again.

"Did you do that?" Santana whispered.

"I don't know," I whispered back.

"*Al-salam maak.*" A strange voice lifted above the mutter of furious djinn. A feminine voice, saying, "Peace is with you."

I squinted into the gloom, watching a figure part the smoky sea. Scarlet-skinned and clad in a red silk robe, she approached us. Her dark garnet eyes burned with a strange white flame. Abdhi had been right about something: she didn't look ten thousand years old. She walked without a hunch, or any sign of age, and had very few lines and wrinkles on her mesmerizing face. I couldn't tell if she was beautiful or not—she was beyond those parameters. But she had a regal quality about her, in the strength of her jaw and the high cut of her cheekbones.

I bowed to her, on impulse. "*Al-salam maak.*"

"I will speak in your tongue, for simplicity's sake, though I commend you for greeting me in kind," she said, smiling. Her voice had a faraway, musical timbre that surrounded me. "My name is Safiya, though many know me as the Storyteller."

"There's no way you're ten thousand years old!" Santana blurted out. "You look younger than my mom."

Safiya laughed softly. "I am far shy of ten thousand years—that is hearsay and hyperbole, to heighten my mystique, no doubt. I would reveal my true age, but a woman of my maturity must retain some secrecy. Regardless, we djinn do not age in the same manner as mortals, and I do not age in the same manner as other djinn."

"Why not?" I prompted, eager to learn more of this mysterious being.

"I was created in Erebus's primary Purge Plague and am thus

imbued with certain qualities that later iterations lack. It is the same with you magicals and your predecessors. I suppose, in that analogy, I would be a Primus Anglicus, while you are diluted descendants." She gave a small, graceful nod. "I mean no offense; I am merely attempting to explain my existence in a way you may better comprehend."

Santana stared at Safiya. "A Purge Plague?"

"Akin to the Purging of a beast, but en masse. Erebus made it so," Safiya replied. "And we are not so simple-minded as most Purge beasts."

"Safiya, Safiya!" one of the furtive shadows hissed.

Safiya glanced at him. "Yes, Rasul?"

"He is Raffe Levi, the son of Leonidas Levi. He holds Kadar within himself, the son of Zalaam." The one who'd spoken came to stand beside Safiya, his form solidifying into a familiar red body and black smoke.

"Ah, I see." Safiya looked back at me. "This is Rasul. He belongs to the same djinn lineage as Kadar and was formerly entwined with his own Levi. I suppose he is family to you."

That was a lot to process. "Rasul, is it?"

The djinn shuffled forward. "Yes, I am he. I resided inside your great-great-grandfather, Javad Levi."

"Is that why you're here, enjoying your... uh... retirement?" I fumbled the word. I didn't want to insult one of Kadar's ancestors.

"Yes. When Javad died, I was freed. I had no desire to return to Persia, in case I became entrapped again. Instead I came here, where all the freed djinn come, no matter where they originated." Rasul dipped his head, and I did the same.

I put out my hand. "It's good to meet you, Rasul."

He shook it. "It is a pleasure to meet you, too. I shared a remarkable bond with Javad. Even now, I miss him. When one has been bound to another so closely, there will always be an emptiness after they pass."

"It's nice to hear about a Levi and their djinn getting along." I thought of Kadar and wondered how he'd feel when I wasn't around anymore. If he'd thrown himself from that building, as he'd planned, would he have ended up here? Or would it have killed him as well as me? I didn't know the rules of suicide in the djinn world. Perhaps it spelled their death, too. Otherwise, why would Kadar have done that? It'd certainly felt like he hadn't intended to survive, though I was buried deep at the time.

"Javad and I were close from the moment he was born, and I was tied to his being." Rasul gazed at me wistfully, as though seeing his host's face in mine. "I even contemplated following him to the here-after, but, after I found my way here, Safiya urged me to remain."

That answers your suicide question, Kadar hissed inside my skull. *I was planning to go with you, just so you know. I wouldn't splatter you and make a run for it. If I'd wanted that, I'd have done it years ago.*

"Now that you have had something of a family reunion, perhaps we ought to return to the matter at hand. Namely, why are you here?" Safiya ushered Rasul backward and once again took center stage. "This is a sanctuary for free djinn. You do not have a free djinn. Unless you are here to sacrifice yourself for his freedom?"

That took me aback. "No, that's not why I'm here."

"It happens from time to time, revealing the occasional selfless mortal." Safiya's white-flamed eyes flashed.

"I'm not here to sacrifice myself, but I *am* here to help Kadar. I do want to help the rest of the djinn, too—not just the one I exist with," I explained. "You're all suffering because Erebus cut you off, and we need to find a way to fix it. That's why I'm here, to see if we can put our heads together and figure out a solution."

She sighed. "I feared that may be the case."

"Feared? Why?" Santana cut in. "Surely it's good that someone is coming to ask for your help to fix a problem that's plaguing you all? I've stayed up night after night with Kadar, and it's not getting any better for him. He's small fry compared to some of you, so it must be kicking your backsides."

Safiya raised her eyebrows. "*You* stayed up with Kadar?"

"It's not like Raffe could. Every time Kadar comes to the surface, Raffe conks out, and I won't leave either of them hanging. I love them, and I'll stay up every night I have to until they're better," she replied.

My heart swelled. I felt Kadar bristle inside me, too, evidently pleased that she'd bundled us together.

"You love *them?*" Safiya sounded dumbfounded.

Santana lifted her chin. "They're stuck together. If I love one, I have to love the other."

"Then you are, perhaps, as much of a rarity in this world as I." Safiya smiled curiously. "Nevertheless, that does not mean I am any more willing to help you. I have been asked for help since this affliction began, but I worry for my kind, specifically those with magical hosts they are bound to."

"Why them, specifically?" I urged.

"Because they do not understand what it will take to rid themselves of this dire ache." Safiya's shoulders sagged, and her black smoke thinned out. "So, I have decided upon the safest course of action. I have encouraged all djinn to endure, in the faith that Erebus's power will eventually return."

The winds whipped up again, though they didn't howl so much as whimper. The djinn were afraid, and they had every right to be.

"Then your faith is misplaced, Safiya," I said. "I don't mean to be rude, and I don't mean to defy your authority, but Erebus has taken on a personal project involving the city of Atlantis. I don't have the details, but I am certain that it will take a while. Longer than you, or I, might have."

Safiya's eyes flashed brighter, and whorls of sand twisted up around us. "He is pursuing this path again?"

"Yes, that's what he's up to," I replied, squinting. "I didn't know he'd tried before. Can you tell me why?"

"Sadly not. I only know that it relates to reaching that ruined city; his reasoning has always been unclear. At least now I understand why we have been separated from his power." Safiya's smoke billowed wildly, her skin pulsating with obvious rage. "And no, this is not his first attempt at Atlantis. However, if we are suffering this way, he has reached much further in his quest than ever before. It is my guess that he has succeeded in the part where he must take a human form. He tried that once before and failed. Yes, that must be why we have been cut off and are suffering."

"Surely you already know that? You must've already known about the human body thing, right? Aren't you all connected to his brain or something?" Santana squinted in confusion.

Safiya sighed. "A common misconception. The djinn are connected to each other, but we are not connected to Erebus's mind unless he desires it and wishes to send messages to us. When he shut us out and the illness began, we had no sense of why. But now I understand. So, I suppose we must sit and talk awhile… There is no other option now."

I sat cross-legged on a patchwork of intricately woven rugs, with the warmth of a fire taking the chill from my bones. Santana sat beside me, clutching a satin cushion to her chest with a heavy woolen blanket draped over her shoulders. Without a word, she took the edge and put it around me, and the two of us huddled inside. Kadar may have kept me relatively toasty, but nothing beat having Santana near. Even if I'd been roasting, I would've bunched up next to her.

One of the bioluminescent pools glowed nearby. The palm fronds swayed in the breeze while the fragrance of desert rose mingled with the earthier scent of woodsmoke. Abdhi sat opposite us, keeping a reverent distance from Safiya, while the rest of the free djinn stood or sat close by, listening in on our conversation.

"As I mentioned, I was created from Erebus's primary Purge Plague, many thousands of years ago. One moment I was energy, drifting in nothingness, and the next, I was forced into sentience through an innocent magical. She died, as the rest of the mortals in that first wave did. Our power was too great for them to survive."

"Were there other djinn like you?" I asked.

She nodded. "Yes, but they are long dead now. As they passed into the ether, returning to the Chaos from whence they were birthed, Erebus created more of us, though he granted us less power than before. No doubt he feared an uprising, either from us or from Gaia herself to protect her own creations, if he kept killing them the way he did during that first expulsion. I imagine that was his way of preventing punishment befalling him, by promising to find an alternative method and undoubtedly claiming that the first bout of killing had been an accidental effect of our release into the world."

"So you're the only one of your kind left?" Santana queried.

"Indeed. I am the last of the first. All these djinn around you now, and within the wider world, are echoes of that initial glory. However, his intention never faltered—that has remained constant. We were made to be Erebus's eyes and ears in the mortal realm, watching and listening and working in his name, covering all corners of this earth."

Santana tapped her lip with a finger. "His network."

"Yes, his network of unwitting emissaries." Safiya sighed. "But, with all Child creations, there were unavoidable flaws in our conception. Flaws he is not able to undo, even now, or we would not be what we are."

I frowned as I held my hands up to the fire's warmth. "Flaws? What kinds of flaws?"

"We are bound to his will, and we rely upon him for our power, but he cannot intervene or negate the spells that we perform of our own volition," she explained.

"I'm guessing that doesn't work in your favor now, though?" Santana pressed, leaning forward.

"Sadly not," Safiya replied. "Erebus has never succeeded in gaining a mortal body before. As long as his being is restrained in human form, the djinn will continue to be separated from his power, and we will slowly decay and fade back into the ether we emerged from. We cannot stop him, and we cannot prevent our own demise. It is the tragedy of the perpetually subservient."

I raised a nervous hand. "Is it okay to speak in front of... them?"

"They are free djinn, hiding here to avoid the call of Erebus. They hold no love toward him, and he evidently holds no love toward them. Anything you say here will be treated with utmost discretion and will not leave this city," Safiya promised.

Funnily enough, I believed her. What djinn would be mad enough to defy their matriarch? Erebus might've been their "father" in a sense, but he was an absentee father if I'd ever seen one. Which made Safiya the single mother, trying to figure out what was best for all her children.

"I guess that's one advantage of being cut off, right? He can't hear you, even if he wanted to?" I hoped.

She lowered her head. "A very small advantage, yes."

"There has to be *something* you can do to prevent your demise, as you put it." Santana leaned even farther, to the point where I worried about the flames.

Safiya lifted her gaze, the firelight intensifying her burning stare. "There is one way, though it is only to be used in the direst emergency. This certainly qualifies." She took in a deep breath. "If the djinn gather with one objective, we can go to Tartarus and speak with Erebus to gain more control. In truth, it would do more than that—it would free us from our maker altogether if we all chose at once, as a collective."

"Wouldn't that put you in the same position you're in now?" I couldn't figure out how it would help them, since they'd still be cut off from Erebus.

"A valid inquiry. We would be excised with a quantity of his power flowing into us and staying there. As such, we would no longer be subservient to him. Those bound to magicals would be extricated immediately upon Erebus relinquishing his hold—it would be like wiping the slate entirely clean and starting again. Ultimately, it would leave us all as weaker entities, but we would be truly free."

A bristle of nervous chatter rose as Safiya spoke.

Free? Extricated? That means... I would be able to have a family with Santana.

My heart lurched at the prospect. I knew that attempting to remove a djinn usually resulted in both parties dying, but this would be different. This would be, as Safiya had said, wiping the slate clean. I imagined the wrench would still hurt, but if it meant I could have a future with Santana, I'd go through every pain under the sun to make it happen.

Traitor. Kadar's voice ricocheted through my brain. A second later, he ripped through me without warning and took over. "You're talking about staging a coup, you vile bottom-feeders. I ought to tear every one of your heads from your shoulders, pluck your hearts through what's left of your throats, and stick them on a sacrificial altar to Erebus for this betrayal."

"You are young, Kadar." Safiya's tone softened. "You have not been made to bow and scrape beneath his autocracy. You have not experienced the shared misery, witnessed through the djinn's hivemind."

Kadar bristled with anger. "You are what you are. You would not exist without Erebus. You ought to kiss his boots instead of whining about injustice."

I fought back, trying to claw my way up from the depths Kadar had shoved me into. "Kadar, think about what—"

He forced me into submission again, just as he'd done at Ignatius's—locking me down so I couldn't get out. "This isn't your fight, and you don't get a say!" Kadar yelled. "You do not owe Erebus as we do, so keep your nose out of it. If you do not, I will cut it off to spite us both."

Kadar, think about what this could mean for me and Santana. I tried to get him to listen, but he was too far gone.

And what about me *and Santana?* he replied violently. *Or do you not give a damn about me anymore?*

I sat silently and retreated to the corner of my mind that belonged solely to me. Kadar couldn't get in here. I'd built it long ago when I realized he could read my every thought and delve into my brain whenever he liked. My safe haven in this safe haven of Salameh. He wouldn't stop me from hoping, not if it meant we both got to survive and live on our own terms. Why couldn't he see what was being offered?

We'd miss each other, sure, but the world would be our oyster—separate entities, at long last. And we could still be in one another's lives if we wanted, the "if" being the important part. No more forced symbiosis. He should've jumped for joy; I certainly wanted to. When Kadar glanced at Santana, she had tears in her eyes. No doubt she understood what this meant, too, especially after Kadar's earlier outburst.

This separation sounded like a viable way to have a family with Santana. If Erebus was forced to relent, the djinn would be healthy and continue existing, though they would be less powerful. But who wouldn't exchange that for freedom from Erebus's shackles?

Kadar... that was who.

"Stay down! I've had just about enough of you!" he bellowed. And with that, the doors locked on my safe haven, shutting me inside. Judging by his ire, I didn't know when, or if, I'd emerge again.

TWENTY-ONE

Kadar

———

S antana, Santana, Santana. Raffe's head spun with nothing but her. My head, too. In our shared blood, she throbbed endlessly—an insipid disease that neither of us wanted to cure. But sometimes, he just couldn't see the wood for the trees.

I'd been with him longer. *I'd* been part of him since birth. One whisper of getting free of me, and he'd jumped for it. Coward. Wretched weakling.

How's that for gratitude? I kept this fool warm when he should've shivered. I gave him strength when he'd otherwise have gotten trampled. I focused him when distraction snapped his attention the wrong way. And I gave him the bad-boy edge that kept our woman interested. Santana would've been yawning if I hadn't brought some spice to our trio. Sometimes, I sensed her yearning for me to come out instead of Raffe. But, selfish to a fault, Raffe thought it was all about him and his wants.

Maybe I could forgive that. Raffe dreamt of freedom when he thought I wasn't listening. He entertained his idealistic mental pictures of a future without me. And liberation wouldn't have been so bad, all things considered. I wouldn't mind sowing my wild oats, so to speak, flexing this djinn muscle however I liked, not worrying about my host losing his mind. But breaking loose of Erebus... I had my unhinged moments, but that was pure madness. And these ingrates needed to hear that.

"You have been out here too long. It has addled your pathetic minds. What you have is a façade of autonomy, when you should accept the nature of our being," I hissed at the crowd, smug in Raffe's silence. I'd buried that chicken deep. A door worked both ways. He wanted to lock me out of a corner of his mind? Fine. He could stay there and think about what he'd done.

"We belong to our king, our leader, our creator. Do you know what gods do when their subjects rebel? They spit in their faces and destroy them for lack of gratitude. If you think Erebus will be any different... let's just say if you go to him and demand this, then you deserve to have your brains crushed against these walls."

"Erebus is no god," Safiya replied coolly.

Silly cow, thinking she owned the place because she'd lived the longest. So what? To me, it just meant she hadn't had the courage to die. We didn't need a matriarch. The djinn had a leader. We were built to follow Erebus, not this dissident.

My eyes burned into her. "What is a god but a creator with exceptional power? Erebus is our creator. Therefore, he is our god. Defy him at your peril, but know this: you'll be to blame for what comes after. If he obliterates us, that's on your shoulders."

A rumble of apprehension circled the crowd of djinn. Despite Safiya's protestations that the Salameh djinn didn't care for our king, it seemed she'd overshot her estimations. Not surprising, considering her arrogance. Haughty old crone. To even suggest mutiny against Erebus spelled conceit.

"Would we survive in our weakened state?" one djinn shouted. A big, bulky Marid, towering over everyone. "We have all made enemies."

"What if it doesn't work?" another cried, bearing the same red flesh as me. "What if he cuts us off completely, and we die anyway?"

A third pushed to the front, all pomp and circumstance. Ifrits always had a sense of perceived superiority, and it showed. All djinn had innate knowledge of the diverse race they came from, separate from the network, so I didn't need to be connected to the hivemind to know the traits each type was known for. "You told us to wait. Maybe that's the safest path—to trust Erebus and pray he is restored to his former glory soon."

"And be under his thumb for the rest of our days?" a Si'lat agitator retorted, their body a mass of seething black smoke with only a hint of red. "When will we ever have another opportunity like this? This would mean true liberation."

"I don't know about you, but I don't want to be stuck in a cycle of waiting to be called, never allowed to exist as I wish." Another rebel stepped in. Another Marid, throwing their weight around. "Why should he subjugate us, just because he created us? That was his choice, not ours. It shouldn't give him the right to retain control."

My eyes flitted from speaker to speaker. They seemed split on the issue. Ironic, considering I wanted to split the agitators in two, starting with Safiya. Cut the head off the snake, and the rest might have the decency to die. Who did she think she was? Even if she were thousands of years old, Erebus had millennia on her. If this was a contest of who'd lived longest, Erebus would wipe the floor with her.

"But we're all used to drawing power from Erebus," another chimed in. "What if we can't function properly when it's gone?"

"What if we all die anyway, because Erebus never returns to his full power? Wouldn't you rather have a fighting chance, decided by us?" A rebel glowered at the objector, so I glowered at *him* to even things out. I let my smoke billow in dense waves.

"Our best chance is not betraying our creator. I'm not going to die a traitor, and I won't be bundled into a rebellion I want no part of." I glared around the crowd of djinn, challenging them all with my eyes.

"The way I see it, we have a choice," Safiya cut in. "We can stay as we are, bound to Erebus with the prospect of having our full strength returned to us, or we can be free with lesser strength. The latter means we also rid ourselves of this pain and insomnia."

"But this pain and insomnia are short-lived. If we tough it out, Erebus will return to his Child form and restore us," I barked back.

Santana scoffed. "When did you get so gung-ho about this, Kadar? Let's not forget that you tried to throw yourself—and Raffe—off a building a few days ago. You tried to end your lives because you couldn't hack it anymore. That doesn't sound like 'toughing it out' to me."

"I would have tried harder, had I known you and Raffe would land me in a mutiny," I snarled. "I told you before. The only way to end this affliction is through death or Erebus. I attempted death, but you were too stubborn to let me succeed. Which means I now choose Erebus. I choose to wait on him and have faith."

Safiya gave me a pitying look that made me want to drown her in one of those glowing pools. "It is as I feared. The longer Erebus holds us apart, the greater the pressure upon his creations. If he is seeking Atlantis, it will take much too long to return to his true form. Already, some djinn have begun to lose their minds. I see that you are no exception, Kadar."

"I survived!" I snapped.

"Only thanks to Finch." Santana turned to me, her face hard with wrath.

"Nevertheless, I lived, and I'm glad I did, so I can talk some sense into all of you before Erebus rips the sense, and everything else, out of your carcasses." I glared back. "I will not choose to be feeble. I choose to receive my power from Erebus, as I always have, pain and insomnia be damned. If we can't deal with this for a while, then maybe none of us deserve to live."

Abdhi stood sharply and puffed his chest. He clearly had something to say, but I would rather listen to the Queen of Idiocy than a sorry excuse for a djinn who'd allowed himself to get stuffed into a little lamp for the rest of time. His "mistress" at the Dubai Coven probably hadn't let him speak in months. Now, we had to suffer for it by listening to him harp on.

"Release Raffe," he demanded. "Let the young mortal speak."

I smirked. "Raffe can't come to the phone right now, so get back in your lamp, you worthless wisp. You aren't ten feet tall anymore. The worst you can do is huff and puff and blow hot air out of your ass."

"I can still flatten you, you impertinent imp." Abdhi's fiery eyes flickered.

"Is that supposed to scare me?" I laughed icily. "Your leash is showing. One little tug from that uppity mistress of yours, and you disappear back to Dubai. That's hardly frightening."

Abdhi clenched his hands to fists and brought them up to his face. "You will regret your insolence."

I laughed harder. "Ooh, allow me to tuck my tail between my legs and bow down. I don't give two hoots how old you are—how old any of you are. It won't match up against youth. That's the trouble with you old fogies; you struggle to grasp the concept that young people have wisdom, so you try and lead us all into more and more chaos. A bunch of donkeys leading lions."

Safiya had disappeared from her spot on the rugs.

"And you forget that we have lived long enough to understand what needs to be done, for the sake of everyone, not just ourselves," Safiya whispered behind me.

I whipped around, startled by her blinding speed. The old gal had skills I hadn't anticipated. Before I could react, her hand slammed into my forehead.

Intense light flooded my head. I had no hope of fighting it—she was too damn fast. I sizzled away, driven down. I felt the door to Raffe's secret hideaway unlock, immediately freeing him. I howled and screamed inside him, but it made no difference. I was trapped now, and he was loose.

"This is the second time Kadar got his ass kicked in less than a day," Santana exclaimed softly, trying to sound amused. But her eyes gave her away. I could see them, through Raffe. She was worried, and she had every reason to be. If these morons staged a coup against Erebus and he retaliated, she'd lose Raffe and me both.

Raffe might've been willing to risk it, but was she?

TWENTY-TWO

Kadar

I sank lower. A bitter stone, with Raffe's anchor dragging me down into the darkest depths of his subconscious. This was now my prison, though I would make a jailbreak soon. I had the good fortune of Raffe not having the clout to keep me here, as much as he'd have liked to believe otherwise. And he wouldn't have other djinn saving his skin every time I did something they had no taste for, either. Paltry bodyguards at best. Irksome annoyances at worst.

I can still hear you... My voice wriggled into Raffe's mind.

I don't mind if you can, Raffe replied. *You got out of hand, but I don't want you suppressed in there. I'm not my father.*

Could've fooled me. I feel everything, Raffe. I feel your excitement. You want to be rid of me. I didn't give in to those emotions, but tiny pulses of shame twinged inside me.

That's not true. I felt Raffe exhaling. Sharing a body had become second nature. His actions, my actions, what was the difference? *It's not that I want to be separate from you, but think about it—this might help you gain your own form. You wouldn't have to depend on me anymore, and you wouldn't disappear because you happened to piss off another djinn. In fact, you'd never have to be pushed down again, and neither would I. No more sharing. We'd be two separate beings, able to do what we wanted, when we wanted, without consulting each other.*

I don't depend on you! I shot back. *Who do you think you're kidding? You're the one who depends on me. You'd be no better than a slug in the dirt without me to give you some oomph.*

He sighed. *You know what I mean. We could live separate lives.*

Who says I want that? I created a surge of adrenaline, just to mess with him. His heart raced, and I sensed his lungs working faster to push oxygen around his already alert body.

Don't pretend you don't, he answered. *You're only part of me because of a curse. I'd miss you—of course I would—but I'd accept your absence, knowing you were free, and I was free.*

I snorted. *And give up Santana? You're forgetting something, pal. You brought her into our lives. Your heart and mine are intertwined; what you feel, I feel. You made me fall for her with all your incessant sappiness. Don't think you can just take her for yourself and push me out of the picture.*

I don't want you out of the picture. Separation doesn't mean... complete separation. I felt thoughts flitting through his mind as Raffe searched for the right words. *We could be like brothers if you wanted. It'd be your choice, because you'd have a choice.*

I didn't know what to make of that. *What, some messed-up, weird kind of family?*

If you wanted that... yes. The three of us. His stomach fluttered, as if cannibal butterflies fought a battle royale inside his belly. *That way, Santana won't risk her life to have children. If you care for her, like you say you do, then we should be on the same wavelength. This is her life at stake, and we're the ones with the axe over her head. If we do this, you get to keep your life, I get to keep mine, and she gets to keep hers. Everyone wins. Think of her. Erebus doesn't care if she lives or dies, but we do. We love her. If we don't do this, then we let her down in the worst possible way. Look at her and tell me you don't see the hope in her eyes.*

I peered through his vision at Santana. Sure enough, her eyes swam with bittersweet tears. The liquid result of human frailty. A physical cue of a mortal in distress. That should've been kicked out of human genes centuries ago, but they'd clung to it for some unknown reason. It did nothing to pique my sympathy... not much, anyway. Maybe a spasm of it, in a very distant corner of my mind. Djinn didn't need that sort of thing. Perhaps I'd been in this body too long; perhaps I had allowed it to weaken me.

That doesn't mean I agree to this insanity, I said at last, the silent words passing to Raffe. This conversation had taken place rapidly, over the span of no more than a moment or two. The other djinn hadn't noticed. They were too busy wallowing in distress and lapping up every word the old crone had to say, while Safiya stared at Raffe with a dose of fake pity. Anything to win him over.

Abdhi settled down. Arrogant worm. I would've torn him to shreds, given half a second longer in my full form. I'd have ripped that meddlesome hag a new one, too, if I'd been ready for her attack. The taking-me-by-surprise trick would only work once. I wouldn't be fooled again.

Safiya took a deep breath. "Separating ourselves from Erebus may be our only choice, going forward. We cannot afford to wait for his restoration, for we will surely fade away in the lengthy interim it will take him to reach Atlantis. This is the only way to ensure our survival."

I thought about that for a moment. Fading away didn't sound good, and it didn't sound like the traitor was lying. Listening to her, a small spark of something like possibility ignited.

What if we really could pull this off? Erebus had created me, sure, but I wasn't old enough to be connected to the djinn mainframe. I didn't feel the full weight of his power. Not yet. Would it make much difference, when it boiled down to it? Plus, I loved Santana. I wasn't ashamed to admit it. She'd lit a fire under this djinn. And Raffe was right: I didn't want her light sputtering out because Raffe couldn't keep his mitts to himself.

She could live, and never worry... I forgot to block my thoughts from Raffe.

That's right, she could. Isn't that worth trying? he replied.

I cursed and recoiled from our shared mental transmission. He made an annoyingly valid point. I was loyal to Erebus, but I didn't love him the way I loved Santana. I wouldn't have run the gauntlet of every hell for him. Santana had only to ask. Sure, I'd put up a token resistance, but I'd still do it. The nights we'd spent with her arms around me—actually me, not Raffe—talking me through my pain and holding me when the tremors came... she was worth the risk. She'd crept in and entrapped me. Losing her would be worse than losing Raffe.

When had I become such a sad sack? Likely, the moment she showed she cared for me *and* Raffe. The beast as well as the host. If Safiya could really rally the troops and do this, maybe a window of opportunity would open. One that hadn't been there before. The chance to steal Santana away from Raffe. I could have her all to myself, at last, and have her arms around me every night.

Yes, I'd say that is worth risking everything for. This time, I wanted Raffe to hear.

TWENTY-THREE

Raffe

"We must discuss this amongst ourselves, Safiya," a wizened djinn stated from her place at the helm of an equally shriveled group. They hadn't aged nearly as well as the Storyteller, and I guessed them to be the elders.

"Of course, Mahmoud." Safiya bowed her head as the elders left together. They walked past the glowing water into the darkness of the desert, where they stooped and muttered, their wildly gesticulating hands the telltale sign that they weren't in total agreement.

The rest of the djinn dispersed to have conversations of their own, leaving Safiya by the fireside with only myself, Santana, and Abdhi for company. Safiya had resumed her position after sending Kadar away. Santana retreated into herself, wrapping the blanket tight around her body as she stared into the flickering flames. No doubt she feared Kadar might appear again. I thought about taking some Lullaby Weeds to ensure he couldn't, but I didn't want to be knocked out, too. Not just yet. This momentary peace presented the ideal opportunity to broach our third reason for being here—Finch's request.

"Safiya?" I said.

She lifted her solemn gaze to me, white flames sparking. "Yes?"

"We've actually got another question for you." I shuffled forward.

"Oh? What might that be?" She tilted her head, her features thoughtful.

"What do you know about the connection between servants of Erebus and the djinn?" I pulled the stolen book from my bag and pushed it toward her. "I've scanned the index of this thing, but there doesn't seem to be a section about it. Maybe I'm reading the wrong part, I don't know. But I figured you'd know more about that kind of thing than a book. Kadar said you might."

Safiya narrowed her eyes. "He did, did he?"

"In one of his less aggressive moments," I replied sheepishly.

"And what specifics are you most interested in? The lore of Erebus's servants could take me hours to work through." She waited patiently, her intense gaze never leaving my face.

Santana answered, a second before me. "Do any of the servants survive their service with Erebus? We've got a… friend in trouble, and we need to know if he'll be okay." She peered over her blanket like a tortoise in its shell, rocking slightly to keep the chill away.

So you do *think of him as a friend.* I'd known Santana cared about Finch, deep down. And he cared about her. They fought like cat and dog, but they'd protect each other when it came down to it.

Safiya closed her eyes, though the white flames seared through her eyelids in an unsettling way. They opened shortly, and her brows knitted. "No… they do not survive his service. They all die obliging his whims and requests, one way or another."

"Are you sure?" Santana's voice sounded strangled.

"I am quite certain. I have scoured the history and found no evidence of a survivor of long-term service, as I imagine that is where your concern lies. Those to whom he offers limited deals live, but their services last a matter of days or weeks—they do not meet the criteria of true service," Safiya explained sadly.

Her words punched me in the gut. If that was true, Finch was screwed. Well and truly screwed. But a doubt nagged the back of my mind. "I thought you couldn't delve into the djinn mainframe anymore, with Erebus restricting you all. How can you be certain?"

"The other djinn are locked out of our shared knowledge, but I am not. Being of the first wave, that cannot be taken from me—I aided in its creation, as all the First did, so it is innately within me."

That wasn't what I'd wanted to hear. I'd wanted a shred of hope, not blunt, brutal conviction.

"*Nobody* has lived? Nobody?" Santana breathed, her eyes scrunching up.

"Actually, that is not exactly correct." Safiya raised a hand and lifted a solitary finger. "I discovered one exception, but it may be of little use to you and your friend."

Santana threw off her blanket. "Tell us anyway!"

"Very well, but don't say I did not warn you." Safiya sighed and lowered her hand. "The sole survivor of Erebus's long-term servitude was a Necromancer. He saved a Marid from an abandoned lamp while on a mission for Erebus, unraveling the curse that had bound him to the object. In return, that djinn aided the Necromancer in escaping Erebus's service."

"A... Necromancer?" She was right. That didn't help us much—but it meant it could be done. I needed to know more, though it was a long shot. "How did he get out of it?"

Safiya closed her eyes again, then returned a moment later. "The djinn imbued a special amulet with part of his restored magic. As you know by now, Marids are tremendously powerful in their raw form.

He blended his magic with some of the Necromancer's Chaos, binding both to the amulet. With it, the Necromancer was granted the ability to revive himself. In case you did *not* know, Necromancers cannot resurrect themselves. Only one can... this one."

Santana made a strained noise, halfway between a gasp and a shriek. "It's Davin. She's talking about Davin." She looked to me with panicked eyes. "Remember Marie Laveau's church? Finch stuck a knife in Davin, and Marie's Voodoo hounds tore the living daylights out of him. He should've been dead, but that asswipe came right on back. And after Harley battered seven shades of crap out of him at that shady hotel? He popped up again in Elysium, as if nothing had happened."

My stomach churned with dread. "You're right... Holy crap, you're right!" Of course that snake had found a way to cheat not only death, but Erebus. He served himself, doing whatever he had to in order to survive.

"Only in death is the servant free of Erebus," Safiya continued, her scarlet skin rippling. The wind whipped up again, as if reacting to her anxiety. "And given that, as I said, Necromancers cannot resurrect themselves... well, this individual—the Necromancer—had to manipulate a few rules to achieve it."

"Hang on, hang on, hang on." I raised my hands, trying to keep hold of all these dangling threads. "You said Erebus can't intervene with djinn magic? Does that mean—"

"Erebus cannot do anything about his errant former slave." She nodded, finishing my sentence for me. "The amulet is bound with djinn magic, as I mentioned, which makes it indestructible. At least by Erebus's hand. Another could destroy it, perhaps, but they would find it exceedingly difficult. Anyway, it serves to shroud him from Erebus's gaze and provides him the necessary means to move unseen."

Santana edged closer to me and leaned against my arm. "That's probably why Davin keeps gunning for Finch. He's clearly got major beef with his former boss, and he'll want to do everything he can to screw with Erebus's plans."

I nodded, my stomach roiling. "And since Finch is involved in those plans, he's moved to the top of Davin's most-wanted list—to ruin Erebus's endgame."

"I am sorry I have nothing more comforting to offer you." Safiya dipped her chin to her chest, white veins pulsating beneath her red flesh.

"At least you've given us a clue about Davin. That's more than Erebus did," I replied. But would knowing Davin's motivations really help us, or Finch? I had no idea. I needed to mull it over, see if we could coax some loophole open to aid our friend.

Unfortunately, now wasn't the time for that kind of mulling. The elders had stopped flailing wildly and were heading back to where we sat. I felt Santana's tension, and she likely felt mine. What answer had they come to? It took all my willpower to stay still and wait for them to speak.

"Mahmoud? What conclusion have you reached?" Safiya jumped in, her tone discreetly hopeful.

The wizened djinn sketched a bow before replying. "We have conversed at length and agree that the best course of action is to forge a collective and assert ourselves against Erebus, by going to Tartarus to confront him and sever ourselves from his power. However, we must give everyone a voice in this, considering what the consequences may be. First, we must summon all the djinn in the world and discuss it further once everyone is gathered."

If this all ends in a blaze of misery and viscera, you will be the one responsible. Kadar made *his* voice known. *Fortunately, we may not live to* be held accountable. *If Erebus rejects this, I will be obliterated, and you will suffer the wrench of my departure.*

Can you be positive, for once? I shot back silently.

I heard him chuckle coldly inside my skull. *I just want to get in an "I told you so" while I have the chance.*

"I entirely agree," Safiya said. "Everyone must have the opportunity to choose. I will summon the djinn so we may hold a forum."

She raised her arms. White light, tinged with a reddish hue, slithered from her eyes and down into her chest. Her heart ignited as the light burst from her, her every pulse visible. The sheer force of the explosion bent her backward at an impossible angle, and we beheld the spiraling vortex of raw energy as it tunneled through the night sky. It seemed to pierce the atmosphere, glowing ripples palpitating outward in a steady rhythm.

The desert responded. Black clouds rolled in, and thunder roared in the distance. Cold spits of rain splashed my upturned face. A wall of sand raced over the dunes, and forks of red lightning splintered through, briefly illuminating eerie flying shadows, all headed in our direction. The winds screamed a rallying cry as the gathered djinn lifted their hands, their own hearts igniting in kind, all linking together as one. Glancing down, I noticed my own heart glowing through my skin.

Have you literally had a change of heart? I asked Kadar.

What can I say? Where Santana's life is concerned, I can be persuaded to put aside my moral compass, he replied. *Let's just hope it doesn't get us all killed, shall we?*

I glanced at Santana. Her eyes were fixed on the sky, her head tilted upward, highlighting the smooth curve of her neck and the serene beauty that gleamed from her when she was deep in thought. Not that she wasn't always beautiful. I'd seen her first thing in the morning, her hair sticking up and her eyes puffy, and thought she was the most stunning woman to ever exist. I followed her gaze to the shadows falling from the storm clouds. My heart lurched in fear, but I reminded myself that this was a good thing. The djinn were heeding Safiya's call. Maybe, just maybe, she'd convince them to agree to this insane idea.

Wispy tendrils of smoke twisted downward, landing in solid djinn form in the oasis of Salameh, wedging in wherever they found room. Flying figures hurtled in from the sandstorms, carried in on the winds, while other djinn appeared out of nowhere. Before our eyes, thousands of red-eyed djinn stood, stretching so far that they filled the city and beyond, some perched on the dunes out of necessity.

Looks like Daddy decided to join us. Kadar pulled a few strings, making me turn my head toward the latest arrivals. Sure enough, Zalaam stood there, his heart aglow, his eyes burning.

Fight Erebus, I silently urged, to no djinn in particular. *It won't be easy, but nothing worth doing has ever been easy. Fight your master and be free!*

If they didn't, then all our hope would disappear, and so would they. Along with my chance at a normal life with Santana, slipping away like the sand of this desert running through my fingers.

TWENTY-FOUR

Finch

Ah, the Great White North. The Great White Nothing was more like it. One good thing came out of Canada: maple syrup. Maybe ice hockey too, and I didn't mind staring at a moose or a beaver from time to time. But definitely not the weather, which was freezing off my extremities at this very moment. And definitely not Ryann's favorite serial killer—the boyfriend, Adam. He might've come from the French part. I'd never bothered to ask.

Snow charmed a lot of people, people who hadn't trudged through it across harsh terrain for the last two hours, trying to find a crashed airplane. Icy flakes wafted endlessly from a dark gray sky, making this entire trek ten times as grim.

The town of Churchill squatted in the distance, and puffs of black smoke rose from the trains that rattled in and out, bringing cargo to the banks of Hudson Bay. Calling it a town might've been too generous. The uniform gray-and-white buildings with hints of rusty red reminded me of some Scandinavian, middle-of-nowhere glimmer of civilization.

A couple larger buildings cropped up ahead—factories or depots of some kind. One stood right on the edge of the water. A monolith of industry. No idea what it was for, though I'd seen oil tankers on the horizon, so maybe it had something to do with them. I cast one eye over my shoulder, in case a polar bear crept up on me.

Polar Bear Capital of the World... A quick phone search earlier, before I'd left Gatsby's Speakeasy, had revealed that sweet nickname. Of course this Nash fella would be hiding out here with some of earth's most vicious predators.

I wasn't having much luck getting cell signal out here, which meant no contact with Raffe. Freezing my plums off in the wilderness, freaking out about polar bears, and not being able to find this friggin' plane carcass created the perfect melting pot for a foul mood. And my gremlins didn't let me forget about Lux. Oh no, sir. That meeting had left me reeling, on top of Erebus's quaint dinner. Weren't there other poor suckers on this planet they could mess with instead? Six billion people, and they chose to toy with little old me.

What *did* Lux want from me? Did she expect to turn me into some kind of double agent? Clearly, she wanted me to tell her about Erebus's movements and his progression toward Atlantis, which meant I hadn't seen the last of her. Frankly, I should've been more worried about her popping up than ravenous bears.

I stopped on a slippery rock to catch my breath, the surface worn smooth from years of battering by the stormy waters beyond. Breathing here felt like dragging in shards of ice instead of air, and the shock on the back of my throat made me cough.

I hate you, Erebus. I really, really hate you.

Then I saw it. Below, partially hidden by the endless array of snow-covered rocks and sparse trees, the silvery shine of a downed plane caught the wintry sunlight. The last known location of Nash

Calvert. Naturally, Erebus hadn't bothered to teleport me anywhere near this plane. He'd wanted me to sweat for it. Sadistic asshole.

I clambered across the intersecting rocks and down to the crashed plane. It had some graffiti scrawled on it—the signature of bored teenagers with nothing better to do. With no Wi-Fi and no signal, it was only to be expected. Judging by the word "cargo" slapped on the side of the plane, this silver bird had carried freight before its untimely demise. And, though it was pretty sizeable, it looked truly abandoned.

Come on, Nash, where are you? I approached the plane and sent out some magical feelers. Fortunately, Erebus had instructed me on a spell I could use to break through any secret interdimensional walls.

I pressed my hands to the plane and spoke the words: *"Removere velamen. Illud trahere seorsum. Ostende mihi verum. Videbo. Ne abscondas. Latitudo autem ante faciem meam ad quæ revelanda erat."*

Nothing happened. I tried again, which resulted in nothing again. A few faint sparks drifted to join the snow, but that was it. If Nash had ever hidden himself here, he was long gone.

An expletive tingled on the end of my tongue. My patience had worn so thin it was borderline transparent now. My gremlins weren't helping. My Child of Chaos meetings had set them off again, wilder than before, and they had a grand old time in my head, making a mockery of logic and focused thought.

They were responsible for the paranoia about polar bears. They kept whispering that I would get munched, feel my skull pop like hard candy in a set of jagged jaws. And when I'd managed to talk myself out of that pit of fear, they lashed me with Lux's expectations, images of Ryann being splattered across San Diego, and mutterings of Raffe failing his task in the UAE, resulting in Erebus splattering me once I'd done everything on his extensive list.

I couldn't handle the barrage of images. My control slipped further with each tormenting hiss in my head. If I didn't find Nash soon, I would wade into the bitter water of Hudson Bay and never come out again, just to shut them up for good.

Moving away from the plane in an even fouler mood, I spotted a fisherman up the bay. He sat perched on a huge rock, his rod dangling in the water. I dug a photo from the top pocket of my pathetically thin coat—about the only helpful thing Erebus had given me. The photo, not the coat. The coat was mine, the only cold-weather item I owned. However, it worked for San Diego cold, not Canadian frostbite cold.

"Excuse me!" I shouted to the guy. He looked middle-aged and was dressed in a puffy orange jacket complete with a furry hood that turned me green with envy.

He glanced down at me, then set his rod on a mount. "Hello there!"

I hurried toward him as fast as my legs, and this terrain, allowed. "Could I pick your brain for a minute?"

"By all means, my friend." The man smiled with Canadian warmth. "I'm not doing much; the nibblers aren't nibbling."

Lucky for them...

"Here, you have yourself a sip of this. You're about to catch your death. This weather often catches folks unawares." The man unscrewed a thermos and poured some coffee, then handed the filled cup to me. I had no pride left to refuse, so I practically snatched it from him, letting the heat radiate into my frozen hands. After giving myself a moment to enjoy the warmth, I handed him the photo.

"Do you recognize this guy?" I asked. "He might be using the name Nash Calvert."

The man scanned the photo. "Nope, I'm sorry to say I don't recognize him. And I don't know any fella out here by that name. It's a small town, my friend, so I would have heard it. It might be that he's going by a different name."

"You could be right." After all, he wouldn't be much of a runaway if he went and used his real name. *Yeah, dumbass.* My gremlins gave me a kick, just to make me feel twice as stupid.

"Try asking along the bay—I don't go into town much these days, so it might be that he's a newcomer I've not had the pleasure of meeting yet," the man said. "And take this with you. You need it more than me, from the looks of you." He took a woolen blanket from his pack and handed it to me. I took it gratefully and threw it over my shoulders before reclaiming my photo. Someone in this godforsaken place must have seen Nash. He may have been the king of hide and seek, but he had human needs—food, water, etcetera. He had to have left his hole at some point.

"Thank you." I wrapped the blanket tighter around me.

"Think nothing of it, my friend. I hope you find this fella."

I sighed. "Yeah, me too." He didn't bother to ask why I was searching for the guy, and he hadn't thought twice about giving up a blanket for me—a total stranger. Either the cold had dulled his brain to dimwitted proportions, or this was the fabled Canadian trust and friendliness in action. This would never have happened in San Diego, for sure. Maybe I just wasn't used to folks doing favors for others, no questions asked.

I pressed on up the rocky bay, passing beachcombers and fishermen and folks taking their soggy dogs for a walk. I showed each one the photo and received similar replies. Nash had covered his tracks. With every disappointing response, my gremlins got rowdier. My clothes were drenched in sweat, and I couldn't tell if I was roasting or frozen to the bone. My mouth dried, my hands shook, and my brain bombarded me with worst-case scenarios. Worse, it showed no sign of letting up.

Finally, after another hour of walking and shoving Nash's photo in people's faces, I sat on a nearby rock and held my head in my hands. Closing my eyes didn't help fend off the gremlins. Neither did deep breathing. And I refused to bother with any new-age meditation—that amounted to a pile of horse crap for me. My temples throbbed, as if readying themselves to explode.

Tears stung as I lifted my head, staring out at the bleak ocean. Gray water churned beneath a gray sky—everything gray, everything hopeless. Being alone didn't help. If I'd had someone here, they'd have talked me out of my wallowing, or given me something else to focus on.

"Hey!" A voice pierced the air. A young woman wandered across the rocks with a big, slavering Newfoundland plodding alongside. Her pale face poked out of a furred hood, her nose pink from the cold. With all that padding, I couldn't help but think of a caterpillar.

I pointed at my chest. "Me?"

"Yep, you. I just passed my neighbor with Beethoven here, and he said you were looking for someone?"

"Beethoven?" I smiled despite myself. "I love that movie."

She chuckled, the fur of her hood fluttering in the icy wind. "Me, too. Otherwise this lump would've ended up with some other name, wouldn't you?" She scratched the dog between its ears. "So, who's this person you're looking for? I work at the police station, so there aren't too many people I don't know."

I pulled out the photo without much hope. "This guy."

"Oh, that's Ed Gillespie."

My jaw damn near disconnected. "What?"

"That's Ed Gillespie. He drifts in and out of town, but he's got a cabin and some land up yonder." She pointed away from the bay. "Is he a friend of yours? I've got to say, he's never been overly sociable. Keeps to himself." Her voice took on an officerly note. No doubt a force of habit, in her line of work. Though I couldn't imagine she dealt with much crime up here: a few disorderly seals, maybe, or a gang of dumpster-diving bears.

"Uh… more like family business. I'm his cousin, and our grandma just died." The lies rolled off my tongue. "We've been trying to get in touch with him for days, but there's not much signal up here, and I figured face-to-face is best, anyway."

"I'm so sorry to hear that." She ruffled Beethoven's fur absently. "Well, if you follow the railway lines from town, to where the woodland gets real dense, you'll spot a forest track a few miles down. It's got a white signpost with a wolf carving. That'll lead you right to Ed's cabin. Last I heard, he was home."

Last Erebus heard, Nash had an interdimensional bubble in that crashed plane, and look how that turned out… I banished the snark, choosing gratitude instead. This caterpillar woman may have saved my skin. At the very least, she'd given me enough to stop me from making good on my impulse to wade into that gray water.

"Thank you, Miss—?"

"Call me Reeann—that's with an 'ee' not a 'y,' though I suppose it doesn't matter since it sounds the same." She extended a gloved hand and laughed, her blue eyes twinkling.

Of course that's her name. "I'm Steve," I lied, shaking her hand. A wolf-whistle pierced my brain—one of my Puffball-looking jerks having a joke at my expense. I winced as the delusion splintered through bone and flesh, making my ear canals quiver.

"You okay there, Steve?"

I nodded. "I'm fine, just a bit chilly. Can't feel my fingers anymore. But who needs all ten, right?"

"You know, you shouldn't be wandering alone out here without the right gear. Why don't you come by the station with me and I'll get you outfitted properly before you head up to Ed's? I need to drop in anyway to pick up a parcel. I don't mind the company, and neither would Beethoven." The dog barked in agreement, its dopey face staring up at me. The officer wore the curious sort of smile that I'd only ever dreamed of Ryann—with a "y"—mustering for me.

Is she... flirting with me?

I narrowed my eyes in suspicion. "You're not... Lux, are you?"

"Pardon?" Confusion rippled across her features.

"Never mind. I thought I knew you from somewhere. Ignore me. I'm going crazy." I gave a dry laugh. *Oh, if only she knew how true that was.*

Her expression returned to a kind smile. "What do you say, then? Cup of coffee, warm coat, maybe some cookies if I can rustle something up?"

"That's a very kind offer, it really is, but I'm in a rush to find Ed." I stuffed the photo back in my pocket. "Although, if you find a body out in the woods, dead of hypothermia, you can go ahead and identify me."

"Are you sure you can't leave it a while, until you're warmer?" Her brow creased with concern. "Ed usually stays in the cabin for a week or so when he drifts back into town, so I doubt he's going anywhere."

"Sorry, I really can't. We have to catch a flight to the funeral. It would kill him to miss it, they were so close. I'd hate to miss it, too."

"Fair enough. Family's the most important thing in life, though it's hard for me to imagine Ed being close to anyone, loner that he is." She looked a touch disappointed, and clearly not ready to give up on whisking me away for coffee. "Can I at least coax you into swinging by on the way back? It'll save me from organizing a search party."

I nodded, though I knew I'd probably never see this woman again. "Sure thing."

"You take care of yourself, you hear?"

"I will," I replied. "Scout's honor." As if I'd ever been a scout.

"Okay, then. I'll see you again, Steve. Preferably alive." She patted her leg and moved off, Beethoven following obediently. I waited until she was far down the bay before I started walking, though I noticed she looked back every so often, that same warm smile on her lips.

Sorry, Reeann with an "ee" but you and your dog are barking up the wrong Finch. I would never not be wary of easy flirtations. Who knew what lurked beneath that seemingly innocent façade? Besides, there was only room for one Ryann in my life. The one with an ironic "y." *Y? Because I can't get her out of my head.*

Now that I had a goal, the cold didn't bother me as much. I wasn't wandering aimlessly anymore, and, man, did that feel good. Like a good little Dorothy, I would follow this yellow brick road right to Nash Calvert's door. And the walk, though lengthy, gave me a decent amount of time to practice my performance. I planned to offer my help in removing Nash's djinn curse in return for some of his untainted blood, afterward. Plus, I had some ironclad reasoning, primed for persuasion—I would tell Nash I needed the blood to break free of Erebus's service. Which was partly true.

"The details aren't important. Nash just has to sympathize with me. I'll throw in some puppy-dog eyes and bleeding emotions, and that'll snag him hook, line, and sinker," I said aloud, trekking through the winter wonderland along the railway lines with a new spring in my step. Maybe things would work out—no worst-case scenarios necessary.

Provided Raffe succeeds in his mission, that is, my gremlins hissed in the back of my head. *Otherwise, this is merely one step closer to your bitter end.*

I whistled to distract myself, refusing to entertain their negativity. I had faith in Raffe and Kadar. Raffe was my friend. Even if it wasn't his top priority, he'd tap the Storyteller for any resources she had that could free me. Dwelling on that hopeful note provided my mental agony a temporary salve. And I popped two more pills, to be doubly sure. I'd need my wits about me to deal with Nash.

Half an hour later, I arrived at the forest track which interrupted the dense tree line. A white wooden signpost marked it, carved with a black wolf just as I'd been told. Jittering with agitation, I headed down the dirt path, the crowded pines dulling every sound as I walked. It felt like someone had put earmuffs on me, and the effect made every snapping twig and falling mass of collected snow eerie as hell. Ghostly, as if I'd stepped into a different world.

I'd have been a shivering mass of useless on the ground if I hadn't taken those pills when I had. Shadows flitted between pine trunks, the wind rustling the fronds and making them whisper furtively. I clung to my nerve, though my heart thundered in my chest. Anyone could be hiding in these woods, and I'd have no clue until it was too late.

The path expanded into a clearing that looked partway between a lumber yard and a horror-movie holiday destination for unsuspecting teenagers. A cabin sat in the center, adding to the psycho-killer effect.

I readied myself to approach when a sound made me sidestep quickly into the woods, ducking behind the heft of a massive old pine tree. It sounded like whispering. Not the wind in the fronds, but actual, human whispering, followed by the soft tread of feet crunching the snow. Maybe I liked snow, after all—an assassin's nightmare, it made stealth nearly impossible.

Two furry-hooded figures appeared on the forest path, their faces shrouded with ski masks. They tiptoed slowly, a sure sign they were up to no good, whoever they were. I didn't wait to find out. Lifting my palms, I shot two fierce strands of Telekinesis, which hoisted them into the air.

"Finch! Finch, stop! It's us!" a terrified voice rang out. One I recognized.

"Melody?" I emerged from my hiding place. "What the hell are you doing here?"

"Let us down, then we'll talk!" Luke grunted.

Irritated, I set them back on the ground, where they proceeded to push their hoods and ski masks back to reveal their faces. My mouth opened to rip into them, but the words died on my lips. The wind whipped up, and the trees' whispers rose to a deafening shriek. Snapping branches went off like gunshots, the thud of falling snow like a drumbeat. The percussion of danger approaching.

"Someone else is following us," I hissed.

"What?" Melody stepped forward, but I staggered away from her. The pills hadn't done jack. They'd fooled me. Now, all that paranoia and pent-up terror assaulted me, rampaging through my mind. My hands shook so hard they hurt, and my throat closed, while my chest gripped in a vise so tight it felt as if a sumo wrestler had sat on me. I stared, wild-eyed, at Melody and Luke. Only, they no longer looked like Melody and Luke. Their faces twisted into monstrous masks, their fingertips growing claws as they neared me, their teeth pointed and sharp.

"Get back! Get back!" I howled.

"Finch? What's going on?" Melody's mouth curled into a sneer. "Finch?"

Luke peered at me, his eyes entirely black. "Are you okay?"

"Get back! Get away from me!" I stumbled away, my hands too shaky to form a single strand of Chaos.

Deep down, I knew what I was seeing wasn't real. But it didn't matter. The rocks of reality had turned slippery under my grasp, and now I plummeted into a mania I couldn't escape.

TWENTY-FIVE

Finch

This isn't real. This isn't real!

I squeezed my eyes shut and staggered backward from the path. I collided with a pine tree, and I felt a shower of snow collapse onto my head. The cold blast added to my overwhelming terror. My breath came in short, sharp gasps.

Everything went into overdrive, and my mind filled with dark and grisly images of what Erebus had planned for me. Fountains of blood, my head rolling like a ball, black veins eating me alive from the inside out. Perhaps this was a premonition—a warning of what would come after the Atlantis mission. My whole body shuddered in response, no longer under my control.

I understood the position Kadar had been in, standing on that rooftop. All this pain, confusion, fear… I couldn't take it anymore. And I couldn't suppress it anymore, either. The pills had stopped working. They'd been my lifeboat, and someone had taken a massive pin to that boat, sinking it so I had no choice but to let the current take me.

"Finch?" I heard the crunch of footsteps and Melody's soft tone.

"Stay back!" I yelled. "You're not real!"

"It's me, Finch." The footsteps got closer, and the pine trunk at my back prevented me from fleeing. I couldn't bring myself to open my eyes. I didn't want to see Melody's face all twisted up again.

A second set of footsteps echoed the first. "Finch, it's us. What's going on? Are you hexed?" Luke spoke, calm as ever.

"I wish." I grasped my skull with both hands, pushing inward. Throbbing agony jabbed red-hot pokers behind my eyes, as if trying to push my eyeballs out of their sockets. The gremlins were in attack mode, pounding my cranium as if they could escape if they could just make a crack wide enough. For the first time ever, I feared they might actually succeed.

"Finch, I'm going to put my hand on your arm, okay?" Melody said.

I shook my head, tears squeezing from my clamped-shut eyes. "No! Don't touch me!"

"I need to, Finch. Listen to my voice and focus on it. Hold on to it and stay with us, please."

A hand clasped my wrist. I flinched, trying to yank it back, but Melody held tight. Warmth spread up my arm, like something between syrup and hot massage oil. I fought it every step of the way. This was a demon come to punish me, not the real Melody.

The warmth slithered up my neck and entered my mind, pooling in my brain. Instead of darkness and gremlin delusions, an image of sunset at the monastery burst to the forefront of my thoughts. The scent of lemon trees found its way into my nostrils, and the balmy heat of the Grecian evening wafted over me.

Figures sat at the long, wooden dinner table where we'd gathered that first night on the island. Melody, Luke, and Mr. Abara, but that was where real memory ended. Harley sat to my right, and Tobe on my left.

You shouldn't be here... Why were they here? The confusion gave my brain a fleeting respite from the panic.

"I missed you, Finch," Harley said, reaching for my hand. "I'm so glad you came back."

Tobe smiled, flashing his fangs. "You are safe here with us, Finch."

"You are strong, boy." Mr. Abara lifted his glass to me. "More than you think. You've endured Etienne's tasks, and succeeded. Don't be defeated by this."

"What's happening?" I rasped.

"I calmed your mind with a transformation spell," Melody replied. "A variant of Euphoria, which helped me put you in a safe place in your mind. Whatever is happening to you can't reach you here."

I raked my fingernails across the wooden table. It felt real. Eerily real. "Are you really with me, outside... this place? Did you follow me to Canada?"

"I'm with you. I think you're seeing things that aren't there, but it's really us." Melody's eyes glinted with tears. "You need to tell me how to help you—the real you. Was Luke right? Did someone put a hex on you?"

I sagged into my chair. "It's not a hex. That would be simpler. Katherine even tried to convince me it was, a long time ago, but it isn't. This is me. This is what I've been dealing with my whole life, though recently it's... gotten out of control."

"What is it?" Melody pressed.

"I suffer from... a delusional disorder." My voice faltered.

She nodded in understanding. "And it's getting worse?"

"A lot worse." I nodded. "I don't know why, but my 'gremlins,' as I call them, won't quiet down. I have pills that are meant to help, but I keep taking more and more and it doesn't make a difference. It shuts them up for an hour or two, most of a day if I'm super lucky, but then they come back with a vengeance. Like they're pissed at being forced to shut up."

"These pills. Do you have them?" Melody asked.

"They're in my jacket pocket."

"Okay, I'm going to give you two, and then I'll draw you out of here. Keep listening to my voice, and use it as an anchor to center yourself." She held my gaze. I wanted to stop her and tell her I'd already taken two and ended up like this anyway. But I figured I was already in for a dime; I may as well make it a dollar.

A minute or so later, the monastery terrace melted away. Freaky, in and of itself, to watch everything disappear. It gave me major flash-backs to my first taste of the orange poison in the tower. As it faded to nothing, I braced for the gremlin onslaught... which didn't come. With my eyes still closed, I heard the wind whistle through the pines and Melody's strained breath, but no jumped-up Puffballs trying to tip me over the edge.

"Finch? Can you hear me?" Melody spoke.

I nodded slowly. "Yes."

"Open your eyes."

Hesitantly, I urged my lids up and peeked out. Melody crouched beside me. No twisted demon face, just cheerful Melody with her adorable hamster cheeks and earnest expression. Luke stood behind her, looking more worried than she did. He probably thought I might leap forward to strangle her or something.

"Anything weird?" she asked.

"Nope... just Canada." I managed a ghost of a smile.

Luke folded his arms. "Does somebody want to tell me what happened?"

"Go easy, Luke," Melody warned. "He's dealing with some terrible things in that head of his. I only saw a few bits and pieces, but it'd floor a weaker man. A world of nightmares that he can't escape."

"What?" Luke's tone switched to concern. Actual concern… for me. Now *that* was weird.

I sighed wearily, feeling like a sack of heavy, lumpy spuds. "I have a mental illness. I was born with it, I think. The old nurture versus nature argument. Maybe it came later, maybe Freud would slap some Oedipal nonsense on me or put it down to abandonment issues, I don't know—but I've had it ever since I can remember."

"Your gremlins, right?" Melody prompted.

"Right." It sounded odd to hear someone other than my sister call them that.

She leaned from her crouch to a sitting position in the snow. "And they've gotten worse?"

"Way worse. I used to be able to keep a lid on them, but that lid has blown off, and, like all stray lids, I have no idea where it went." I clenched and stretched my hands, trying to feed some warmth to them.

"When did this start?" Melody asked.

I chuckled faintly. "Shouldn't I be reclined on a couch for this?"

"The snow will have to do," she replied somberly.

"Honestly, they've been more vocal since Elysium, but I still had some control," I explained. "My pills worked like plugging a leaking dam with my finger. Then, after the monastery, the floodgates opened, and no amount of finger-plugging has been able to shut them again."

Melody's eyes widened. "It might be the orange poison you ingested."

"Huh?" Luke grunted.

"The orange poison alters your state of mind, and map-making does the same thing once you've gotten the hang of it." She paused, as if putting her ideas together. "Now, this is just a theory, but hear me out—maybe the pills aren't working anymore because your mind is no longer in the same state. They were geared toward quieting your gremlins, the way you used to be. But your mental chemistry has changed, so it stands to reason they wouldn't be as effective anymore."

I stared at her. "You know what, that actually makes sense. But, if that's true, then I need a straitjacket and a padded cell before the delusions get worse."

"Not necessarily." Melody put her hand on my forearm. "I know what it's like to feel like you're losing your mind. When I became the Librarian and all the world's knowledge poured into my brain, I thought I'd completely lost the plot. It's not exactly the same, but I understand, to a degree, the strain of sifting through waves and waves of information that aren't supposed to be there."

"Is that how you learned the safety pocket trick?" I brushed away snowflakes that had landed on my eyelashes.

"You mean what I did to you a moment ago?" she replied.

I nodded. "Yeah, that."

"It's a coping mechanism I learned, yes. You may find it useful, too." Melody gave my arm a reassuring squeeze that made Luke glower. "That 'safety pocket,' as you call it, is in your head now—a small bubble that can't be penetrated by the gremlins. All you have to do, when things get overwhelming, is retreat there until you calm down. Think of it, and your brain will take you there."

"But the beasties will come back?" My heart sank at the thought.

She creased her brow. "They will, but at least you'll have another way to manage them when the pills don't do what they used to. Who knows how long it might take Dr. Krieger to create pills that fit your new brain chemistry? If it can even be done, considering the way your mind has changed, without making you a zombie or borderline tranquilizing you."

"You got any transformation spells that'll give me a whole new brain?" I asked her dryly, hating that my most important organ—debatably—continued to fail me.

"I'm afraid not," she replied. "If I did, you wouldn't be you."

I snorted. "I'm not too fond of me right now. I could live with that."

"Even so, your gremlins don't define you. *You* define you. I know you're probably tired of fighting and people telling you to simply cope with it." Melody took a breath as snowflakes settled on her dark hair. "But you've never seemed like the kind of guy to back out of a fight because it gets hard. You're brave, Finch. Now, after glimpsing your mind, I know just how brave you are."

"Careful, you'll make me blush," I joked halfheartedly. "I definitely needed a couch for all this brain-shrinking."

Luke crouched suddenly. "I hate to break up the heart-to-heart, but we've got company." He gestured toward the cabin clearing, where a figure had emerged. The man carried a bundle of logs in his arms, and we watched him pause beside a woodshed before disappearing inside.

"That's him," I whispered. I'd seen his photo enough in the last few hours to know.

"Who?" Luke replied.

I frowned. "So, you guys followed me without even knowing why? I figured you'd bugged me or something."

Melody flushed pink. "We followed you because we were worried about you. You took off out of the blue. Luke spotted you leaving in a cab, and we went after you, all the way to Gatsby's. We waited downstairs, after the host said you'd gone to dine with a Mr. Erebus, and after some time I sensed a disturbance—"

"In the Force?" I interjected automatically. Hard to resist such a perfect opportunity.

"No, not in the Force. Although… I suppose Chaos is like the Force," she mused. I hadn't expected her to be a *Star Wars* geek. "Anyway, I felt a surge of energy and realized you'd portaled out of Gatsby's. I managed to track the portal signature here, though it took us some time to find you with a chalk door instead of a portal. I had to do some magical improvising, and some delving into my mind palace, to hit the right spot. You know, considering it is nigh-on impossible to chalk door to somewhere you've never been. I suppose being the Librarian comes with some perks in that respect."

"Who's the guy?" Luke cut in.

"His name is Nash Calvert. He's the key to Atlantis," I replied, relaying the rest of the intel about him being a Sanguine with a djinn curse on his blood. One I had to remove, somehow.

Luke fixed his gaze on the woodshed, visibly flipping into mission mode. "How are you going to get him to give up the goods?"

"Lie through my teeth." I smiled anxiously. "I'd go in guns blazing, telling him I need it for Erebus, but Erebus warned me not to mention him. So, I can't even name-drop for a bit of leverage—well, not outright, anyway. I guess the E-man fancies keeping up an air of mystique. Wouldn't do for the key to know who wants him, and why. But I figured I could get this guy to sympathize with me, tell him I'm a servant of Erebus who needs help getting out of a deal. Erebus might not like it, given his orders, but it's my best option."

"Unless Nash knows Erebus, and Erebus knows that mentioning his name, in any capacity, would make Nash refuse to help," Melody said thoughtfully. "Maybe they have bad blood, if you'll pardon the pun."

I raised my eyebrows. "Huh… I hadn't thought of that. Once again, you make a lot of sense, Winchester. Anyone would think you've got some knowledgeable insight that the rest of us lack."

"Well, she is the Librarian, dumbass," Luke piped up.

"And I was being sarcastic. I guess that's too much wit for you?" I shot back.

Melody fidgeted with the toggles of her hood. "Are you sure that lying is the right—"

She didn't get to finish. An ear-splitting howl ricocheted through the woods as a furry beast erupted from the tree line, its white coat having been camouflaged by the snow. It leapt through the air and landed on the path, showing its enormous size. It had the face of a husky but the heft of a dire wolf—massive and savage, and likely ready to tear out our throats. As if sensing my terror, it lowered its head and bared its fangs, a growl thrumming in its throat.

"That's not your everyday wolf," I managed to say, my voice shaking.

"You're damn right." A figure stepped out of the trees, pointing a rifle at us. One moment, Nash had been in the woodshed, now he was here. Clearly, he'd used this enormous wolfdog as a distraction to sneak up on us.

Well, well, well, Mr. Calvert... you're one slippery devil.

TWENTY-SIX

Finch

———

"Who are you?" Nash growled, matching the rumble of the massive husky. *My, my, aren't you two a match made in heaven?* Evidently, they came as a pair, down to the icy blue eyes and shock of silver hair that sprouted from under Nash's woolen hat. It reminded me of my bygone platinum days, but it turned out strawberry blonds had more fun.

"You'd loosen these lips more if you didn't have a gun pointed at us." I lifted my palms in a gesture of goodwill.

Nash stepped forward, bringing the rifle barrel level with my eye. "Funny guy, huh?"

"Just trying to stop you from blowing our heads off, or having White Fang here turn the snow red." I shrugged. "No need to get trigger happy. We come in peace."

"I'll make the demands here, buddy. Who are you? I won't ask again." Nash peered down the rifle's sight, finger flexing on the trigger. One of these days, I'd go on a mission and be welcomed in with coffee and cookies.

I glanced back at Luke. "Hey, pal, whenever you feel like stepping in, that'd be swell."

Understanding dawned on his stern face. His hand shot up, his wrist twisting suddenly. The rifle flew from Nash's grip and vanished into the trees.

"What the—!" Nash stared down at his empty hands while the husky's growl deepened. Nash's icy eyes flashed with anger. He delved into his coat and whipped out three knives. He raised his arm to hurl them, and Luke twisted his hands again, wrenching the knives from Nash's grasp and burying them in tree trunks with a trio of satisfying thunks.

"Better late than never." I cast a grin at Luke, who rolled his eyes.

"And only fools rush in."

I turned my attention back to Nash. "Will you play nice now? I said it once, I'll say it again—we come in peace. There's no need for this to get nasty."

"You're on my property without permission. I'd say that's cause to get a little nasty." Nash threw up his hands. Fire erupted from his palms and exploded in a volley of fireballs. I dove, hitting the powdery snow face first. Meanwhile, Luke pushed Melody out of harm's way, playing the hero and getting grazed across the shoulder by a fireball for his trouble.

"Don't be an idiot, Calvert!" I yelled, flipping onto my back. "We just want to talk!"

Nash aimed a fireball at my head.

Groaning, I raised both hands, unleashing a powerful strand of Telekinesis from my right and a torrent of Fire from my left. The latter drew a barrier around the husky, taking it out of play. The dog whimpered, pawing the dirt as it huddled to avoid the fierce flames. It lifted its blue eyes to its owner, as if he'd know what to do. Unfortunately, at that very moment, my Telekinesis wrapped around Nash and flung him away from his dog and any other tricks he may have wanted to pull. The flames sputtered out, unable to feed on snow.

"Stop it, all of you!" Melody hoisted herself to her feet. Nash recovered and ran forward, looking twice as furious. "There's no need for violence. Nobody has to get hurt here. Nash, all we want to do is talk. Please, listen to what we have to say."

"Why should I?" he snarled. The husky huddled against his leg, teeth bared.

"Because I know you're alarmed and frightened by what my friends here have just done, and I know you don't really want to do us any harm." Melody stood her ground, evidently getting a read on Nash. "I can feel your reluctance. You're not a violent man, Nash. So why don't we all calm down and try to pretend we're rational people who don't want anyone dead."

Nash narrowed his eyes. "Empath, are you?"

"I am, but I am more than that. My name is Melody Winchester, and I am the new Librarian. Telling you that is an enormous risk to my safety, but I hope you will take that as a sign that we mean well," Melody replied, shocking Luke and me. "We only want to talk. We aren't here to rob you, or hurt you, or anything like that."

A stalemate stretched between us all. I stood, dusting snow from my pants. Nash hesitated, his gaze flitting from Melody to Luke to me and back again. I mean, who could honestly look at Melody and her chubby cheeks and think she wanted to cause trouble?

A lifetime later, Nash lowered his hands. He used one to ruffle the husky's fur, apparently signaling the beast to stand down. It visibly relaxed, concealing its fangs as its demeanor shifted to fluffy puppy. Steam rose up from its pink tongue as it lolled from its mouth, giving no indication that it still wanted to send us all to kingdom come.

"You understand my wariness. A man's property is his empire, and those who enter unannounced don't tend to have good intentions," Nash said. "Especially those who sneak up and hide in the trees. You see how it looks to a fella?"

"Well, that's why you ask questions first and shoot people later, when you don't like what they've got to say," I replied sharply. Men who waxed lyrical about property and empires tended to have a dose of the high-and-mighties, and I loved taking that kind of person down a peg or two. "Glad to see you've got the common sense to back down when you can't win, though. Luke and I would have floored you, anyway… and your little dog, too."

Nash scowled. "Excuse me?"

"Ignore him. He rambles when he's nervous, and I think your dog scared the living daylights out of him," Melody cut in before I said anything we might all regret. She shot me a *Seriously, Finch?* look that made me smirk.

"Biggest husky I've ever seen," Luke murmured.

I shrugged. "Doesn't look so bitey now, though."

"That's because I don't want her to bite… for now." Nash crouched and stroked the dog's face. The beastie lapped it up. And literally began lapping Nash's face, giving him a tongue-bath.

"You want us to give you some privacy?" I laughed, ignoring another warning glance from Melody.

"I guess every group has a joker. Not my taste in humor, though. Too lowbrow for me," Nash replied coolly. "And this is not just any husky, though I'm guessing you've figured that out by now. This is my Familiar, Huntress."

Melody's face morphed into excited-chipmunk mode. "I've read so much about them, but I've never met a real one!"

I scoffed. "Aren't they just souped-up pets?"

"No, they're so much more!" Melody explained enthusiastically. "They're extremely rare in this day and age, and have special abilities of their own, acquired through a series of magic rituals. They share a unique and complex bond with their magical, forged over years and years. A bonding of souls, in a manner of speaking, which is so strong that it causes immense pain to the magical if the Familiar dies, and vice versa. It's supposed to be worse than the pain of a Purge."

Nash smiled faintly. "Huntress and I were lucky to form that bond quicker than most. I've had her since we were both pups."

"Not that this isn't fascinating, but do you think we could take it inside?" I piped up. "I've been trudging through this great white pain in the ass for hours looking for you, and these chops won't function if they're frozen shut."

"That wouldn't break my heart," Nash retorted, then peered at Melody. "Is he always so charming?"

"Oh yes. Always." She chuckled. "But he's not a bad guy, I promise. You know how people get when they're frozen solid."

"You should've worn a better coat," Nash retorted.

"Yeah, yeah, I know I'm underdressed. Who knew Canada got so cold?" I tried to rein in the insults, considering I needed to win this guy over.

Melody rubbed her palms together pointedly. "So, how about some coffee?"

"Guess it wouldn't be very neighborly of me to say no, now, would it?" He led us into the cabin, Huntress padding obediently at his side.

TWENTY-SEVEN

Finch

———

"Cabin" might've been the wrong word for the vibe Nash had going on. I kicked the snow from my boots before entering to be a polite guest, and my stunned gaze rested on what could only be described as a workshop.

"Who's on the naughty list, Mr. Claus?" I asked, catching Nash's eye.

He gave a hint of a smirk. "I might switch you over, after the stunt you pulled out there."

"What else is a guy supposed to do with a rifle stuffed in his face?" I replied. "Isn't that right, Luke?"

Captain Beefcake shoved his hands in his pockets. "Don't bring me into this. I'm only here to protect Melody."

"I didn't realize the government hired bodyguards for the Librarian." Nash hung his coat on an iron hook by the door. "But I'm out of the loop. I don't involve myself in magical society much these days."

"They don't." Luke crossed to where Melody stood gaping at Nash's workshop. "I'm a private hire."

"Sensible." Nash seemed to approve.

A roaring fire burned at the opposite end of the vast cabin, and I enjoyed the warmth sinking into my frozen body. The entire building was open plan, most of the space taken up by long wooden tables and miscellaneous machinery. Knives hung on racks and in various states of construction on the workbenches. Bone handles, wooden handles, semi-precious handles with gold and silver inlay. Beautiful specimens, and, weirdly, not unsettling even in their multitude. They were too pretty to scream slasher-movie killer, and I didn't see any random limbs or bits of bodies lying around.

"Do you make knives for a living?" Melody turned to Nash.

"It's a hobby. Keeps me sane through the long winters." He brushed his fingertips along the nearest workbench. I stayed alert, in case he decided to have another go at thrashing us.

"You haven't always been here, though, have you?" I remembered the plane carcass with the spark fragments drifting off it.

He cast me a wary look. "This is my main base of operations, but it serves to have outposts and hideaways that I can retreat to, if needed. That's the trouble with Canadian hospitality—folks always want to drop by and bring me pies and things, so I have to maintain a reputation for drifting in and out of town."

"I take it you don't give everyone such a warm welcome?" I gave him a sweet smile.

"I have to defend my property from strangers. Especially magical ones." His face hardened. "There aren't any magicals in this town. Huntress sensed you the moment you stepped on the path. That's why you got the hostile treatment."

I picked up one of his knives and turned it over in my hand. "I guess that makes sense. Is that why you hide out here, because there aren't any magicals?"

"You ask a lot of questions." Nash took the knife from my hand and set it back down on the workbench, as if I'd tried to snatch one of his children. "Before I answer any more, I want to know who you are and why you're here. You can tell me while I get the coffee going." He walked to a rustic coffeemaker and began to brew a pot, leaning expectantly against the sideboard.

"My name is Wade Crowley," I said, sinking onto a varnish-stained stool. "You already know Melody, and that's her guard dog, Luke Prescott. Not as menacing as yours, but he does the job."

I had to lie about my identity, considering Melody's former warning. If Nash got a whiff that I was involved with Erebus, and they did have bad blood, he'd be off like a shot. I didn't want to risk him knowing who I was and what I'd gotten myself into.

Melody frowned at me but said nothing.

Luke, on the other hand, sighed. "I'm a bodyguard, not a guard dog."

"Sounds like six and two threes to me." I chuckled, swinging my feet like a kid. Thanks to Melody, the gremlins had gone underground. The mental freedom felt amazing, making me lightheaded. Even if I knew it wouldn't last.

"Crowley, eh?" Nash folded his arms across his red-and-black flannel shirt, the uniform of any woodsman worth his salt. "Impressive name to bandy about. I heard you were involved in Katherine Shipton's demise last year."

"Ah, so you do get the news here?" It appeared he wasn't quite the recluse he made himself out to be.

"I dip my toe in from time to time." He lifted his shoulders in a half-assed shrug. "Now for the million-dollar question—what are a Crowley, a Winchester, and a bodyguard doing here, harassing me?"

Melody stepped in before I could say a word. "We need your

Sanguine blood for a spell, to save our friend who's being forced to live with a horrible and violent djinn. And we're willing to remove the djinn curse on you, if you agree to help us."

Whoa there, Winchester. That left me reeling. Melody had clearly done her research on Raffe, which I hadn't anticipated.

Nash lowered his head, deep in thought.

"Nash?" Melody prompted.

He lifted his head. "Can you guys excuse me for a moment?"

"Of course," she replied.

With a conflicted expression, Nash walked away toward the back of the cabin and disappeared through a doorway in the back wall. Huntress padded after him, leaving us alone in the kitchen-slash-knife-factory.

Luke jumped in right away, his tone hushed. "Wade Crowley? Are you serious? You think he won't find out?"

"I couldn't tell him I'm me, could I?" I hissed back. "The deal I struck to kill Katherine was supposed to be secret, but it got around."

"That's exactly my point." Luke heaved a strained sigh. "If Nash has seen your photo in the news, he'll wonder why you're lying. Deception won't get us anywhere. And, I hate to say it, but that goes for you too, Melody. Why didn't we just tell him the truth, upfront?"

Melody leaned against one of the workbenches. "I did what I had to, based on my judgment of his emotions."

Luke looked exasperated. "Is this about going to Atlantis again?"

"Huh?" I gaped at Melody. Evidently, they'd been having a lovers' quarrel I hadn't been party to.

Luke grimaced. "Melody is still determined to go to Atlantis, even now that Erebus wants to, too, which makes the entire endeavor ridiculously dangerous. I've been trying to dissuade her for days, but she won't listen to reason."

"Let's shelve that for a minute." I could only deal with one piece of stress at a time. "Why did you swoop in with that? I had an excuse ready and waiting."

"Yours wasn't going to work," Melody replied bluntly. "Mentioning a spell to free you from Erebus would've made him suspicious, and Erebus explicitly told you not to say his name—he had to have a reason for that. We're better off pinning this on Raffe, since Nash has been on the receiving end of a djinn curse, too. It's familiar territory for him, and it'll play on his sympathies."

To my shock, that made perfect sense. "Oh, you're good, Ms. Winchester. Very, very good."

"I try." She beamed and tapped the side of her head. "It's not all a mess of information up here. Brilliance finds its way through, from time to time."

"I still don't like lying," Luke countered, though he looked grudgingly impressed.

Melody gripped the edge of the workbench. "Neither do I, but sometimes it's necessary, for the sake of the bigger picture."

I shuddered. "Don't say that."

"What?" She frowned in alarm.

"The bigger picture. It's too… Katherine. Gives me some nasty flashbacks." I ran a hand through my still-damp hair, praying the mention of my mother wouldn't bring the Puffballs back.

"Sorry." She blushed furiously. "I meant, for the sake of reaching Atlantis and finding out what Erebus wants there."

"Why are you so interested?" I countered.

She sighed, giving me a look that made me feel like I'd said something idiotic. "You know why, though it seems you've got a leaky memory. I told you back in Greece, Atlantis is the one gaping hole in my knowledge. It's beyond the reach of the Librarian, which is an oddity in itself. In a way, it feels like my duty to find out what's there and fill in that gap. And I'm intrigued as to why Erebus is so eager to find the place. Maybe his reason and mine aren't so different."

"Knowledge for its own sake isn't worth your safety, and Erebus wanting to go there too isn't something we should investigate. Leave that to Finch and get the details afterward. That's the logical way to proceed," Luke protested, but Melody offered him a pained glance.

"I can't hide for the rest of my life, Luke, and let all this knowledge go to waste or make someone else do the hard work for me. I want to make myself useful. And it's not as if I'll be alone. I have both of you."

My heart pounded. "You think Erebus will take me with him?"

"You don't?" she replied, her tone genuinely curious.

"I hadn't thought that far, but… knowing him, you're probably right." My mind drifted to Raffe, and I prayed he was finding success in the UAE. Maybe, if he found an escape route, I could get out from under Erebus's thumb before it came to that.

Nash came back into the room with a tiny potted bluebell in one hand and a syringe in the other. The syringe was filled with red liquid. Thick, viscous… definitely blood.

"You planning on doing some gardening, buddy?" I joked through my anxiety. Etienne had instilled a healthy fear of potted plants in me at the monastery. If these babies started screaming, I couldn't be held responsible for my actions.

"No, I want to show you something." Nash set the plant on the nearest workbench and rested the nib of the syringe on the edge of the pot. He'd rolled his right sleeve above his elbow, revealing a Band-Aid across the crook of his arm. It appeared he'd drawn that blood fresh from the vein a few seconds ago.

Huntress sat in the center of the room, watching us all intently.

Dogs were meant to be cute, not hella creepy. Its eyes were solemn, the emotion impossibly human.

I forced my attention back to Nash. He pushed the plunger, and a few drops of blood dripped into the soil. Black threads spiderwebbed up the thin stem of the plant, spreading out into the flowers. The bluebells trembled for a moment before the petals curled and turned gray. Fragments broke away like ash, falling to the soil.

"Why did it die?" I asked, a creeping dread slithering through my belly, climbing into my chest.

Nash set down the syringe and gestured to the Band-Aid on his arm. "You know about the particular power of my Sanguine blood, or you wouldn't be here. And you know about the djinn curse." He paused. "But what you don't know is that I asked a djinn to curse me in the first place, to keep blood-hunters away."

"Blood-hunters?" Luke peered at the dead plant.

"Sanguines have been hunted to near-extinction. The handful of us remaining are still targets, especially a Sanguine with a bloodline like mine. That's why I've taken to living off-grid, away from anyone who might try and steal my blood from me," he explained. "I sought the djinn because I wanted my blood to be unusable to anyone who came looking. I made sure the news of my blood curse spread, to reduce the risk of people hunting me."

Another fragment of bluebell fell. "But if your blood does *that* to a plant, what's it doing to you? Or does it only turn lethal once it's out of you?" I asked.

"No, it's killing me slowly." He dipped his chin to his chest. "But I made the decision, a long time ago, that it was better to live a free and short life than a long and miserable one of constant pursuit—or a much shorter one, if I wound up getting my blood drained for some crazy, evil magical's spells."

"Goodness... that's... that's awful." Melody gathered her fluffy jacket closer, as if she'd felt a sudden chill.

Nash tugged his sleeve down. "It was the only way. Besides, I'm not eager to live longer than Huntress. As my Familiar, her life is extended beyond normal canine parameters, but she still won't live as long as a human. When she goes, I hopefully won't be far behind her." He had to be in his mid-thirties, at least, which meant Huntress had been alive a hell of a long time.

The husky whined quietly, breaking my damn heart. One man and his dog, against the world and all its bloodthirsty hunters. For the second time this week, I found myself understanding the inner workings of someone under a lot of strain. Kadar had thrown himself from a building because he couldn't take the pain anymore. Nash had sentenced himself to slow death because he couldn't take the constant terror and pressure of persecution. Both had valid reasons, but to make the choice that Nash had made... that took some serious guts.

Now I understood why he'd gone on the offensive when we'd sauntered down his forest track. Strangers weren't simply a nuisance for him; they could signify his death. Even with his blood cursed, it was likely a force of habit to attack first and ask questions later.

"I'm sorry, man." I found my voice, looking at Nash with a newfound respect and admiration. He'd taken his fate into his own hands, choosing freedom despite the high price. If Raffe came back with good news, I hoped I'd have the strength to do the same.

TWENTY-EIGHT

Raffe

The desert turned to fire and shadow. Djinn as far as the eye could see. Ruby eyes glinted toward Safiya and the central flames she had raised to keep us mortals warm. No doubt they wondered why they'd been summoned with such urgency. Nerves shivered through the collective.

"Raffe, Kadar, Santana." Zalaam broke ranks to greet us, wearing his warped version of my father's face.

"Glad to see you out of the infirmary," Santana replied.

He smiled. "As am I."

"Zalaam." I bowed politely. "I didn't expect you to come."

Zalaam put his hands together, as if praying. "The Storyteller called. That cannot be ignored."

"But you were down for the count," I said, trying to figure out how deep my father was buried.

"Weakness is no excuse for refusing to heed Safiya's call. When the oldest djinn requires our presence, we attend," Zalaam explained.

Santana stared at him in curiosity. "How did you get here so quickly?"

"Raffe's father had an emerald in his possession. I used it to bring us here, following the signature Safiya released into the remains of our network." Zalaam pressed a palm to his glowing heart. "Do not worry for him—your father is resting as we speak, letting me endure the sickness for us both. I have more strength than he does, even in our current predicament."

Safiya raised her hands to silence the rowdy djinn. They dipped their heads reverently, as if the principal had just entered the assembly hall. Still, a few concerned whispers hissed around the vast army of djinn. The voices susurrated, until I couldn't distinguish between the desert winds and their hushed tones.

"Gratitude for your swift arrival!" she bellowed, her voice carrying far and wide. Evidently, age hadn't affected her vocal capacity. "I know you are anxious to understand why I have called you. Ordinarily, I would have delivered the message via our hivemind, but, as I am sure you are aware, that has become somewhat limited this past week or so."

The gathering thrummed with concern. Most of the djinn stood on their own two feet, bearing only hints of the illness—dwindling flames in their eyes, their red flesh rolling and phasing between scarlet, black, and veins of white. Some, however, had to be held by their closest neighbors. Older djinn, I suspected, as their faces were creased with wrinkles.

"I have summoned you to implement a parliament—the likes of which has not been seen since the dawn of the djinn and the rush of that First Wave," Safiya continued, her voice strong. "You will appoint three spokespeople from each of your kind and discuss a very serious matter amongst yourselves before delivering an answer to me."

"What matter?" a voice called. The atmosphere stilled until you could've heard a pin drop.

"Erebus has severed his ties with us by restricting himself to human form." Safiya's white-flamed eyes burned brighter in anger. "He has forsaken us, not caring about the toll his action will take upon us all. Already, some of us suffer more than others, and it will not be long before we begin to fade irrevocably. As such, we must take an unprecedented step to free ourselves from this sickness that has been inflicted upon us by our creator. We must rally, as one power, and go to Tartarus to demand that Erebus dissolve his relationship with us entirely. We have the numbers to make him listen. We must go there to sever our ties with him, as it is the place where he conjured us into existence before sending us out into the world."

"We'll die!" a shrill, terrified djinn shouted.

Safiya shook her head. "No, we will not die by being separated from Erebus's source. If he agrees, in the face of our combined ire, the ultimate dissolution of our ties will result in an expulsion of Chaos. In this case, coming from Erebus's Darkness. We will each own our own piece of that Darkness to fuel our bodies and abilities—a separate fragment for each of us."

"How can you know that?" a Ghul rasped.

"Because it has been done before, with the creations of other Children. Namely, Eros and his Fée. They retained a fragment of their creator's power, the same piece that was given when they were brought into being. It will be the same for us," Safiya replied. "I will not lie to you: we will be weaker beings, but we will be independent of Erebus, ensuring this illness that affects us all will never come over us again. It also means we will no longer be dutybound to answer when he calls. That will be a matter of personal choice should he request your aid, from the moment of our separation onward."

"We would be truly free?" A female djinn stepped forward, folding her black wings behind her like a dark angel. An Ifrit, from what Abdhi had told us.

"We would," Safiya confirmed.

Another djinn, hunched and twisted, scuttled forth from the gathering. A Ghul, I guessed. "You lie. We *will* die. Erebus will never allow a rebellion. Even if he doesn't kill us all, he will kill some of us to send a message. To go to Tartarus would be suicide."

Safiya's robes billowed backward as a rush of wind spiraled around her. "I have it on good authority that he is presently distracted with personal complications, which means now is our best moment to strike. He will not want any delay of his private project's timeline and is more likely to agree now to save himself the bother."

"Or kill us for the same reason!" Another Ghul hobbled out on all fours.

"I understand your qualms, as I share them. However, if we do not act, we will all die anyway," Safiya urged. "This personal project, to my knowledge, will keep Erebus trapped in human form for longer than we have. By the time he is done, we will all have faded back into the ether. It affects him little, for he can create more of us when he returns to his true form, but it will be too late for us. To him, we are expendable. We must show him that we refuse to be superfluous."

A beautiful djinn emerged then, though her legs were furred and hoofed. A Ghul in another form. "And if we consent to do this, what would keep Erebus from smiting us in our weaker forms? I rather like being powerful."

"Abdhi was right about the Ghul," Santana whispered. "Who in their right mind could look past those legs and think that was a normal woman? Even if I don't shave for weeks, my legs aren't that bad."

I chuckled. "Maybe they cast magic to fool the men they're trying to capture."

"You must listen," Safiya insisted, silencing Santana and me. "There are two choices ahead of us: we risk death waiting for Erebus, or we take matters into our own hands and exist as weaker individuals with our own lives, free of any connection to Erebus. Power is all well and good, but you cannot use power if you no longer exist."

She's good. I'll give her that, Kadar muttered. *She's even got me considering it.*

We should all consider it, I replied.

He snickered in my head. *You're only saying that because of your fiery* señorita.

That is my main reason, but the more Safiya talks about it, the more it makes sense. I meant it. Safiya was extremely persuasive, and she made a skilled argument. She didn't feed the djinn any lies; she'd given them cold, hard facts in the hopes they'd make the right decision.

Well, brace yourself. These djinn could talk the hind leg off a Ghul, and a few will probably lose a limb or two before they reach any kind of answer. Kadar sighed. *Think of it as the worst Christmas dinner you have ever encountered, and all the family members are here, every single one with their own opinion. There'll be tears before bedtime, I guarantee it.*

"I will leave you to discuss this matter," Safiya concluded. "Come dawn, we need a decision."

The djinn separated into their respective groups, arguing amongst themselves about who ought to be the three chosen spokespeople. Kadar was right. There'd be hours of bickering and handwringing before the sun rose, and I had no idea how this would play out.

"She cannot be serious," Zalaam whispered. "This is tantamount to suicide."

"And hoping that Erebus will return to his true form before you all die isn't?" Santana hissed back. She had a point.

Zalaam balled his hands into fists. "I would not expect you to understand. This is sheer madness."

"Kadar doesn't think so." I held Zalaam's fiery gaze. "He started off thinking the same as you, but Safiya won him over."

"Nonsense," Zalaam spat.

"It isn't nonsense. If this goes ahead, and Erebus dissolves these ties, every djinn bound to a magical will be freed, as well. It'd be a clean slate for him, and for you, and for every Levi to come," I said. "Kadar could live his own life, and so could you. And I'd never worry about the woman I love dying in childbirth, and no Levi after me would, either."

Santana's eyes widened, glimmering with sadness and hope. "You've really been thinking about that a lot, haven't you?"

"How could I not?" I replied, shuffling awkwardly.

Zalaam clicked his tongue. "Ah, so that is why you are so eager, is it?" He stared at Santana, who still looked at me with that painfully conflicted expression. "You think this will grant you a normal life and free my boy at the same time?"

"It *will*," I insisted, ignoring the desert chill creeping into my bones. Kadar had stopped warming me up, likely out of stubbornness.

"No, it will not." Zalaam's black smoke wisped upward. "Even if Erebus dissolves his bond with us, it will do nothing against the curse placed upon the Levi family. The sorcerer who executed the curse was no ordinary magical—he was a spurned djinn. And Erebus cannot break a djinn curse, even by dissolving our ties to him. It will remain in place, and the Levi men will continue to be born with djinn inside them. For us linked to the Levis, we will only be free when our magicals die, as has always been the case."

Abdhi hovered nearby, shamefaced. And the hopeful shine in Santana's eyes dimmed.

"Abdhi? Is that true?" I demanded.

Abdhi toyed with the strands of smoke twisting from his fingertips. "I'm afraid I don't have the answer to that, Raffe. You would have to ask—"

Safiya walked toward me, silencing Abdhi. "I heard Zalaam's words to you, and I am sorry to say that they are true. If a djinn is bound by another djinn's curse, it will not break upon the occasion of Erebus freeing us. I had to conceal that from you earlier, when I told you otherwise, and I am deeply remorseful for that. I did not want you to lose heart."

"You don't think you should have told *them* that?" My voice came out strangled, my heart crushed to pieces. I'd been so sure.

What, did you think she wouldn't lie by omission to get the other djinn on her side? Or us, for that matter? Kadar scoffed, though he couldn't hide his disappointment. He'd bought into the hope, too—I could feel it, swimming through me.

Safiya sighed and put her hand on my shoulder. "I did not wish to say anything in front of the other djinn, as your situation is somewhat unique. The curse upon your family is ancient. I did not want to single you out, and I did not want to instill doubt where there need not be any. Other djinn who are bound to mortals may be freed by this action, as they have not been tied to the djinn for as long as your family has. Providing Erebus agrees, that is."

"I need some air," I panted, ready to run away from this oasis.

"Raffe, breathe. We can talk about this." Santana reached for my hand, but I recoiled.

That's right, get your ass as far from here as you can. This is not intended to serve us. We were fed a lie, and I ought to tear out her tongue for lauding us with false promises, Kadar snarled.

"You needn't despair, Raffe. There may be a way to resolve your problem, but that is not our priority at the present moment," Safiya urged. "We will find a way after this is done."

"How? Do not claim you will unravel the curse yourself," Zalaam interjected. "We do not even know which djinn cursed the Levi family. That secret was lost many decades ago. I highly doubt even you would be able to unearth it."

Safiya smiled strangely. "I will do what I can and inquire where I must."

"Another empty promise?" I wheezed, desperate for some space to think.

"I will not lie to you. The odds are slim, but that means there is still a chance."

"Raffe, it will all be okay," Santana cut in. "Let's just go for a walk and talk this through."

I shook my head, preparing to flee. "No. I need to be alone. Don't follow me."

"Raffe, come on, we can—"

"I don't want to talk! I want to be on my own. I can't even think here, with all this djinn energy all over the place." I offered her an apologetic look, but I really did mean it. I couldn't talk about this... yet. The wound was too fresh.

Safiya removed her hand from my shoulder, and I ran. I didn't need to hear any more. Safiya had known the truth and she hadn't said a word. She had let Kadar and me think it would all be fine. That it would be a clean slate, regardless of the intricacies of Erebus and djinn magic. Well, I wouldn't believe in false hopes again, because it only hurt that much more when the dream came crashing down.

TWENTY-NINE

Kadar

always said you should never trust a djinn. I fed my thoughts into Raffe's head. We stalked together through the darkened desert, the oasis at our back. Nobody had followed us after Raffe had gone all dramatic and made a dash for it, and that suited me fine. I didn't want to be around anyone right now, either. Safiya gave us hope, and now I wanted her head on a pike. "Fuming" didn't even begin to cover it. "Livid" might've been more fitting.

"Shut up!" Raffe barked. "Now's not the time to be a smartass."

I'm just saying... I told you so. Surprisingly, being right didn't make me feel smug. For once, I hadn't wanted to be. Raffe might not have known my private thoughts, but the prospect of having Santana all to myself had been tantalizing, and Safiya had whisked that plump morsel under my nose and snatched it away again. I hated her for that. Loathed her, in fact. Stupid old witch, trying to pull the wool over our eyes.

"Please… just stop. I don't want to hear 'I told you so.' I don't want to hear any of it." Raffe lowered his head against the biting wind. "You might be inside me, but you've got no idea how this feels."

Why, because I'm a heartless monster? I replied.

"You *know* I didn't mean that." Raffe rubbed his eyes, weary to the core. He wasn't the only one. "I realize it sounds stupid, since I only started believing in the possibility about two seconds ago, but Safiya made me put all my eggs in this basket."

And now there's yolk all over the place? I offered a bitter laugh, but Raffe didn't bite. He wasn't listening to me. No, he was on the Santana train, bound to nowhere good, and he wouldn't be getting off until he was ready to stop wallowing. Mortals loved a satisfying wallow—like hippos in river slime.

"My whole future with Santana rested on this, and now it's gone. This freaking hurts, Kadar." Raffe came to a sharp standstill, heaving ragged breaths.

Easy there, pal. I know it hurts... I feel it, believe it or not. My heart is your heart. I sense when someone has taken a sledgehammer to it. I tried to offer some comfort. What could I say, I had a soft spot for the guy. Years joined to him would do that. He'd snuck in and lodged his prongs deep. It was like brushing past a shrub and getting a pesky burr on your back. And, call me sentimental, but I wouldn't pluck him off even if I could. I might have wanted him to pluck off from time to time, but he and I were one.

What have I turned into? My worst nightmare—a soft djinn. Ugh, spare me. I kept those thoughts to myself.

"This sucks, Kadar." Raffe breathed into the chilly night.

You know, it's not all bad, I mused so he could hear.

"What do you mean?" Raffe snuffled. Yeesh, if he started the waterworks, I'd have to lock myself away until he got his act together.

The thing is... I hesitated, terrified of going full sap. But he needed to hear this. And I needed to say it. *The thing is, Raffe—even if we could separate, I don't know if I'd actually go through with it.*

"You wouldn't?" Raffe sounded shocked, his brainwaves thrumming with surprise.

I laughed quietly. *I've been with you since you were born. I existed before you, but not long enough to get used to it. I'm still a kid, in djinn terms, though don't go spreading that around or I'll singe the skin off your tongue. Being with you is pretty much all I've ever known. Nobody knows you better than I do, even Santana—much as she'd argue against that. Hell, she'd probably set up a quiz to test the theory, and I would have to embarrass the crap out of her.*

Raffe chuckled despite himself. A good sign he was coming out of his wallowing hole.

You and I share all the fleshy goop of a body, the pulsing gray matter of a brain, and the intangible whatever of a soul. I know you down to your bowel movements, much as I wish I could be anywhere else when those rumblings get busy. I snickered, feeling Raffe bristle in disgust.

"Kadar, seriously," he complained, but I ignored him.

We share a past, from you crapping your diapers, wiping your snotty nose, and skinning your knees to the here and now—this present that we share. I paused. *But we have a future, too. A future that I don't mind sharing with you, even though we sometimes hate one another's guts. And, for the record, when it comes to your bowel movements, I REALLY hate your guts.*

"Can you leave my bodily functions out of this? It's taking the positivity out of what you're saying," Raffe complained. Whiny little man-child that he was. *My* whiny little man-child.

Hey, I'm just trying to emphasize that I'm with you through the rough and smooth. We are two halves of a whole, like a brain split down the middle. And, you know what, I'm okay with that. I sighed begrudgingly. *Besides, I doubt I'd have a chance with Santana on my own. She likes the two halves.*

She gets the sweet and the spice, wrapped up in one. At least, this way, she stays in my life. And so do you. I may be a whippersnapper in djinn terms, but I'm too old to learn new things, like living without a host.

"That was almost cute." Raffe smiled, his body sparking with new motes of optimism.

Careful, I warned. *Call me cute and I'll have to get ugly.*

"Inspiring, then," he replied.

I can cope with that. I put my feelers toward his heart, which slowed to a steadier pace. *And it's not a total loss with Santana, either. She has a smart head on that fine, fine figure of hers. She isn't worried about the future. She just wants us. At first, I thought that was mortal stupidity, but maybe she has other plans.*

"Santana has other plans? What other way could there be with her and me?" Raffe switched back to avid wallower, which instantly riled me up. I hated him when he went all pathetic. It made us both look bad.

"Maybe you could ask me, *mi amor*, instead of pushing me away." A voice cut through the air as a figure emerged from the darkness. The woman herself. Santana Catemaco, Mexican queen of my dreams. Damn, she looked good. Good enough to eat. Another reason things might not work out if I tried to steal Santana for myself. I hadn't tasted human flesh in a long time, but the craving never truly went away. And she would taste delicious. One crazy moment of temptation, and she'd be barbeque. Raffe keeping me in check served us all better.

Raffe hung his head. "What other way can there be, *mi ciela?*"

"We could adopt. I've been thinking about it more lately, and it makes a lot of sense. There are so many children in this world without a family, and I could love them and give them a place to call home, with you," she replied. "Who cares if they come from my friggin' womb? I certainly don't. They don't need to look like us to be loved by us, Raffe. That's why I'm not worried about our future. We can build a big family with kids who need our help."

Raffe, stubborn as ever, shook his head. "You'd be happy with that? I don't believe you. I've seen the photos of all your nieces and nephews, and the way you talk about your Mexican heritage. I don't want to deny you your own children because of my curse. What if you change your mind one day? What if you feel unsatisfied? What if you resent me because I can't give you what you want?"

Then you don't know her at all, I whispered instinctively.

"Then maybe you don't know me at all," Santana echoed sadly. "I love *you*, Raffe. I don't love imaginary children we don't have. I want a family with *you*, you dope. And I don't care how that happens, as long as we're both alive and in love and together. Just because my children won't be born in Mexico doesn't mean I won't share my history and heritage with them. And I'd hope you would share yours with them, too."

"I just wish it didn't have to be this way," Raffe mumbled. "I feel so guilty, whenever we talk about the future. I don't know if that will ever go away."

"Raffe, listen to me." She moved closer and grasped his face in her hands. I felt his heart lurch, filled with the usual warm fuzzies that she instilled in him. "I love you. I don't want to lose you. I almost did, on that rooftop, and it nearly killed me. So, you can think again if you plan to end this relationship because of something I don't care about, or if you think I'll just let you go. I love you too much. I *can't* be without you. Please, don't make me."

Raffe gazed into her eyes while I piggybacked on his vision. "I thought we could be free. I thought I could fix this."

"We *are* free, *mi amor*, and if it's not broken, it doesn't need fixing."

Santana kissed him, sending shivers through me. The best kind. "*Dios mio*, I even love Kadar, in my own weird way. I'd miss him if he disappeared. He is a part of you—a big part—not some tumor that needs removing. I am happy to love both of you, until the end of our days."

"But…" Raffe faltered.

"If you mention children again, I will kiss you until you shut up." Santana smiled. "When we reach that point in our lives, we'll find some kids out there who need us. I mean, look at Harley and Jacob. If they'd been adopted by the Smiths from the get-go, just think about how different their childhoods might've been. We can be the Smiths in that scenario. I don't need my own baby. I genuinely don't. This isn't a lie to make you feel better—as long as I have you, and we have kids around us someday, I'll be the happiest woman alive. So don't you give up on us, because I won't want any of that without you to share it with."

Time to heave up whatever you've got in that stomach, I chimed in. It wouldn't have been right to just let them have a sappy moment. That wasn't my style.

Raffe chuckled. "Kadar wants to barf."

"Well, Kadar can shut his trap for a while. He's caused enough fuss tonight, and he's not ruining this for me," she replied, which made me grin. I liked her sass.

"Do you really mean it?" Raffe focused his attention again.

She nodded. "I really mean it. I want you, and whatever family we end up with. I don't give two hoots that they won't share our genes. Between us, our babies would probably be crazy, anyway."

"Then… I believe you." Raffe tilted her chin up. "I won't try and push you away anymore. And I won't keep wishing things were different, though it might take me some time to fully come to terms with it."

Attaboy! I cheered.

"I love you," Santana breathed.

"I love you more. I don't ever want to be without you, either." Raffe leaned in and kissed her slowly, prompting me to connect to his nerve endings so I could feel what he was feeling.

She sank into our arms and pressed close, matching the passionate rhythm of his kiss. Her arms looped about our neck, and her fingertips ran through our hair. Giddiness pinballed through our shared veins, while the warmth of her chased away the icy chill of the desert, leaving a contented glow.

For a fleeting moment, no barrier separated me from Raffe. He was me, I was him, and we were kissing the woman we loved. And I found myself thanking the djinn who'd bound us together. Without this curse, I would never have known what it felt like to love and to be loved.

THIRTY

Raffe

W e couldn't stay out in the desert forever, much as I'd have liked to kiss my love until the sun came up. I'd had some sense knocked into me by Kadar and Santana. Just because severing ties with Erebus didn't benefit me, per se, didn't mean it wouldn't benefit the djinn. They deserved freedom. It was selfish of me to wallow in my personal gripes, when they had the possibility to end their collective enslavement to their creator. Even if it meant Kadar wound up weakened, too, without the independence payoff the others would receive.

Feeling much better than I had, I returned with Santana to the oasis. And it looked as though our timing couldn't have been better. The various djinn had all returned to the center, though they still muttered amongst themselves.

"Which way do you think they've decided to go?" I whispered to Santana.

"Hard to tell," she replied.

I'm going to say fifty-fifty, which means another tedious few hours of pointless discussion, Kadar interjected. *They'll come back again, and again, and again, until they have the majority that Safiya clearly wants. Politics are the same with every advanced species.*

Zalaam made a beeline for me, leaving the gathering of what I presumed were Qareen—the type of djinn Abdhi had mentioned Kadar might be.

"Leonidas urged me to follow you, but I convinced him to give you some peace and quiet to attend to your thoughts," he said. "Although, I feared you would not return in time to hear the verdict."

"I needed a moment to have some sense kicked into me, that's all." I flashed Santana a grin, which she returned. "Where do you stand on all this?"

Zalaam puffed his chest out. "Actually, there have been many persuasive arguments while you were gone. And, I hate to say it, but I think I may be coming around to the idea."

"Seriously?" Santana blurted out.

"I am quite serious, yes. I merely hope it does not get us all annihilated." Zalaam's red eyes flickered with concern. "But, as many of my fellow djinn have hammered into my brain, even so a swift annihilation would be better than enduring a slow, unavoidable death. Perhaps this sickness is making me lose grasp of my faculties, but I have begun to agree. I will not spend my last days wasting away in a coven infirmary. It lacks dignity, and if we are to die, a djinn must die with dignity."

"That's a noble sentiment." I glanced at the rest of the djinn, trying to gauge which way they would swing. It really was impossible to tell.

"The two of you seem alarmingly happy, despite our dire straits," Zalaam commented, scrutinizing Santana and me. "That must have been quite the epiphany you had out there."

Ah, is that what the old folks call it? Kadar joked, making my cheeks flush.

"We had a lot to discuss," I managed to say, burning with embarrassment. "And we managed to resolve our problems."

"Ah. I had no idea there was trouble in paradise." Zalaam's lips curved into a smirk.

"Not anymore," Santana cut in. "We're peachy."

Zalaam nodded, still smirking. "I am pleased to hear it. I do not think Leonidas could have abided a mopey son had things gone awry. And he has a great deal of respect for you, Santana—I am sure he will not mind me saying so. We would not have wished to go through this rigmarole with some other young lady, on the slim chance Raffe ever managed to dig himself out of his pit of despair to attract another mate."

Santana stifled a giggle. "Good to know."

"It surprises me that Raffe is not as competent with women as his father was during the prime of his youth," Zalaam went on, making me wish for quicksand beneath my feet. Kadar cackled internally. "Though perhaps that is more a failing of Kadar than Raffe. The animal magnetism often rests with us, rather than our hosts."

I'll show him animal magnetism! Kadar yelled. *I'm beast enough to wrench out his heart and stuff it down his throat, if he doesn't keep his opinions to himself.*

The elected djinn stepped forward before Kadar could make good on his threat. He hadn't liked having his sex appeal questioned by *his* father. Even now, he broiled in my belly, using my intestines as a punching bag. I ignored his tantrum, focusing on the djinn as they prepared to make their decision.

The city of Salameh fell silent, and it felt like everyone held their breath. I certainly did. A motion like this could be huge—the biggest scheme ever taken on by the djinn as a collective. The atmosphere grew thick with anticipation, with anxiety and excitement mingling in the breeze.

Safiya stood and addressed the trios of spokesdjinn. "Have you reached a conclusion?"

The Ifrit council went first. "We have made the unanimous decision to unite against Erebus and go to him in Tartarus. We choose not to serve him again, no matter the consequences."

The Marids went next, towering over the oasis like shadowy megaliths. "We also choose to unite against Erebus, though we have an addendum to the words of the Ifrits. If Erebus grants us freedom, we may choose to serve him on our own terms, in return for additional power."

Thirdly came the Qareen. "We are in agreement. We will unite against Erebus and win our liberation. But, like the Marids, we have an addendum. We may choose to align with mortal beings if we desire, as we have done in the past. That is who we are, and we see no reason why that should change."

"That makes perfect sense," Safiya replied.

The rest of the djinn made their cases, and ultimately each group chose to unite against Erebus, with a few tweaks to suit their own kind, but nothing that made their decision contradictory or void. The forum ended with the invisible Hatif. In fact, I'd thought we were done when an eerie voice whispered into the silence.

"We Hatif agree with this course. Our brethren of physical forms, you would survive longer than we creatures of sound and spirit. Many of us are already lost. We will not lose more." The strange voice seemed to come from all directions, impossible to pinpoint. "We will have freedom. We will join this fight, to ensure that we never suffer like this again."

Hold on to your backsides, everyone... we're headed for a savage ride. Kadar sounded stunned by the unanimous will of the djinn. I couldn't deny it—they'd shocked me, too. But Erebus had brought them to this. He'd cut himself off from them without a single care for their wellbeing. What else were they supposed to do to save themselves? Knowing Erebus, they hadn't even crossed his mind, and he certainly wouldn't have anticipated this.

It gave me an odd satisfaction to see them all take the risk of standing against him, when they could just as easily have bowed down. My admiration had grown tenfold, steeling my resolve to send Finch on the road to freedom, as well. If these djinn could take fate into their own hands, I had to help my friend do the same.

Erebus was definitely going to get a nasty wake-up call.

THIRTY-ONE

Raffe

"What happens next?" I whispered to Zalaam.

His eyes flared. "Everyone gets what they have asked for. We face our creator in his otherworld—the place our sentience was formed—and we demand to be separated from his power."

Santana shifted uneasily. "Erebus won't like that."

"No… no, he won't," Zalaam replied.

Safiya raised her arms, and the gathering quieted once more. "The decision has been made. We will go to Tartarus and seek our liberation. We must make haste. There is no reason to delay."

From her robes, she removed an emerald the size of an ostrich egg. How she'd hidden it so easily, I had no idea. Safiya had a few tricks up her ancient sleeves.

"Hang on, what about—" My words evaporated like a speck of water in the desert's daylight heat as Safiya lifted the emerald. Green light exploded in a violent wave that enveloped Salameh and the djinn on the outskirts. I'd wanted to ask Safiya to leave me with Santana, but I'd been too slow. Wherever the djinn were going, I was going, too, thanks to Kadar.

Take her hand, or I will! Kadar barked in my head. I quickly grasped Santana's hand. I didn't want to strand her in the desert. Only after our bodies started to twist upward, disintegrating, did I realize Erebus's otherworld might not be the greatest place for her, either.

What was that for? I hissed at Kadar.

You want her to burn to a crisp when the sun comes up? Chalk doors don't work in Salameh, and she'd have lost her way in the desert long before any rescue came. This is for the best.

You better hope you're right...

As my very being tore apart on a molecular level, the world shot past at lightning speed. Desert landscapes, towering cities, lush greenery, and expansive oceans whizzed by, then turned to darkness. A crackle of sparks erupted around my fast-moving form, letting me know we'd passed from the real world to... somewhere beyond. Tartarus.

I landed with a jolt, finding Santana beside me, her hand still in mine. She looked pale and gripped my hand harder as the shock of the portal wore off. The darkness had disappeared, too, which was another surprise. Last time I'd been to Tartarus, when we'd come to stop Katherine's ritual, I'd seen a world of shadow and danger, with Purge beasts snapping and snarling from all angles, shrouded in perpetual night. But this world... I wondered if Safiya had hit the emerald wrong or something. It didn't look anything like the Tartarus I knew. It looked... empty. That was the only way to describe it.

A vast expanse of bland nothing stretched as far as the eye could see, flat and barren. Dirt that grew nothing, no Purge beasts to speak of, everything illuminated in an anemic glow. A hill rose a short distance away, again lacking any signs of life or Erebus.

I sought out Safiya, still holding Santana's hand. "Are you sure this is the right place?"

The djinn muttered amongst themselves, seemingly as confused as I was. Even if they'd never personally visited this otherworld, they'd have known it by reputation.

Looks like the grand old witch messed up, Kadar muttered. *She's brought us to some abandoned otherworld, the stupid hag.*

I ignored him and continued looking around. In this flat emptiness, I finally saw the full extent of the djinns' formidable numbers. Before, I'd had my doubts that the djinn could persuade Erebus to liberate them, but seeing them en masse—now, I doubted that Erebus could refuse.

I gave Santana's hand a squeeze, to try and coax her out of her shock. But she didn't look back at me.

"Hey, you're okay. We're going to be okay," I whispered. "Kadar and I will protect you. I know this is weird, but I couldn't leave you in the desert. Whatever happens, we'll get you out if things take a turn."

She gave a faint nod, but I couldn't tell if she was convinced.

"This is Tartarus," Safiya replied confidently, bringing my attention back to her. "Though I understand your bemusement. I share it. This is not the way Tartarus ought to appear, nor has it ever looked this way when I have been summoned by our creator."

"Might you have pulled us in the wrong direction?" Abdhi swayed, clearly nervous. "Transporting thousands upon thousands of djinn is no simple task, Safiya. Perhaps there were too many and something went awry."

Safiya shook her head. "No, this *is* Tartarus." The flames in her eyes brightened. "Oh, that foolish Child."

"What is it?" Santana asked, finding her voice. She leaned into me, a bit of steel coming back into her eyes. *That's my girl...* Even in the darkest of times, nothing shook her for long.

"His otherworld has responded to his new form. Their realms are innately linked to their beings, created to emulate their wishes and their natures," Safiya explained, her tone somewhat awestruck. "Now, his otherworld does not recognize *its* creator. It is... lost, in a sense, and has reverted to its initial state of vacancy. A true blank slate. I did not think it would happen so quickly. Indeed, I did not think this would happen until we djinn had all crumbled to nothing, but it seems I was serendipitously mistaken."

Santana frowned. "Wait, does that mean Erebus isn't here?"

"It appears so," Safiya replied, a small smile tugging her lips.

"Then what possible reason could you have to smile?" Zalaam interjected sharply. "If Erebus is not here, you have brought us on a wild goose chase. How can we demand freedom of him if he is not home for us to confront?"

The djinn collectively grumbled in agitation, but Safiya took it in stride. In fact, she seemed eerily calm.

"Fear not, my brothers and sisters. You need not be alarmed by this alteration in proceedings." Safiya addressed the entire army of djinn. "Indeed, this lends itself to our advantage. It removes all the risk and doubt we have harbored regarding our separation."

"No offense, Safiya, but how?" I asked.

She doesn't know what she's yakking about. She's bluffing because this has all gone wrong, in the most spectacular way. Kadar bristled inside me. *If the djinn suspect she's made a mistake, they'll wrench her limbs out of their sockets and use them to beat out a samba.*

Safiya turned to me. "Follow me, and I will show you." She set off without waiting for a reply, trekking across the empty landscape toward the dusty hill. The djinn followed, because what else could they do? Safiya had brought them here with hope in their glowing hearts, and they wouldn't leave until they were satisfied. Santana, Zalaam, and I fell in with the crowd, sticking close to Safiya.

"Does she know what she's doing?" Santana whispered. "It's kind of a relief that Erebus isn't home, but… I thought the djinn needed him to break free?"

I put my hand on the small of her back. "She seems to have an idea. Maybe she knows something we don't."

Santana seemed to grow stronger by the second, recovering from the initial shock. "What's the point in living for thousands of years if you don't pick up a trick or two, right?"

"That's what I'm thinking."

She glanced at me. "Thank you for not leaving me in the desert. I might not know what she's got in mind, but I wouldn't have missed this for the world. Seeing all the djinn here, it's pretty damn impressive."

"I'd never have left you behind," I insisted.

"I know, but you might've made a silly decision in the moment, thinking I'd be safer in the middle of nowhere." She managed a smile. "I'm glad you didn't."

We're not out of the woods yet. It might still be a stupid decision, Kadar chimed in. *But at least we'll all go up in flames together, eh?*

That's not going to happen, I replied inwardly.

Roasty-toasty Levis and Catemacos. Kadar laughed coldly, but I felt a shiver of hope bristling through my stomach. His hope.

At the top of the hill, after a thigh-burning climb, a morsel of architecture finally appeared. Crumbling ruins, sitting at the summit. The withered remains of vines continued to strangle the decrepit pillars, but little else adorned the hilltop. A few tumbleweeds bounced along on a faint, cool breeze.

"Is this supposed to make sense?" a towering Marid muttered frostily.

"It will." Safiya entered the ruins and stopped in front of a block of gray stone. An altar of some kind. Or, it had been, once. Gently, she touched her fingertips to the block's surface. Red light slithered underneath, and the top of the altar screeched open with a grating of stone on stone. Her hands delved inside, then receded a moment later. Hovering above her palms swirled a ball of red-and-black matter, part liquid, part smoke. A bright crimson glow pulsated in the center.

"What's that?" I asked, resisting the urge to step back. Bad energy reverberated from the swirling orb. Santana trembled slightly, which wasn't like her at all. Her eyes widened, and she appeared unable to tear her gaze from the bizarre substance.

Safiya grinned. "This is us, in our basest form. The primordial soup from whence we were formed. The experiment that allowed us to exist. The Nexus of Erebus."

The djinn gasped, their smoke billowing wildly.

"The who-said-what-now?" Santana whispered, sweat glistening on her forehead. She looked calmer, but I sensed lingering fear in her. It prompted me to put my arm around her waist and pull her closer. Here, she was a fish out of water, surrounded by djinn in Erebus's otherworld. Not exactly a comforting position to be in. But she was taking it all in stride, making a decent show of being brave.

"It is the connective tissue binding us to him. He formed it, and us, from his own body. It is us, and him, combined." Safiya moved toward the center of the ruins.

I frowned. "How do you know this?"

Zalaam cut in. "More to the point, how did you know it was here?"

"I have researched our origins for thousands of years," Safiya replied. "But I was also one of Erebus's first. When I was created, I erupted from this Nexus and stood on this very hilltop to hear the instruction of our creator. Once he had spoken of his desires for us—his creatures—he sucked us back into this orb and sent us into the world in a Purge Plague. On one occasion, when he summoned me to perform a task on his behalf, I watched him remove the Nexus from the altar and stood in this very spot as he created more of our kind."

"What if he comes back?" A Ghul sniveled, dripping black goo onto the ground.

Safiya smiled. "He cannot."

"Pardon?" I gaped at her.

"In his human form, his otherworld has no choice but to reject him. He may portal in, as we have, but he has no power over this realm any longer." Safiya's eyes flashed again. "However, *we* do. We are of his essence, and we are of his Darkness. We are more Child of Chaos than he is, at this moment—specifically, more linked to the energy that he has abandoned."

Santana folded her arms across her chest. "Sorry, Safiya, but this isn't making any sense."

"Observe, and perhaps it will." Safiya closed her eyes and sent energy surging into the ball. The pulsating red glow in the center brightened, and then… it stopped pulsing and became a constant, vibrant red light, less like a heartbeat and more like a beacon. A moment later, the swirling black edges of the orb spiraled into the red center. A brief pause lingered in the air while everyone held their collective breath. The red light faded to black before the entire thing exploded like a decayed star finally turning supernova. Powerful rings of searing scarlet energy burst outward, rushing past us all to fill the entirety of the otherworld before vanishing.

"I don't get it. What happened?" a Si'lat asked in a frightened voice.

"We are free," Safiya explained with a triumphant grin. "I have performed precisely what Erebus would have done to liberate us. You will feel your new weaknesses in the coming days, but you will also feel the effects of the sickness begin to ebb. And now, we control Tartarus."

"What did you say?" A Qareen edged forward, face aghast.

Safiya bent down and brushed her hand over the barren earth. "Watch and you will see." Her eyes closed, and a tiny spark of red leapt from her palm. Where it fell, a small plant with scarlet petals and a blood-red stem emerged. "Tartarus responds to us now. It recognizes our energy as that which it lost. We have taken Erebus's place as this realm's creator, free to shape it in our image and do whatever we care to with it. This is our world, brothers and sisters—this can be our home, built as we see fit. This is our land of hope and glory."

Holy human on a stick... she did it. She freed us and seized Erebus's otherworld from under his nose. Kadar sounded dumbfounded. I shared in his awe. Safiya had led the djinn here with a promise of freedom, and she had not let them down. A leader who had actually followed through with her intent. It struck me right in the heart, making it swell with something like pride. Even though I'd never thought of myself as being djinn, the djinn were an innate part of me. And I'd never felt closer to Kadar than I did in that moment—the moment the penny dropped for him. He may not have been free of me, but he got to see his people liberated. It filled us both up with joy, so weird and wonderful that I wanted to cry or yell or punch the air.

Another djinn shuffled closer, observing the plant. "But what if Erebus comes back to claim his otherworld?"

"He cannot, if we choose to deny him entry." Safiya touched the red petals. "We are the rule-makers, and we are the sovereigns of this world now. If we seek sanctuary, we have only to send our energy into this realm and insist it deny Erebus access. He may only be able reclaim it if, or when, he returns to his original form, as the otherworld will likely recognize his authority again and register his superiority over us. But I have a feeling that will take quite some time. His personal project will prevent it from happening imminently. Even on that occasion, he will not be able to undo what I have done this day—I have liberated us, and he cannot alter that. Those are the rules, formed when he made us. He cannot unravel djinn magic."

You sly, delicious minx! Kadar cheered inside me. Safiya had put the pieces together so perfectly, taking a dire situation and making it into something incredible. Her fast thinking had brought this into being. The greatest thing to ever happen to the djinn in all their history. I hoped it would stay that way, for their sake.

The djinn murmured excitedly as Safiya slowly stood. She had barely risen when she collapsed to the ground. Their excitement hushed, and their eyes all turned toward the Storyteller, who lay limp and motionless. I gasped and Santana froze at my side, the two of us staring at the Storyteller in confusion. Abdhi swept forward and quickly scooped her up in his muscular arms.

"Safiya? Safiya, is it the sickness?" he asked, scanning her for injury.

Her face turned toward his, wearing an expression of contentment. "No… it is not the sickness."

"Then what's the matter?" Abdhi pressed.

"I… gave my life so you all might… be free."

I rushed to her side, with Santana close behind. "What did you do?"

"Changes of this magnitude… require payment… and I was… the only one with the… strength to offer the sum," she wheezed, coughing violently. Black smoke rippled from her mouth. "I have lived… long enough. It was time… I gave back to my kind. And what finer… way to end one's life... than with a gift... to those I have watched... all these years?"

She gave herself... for us? Kadar sounded crushed. An unsettling feeling for me; Kadar didn't venture into that realm of emotion very often. It filtered through to my own emotions, making my chest clench in a vise of panic for the ancient djinn.

Realization may have dawned for Kadar and me, but Santana was the one who spoke. "Did you know this would happen all along? Did you plan to sacrifice yourself for this?"

Safiya smiled at Santana. "From the moment... I realized Erebus was not here... sweet girl. That was... when the thought transformed into... reality, and I knew I would... have to give myself in return... for this liberation. I could... not ask another to do this... in my place."

You did this without a single pause. My heart lurched in admiration and sadness. *You knew this would happen, you knew you'd have to die, and you kept right on without fear.* She hadn't faltered once. She'd stuck her hand right into that altar and drawn out the Nexus, and she'd used herself to bring them out of enslavement. No hesitations. I felt Kadar's increasing respect for this woman rushing through our shared veins, and when I turned to look at Santana, I saw that same emotion written across her face. The highest of regard. How could any djinn or human look at the Storyteller and not feel that? A human could go through their entire life and never witness a genuine martyr. And I felt honored to have witnessed this. Honored and heartbroken.

"But we can't do this without you," Abdhi murmured, staring help-lessly into her eyes. "We don't know how to be free without you to lead us. How do we use your gift?"

"I have thought... of that, too." Safiya lifted her shaky hands and touched the sides of Abdhi's head. Scarlet light shot from her palms and into Abdhi's skull. His eyes lit with such ferocity that I had to look away.

What is she doing? I whispered to Kadar.

Handing over everything inside her head. Passing on her knowledge, he replied.

Sensing the dying of the light, I looked back to find Abdhi standing at his full Marid height, holding Safiya in his enormous arms. She looked so small and vulnerable, her life clearly waning. Whatever she'd done had freed Abdhi from his lamp ahead of time. If she really had succeeded, I guessed those trapped in lamps and the like would return to their original states in due course, but she'd expedited it for Abdhi. The Storyteller's strength and fortitude was beyond anything I'd ever seen, but that didn't alter the pain of knowing she wouldn't live to see what she'd purchased with her life. It was like the old adage of planting an oak tree, knowing you'd never get to stand in its shade, but planting it anyway for the generations that would come after.

"I feel your memories." Abdhi's voice strained. "Your thoughts, your past, your hopes… are all in my head."

Safiya chuckled softly. "My last gift… to you. You must lead them now. Make this world your own, and make it… the perfect sanctuary for… djinn. We will never bow or obey again, unless… we choose to."

All of this had happened so quickly that my brain could barely keep up. Kadar remained inside me, but then, I'd known that would happen. Even so, some of my weariness had begun to fade.

Can you feel the change? I asked Kadar.

I… think so. The pain is lightening, like sweating out the last of a fever, he replied.

The other djinn seemed to feel the same. Across the vast gathering, I heard mutterings of, "I can breathe easier," and, "The agony is not as strong," and various iterations of the same sentiment.

"You should have warned me," Abdhi murmured, sinking to his knees so all could see his precious cargo. "You should have told us of your intended sacrifice. Others would have given themselves in your place."

Safiya moved her hand down to his cheek. "Precisely. Someone would… have tried to be heroic and do what I… had to. Someone younger… with so much more… life to give than I do. The truth is, Abdhi… I have told stories all my life, and… it was time I became… the heroine of mine."

"You really did this for them?" I looked around at the stunned faces of the crowd. I knew my question was a little redundant, but I wanted to hear her reply. I wanted to understand why she'd done this, without a thought for her own existence. I had to.

Safiya nodded weakly. "We were born to be slaves… but… we deserve more. All I ask, in return for… my sacrifice, is that… you use this gift well. Be free, be happy… and build a world… for yourselves. And if Erebus comes back in his Child… of Chaos form, and the otherworld does… recognize his authority and remove you… then rebuild elsewhere. He cannot… stop you now."

A death rattle wheezed in her chest. A moment later, her body went limp, and the light in her eyes faded. Her skin flaked into ashy fragments, then drifted into the air where they turned to smoke and disappeared—until there was nothing left of her, and Abdhi's arms lay empty of the Storyteller.

"You heard her." Abdhi looked up, black tears sliding down his cheeks. "We mustn't waste what she has given. Let's build this new world, to ensure her last act was not in vain." Solemnly, he turned his face to the gray sky. Beneath the scarlet skin of his chest, his heart glowed.

The other djinn turned their faces up as their hearts glowed vividly. Tears sprang to my eyes as I watched them mourning her. All of them. And I had the feeling that Kadar was, too. Those tears weren't entirely mine.

Safiya had given her life for the djinn's independence from Erebus. They would be weaker, and the addendums they'd sought would be null and void, but now they had a world to call their own, away from anyone and anything that might try to harm them or bend them to their will. Here, they could come and go as they pleased, knowing they had a safe haven to return to. And Safiya had done all of this for them without pomp or circumstance, or any expectation in return.

After thousands of years, her own story had finally ended. Now, the djinn would have to write their own book, starting afresh, living out the promise to make it a good one in her honor... preferably without eating any humans.

THIRTY-TWO

Finch

I stared at the dead bluebell. It didn't inspire optimism. Nash might've had good reasons for making his blood unusable, but the problem was—*I* needed to use it. Sure, I'd developed some respect for the guy, but I didn't know him. And, unfortunately for him, I had to look out for myself and my people first.

"Look, we wouldn't ask if we weren't desperate," I told him, setting my jaw and nerves.

Nash scraped a stool from under the workbench and sat. "I get that, but I won't just give up this djinn curse for one person. If I do that, I open myself up to hunters again. And if it comes down to my life or someone else's, I'm sorry, but I have to put Huntress and myself first."

Seems like you and I have something in common...

"But our friend is in dire need." Melody knelt beside Huntress and scratched between her flicking ears. "Only you can fix him. Please, Nash. Could we offer you protection in return for your help?"

"You think you're the first to offer that kind of exchange?" Nash rested his head on his hand. "I'm not saying you'll stab me in the back. You seem like good people. But I've been double-crossed so many times. I can't risk it anymore. There's no safe place for me in this world, as long as I've got this blood in my veins."

Melody met his gaze. "I'm the Librarian, Nash. I can find a solution to protect you from the hunters—so you don't have to cut your life short, either at the hands of hunters or this slow-killing curse. I swear, I won't stop looking until I find a way, if you agree to help us."

"Even if you could, it's not like you've got a djinn handy to remove the curse," Nash replied.

A lightbulb went off in my head. "But we need your blood in order to save our friend, who *does* have a djinn inside him. That's why we're here. You might know of him—Raffe Levi? Another of the soldiers who took down Katherine in the Battle of Elysium. A brave warrior, one who wants to be freed of a curse far worse than yours."

"Raffe Levi?" Nash frowned. "The name rings a bell, but how can his curse be worse than mine?"

"Because it affects generations upon generations of his family and kills innocent women in childbirth." A bubble of determination rose in my throat, and a tiny bit of acid guilt. This wasn't why I needed his blood clean and functioning, but I had to put on a believable show. "Raffe's djinn needs amputating, and he's the one who can break your curse. We can do this. Melody can find a different way to keep the ol' black spot off you, and we can save Raffe and make a little djinn very happy, all at the same time. Come on, Mr. Claus, doesn't that sound like Christmas to you?"

Nash hesitated. "You're asking a heck of a lot from me, Crowley. I don't even know you."

"No, but you're not a hard-ass," I replied. "It's all well and good, hiding and staying off-grid, but what's the point of any life at all—long or short—if this is all you do? We're offering you a potential way out. A permanent fix to the hunters. And all you have to do is let us remove your curse so you can help us. From where I stand, that's a win for everyone."

"It's that 'potential' part that's not quite selling it to me." Nash sighed. "What if Melody can't find a way to protect me? Will she get Luke to bring in a colleague—give me a bodyguard for the rest of my days? Because I've already got one, and that's not much different than the life I'm leading now. It's not a win for me, more of a break-even with significant risk."

"Better than a loss," Luke chimed in, right on the money.

Silence unfolded across the cabin. Even Huntress quieted to only the softest of pants while Melody continued to fuss over her. Nash picked up one of his half-made knives and ran his fingertips over the smoothed bone handle like he wanted to take it out for dinner. I saw the cogs whirring. Our hermit friend was weighing his options. Do nothing and be safe in his selfishness, or help us and risk putting a target on his back again. No judgment from me, though—he and I were in twin canoes, about to lose our respective paddles. I'd understand if he stood his ground and said no… I just hoped he wouldn't.

And that is one hundred percent your *selfishness talking. You'd throw this plaid sucker under a fleet of buses to gain your freedom*, a whisper hissed inside my head. The gremlins were back, less than an hour after my last dose. And that had been a double dose, to top up the one before it.

I dug my fingernails into my palms. The twinge of pain lodged me in reality, and I needed to hold on to reality for a while longer. Just until Nash agreed. He was teetering on the edge of yes; I could see it on his face. I thought about finding that pocket of calm Melody had tucked away inside my noggin, but that would mean abandoning ship.

If I did that, Nash would have questions, and that might make him think twice about putting his faith in us. It wouldn't have been the first time someone encountered my dark side and turned tail.

"If it gets really bad, we can always find another djinn to restore the curse." Yup, I was scraping a grimy barrel now. But only because I had no idea how long I'd be able to fight the gremlin tide. If faces started getting twisty and demonic again, Huntress might turn me into fleshy ribbons to protect her soul-partner.

"But it shouldn't come to that." Melody swept in. "I have an entire world's worth of information in my head, from centuries of magicals and Chaos. Trust us. We'll get you out of this predicament, if you get us out of ours. Our friend's life depends on it. I know that may not mean anything to you, but it means a great deal to us."

Nash sighed. "I've got to say, your timing is weird."

"What do you mean?" I prompted.

He glanced at us as if debating whether to continue. "Well... I've been feeling worse lately. This curse is meant to keep me good for another decade or so, but... I feel messed up. It's harder to get out of bed in the morning, and it ain't because of the cold. It's why I moved back here from another outpost—I couldn't maintain an interdimensional bubble. It took too much out of me."

Erebus's separation from the djinn must be affecting him, too. I knew Erebus couldn't interfere with djinn magic, but maybe the magic itself weakened when the power source wasn't providing the juice. But I couldn't say that without revealing that our need had something to do with Erebus.

"You've been sick?" Melody pressed.

Nash peeled back the Band-Aid on his arm, revealing cracked, dark threads of collapsed veins. "Yeah. I don't bounce back so easy. Even walking in the woods leaves me breathless."

Melody and I exchanged a glance, evidently on the same wavelength.

"And if you find a way out of this, then… ah man, I don't know. It's a lot to give up, and it's a big gamble for me." He covered up his wound again. "But this curse has definitely sped up, and I wouldn't want to die with unfinished business."

"Unfinished business?" Luke narrowed his eyes. "What kind?"

"Personal stuff." Nash's grip tightened around his unfinished blade. The grim expression on his face told me it was more than finishing his knife collection. No, I'd seen that look before… he was referring to a vendetta. One burning him up inside.

A noise outside made all our heads whip around. An oh-so-human scuffle of feet, crunching in the snow. The spike of terror that jolted through me tipped the fragile balance. The floodgates tore open, and my brain sailed away on the unleashed torrent.

I envisioned a horde of demonic magicals in the clearing, palms raised and ready to pound us into oblivion. A second later, Erebus's distorted figure loomed over me. He stood on the top of Mount Sisyphus in his otherworld, gesturing to ten wooden posts he'd erected, complete with eleven dangling figures all strung up by their arms. Blood splattered across them, their bodies ragged with open wounds: Harley, Ryann, Wade, Melody, Luke, Saskia, Garrett, Tatyana, Kenzie, and Kenzie's mom and sister. Purge beasts crouched in front of each person, awaiting orders to execute.

"You have disappointed me for the last time. I warned you, did I not? I warned you until I was blue in the face, and it made no difference. You understood the stakes, and yet you chose to fail me," Erebus hissed in my ear, back in his floaty Child of Chaos form.

This isn't real… it can't be… Erebus is still in human form. But I no longer knew what was what—the lines had blurred beyond recognition. I felt the hot-and-cold prickle of Erebus's breath on my neck. I heard the roar of the Purge beasts below. I smelled the metallic tang of fresh blood in the air, and the foul stench of the creatures waiting to kill the people I cared for.

I tumbled off my stool to the floor, then clung to it, using it to pull myself upright. Burying my face in my knees and wrapping my arms around my legs, I cowered as the panic and nightmares hit me in wave after wave. Closing my eyes wouldn't have helped. The nightmares played out in front of me, phasing in and out of reality and the cabin surrounding me.

Just then, Huntress charged me, her white coat and husky face morphing into a gigantic hellhound with bared fangs that dripped blood. The scent of sulfur and fire washed over me. I screamed, lifting my hands in preparation to unleash a blockade of Telekinesis.

"Calm down!" Melody shouted, tugging Huntress away before skidding to her knees at my side. "Find the monastery. Find it and stay there until I can get you out again."

"I can't... I can't do it... I can't control anything..." I wheezed, struggling for air.

Melody grabbed my face. "You have to!"

Black eyes stared back at me. I saw sharp fangs slide from under Melody's lips. I watched, horrified, as her skin turned ashen.

"You're one of them! Your face—you're one of them! You want to kill me!" This time, I did squeeze my eyes shut, to block out her evil face.

"What's the matter with him?" Nash came over, Huntress padding close to him. I heard her paws click against the hardwood floor.

"He has a delusional disorder, and it's getting worse. He has pills, but they don't work anymore. I gave him a safety bubble in his mind, to take him out of the delusions, but I… I think he's too far gone to reach it." Melody's words tumbled out.

I peeked through my lids to see Nash glare at the door behind me. "I take it you've seen this before?" he asked.

Melody nodded. "I don't know why they come on, but they seem to be intense panic attacks. He hallucinates, too, which is why he's saying we're out to kill him. These attacks hit him hard. I've seen it once, and that was bad enough."

"What if he's not entirely paranoid?" Nash hurried to the door and flung it open. "You all heard that noise."

"NO! Don't let them in!" I howled, feeling an icy blast on the back of my neck. I didn't have time to deal with it, as the nightmares swamped my vision. The cabin disappeared, leaving me on the mountain, watching my friends hang from their wooden stakes, broken by torture.

"I warned you, Finch." Erebus appeared in front of me. "Now you will watch as they die, all because you did not obey. You had the power to save each and every one, and you failed them, as you failed me. Their deaths are on your shoulders. Not that you will have to live with it for long, but guilt of this magnitude *will* follow you into the hereafter. If it does not make you into a poltergeist."

"No…" I sobbed, hot tears streaming down my cheeks. "I didn't fail… I didn't."

"Too late, Finch." Erebus clicked his fingers and the Purge beasts leapt forward, fangs and claws bared to murder my friends and sister in cold blood. And I couldn't do a single thing about it. I sat there, shaking and sobbing, frozen to the spot. Just the way Erebus wanted. A hellhound's jaws opened to sink into Harley's throat, her head limp, too weak to fight back…

"Crowley, swallow this!" Nash's voice wrenched me out of the nightmare before the hellhound finished the job. Cold glass clinked against my teeth. Luke had his thumb and forefinger pressed against my cheeks, forcing my mouth open. Both men looked like demons, their eyes black, their skin gray. I writhed to escape them, but Melody sat behind me with her arms around my chest, pinning my arms. Tepid, thick liquid spilled down my tongue and into my throat, as Nash clamped his hand over my mouth and nose.

Suffocate or swallow, my gremlins chorused. *We suggest suffocate. They're trying to poison you.*

Next thing I knew, Huntress leapt up. She barked so loud, right in my face, that fear of her overtook everything else. Instinctively, my throat swallowed, swiftly carrying the liquid down into my stomach. I waited for the pain and dissolving of tissue to start. Instead, a cold sensation unfurled in the pit of my belly and climbed into my chest, working into my limbs and up to my brain. Not an unpleasant cold—more like sinking into a chilly pool on the hottest day of the year.

As the cold reached my brain, the gremlins halted in their tracks. I literally felt them stop. The vision of Tartarus evaporated, taking the terror and grief with it. Then, the gremlins themselves dissolved, disappearing into the recesses of my mind. It was almost the same sensation I'd experienced when I first took my pills, so many years ago.

"What... did you do to me?" My gaze shot to Nash, my body still trembling from the aftershock. Hesitantly, Melody let go of me.

Nash sank back on his haunches. "I've got a pantry of magical potions I collected on my global travels. What I gave you was a special blend, learned from a page torn from an ancient book when my ancestors fled their homeland." He gestured to a cupboard door, which had been flung open while I was in Tartarus. "They called it Medela; it helps with mental difficulties. It'll keep the nightmares away, and your mind clear, as long as you take it. It's not a cure, but it's better than what you've had."

"What?" My mouth dropped. He didn't know that I knew he had Primus Anglicus blood. Which meant this was an Atlantean recipe, torn from an Atlantean book. A medicine that had been out of my reach, unknown by magical physicians. And I'd seen my fair share.

"It means you won't need those pills ever again, once you learn to brew your own. I'll teach you," he replied kindly. "You took a heck of a turn there, pal. Nobody should have to go through that."

"Medela? That sounds so whimsical." Melody looked awestruck.

Nash nodded. "It's got benefits, but I'm not sure about it being whimsical. Like I said, it only seems to work on mental afflictions. There might've been a companion recipe to help with physical illness, on a different page, but my ancestors only stole the one, so we'll never know."

"And you'll teach me to make it?" I rubbed my arms to usher away the chill.

"I said so, didn't I?" Nash replied.

"And the ingredients are here? Easy to find?" I didn't want to give away what I knew of Nash's heritage.

Nash frowned. "They can be, yes. The issues that cause your attacks won't ever truly go away, because they're part of you. But you have a surefire way to control them with Medela."

Screw you, gremlins! I am Gizmo, I have my red Ferrari, and I've just Rambo-ed your asses back into the shadows you crawled out of, you slimy creeps! No one's feeding you after midnight anymore! I could've punched the air. I would have, if I wasn't petrified of Huntress savaging off a hand thinking I'd gone into panicked, demon-seeing mode again.

"Thank you, Nash. I mean it… thank you," I gushed. If ever there was a time for gushing, this was it.

"Don't mention it. I can tell you're a decent guy, Crowley." Nash smirked. "I wouldn't want you thinking all I do is sit on my ass and look out for myself."

Ah, crap... He thought I was a good egg, while I was full-on lying about who I was and why I was here. Still, at least the gremlins weren't having a dig and making me feel a million times worse with their endless chatter. Nothing but blissful silence filled this old gourd. Frankly, I wanted to bathe in that Medela stuff.

"Do you feel better?" Melody craned her head around my shoulder to look at me.

I chuckled. "A lot better, yeah, so it was probably good you stopped the bear hug when you did, or Luke's face would definitely end up staying that way."

"What?" Melody glanced up at Luke, who shifted uncomfortably. Her cheeks turned beet red. "I just didn't want you hurting yourself."

"I appreciate it," I replied. "Though I'm not the biggest fan of physical contact. Well, unless it's coming from Tobe."

Melody's embarrassment faded. "I totally understand why you all love his hugs now. He's so… fluffy!"

"Yeah, well, don't turn him into one of your jackets." It felt good to joke.

"I wouldn't!" she protested.

"Don't, you'll make her self-conscious," Luke chided, apparently recovered from his green-eyed monster attack.

I raised my hands in mock surrender. "Hey, I've just been swarmed by dark mind stuff. I need to make sure my humor synapses are still firing on all cylinders."

"Doesn't look like they took any damage," Nash said, ruffling Huntress's fur.

"If he had any in the first place," Luke added wryly.

The door burst inward.

"Looks like you're having a lovely get-together. What a shame I missed the invite."

Davin stood in the doorway, smug as ever. Before anyone could move, he launched a small cloth pouch at Huntress. It struck her face and exploded into a blinding, acrid swell of thick green smoke that threatened to choke us all.

THIRTY-THREE

Finch

For the love of Kevin Bacon! Davin had followed us here, likely using a tracing spell like Melody had. Either that, or he'd been keeping tabs on me somehow. He'd shown up one too many times for it to be coincidence. Every time he popped up, the element of shock ebbed. In fact, I would have been surprised if he hadn't shown up.

Choking on the bitter smoke, I released Air from my palms, sweeping the dense green fog away as fast as possible. Huntress wheezed and spluttered, her limbs stiff and her body shaking.

"Davin?" Nash stepped forward, his gaze flitting between that stuck-up dingleberry and his suffering Familiar. Recognition washed across the Sanguine's face. Cold, bitter recognition.

"Long time, no see." Davin chuckled, launching a blast of Telekinesis that sent us all flying backward.

My hands twisted wildly, conjuring four pockets of Air in rapid succession. The first caught Melody before she careened into a table full of knives, the second missed Luke completely, and the third buffered the collision between Nash, Huntress, and the wall. I missed my own and slammed into the kitchen counter, which brought pots and pans crashing down onto my head.

I jumped up, ignoring my dizziness. Nash joined me in the center of the cabin, where I cast him a side-eye. "You two know each other?"

Nash attacked with a volley of fireballs, which Davin ducked effortlessly. "You remember those hunters I told you about?"

I added a lasso of Telekinesis to the fight, grasping Davin around the ankles and yanking him to the floor. "Yeah, I remember."

"Well, you're looking at the worst of them." Nash sidestepped a tendril of Telekinesis as Davin hauled his ass back up, snatching a clutch of knives from the nearest workbench. He hurled them full speed at Davin's head. The British donkey managed to duck two while Telekinesis whipped the last two away, letting them *thunk* harmlessly into the wall.

Luke launched himself in front of Melody. Using his Magneton abilities, he lifted the knives from the workbenches and the metal pots from the kitchen, heaving them all at Davin. Davin's eyes widened; he sent up a wall of Telekinesis to protect himself from the onslaught. One knife slipped through, grazing Davin's shoulder before disappearing into the snowy world beyond.

"There's no need for battle, Nash." Davin dusted off his fancy suit jacket, safe behind his protective shield. "I have a djinn ready and waiting to break that curse. Come willingly, and nobody suffers."

"I'd rather eat squirrel guts!" Nash snarled, unleashing a powerful torrent of Fire. Huntress sprinted alongside the twisting flames, launching herself at Davin's neck. Somehow, she sailed through the Telekinesis shield, her jaws snapping.

But Davin was ready for her. With a flick of his wrist, the husky arched backward through the air. She landed on all fours, skidding back like a ninja, her claws raking the floorboards.

"I've always been more of a cat person." Davin smirked, raising his palms to strike.

Of course you have. No offense to cat lovers, but I'd never seen an evil person choose a dog over a cat. After all, the pet matched the owner, and cats could be egotistical little assholes.

Huntress stalked backward, planting herself in front of Melody. It gave Luke some backup, though he wasn't doing too badly with his Magneton abilities. Another flurry of knives flew, keeping Davin on his toes as he tried to fling them away.

"Listen here, Calvert. I have no intention of leaving without you and your blood, so you might as well make things easy. Do you want their blood on your hands, as well?" Davin showed signs of frustration, running a hand through his oily mop.

"I told you last time, and I'll tell you again: go to hell," Nash shot back, adding a massive ball of Fire to underscore his point. Davin sidestepped, the fireball searing close by his face.

Davin's eyes narrowed. "I think you should reconsider."

"Why do you think I put this curse on myself in the first place?" Nash spat as I lashed everything I had at Davin: Fire, Air, Earth, and Water, with a hint of Telekinesis to really pack a punch. It forced Davin to dart outside and use the wall for cover to avoid a five-point obliteration.

"You did that because of Davin?" I asked, as Luke joined us. Huntress had taken up the reins of Librarian protector, crouched and prepared to spring if necessary.

Nash's mouth twisted up. "He's been hunting me a long time. He's the reason I hide. He's my unfinished business."

"You and me both." I sighed.

"You?" Nash sounded confused. "What beef do you have with him?"

I sent a snake of Telekinesis to pull Davin back into the room. "It's a long story. If we survive, I'll tell you everything."

We might have been evenly matched, the three of us against Davin. But Davin still had tricks up his sleeve. As he staggered back into the cabin, tugged by my Telekinesis, he started lobbing smoky pouches at us. They exploded on the ground, releasing thick masses of fog that I couldn't sweep away fast enough. Davin disappeared in the haze. Not a comforting feeling. I couldn't see Nash or Luke anymore, either.

Bursts of light cut through the smoke, like we were in a war movie. Tremors shuddered through the floor. I shot back, aiming my magic at the epicenter of the blasts, but if I managed to hit Davin, I had no idea. We were in the dark, literally.

"Nash. All you have to do is come with me, and we can stop this nonsense!" Davin's voice echoed through the fog.

Two blasts went off simultaneously—one from my Fire, one from Nash's. At least, that was my guess. Luke only had Magneton abilities, and if he used them, me and Nash might've ended up looking like porcupines.

"Go to hell, Davin!" Nash roared.

"Have it your way." Another flash burst through the haze, followed by a howl of pain. It sounded like—

"Luke! What's happened? Luke, are you all right? Luke!" Melody screamed. An agonized groan answered. I heard the scuffle of feet and paws on the floorboards and cursed under my breath.

"Melody, stay back!" I yelled, but the scuffling continued.

"Luke! Where are you?" she called hopelessly.

A bark splintered the air, followed by muffled sobs. Huntress had found Luke, by the sounds of it, and it didn't sound good. But I didn't have time to dwell on it, as something snagged my leg and pulled me down. I hit the deck with a hefty thud, my back smacking the floor and knocking the wind right out of me. I rolled away immediately. A cold laugh hissed through the fog.

Davin's voice followed. "I will kill them all, Nash. It is your choice."

"You don't seem to hear me, Davin. I'd plunge my own knife into my chest rather than let you take my blood!" Nash bellowed back, though I had no clue where he was. His voice echoed all around, the smoke confusing my bearings.

"Now, don't do that until I've lifted your curse. That would be foolish," Davin replied. I rose to my hands and knees, peering underneath the smoke to see if I could catch a glimpse of feet—Davin's shiny brogues stood out a mile off. But even near the ground, the smoke rolled thick and impenetrable, and no amount of Air-wafting could dissipate it. There was too much of the stuff. It made it hard to breathe.

A violent detonation of Telekinesis struck my face and sent me sprawling. Nash grunted nearby, and then came the scrabble of someone trying to make their way across the floor. Melody, presumably, trying to find her way back to Luke, if that blast had separated them. Huntress barked again, giving Melody a direction to follow.

Purple threads slithered through the fog. Necromantic magic. I built a wall of Telekinesis to defend myself, but the purple threads crept through. More explosions of fire ricocheted in the smoke, but it was impossible to hit a target you couldn't see. Especially one as sneaky as Davin.

One of the violet threads touched my upraised palm, and a brutal jab of icy energy shot through my arm. It stole the breath from my lungs, and my throat strained for air. My limbs sagged and everything slowed, my bones aching as if I'd just been diagnosed with arthritis.

My hands turned a sickly gray-blue color, and liver spots speckled my skin. Davin was trying to kill us by decaying our cells—speeding up the aging process. A new skill he'd evidently learned between this meeting and our last one. Through the fog came the wheezing of strained breaths and panicked gasps. Davin had saved the best for last, and we couldn't fight it.

"Last chance, Nash. I won't kill you, but I will kill the others." Davin laughed bitterly. "I've wanted to put an end to Finch for a long time."

"Finch? Who's Finch?" Nash rasped.

Davin cackled louder. "Oh dear, it looks like someone has been telling porky pies. What name did he give you, hmm? Not that it matters. He'll be dead in minutes."

I couldn't respond. A zombie groan was all I could muster. The gray-blue skin and liver spots had rapidly spread, and everything ached. I felt my cells dying, one by one, my heart slowing to a perilously snail-like pace. Luke and Melody were likely in the same predicament. Nash, too, though he'd get out of this alive. Until Davin finished with him.

Davin wanted him for the same reason Erebus did. No PhD required. The details about why were as fuzzy as Erebus's details, but they'd entered the same race and were fighting to cross the finish line first. Perhaps Davin wanted to piss Erebus off. Perhaps he had his own reasons. Either way, once again, Davin had ruined Erebus's plans. And we would die for it.

"Clock is ticking, Nash," Davin said. "You volunteer, and I release them. If you don't, I kill them, and I take you. It is very simple."

"Why would I trust a word from your mouth?" Nash shouted. "You'll just kill them anyway."

"Maybe you caught me in a generous mood." I could just picture Davin puffing his chest, smug that he had what he wanted, right there in the palm of his hand.

"You just said you wanted to kill Finch. If he's the Finch I think he is, you said it yourself—you've wanted him dead a long time. Makes sense, considering he killed his mother, your Ryann." Nash's breath rattled dangerously. Well, the jig on me was definitely up. At least I wouldn't have long to bathe in the shame of lying.

"Fine, I'll spare the other two, and that dog of yours," Davin countered. "Finch doesn't get a free pass, I'm afraid."

Bright light flooded the house. Pure white energy pulsed through the fog, dissolving it instantaneously. A weird flapping sound came through the thrum of intense power—like rustling feathers complete with a rush of warm air. At first, I thought Davin had done something, until I heard him cry out in pain. I looked around, now that I could finally see, and caught a glimpse of Davin's hands shooting up to cover his eyes. This light hadn't come from him.

Lux... It had to be her. White light, powerful as hell, burning the eyes of a Necromancer—who else had that sort of oomph? But I couldn't shout that from the rooftops. She wouldn't take kindly to me spreading her name around. Children of Chaos weren't supposed to involve themselves in the mortal realm.

Well, well, aren't you a little renegade? I had no problem with that. I just wondered what this rescue would cost me.

THIRTY-FOUR

Finch

Huntress barked furiously as she bounded toward the open door. Davin staggered around the cabin, groaning and covering his blinded eyes. He left a gap for us to slip through. Lux had given us a helping hand; we couldn't waste it. I checked my arms, but the gray skin and liver spots had vanished. Our angel of mercy must've broken the link between Davin's magic and our decaying cells.

"Nash, help me with Luke!" I raced for the slumped bodyguard, my body young and energized again. Melody knelt beside him, cradling him, but she let go as we came to his aid. Nash tugged Luke's arm over his shoulder, and I took the other.

Between us, we hauled Captain Beefcake, who weighed a ton, toward the door where Huntress stood guard. She'd stopped barking, no doubt realizing the sound gave away her location. Melody hurried after us, and the four of us edged through the entryway into the sting of the Manitoban winds. I glanced back, watching Davin struggle. His arms flailed, giving me a glimpse of his unseeing eyes; a spiderweb of red veins branched from the centers.

What the hell did you do, Lux? It looked like she had actually burned his eyes. His grunts of pain cemented the notion. Why had she suddenly decided to help? Not that I minded, but the last time I'd seen her, she'd chucked me out of the room on my ass and promised to flay me if I told anyone that we'd spoken. That wasn't exactly the basis for a shiny new friendship.

"We need to get into the woods, use trees as cover," Nash instructed, panting heavily. His legs buckled for a moment, his face paling as he caught himself.

"Are you okay?" I eyed him with concern.

He winced. "It's the curse. I don't have the strength I used to."

"Let me take him. You worry about yourself. Same to you, Melody." I wrapped a strand of Telekinesis around Luke's waist and hoisted him up. His body floated as I dragged him along. He still weighed a ton, but it felt like carrying someone through water—much more manageable.

"Will he be all right?" Melody stayed close as we ran for the trees, crashing through the undergrowth. Davin might've been blinded, but we were making a racket. And I had no idea how long he might stay blind. Lux really would've broken major rules by leaving him that way.

I shrugged, my arm shaking under the strain of keeping Luke airborne. "He won't be if we stay here."

"We need to go back to my house. Davin can't follow us there," Melody instructed as she trailed Huntress through the ominous forest, the boughs shaking as we passed. Most of the pines were too densely foliaged, if that was a word, to even attempt a chalk door. But Huntress seemed to know where she was going.

The husky trotted across the snow, her head turning back occasionally to keep a blue eye on Nash. He kept pace as best he could, but I heard his every shallow breath. That curse was doing a number on him. All that pain, just to keep Davin at bay.

Huntress made for the nearest trunk and stopped, then nosed the wood. Melody ran to the dog and whipped out a stick of charmed chalk. I had mine, but I also had my hands full with her lover-boy. Behind us, from the cabin, I heard an almighty howl and a couple choice expletives—at least, they sounded like expletives, but they were oh-so-British: "Bollocks, bollocks, bollocks! You despicable blighter! Come back, you buggers! I am not done with you! Tossers, the lot of you!"

"Draw!" I urged, struggling to keep Luke afloat.

Melody scratched a rectangle into the trunk before whispering the *Aperi Si Ostium* spell. The lines fizzed and burned into the tree, creating the doorway that would get us out of Dodge. She yanked the handle and wrenched it open, leaping through first, with Huntress, Nash, Luke, and me darting in after. I brought up the rear and slammed the door the moment we were in the spooky embrace of the Winchester House. I guessed the house didn't have the same security restrictions for Melody, with her being a Winchester and all. She'd brought us right into the belly of it.

Trembling, I dropped Luke like a sack of spuds and sank onto my haunches. Melody knelt beside him, pulling him into her lap as his eyes fluttered open in confusion. Across the hall, Nash collapsed on his backside, gasping as if he'd spent a few minutes in a sleeper hold. Huntress ran to him and began nudging his hand.

"That was close." I tipped my head back, feeling my heart rate return to normal.

"A little too close." Nash fixed his gaze on me. "Finch, I presume?"

I flashed an apologetic smile. "Yeah... sorry about that. People make kneejerk assumptions after they hear my name."

"I'd be pissed if you hadn't saved my ass back there." Nash stretched his legs. "Did the rest of you start aging rapidly, or just me?"

"It was all of us," Melody replied. "A rather unpleasant branch of Necromantic magic. Everyone assumes that Necromancy is for resurrection, but it can actually be used in reverse if the Necromancer is powerful."

"Can you find anything about it in that mind palace of yours?" I asked.

Her expression hardened. "I'm researching as we speak. Nobody hurts my Luke and gets away with it."

Davin had managed to ignite the rage of the sweetest person I'd ever encountered. Maybe Melody wasn't all sugar and spice after all. Right now, it looked like she wouldn't have batted an eye at sugar and spicing the life out of Davin Doncaster. Clearly, getting on the Librarian's bad side was a *very* unhealthy idea. Knowledge was power, and Melody had it by the motherload.

"Finch?" A voice shivered out of a nearby corridor. My favorite voice.

My eyes shot up. "Ryann?"

THIRTY-FIVE

Finch

"Don't get mad." Melody spoke first, taking me by surprise. "I asked Ryann to come after we followed you to Gatsby's, in case we needed help. This is the safest place to be, after all. My family and I can chalk-door into here because of who we are, but nobody else can, and drama tends to... uh, follow you around. I figured I should have someone waiting in case anything got hairy."

"That light must've blown out my brain, because that doesn't make an ounce of sense," I replied, looking between the women as Melody crossed the room to join her. Luke had opened his eyes, which probably meant he was out of the woods. Literally and figuratively.

Ryann frowned. "Which part?"

Man, it's good to see you again. Had my gremlins still been rampaging, just one gaze at her would've soothed the beasties.

"Where do I begin?" I lifted a finger per point, though I only had one. "Let's start with how you got in touch with Ryann. Nice and simple, while I wrap my head around her being here."

"Cell phones, Finch." Ryann smiled, eyes twinkling with relief. Was she happy to see me, too? I hoped so. She wasn't giving me any signals to the contrary.

Melody nodded. "I swiped her number from your phone while you drew the map. You know, in case of emergency. In fact, she was the one who told us you'd gone somewhere—I didn't want to tell you that in case you worried. Anyway, she was held up in a meeting, so she asked us to go and keep an eye on you. After you portaled, I texted her to let her know we were following you and told her to wait here for us in case things went south. Which they did."

"No kidding." I lowered my gaze, realizing I'd stared at Ryann too long. "But how did you even get here, Ryann? Last time I checked, you weren't a magical."

She smiled. "Fortunately for me, I know plenty of gifted individuals. Once Melody texted me to let me know what was going on, I got a message from her mom, giving me the directions to this place, plus instructions on how to get in once I got here. I asked a friend—don't worry, you don't know them—to open a mirror to the San Jose Coven for me, pretended I was on some business, and got a cab the rest of the way here. Simple."

"Nah, seems like a lot of hassle," I muttered. "And, though I realize how dumb it sounds after what just went down, Melody, I'm a little peeved you put me on some kind of security watch. What if you'd been... uh... seen?" I held back the E-word, with Nash listening in.

"He has a point," Melody said. "If we hadn't followed, Davin might not have found Nash... or you, for that matter."

Ryann raised a hand. "Did I hear you right? Davin?"

"Oh yeah... the British Weeble wobbled back up again." I clenched my jaw. If Davin kept invading my life, I'd end up cracking a tooth. "We barely escaped, as per usual."

"Then I'm even happier that you're okay." She grazed her bottom lip with her teeth. "All of you."

I'll take it. I resisted the urge to pull her into a hug.

Melody sidled up to me and whispered, "I truly am sorry for not telling you, but I thought you could use a sight for sore eyes after your mission. I didn't realize it would get that hairy, but on the bright side, there's no safer place for Ryann."

"Yeah, well back-pedaled there, Melody," I replied, but I couldn't stay mad. Those squishable cheeks were too damn adorable. And her earnest eyes spoke of eagerly sought forgiveness.

"Are you sure Davin can't come here?" Ryann's face darkened. Her history with him was almost as grim as mine. I hated to think about the awful things he'd done to her and the Smiths. It burned inside me, even now. Another reason on a long list of reasons to guillotine him repeatedly.

Melody smiled reassuringly. "The magic here is powerful—it's one of the greatest strongholds in the United States. The spirits won't let him cross the threshold."

"S-spirits?" Ryann's mouth gaped. "You mean, the stories are real?"

"They sure are. Haven't you met any yet? They're usually so welcoming." I glanced around, expecting Mary Foster to come screaming from the walls. She wasn't a screamer—at least, she hadn't been with me—but it would have made a hilarious intro. And I could have used a laugh.

"I probably should've mentioned that." Melody shuffled awkwardly. "But, if none have come to say hello, then it likely means they're not that interested in you. They don't always involve themselves with visitors; it depends on how they're feeling."

Ryann looked slightly disappointed. "Oh."

Don't worry, there's at least one person in this house who's interested in you.

"Well, aren't you going to introduce me?" Ryann cleared her throat and gestured toward Nash, who had slung one arm around Huntress's neck. He seemed to be gaining strength from her somehow. No doubt through that Familiar bond they shared.

Nash heaved himself to his feet and walked toward Ryann. "The name's Nash Calvert. I'm here to think about giving up some blood to help a friend of these guys, but I haven't decided yet. So, he's probably a friend of yours, too?"

"Oh, you mean—" Ryann started to speak, but I cut her off. I couldn't have her give the game away unwittingly. And she had no clue what we were talking about. Time for another sterling performance from the one and only Finch Merlin.

"Raffe, yeah." I gave her a telling look, bordering on manic. "Melody might not have had time to tell you, but we got a lead on his curse. We need Nash's super-rare Sanguine blood to separate Raffe and Kadar, so everyone gets to live their own lives and go home happy."

Ryann glanced at Melody, who nodded effusively, like a bobble-head. Luke added a halfhearted thumbs-up.

"You remember what I texted you?" Melody pressed, her voice strangled by the charade. She might've been a lot of things, but a liar wasn't one of them. Luke was way better. He had the right amount of nonchalance... or maybe it was wooziness, considering the blow to his head. I could see the wound, now that we had no smoke and panic to contend with. A big bruise was blooming across his temple.

"About Raffe?" Ryann looked back at me.

I shrugged. "Hey, I don't know what she texted you. I just know that I went to get Nash's blood for Raffe, and these two Muppets showed up as the cavalry."

Ryann's lip twitched into a half-smile. Jiminy H. Christmas, I loved that smile. "Yeah, I remember. I must've gotten confused. I thought she meant Levi and Zalaam—I didn't realize she meant Raffe and Kadar, though that makes a lot more sense now that I think about it."

This is why I adore you. Two seconds, and she'd grasped that we were trying to skirt around the Erebus issue. She probably had no idea why, but I could tell her later, sans Nash. He didn't need another reason to doubt me, and I'd already done a stellar job of making things screwy by telling him I was Wade Crowley.

"I thought I was here to help the Levi guy?" Nash tilted his head, and Huntress copied.

I thought fast. "You are, the younger one. There are two Levis—Leonidas and Raffe. Raffe's our friend, and he's the one who wants to be free. Leonidas seems quite happy shackled to *his* djinn, but that's probably because his doesn't try to kill him." The explanation sounded stilted, but I hoped Nash wouldn't pick up on it.

"That rings a bell." Nash ruffled Huntress's fur. "The Levi curse—that's what you were telling me about, isn't it? I think I've heard of it."

"Exactly." My palms had gone as clammy as an oiled-up blobfish. "I was telling you about it before Davin came in, hex pouches blazing. You know, the whole 'it affects generations' shebang."

"And you told me you were Wade Crowley because you didn't want me making assumptions about you?" Nash squinted, scrutinizing me. "You know, since you're Katherine Shipton's son."

Ah, holy crap... Fear glided up my throat, but I swallowed it. Perhaps *I* was the one jumping to conclusions. Nash had, for all intents and purposes, been a hermit for the past few years. He'd said he dipped his toe into the media here and there, but what if he hadn't heard the part about my deal with Erebus to kill my mother? Journalists had tossed around a dozen theories, and they'd never confirmed anything. And Nash hadn't had much opportunity to shoot the Katherine breeze with random folks who *did* know the truth. So, maybe he genuinely had no idea that, these days, Finch and Erebus went hand in hand.

"I go by Merlin now," I replied, keeping it cool. "But yeah, being squeezed out of that woman tends to give people the wrong impression, though I *did* kill her. And I didn't want you booting us out on our asses before we had the chance to speak properly."

"How come you know about Finch?" Melody still sounded strangled.

Nash shrugged. "I scan online magical feeds from time to time. Names of dangerous criminals, potential hunters—I learn whatever I can from the dark web, so I can make a run for it if I find anyone discussing me or my blood. I found my way onto this cult chatroom, and your name and picture popped up. That must've been about a year ago, but you were on a hit list because you murdered your mother. Since you're still breathing, I'm guessing they didn't catch up to you."

"The Cult of Eris, you mean?" Ryann stepped in, her tone protective.

"Yeah, that's the one." Nash grunted. "Nasty business, but the chatroom disappeared a month later. No trace of it anywhere."

Ryann scowled. "That's because my sister and Wade Crowley have worked nonstop to take down the remaining members of the Cult of Eris."

"Would the real Wade Crowley please stand up?" My joke fell flat, and Ryann gave me a cursory eyeroll for my troubles.

"Most of them are behind bars now, and the rest made deals for their freedom by giving up intel," she continued.

"Which is probably why the chatroom disappeared," Melody

agreed. "They would've sensed their time was up and wanted to erase any evidence, in case they were put on trial. Plotting to kill a national hero certainly wouldn't have done them any favors."

I put a dramatic hand to my heart. "Melody, you've got to stop the flattery, or my head won't fit through the door. I'm no hero."

"Looks like you know something of the situation I'm in, Finch." Nash gave me an appreciative smile, apparently letting me off the hook. "You were pursued; I was pursued. But at least I knew about it. Hey, if I'd known you then, I'd have given you a heads-up, though it looks like you got lucky in the end."

"As if I didn't worry enough about you," Ryann murmured.

My insides went gooey, but I couldn't overanalyze her comment right now. I had too many plates spinning. Davin couldn't get into the Winchester House, which meant I could stow his plate for a moment. And I couldn't deal with Lux until she slunk back into my life, so I could set that plate down too. Okay, so maybe I didn't have that many plates spinning. I only had one actually up in the air. The most important one, for now: getting this curse off Nash, drawing his blood, stowing him somewhere safe, and delivering the goods to the E-man.

And if I dropped this plate, the rest would smash too.

THIRTY-SIX

Finch

Later that night, nestled in the creepy bosom of the Winchester House, our misfit band of merry weirdos reeled from everything that had happened. Namely, Davin, Nash, and the tangled web of lies that could strangle us at any moment. Or, rather, me.

We'd moved to the kitchen. Brighter and less oppressive in décor, it wasn't quite as eerie as the rest of the house, despite the spirits shuffling around on a loop of servitude. Ryann stared at them, half petrified, half curious. Not surprising, since they were her first brush with ghoulies.

Luke lay on a couch by the window, in the "bar" region of the kitchen. Melody perched beside him, armed with magical potions aplenty for his head wound. Nash had sourced them from the Winchester storeroom, mixing vials and serums to speed the healing process. Ironic, considering he couldn't do the same for himself. He'd also rustled up something for me and walked me through the method of making more Medela to keep the gremlins at bay. I hadn't needed another dose yet, even with the added panic of Davin's sudden arrival at the cabin. It looked like this Atlantean concoction had a lot more staying power than my old pills.

"They look cozy." Nash tipped his bottle of cider at the sweet couch scene. I sat at the table with the wannabe lumberjack, nursing my own cider. "Anything between them? Or is it purely professional?"

I shrugged. "Beats me. Luke's besotted with her, but... she's like *War and Peace*."

"Huh?"

"Hard to read."

He burst out laughing, startling me so badly I almost fell off my chair. "You're funny, Finch. That one got me." Huntress nuzzled his hand. "Yeah, I think I agree with you, H."

"You talk to the dog?" I stared at the fluffy pup.

"Of course. She and I are connected, here." He tapped his forehead. "And she thinks there's more to Melody's feelings than meets the eye. H thinks she's fighting her emotions, and you know dogs—they sense emotions almost as well as Empaths."

I frowned at Luke and Melody. Sure enough, they had a glow about them. Luke gazed adoringly into Melody's eyes while she fixed him up, dabbing away the crusted blood with a gentle touch. All the while, *she* gazed down into *his* eyes, a contented smile on her lips. It looked as though they weren't even aware of us anymore. They were in a bubble of their own, progressing to tentative touches—a heart-fluttering brush of the fingertips and the odd graze of Melody's leg against Luke's side as she shifted position.

But it stopped there. No chaste kisses, no handholding, nothing that would've made Nash and me stare desperately into our bottles. They might've been in a world of their own, but they were shackled by this world's duties. Luke to his professional capacity as bodyguard, and Melody to her role as Librarian, which forbade romantic relationships. And if she'd seen Odette's memories, she knew how breaking those rules could turn out—how her heart would break if anything happened to him, and that they stood to lose something real.

"It's banned, right?" Nash brought me out of my sad thoughts.

"What?"

"Relationships for Librarians." He picked at the bottle's label.

I shook my head. "I reckon there are a fair few who've broken those rules, but they're not here. That speaks volumes."

"You think she's worried about a relationship putting Luke in danger?"

Ryann entered at that moment, with bittersweet timing.

"I think anyone in love worries that they'll end up endangering the person they love," I said, watching her walk to the couch with an armful of bandages. "It gets worse if you have some kind of target on your back. Anyone who wants to get to you can use the person you love as leverage. That ups the risk, and Melody's seen enough and knows enough to put anyone off."

"Geez, Finch, you only had one bottle." Nash grinned, but sympathy shone in his eyes. Did he understand? Had he figured out my feelings for Ryann? I tried my best to keep it discreet, but people had a habit of calling me on it regardless.

A house ghost dressed as a Civil War-era nurse drifted through a wall and floated up behind Ryann, who'd just bent to set the bandages on the side table. Ryann stood and turned to leave Luke and Melody to it. A shriek escaped her throat as she came face-to-face with Nursie, who put her hands on her hips.

"Are you medically trained?" the nurse asked. "If you aren't, you shouldn't meddle."

Ryann turned white as a sheet. "I-I-I... you're a... ghost!"

"Evidently, you have no training whatsoever. I would have thought

it blatantly obvious, from a biological perspective, that I am a ghost."
Nursie rolled her eyes. "We prefer 'spirit' or 'specter,' but you are new
here, so you may be forgiven. Now, stand aside and let the professionals attend Mr. Prescott before you cause a hemorrhage."

"It's all right, Ryann." Melody took her hand. "You get used to it."

Ryann stared in abject horror. "I don't think I will."

"Honestly, you breathers are so terrified of death," Nursie tutted.
"Well, take a good look, sweetheart, because this is where you're
headed. And if you insist on helping Mr. Prescott, warm water and
laudanum would be greatly appreciated."

"We don't give people laudanum anymore, Diana," Melody said
softly.

Diana sighed. "Whatever you have, then. You are magical beings—
you must have something in your wizard pantries."

"We've got everything we need here, Diana. But if we need your
help, we'll call you." Melody defused the situation skillfully. With only
a hint of huffiness, Diana floated across the kitchen and disappeared
into the wall.

"Maybe I've been in the woods too long, but I don't find these
spooks weird at all," Nash said, though Huntress didn't share his
ambivalence. Every time a spirit drifted in and out, she followed them
with her eyes, hackles raised.

I frowned. "You don't?"

"It's comforting. With this curse on me, my clock is ticking down
faster than it would otherwise. I guess it's nice to know there's something after, you know?" He stroked Huntress's ears as she let out a soft
whine.

"There's a lot more after this life," I replied. "Turns out, heaven
exists. Or something like it. An... old friend brought my dad back for
a while. Plucked him right out of the afterlife back to Earth."

Nash's expression turned cold. "An old friend? Surely not Davin."

"No, a man named Alton Waterhouse." That was partially true, at least. "He was an incredible Necromancer, but he's dead now."

"Oh… I'm sorry to hear that." Nash relaxed. "Being a Necromancer, did he fear death?"

I tapped my bottle with my fingernails. "You know, I don't know. I was out of it at the time, but I don't think he wanted to go, if that's what you mean. Given the choice, he'd have chosen to live."

"And that's what you think I should do?"

"I do, as it turns out," I replied. "Not just because I need your blood to help my friend. I think every human wants to survive. It's our base instinct. I think you deserve to live the life you were meant to have, instead of trading it for partial safety. That's not a life at all—that's waiting in limbo until the timer runs out."

"You know something, Finch? You talk a good talk, and I think your heart is in the right place, but I get this feeling that trouble likes to follow you around." Nash leaned forward in his seat. "Davin wouldn't have found me if it weren't for you. You and your friends brought him to my door. And that sticks in my throat real bad, pal."

I sighed. "Hey, I'm not disagreeing with you on the Davin thing, and I can't even disagree with you on the trouble thing. But he would've come for you sooner or later. You clearly know him, so you know that he's a resourceful son of a gun. If he wanted you, he'd have ransacked the globe to find you, pulling every string he had. You know that's true."

Huntress nosed his hand, her ears pricked as she listened.

"I could've outrun him," Nash said stubbornly.

"Yeah, maybe. But how long are you willing to keep running? Your legs must be pretty tired by now." I gave a hint of a smile. "If he's who you're running from, who you put this curse on yourself for, then isn't it time you stop and face the music? If you don't, you'll keep playing musical chairs until he finally gets what he wants. You owe it to yourself, and Huntress, to try something different."

"I've tried it all, Finch." Nash hung his head. Huntress sat back on her hindquarters.

"Come on, man. At full power, with this curse gone, you've got the best shot at ending Davin that you've ever had." I pulled out all my persuasive stops.

Ryann made me jump by resting her hands on my shoulders. I hadn't seen her approach. I expected her to remove her hands when she spoke, but she didn't. She left them there, searing my skin. "And do you want to know why you've got the best shot you've ever had?"

Nash mustered a wry laugh. "Sure. Why?"

"Because you've got our help, and we all hate Davin as much as you. Plus, you've got Finch on your side. A guy who'll do anything to help someone in need, no matter the stakes. Have you ever had that before?" she replied.

"No… I guess not." Nash took a long sip of his drink. "I've always tried to do it alone."

"Then you and Finch have more in common than I thought." Ryann gave my shoulders a squeeze, nearly making my heart explode out of its bone cage. "But when it comes to righting wrongs, he won't stop until he makes it happen. I've seen him in action. I've seen his dedication to his missions. You scratch his back, he'll scratch yours. And, together, we might finally get that British weasel to shuffle off his mortal coil for good."

I made myself look at her. *Be cool, Finch.* "Since when do you paraphrase Shakespeare?" *Or not…*

"I dabble," she replied, smiling.

Nash looked down at Huntress, and their eyes glittered with

strange white shards. It appeared they were having a little tête-á-tête. I had no idea what they were saying—maybe deciding which meaty treats they preferred, or whether they would rather chase a ball over a frisbee. All I could do was sit and try not to die of awkwardness while Ryann touched me.

Nash broke the silence. "I said you talked a good talk, Finch, but Ryann talks a better one. A character reference does a lot."

"Does that mean—?" I hardly dared to say it.

"That I'll let you take this curse off me and use my blood to help your friend? Yeah, it does." He lifted his bottle. "Don't make me regret this."

I lifted mine. "I won't. I swear."

"Then we've got a deal." He clinked his drink against mine. "Consider this me scratching your back, as long as you promise to scratch mine."

"Deal." My gut churned, knowing I had pulled him into this on a lie. But I had no choice. And I'd meant what I said about assisting with his Davin problem, which alleviated a tiny smidgen of the guilt. I wanted that slippery hobgoblin dead as much as anyone, and if I could help a fellow misfit out and set him free, all the better.

"So, when do we start?" Nash shifted in his chair. "Where's your buddy?"

I took out my phone. "Glad you reminded me." I dialed Raffe's number and waited. He hadn't been answering, but I hoped that had more to do with Canadian phone service than Raffe going AWOL. He picked up on the third ring.

"Finch?"

"Raffe! Thank Chaos!"

"I've been trying to call you. Where've you been?" He sounded a little miffed.

"Sorry about that. I had to take a little trip up north, and apparently Canada doesn't have 4G yet." I flashed a comical eyeroll at Nash.

"Canada? Why were you in Canada?" Raffe replied.

"I found what we were looking for, and we're ready to take the next step." I kept it vague, but not so vague that Raffe would think I'd lost my marbles. "The key to unlocking our problem has agreed to help us. He's waiting as we speak, so where are you?"

Raffe paused. "You found the key?"

"I did indeed." Man, was I glad I hadn't put this thing on speaker.

"Well, we're on our way back to San Diego. Should we meet you there?"

I shook my head, though he couldn't see me. "No, we're at the Winchester House, waiting on you. Come here instead."

"Waiting on me? Why are you waiting on me?" The poor guy sounded confused.

"It'll all make sense once you're here, and you're going to be thrilled. It'll all be over soon, my friend." I grinned at Nash, giving it the full Meryl Streep treatment. *Aren't I such a wonderful friend? Nope... I suck.* But I sucked out of necessity. Bigger personal fish to fry, and all that. As long as Huntress didn't maul me if the truth came out, I'd count this as a win.

Raffe sighed. "Okay, we'll be there as soon as we can."

"See you soon, *mi amigo!*"

"Yeah... uh, see you soon." Raffe hung up, but I pretended to stay on the line a minute longer.

"What? You're breaking up." I put on a show of straining to hear him. "Yeah, the Sanguine agreed to help you. No, I promise. As soon as you get here, we'll pluck that djinn right out of you, and the two of you will be free. I know... yeah, I know you've gotten your hopes up before, but it's really going to happen this time. I mean it. Okay? Okay. We'll see you shortly. Yep, yep, bye… bye… yep, bye."

"He's on his way?" Nash ran a hand through his silver hair.

I slipped the phone back into my pocket. "Yeah, he's coming."

I'm going to hell for this. Deep down, my doubts ran amok. Nash had helped cure my gremlins, and I was responding by being a class-A douche-hat. Would he really bolt if I mentioned Erebus now? Yeah, probably, if he had any sense. Unfortunately, the thought of disobeying Erebus trumped any qualms I had. I despised lying like this, for sure, but I had no choice. I hated it even more because Ryann had gotten sucked into it. She'd said such lovely things about me, and made Nash believe in me because of it. I mean, maybe she thought I actually had a way to help Raffe with Kadar. Wouldn't that be the guilty icing on the cake?

One thing was for sure, I couldn't have Raffe arrive without knowing the details of the deception. Or he'd accidentally blow this thing to smithereens.

"Can you hold the fort for a second?" I got up to excuse myself. "I need the little boys' room. Cider goes right through me."

Nash pulled a disgusted face. "TMI, Finch."

"Apologies. A man's gotta do what a man's gotta do."

THIRTY-SEVEN

Finch

I hid in the men's bathroom up the hallway, hunched on top of the closed toilet lid, like some bathroom-dwelling Gollum. I waited a couple seconds to make sure no spooky visitors would appear to sate their curiosity. Mary Foster had been weirdly absent since I'd returned to the Winchester House, and I wasn't ruling out the chance that she was waiting for the perfect opportunity to get me alone.

Maybe Cecily had a word with her after all. A stern "back off" from the Winchester matriarch. Nash hadn't gotten so much as a distant swoon from my spectral chum, which wasn't like her at all. It suggested something had happened in our time away. *Poor Mary...* I wouldn't have completed the map without her cheerleading skills. And *she'd* never been inappropriate with me. I'd been the inappropriate one, mentioning garters and knickers, so rude I could make a ghost blush.

Satisfied that I was truly alone, I dialed Raffe again. He picked up on the second ring.

"Finch? Everything okay?" He sounded on edge.

"Yes and no. I need to get you up to speed before you get here. It'll make sense in a second... hopefully." I took a breath and rattled off everything, finishing with, "So Nash thinks we need his blood to separate you from Kadar, and he needs to keep thinking that or he'll run faster than a cheetah on steroids. Plus, we need a djinn to undo said poisonous djinn curse, or all this will be pointless, and I'll be nailed to the wall and sliced up like a Christmas ham."

"What did he just say?!" Santana's voice came through the speaker, nearly taking out my eardrum. "You better hope I heard you wrong, Finch Merlin. You're not pulling us into more crap, I swear to Chaos. We just escaped a bucket of crazy!"

Raffe sighed. "Sorry, Finch, I shouldn't have put you on speaker."

In the famous words of Winnie-the-Pooh—oh, bother. "How far away are you? And what bucket of crazy?"

"We were about to use a chalk door when you called, but it won't open to the Winchester House," Raffe explained. "I might've gotten the directions wrong. As for the crazy, I'll explain when I see you."

"Stay on the line—I'm going to try something." Setting the phone down, I glanced around the bathroom, with its sickly lime walls and unsettling stains. "Mary? Are you there?"

I'd forgotten the defense protocols on this place. Trying to chalk-door to this house without Melody Winchester was like trying to break into Fort Knox with a toothpick. Strangers without an invite were instantly rebuffed. Sort of like a coven register.

Mary floated through the wall moments later, looking sheepish. "Before you jump to conclusions, I must insist that I was not eaves-dropping, nor was I attempting anything voyeuristic. Cecily forbade me from speaking with any male fleshy, unless they speak to me first. As you have called me, I have merely answered." She hesitated. "Although, perhaps you would do me the kindness of not mentioning this to Cecily, if you happen to see her? She has become quite the tyrant, when all I have done is compliment the true ancestor of the Winchester line upon his charming suits. They make him look like a teddy bear." She giggled and quickly covered her mouth, as if Cecily might hear.

"Well, *I'm* pleased to see you. I thought you'd skipped town." I smiled up at her.

"Your colloquialisms are as baffling as ever, my sweet Finch, but I have missed them so." She swept closer, her hands clasped to her breast. "Now, why did you call? Did you simply wish to converse, or is it about that beastly contraption?" She eyed the cell phone on the toilet lid.

"Sadly, it's the beastly contraption, but that's nothing against you. I really did wonder where you were, and I was disappointed when you didn't come to say hey. Not that you'd ever say 'hey.'"

"That warms my cold, dead heart." She sighed.

"What are friends for?" I replied, pleased to cheer her up a bit. "I'd flatter you more, but we need to get down to business. Do you think you could open a little pocket in the interdimensional bubble for a couple seconds, to let my friends through? They're good folks, and I can vouch for them. I just need a word with them before I take them through to Melody and everyone."

Mary's eyes shimmered with sadness. "Because of the dying one?"

"Dying one?"

"The one in the checkered shirt, with the rather pleasing physique and alarming hair." Mary smiled. "He does not look old, and yet his hair is silver. Most peculiar, but then so many youthful creatures color their hair all sorts of bizarre shades these days. I have seen at least one tourist enter the house with *green* hair! Green! Can you fathom it?"

"Unfortunately, I can fathom it. I bet you never saw any green hair in your day, eh, Miss Foster? Except in a freakshow maybe, which probably isn't much different to what you saw. But yes, it's because of the silver-haired one." I paused. "Wait, you can tell he's dying?"

She nodded slowly. "All those near their end are marked, though the living cannot see it. Do you intend to remove that mark? Oh, I do hope so. It would be a grave pity, most literally, to see such a specimen taken in his prime."

"You're making me jealous here, Miss Foster." I chuckled. "But yeah, we're planning to help him. Firstly, however, I need to speak to my friends. Can you do that for me?"

She tilted her head. "You wish me to open a 'pocket,' as you say, for a few seconds?"

"Just long enough to open and close a chalk door."

"That is well within my capabilities, Mr. Merlin. Why, anyone would think I were a dolt, from the way you ask so tentatively." She flashed a mischievous glance before floating to the wall and pressing her palms to it. "I shall enact your request upon your say-so. Would you like to convey the message through that ghastly object, to give your friends due warning?"

"You're an eagle among pigeons, Miss Foster."

She frowned. "Does that mean yes?"

"It does. Sorry." I swiped up the phone and snapped a picture of the bathroom before sending it to Raffe. "Okay, I've sent a picture of where you need to go. Draw the chalk door now. I'm in the men's bathroom on the ground floor, and you need to open it on the far wall, in the photo."

"If this works, we'll be with you soon," Raffe replied. I heard scraping on the other end of the line and nodded to Mary so she could put her spook magic to work. Her palms pressed into the wall, making the sheen of the interdimensional bubble buckle and fizz as it bent to the forcefield. A second later, a doorway appeared, and in walked Raffe and Santana.

The latter wasted no time handing me my ass on a silver platter. "Are you whacked out of your loaf, Finch? You can't trick some guy into giving his blood, and you can't use Raffe in your little subterfuge. Especially when his curse is the one curse, apparently, that nobody can do anything about! Which I don't mind, by the way, but I wish people would stop mentioning it!"

"Whoa, easy there!" I put up my hands in surrender. Clearly, this wasn't entirely about my lies.

"Yes, I suggest you rein in your ire, madam." Mary released the bubble, the forcefield falling back into place as the doorway disappeared. She put herself between me and Santana.

Santana's jaw dropped. "Are you a—"

"A spirit, a specter, an echo of the living. Yes, I am," Mary replied, her tone hard. "And you are not permitted to enter this sanctuary and speak to a dear friend of mine in so brash a manner. I do not care what you think he may have done, and I care little that he is a friend of yours, if you continue to insult him. You will be courteous, or I shall see you tossed from this house like a rag doll."

Raffe stifled a snort. "Do you have a name?"

"Miss Foster. A pleasure to make your acquaintance, as you seem to have less difficulty with courtesy." Mary sketched a dainty curtsey before returning her glare to Santana, who'd turned a troubling shade of red.

"Well, I'm Raffe, and please don't mind Santana. She's had a long day." Raffe took Santana's hand and held it tight, soothing the beast.

"And I have had a lengthy afterlife, but I do not throw my weight about," Mary shot back.

I stepped in before things got ugly. "What's the crazy you mentioned before, Santana?"

"Don't go turning this on me." She shot a dirty look at Mary. "We can talk about all of *that* later. I want to hear what you've got to say for yourself first."

"Look, I know you don't agree with me bringing Raffe into this. If there'd been another way, I would've. In fact, I was ready to tell Nash that I needed his blood to escape Erebus's servitude. But Melody persuaded me that it'd be a bad idea. Nash has some kind of history with Erebus, and any mention of that name would make him shut down. So, she went with the Raffe charade, and I went along with it."

"And here I was, thinking *you* were the most exquisite wretch of them all." Kadar flickered to the surface, making Mary shoot back as if stung. "Are you telling me that Melody is the brains behind this outfit? Melody—the tiny mouse of a human, who'd barely make a mouthful for me?"

I met his eye. "That brain of hers would probably choke you."

"I thought you and I had a glorious friendship, built on corruption and deception, ahead of us. Now, I am disappointed." Kadar tutted, while Mary stared. He turned toward her. "You ought to count yourself lucky, Miss Foster, that you are a specter. I am ravenous, and I imagine you would've been quite the tasty morsel in your day."

Santana cut in. "You wouldn't so much as nibble on her, Kadar. You know that, so quiet down with the threats before I shove Lullaby Weeds down Raffe's throat." She turned back to me. "Look, I'm peeved you used Raffe. Why not Levi and Zalaam? Raffe isn't your pawn, Finch."

"Neither are Levi and Zalaam, but it doesn't sound like you'd mind throwing them under the bus. At least I'm letting Raffe know now, before we proceed. Anyway, a djinn needs to remove the curse, and

Kadar is a djinn, so I guess you could say that Melody's lie created a djinn-djinn situation." I tried to laugh, but Santana's withering look killed it.

"Without even asking him first?" Santana replied. "And why do you think this Nash guy would run if you told him the truth? If he has issues with Erebus, then wouldn't that put you on equal footing? He'd more likely sympathize with you than sprint in the opposite direction."

"But I need his blood *for* Erebus, and I doubt Nash would like helping him," I said softly.

Raffe raised a hand. "For what it's worth, I don't mind."

"Neither do I," Kadar chimed in. "I may be weakened, but my djinn muscles could use a bit of flexing. And I do so enjoy unraveling the masterpieces of other djinn. There's something satisfying about destroying their handiwork."

Santana looked upward in exasperation. "That's not the point!"

"Then what, pray tell, is the point?" Mary recovered enough to muster some pointed inquisitiveness.

"You just went ahead without sending so much as a text to Raffe," Santana replied. "Is it really that hard to say, 'Hey, by the way, we need to lie to get some blood off a dude. Is it okay if I say it's about you?' and then he could choose to agree or disagree? You took that choice away, and now you're backpedaling like mad to keep this going."

"I was in CANADA! The ass-end of it! I had no signal!" I blurted. "Raffe knows that, because he said he tried to call me and couldn't get thr—"

A blinding white flash enveloped me before I finished, over-whelming everything with raw energy. I collapsed and heard the distant cries of Santana and Raffe. But I wasn't in the bathroom anymore...

My grip on reality slipped, and I faded into glowing oblivion, not knowing where I was headed, or what had pulled me in.

I blinked awake to bright light glaring into my eyes. I lay on an altar in a pillared temple of pristine white marble, with winged statues and lemon trees standing guard. *Well, this isn't at all ominous...* Was I trussed up for sacrifice? I wiggled my arms, but I didn't seem to be tied down. Confused, I sat up and took in my surroundings.

The temple rested on an expanse of diamond grass, glinting with beauty and menace. One bare foot on those blades, and my tootsies would be shredded to ribbons. Azure sky stretched overhead, but no sun. The light came from inside the temple and all around, glinting off every diamond blade of grass, and it was painful to endure. I'd landed in an otherworld.

"Welcome." An apparition shimmered, her limbs solidifying into a slender female form. Of course, who else's otherworld would I have landed in? Erebus didn't have this kind of wattage. So, naturally, it had to be the one and only Lux.

"You mind telling me how you summoned me?" I dangled my legs off the edge of the altar. "Last I checked, your hubby is the only one who can do that to me. Even then, I'm the one who has to do the actual traveling, with this thing." I took the portal ring from my pocket, where it always stayed until I had to use it, and waggled it at her.

Lux laughed coolly. "He always has hated expending energy at any cost to himself. I hail more from the 'if you want a job done well, do it yourself' field of thought."

"Still not giving me the details here, Lux." I'd had enough of Children thinking they could do what they liked with me. What if I really had been going to the bathroom? That would've been awkward.

"You were touched by me, at that human place of revels," she explained. "As such, I can summon you at will, much like my husband does. Only, I prefer to create a telepathic link, instead of pulling you physically from the mortal realm and into mine. It saves a great deal of time and effort."

"Come again?" I gaped at her. "I'm not really here?"

She shrugged. "Yes and no. Your mind is here, but your physical body is where I left it, likely drooling and speechless. I would say that is not much of a change for you, but I am above such childish repartee."

"That's like saying, 'I'm not being offensive, but…' and then going on to say something really offensive," I retorted.

"I have not summoned you to indulge in a game of wits, Finch." Lux paced the temple floor, her body shimmering with shards of light. "I have questions."

I grimaced. "Why am I not surprised? It *was* you who helped with Davin, wasn't it? I friggin' knew there would be a price for that."

"I like to ensure that my personal interests are protected," she replied simply. "And I was not the one who came to your rescue. I sent my Sylphs."

"Forgive me if I'm wrong, but I thought intervening like that was a major no-no."

"My creations, as with all Children's creations, provide a get-out clause of sorts. They are our eyes and ears, and, yes, our force in the mortal realm when we can't move directly." Lux shot me a hard stare. "I would have thought you'd be more grateful."

I echoed her hard stare. "I would've, if it had been an act of altruism. But you Children don't go for that, do you? There's always a deal here, an exchange there—it's never something for nothing."

Her glowing eyes flashed with irritation. "Don't tar me with the same brush as my husband, Finch. I help my fair share of mortals, without request for anything in return. I do not make a song and dance about it, which is why you likely never hear of my charitable endeavors. My Sylphs aid many people in times of need. But I do not take the credit, nor do I want to."

"Say that's true—why is it different with me?" I found her incredibly tricky to read, but the note of genuine affront convinced me she was telling the truth.

Lux sighed. "Because, unfortunately, you have something I need. Information."

"About what?"

"I want to know why you went to Canada for this Nash Calvert individual," she replied, returning to business.

"Don't you already know, if you had eyes and ears on me?" I countered.

"My Sylphs could not hear everything, and there is something about this Nash person that blocks their ability to listen," Lux explained. "In this instance, you know more than they could discover, which makes you invaluable to me. There will be rewards for that, if you comply."

I narrowed my eyes. "What kind of rewards?"

"I have yet to decide; it depends on the quality of your information." Lux wandered to one of the pillars and stared into the vast fields of diamond grass. "Now, why were you there? Who is this Nash fellow?"

I was in her world now, and I got the sense I wouldn't be leaving until I spilled my guts all over her temple. Not in the literal sense, hopefully. Plus, I owed her for the rescue, even if I hadn't asked for it. And if she intended to reward me, that put her one step above Erebus in my eyes, who'd never offered so much as a pat on the back for my efforts. Maybe *she* could break me out of my deal with her lover. The notion was enough to loosen my lips a touch.

"Nash is a Sanguine, with blood from two lines of Atlantean Primus Anglicus. You know, the good stuff," I said reluctantly. She'd protected me once—I hoped that would extend to saving my skin from Erebus if he ever found out I'd yakked to his wife about his plans.

Lux whirled around. "A Sanguine of Atlantean descent?"

"Bingo."

"Otherwise known as the key to the Gateway to Atlantis!" Her whole body glowed two notches brighter, forcing me to cover my eyes. "That stupid, stupid fool."

"How so?" I pressed, but she didn't answer. She'd returned to pacing, clearly deep in thought about the crafty doo-doo her husband was wading through. "Fine, I'll just talk to myself."

Still, Lux said nothing. She simply walked, then stopped, then walked some more, and stopped some more, in super-awkward silence.

Well, this is fun... Squirming in the quiet, I changed tactics.

"Since we're sharing secrets, why don't you tell me what this is about? Why is Erebus so set on Atlantis? And why don't you just talk to him about it, instead of using me as your go-between?"

Lux's body sparked violently, making me wish I'd kept my trap shut. "The only way to deal with Erebus is through lies, deception, and manipulation," she spat. "That is how he deals with me, so I pay him back in kind. These measures are the only thing that will get through that dense skull of his, once I confront him!"

I'd poked the bear way harder than I'd intended. Lux was a cold fish most of the time, hovering somewhere between serene and frosty, and I'd never seen her lose it like this. It genuinely seemed something had snapped inside her. One too many betrayals, maybe? Or one too many lies from the being bound to her for eternity? A marriage made in hell.

"Sorry for asking," I mumbled, shell-shocked.

"I am sure you hoped I would have answers for you, but I cannot say more at this time." She recovered quickly, her glowing form settling down. "Nevertheless, you must be careful. If you do not serve me well, and show me due courtesy, you will end up dead, like all the other servants of Erebus."

"What did you just say?" My heart dropped like a stone.

"I believe you heard me." Her eyes bored into my soul. "I will call on you again when I require you. After what you have told me, I will be keeping a close eye on matters."

"All of his servants died?" I ignored the last thing she'd said. That didn't matter to me right now, after the bombshell she'd dropped. Erebus had evidently gotten right under her skin and made her as toxic as him. She was the one who supposedly cared about mortals, along with Gaia, and she may as well have taken a brick to the back of my head with that revelation.

Lux turned away. "Ask your friends, Raffe and Santana. They can confirm. I, on the other hand, tire of talking."

I woke up in the grisly bathroom. Santana and Raffe stood over me, staring at me. And my cheek stung, as if someone had given me a sharp slap to try and wake me up. Judging by Mary's furious face, Santana had been the one to do the slapping.

"Finch?" Raffe knelt. "Are you okay? You zoned out for a minute there."

"A minute?" I looked at him, puzzled.

He nodded. "Yeah, maybe two."

I realized time must've moved differently during my telepathic "call" with Lux. "Sorry about that. I always tell myself not to drink on an empty stomach, especially when there's a lot on my mind. It must've gotten the better of me."

"Are you sure that's all it is? You were really out of it, Finch," Santana interjected, her expression showing a hint of worry.

"Honestly, I'm fine." I mustered a smile. "Actually, it did me some good, because there's something I want to ask you both."

Finally, in this crazy, roundabout way, I would get some answers.

THIRTY-EIGHT

Raffe

F inch was anything but fine. He'd been talking one second, then blanked out the next, the cabinet beside him breaking his fall. As if someone had flipped a literal switch in his head. His eyes went vacant, his head lolled, and then he'd come back suddenly, as if nothing had happened. I wasn't buying it. Finch had his own brand of weird, but this was different. As if it took him by surprise, too. Then again, with the pressure he was under, and Santana not exactly making things easier, who wouldn't break?

"What did you want to ask?" I said, figuring it was better to focus on that. Finch clearly didn't want to talk about what had happened.

"What did you find out about the servants of Erebus?" Finch cast me a thankful look, but an odd note lingered in his voice. An artificial casualness.

Santana sighed and leaned against the wall. "Raffe, you should probably take this one."

"That bad, huh?" Again, Finch's tone seemed... off. He laughed, but it didn't reach his eyes.

"We learned a lot, and a *lot* happened." I took over, knowing I could finally get some weight off my chest. "But, before we get to the servant stuff, there's so much you need to hear. The Storyteller was a huge help, but she is no longer with us. She amassed the djinn to take on Erebus in Tartarus, but when we all arrived, he wasn't there. The Storyteller knew a way to separate the djinn without going through Erebus directly, and gave her life to free them. They'll be weaker now, but they've all agreed that's a small price to pay, considering the alternative."

Finch's mouth gaped wide open. "Are you telling me the djinn are free? Like, legitimately free?"

"I am," I replied.

"They freed themselves?" His eyes bulged.

"They did. I'm not sure how many ways I can say it." I offered a smile. This had to be a bit of a shock for him.

Finch shook his head, halfway between disbelief and admiration. "Son of a nutcracker! Those sneaky devils! Man, why couldn't I have been a djinn? I'd be strutting free right now, if I was. Never in my life have I been more jealous of billowing smoke, flashy red skin, and anger-management issues."

I lowered my gaze, only to raise it again. "But there's more. Tartarus isn't the way it was before. When we arrived, it was… empty. That's literally the only way I can describe it. No darkness, no Purge beasts, nothing."

He frowned. "What?"

"The Storyteller explained that, because Erebus took human form, Tartarus doesn't recognize him as its creator anymore. But it *does* recognize the djinn and their energy. So…" I paused, hoping this might give Finch a boost. "The djinn seized it for themselves. They're going to build a world there, and since they make the rules, they can deny Erebus entry, if he tries to get back in. At least while he's in his human body."

Finch's mouth hung open. "Are you friggin' serious?"

"Yeah, because we'd joke about something like that," Santana interjected.

"Wait, wait, wait. You're telling me the djinn are free, and Erebus is… locked out of his own otherworld?" A hint of a smirk formed on Finch's lips.

"We are," I replied. The news seemed to be having the desired effect.

He started laughing like a maniac. "Oh damn, that's *too* good! Erebus finally lost something he cares about, all because of this stupid pet project! Raffster, you've made my friggin' day!" He clutched his stomach, wheezing. "There must be some insane treasures in that drowned city. If there aren't, it'll be like opening coal on Christmas. Just to clarify, the Storyteller made this happen, right?"

I nodded. "She performed a sacrificial spell, yes."

"Then Erebus can't even do anything about it, right? If it's djinn magic, he can't undo it!" Finch howled louder. "This is perfect, Raffe. Absolutely fudging perfect! I wish the Storyteller were still around, so I could shake her hand and give her a kiss for this—I'm sorry she had to die, of course, but what a way to go out! *Literally* liberating all of her kind. The djinn have serious guts. Ain't that the truth, Kadar, my man?"

Kadar sprang up. "We do, though we never say no to devouring more."

Can you not? I beseeched him, taking the reins again.

It's not my fault if you don't like the truth, he replied with a chuckle.

"Unfortunately, since you're not a djinn, this confrontation doesn't affect your predicament," I went on.

Finch stopped laughing.

"It doesn't affect the Levi curse, either," Santana interjected. "Again, genuinely not bitter about it, but I'm getting sick of hearing about it being lifted. I want to move forward, knowing this is how things will be—me, Raffe, and Kadar, together. That's why I sniped at you, Finch, which was wrong of me. It's been an insanely long day, and people had already riled me up by telling lies before I heard your call to Raffe. Other people, who aren't you. Still no excuse, but... well, I'm sorry."

Finch shrugged, his humor gone. "Apology accepted. Melody's the one who should get an earful of your wrath."

"I'm all out," Santana replied.

"So, the djinn launched a protest and earned their freedom, giving Erebus a bunch of grief alongside, which he may not even know about yet? Good on them. I hope it ends well. I'm cheering them on, for sure. Did you find out anything about the human servants?" Finch turned back to me, still swinging his legs.

I gripped the towel rail, my heart racing.

Tell him, Kadar demanded. *He's got a right to know.*

Give me a minute! I took a shaky breath. "No human servant of Erebus has ever survived a long-term deal."

I waited for the shocked gasp or despairing cry, but Finch sat there saying nothing. Taking that as a cue to continue, I did.

"That is, except one. The Storyteller told us that a Necromancer in Erebus's service had saved a djinn, and in return, that djinn granted the Necromancer the ability to resurrect himself using a charmed amulet imbued with djinn magic. Considering the only way to escape an Erebus deal is death, this Necromancer died and resurrected himself, tricking his way out of servitude by cheating death... and Erebus, I guess."

Finch started to laugh manically again, though his tone was bitter as he rocked precariously on the toilet lid. "It's Davin, isn't it? Go on, land that beautiful punchline."

I nodded reluctantly. "Yes, it's Davin."

"That slimy boglin! That dirty, evil son of a jezebel!" Finch's laughter cut out. Pure, savage rage replaced it. "Is there nothing he can't squirm and cheat and lie his way out of? Death must be kicking itself, seeing that worthless dingbat return time and time again. Man, I'd take a scythe to his friggin' neck in a heartbeat, if I thought it'd do any good! I'd use his head as a damned basketball, shooting hoops for the rest of my days."

Santana and I exchanged a worried look while Miss Foster fled through the wall in alarm. "It means there's hope for you, Finch," Santana said slowly, though he clearly didn't believe a word of her encouragement.

"Don't you say that word to me, Santana. Hope, to me, is only a dangling carrot that I'm never going to bite off the damn rod. You hate lies so much, then don't be a hypocrite." His tone turned steely. "You said it yourself: I'm not a djinn. I don't get a free pass."

"If you could get that amulet, maybe you could do what Davin did?" Santana proceeded regardless.

"What am I, a freaking task-monkey?" Finch's eyes bulged. "If it's not one mission to try and spare my life, it's another. And, guess what, there are no guarantees about what you've just said. It's just another aimless wander into the unknown, probably for no payoff."

"Finch…" I touched his arm gently.

He flinched. "Davin is a Necromancer, and he's way craftier than I'll ever be. He and I aren't in the same boat. Say I go after this amulet —what if it doesn't work? I refuse to get my hopes up again."

"You can't give up now." Santana joined me on the floor and placed a hand on Finch's leg. "That's not who you are. There are so many people in this world who love you, and we'll do anything to keep you alive. Even if we have to get that amulet for you. Even if we have to get a thousand amulets. You're not giving up, Finch. Over my dead body."

He gave a bitter laugh. "Nope, over mine. She was right. I'm going to die… All of this is only to fend off the inevitable for a while."

"She? Who's she?" Santana cocked her head.

"The cat's mother," Finch mumbled, withdrawing into himself.

"Now, you listen here, you sad-sap, and you listen good. I'm about to hit you with some home truths." Kadar burst out, pushing me down. "Are you seriously going to let Davin and Erebus get the better of you? Are you going to lie down and play dead and let those vultures pick at your bones? I've watched you this last year. I don't say this often about humans, but you've got more fight in you than a Marid after they've downed the blood of a hundred enemies. So pick yourself up, you moron, and get on with your tasks. First, the blood—put Erebus off the scent of you wanting to escape your servitude. Second, get Davin, and that amulet, and free yourself. And keep that putrid glob of excrement from rising again. You need help? You've got it, pal."

Finch stared at Kadar. "But—"

"Butts are delicious masses of muscle and fat that are so tender they sizzle when they cook. I don't want to hear about yours, unless you're offering up a slice to feed my appetite." Kadar bristled with energy, giving me a secondhand buzz. "Earlier tonight, I was set against rebellion. Now, I've been forced to see the value of freedom over servitude, and I've seen that come to fruition. Yes, we got lucky, but we were prepared to fight—we went in thinking we'd have to battle it out for liberation. Be as the djinn. Fight him until there's nothing left of you, if that's what it takes. Will you wait for him to end you, or do something about it?"

Nicely done. I had to give credit where it was due. Kadar had made a more rousing speech than Santana or I could have.

"Now, how about we get on with this curse-lifting before I decide to despair of the *entire* human race and leave you djinn-less? Nash won't wait around forever, and he'll think you are doing something utterly abhorrent to this toilet." Kadar's smoke billowed into the bathroom. "Haven't you always claimed to be the king of compartmentalization? Take your own advice, you sorry sack of flesh, while you've still got air in your lungs."

Finch opened and closed his mouth, speechless.

I rose back to the surface. "You have my word that we'll keep up the lie. Nash will get his life back, and after we get rid of Davin, hopefully he gets to live a good one. And so will you. The result of this lie justifies it. So, we're ready when you are."

"What he said," Santana added.

Finch continued to sit for a moment. Without warning, he stood and crossed to the bathroom door. He turned, a flicker of the old, determined Finch on his face. "Then let's go, before Nash thinks I've taken a Howitzer to the can."

All three of us headed for what turned out to be a very homey kitchen. A few ghosts drifted around, but they were almost like part of the furniture, always present. They didn't scare me. I'd seen enough weird and wonderful things to know that ghosts were nothing to be afraid of. Not this kind, anyway. A poltergeist, sure, but this house had placated its spirits. They were like house guests, simply going about their business.

"I thought you'd drowned in there." A stranger in plaid looked up from a bottle of cider. Nash, I guessed. He sat at the kitchen table with Ryann, whom I certainly hadn't expected to see. Luke and Melody sat on a couch across the room. I didn't know them well, but I knew their faces and reputations.

Ryann offered a curious frown. "When did you two get here?"

"Finch came to get us," Santana replied smoothly. "There are so many spells on this house, we'd never have gotten in without him. We were just wandering around aimlessly on the street outside, so we ended up calling Finch."

"You're the one with the djinn problem?" Nash eyed me.

"Yup." I nodded.

Djinn problem? I'll give him a djinn problem, Kadar muttered inside my head.

Cool it, Kadar. This is part of the charade, remember? I warned.

Fine, but if he says anything like that again, I'll—

You won't, I cut him off. *No devouring, no nibbling, no tearing, no flesh-consumption of any kind.*

He laughed. *Spoilsport.*

Nash pushed his cider bottle away. "How do you want to do this, then?"

"I guess you just sit there and let Kadar work on the curse," I replied. Honestly, I had no idea how this worked, but Kadar seemed to. He felt agitated, eager to get on with it.

You do know how to undo curses, don't you? I said internally.

It is one of my specialties. Well, I say that, but it is simply something the djinn innately know how to do. It is in our blood. I am looking forward to this.

Have you ever thought about unraveling our curse? I had to know.

He snorted. *Our curse was placed upon us by a very old and, presumably, very dead djinn. Other djinn in our ancestry have tried to break it and failed. Because it cannot be broken, in case that needed hammering into your head again.*

Would Nash's blood really not help?

Nash's blood may as well be syrup to us. It is useless for our curse. Its value relies on its application as a substitute for a spell ingredient—nothing more, nothing less. Our curse is too ingrained for such simplistic things. There is no spell to undo ours; therefore, his blood cannot be used as an ingredient. Does your small mind comprehend? I sensed Kadar grinning.

Yes, I comprehend. And if my mind is small, so is yours, I retorted. *I only wanted to clarify.*

Well, now you have. And it's time for me to work my expertise. He took over a second later, leaving me as the backseat driver as he approached Nash.

"You ain't going to gouge my eyes out with spoons, are you?" Nash laughed nervously.

Kadar smirked. "That depends on how you behave."

An enormous husky stood from behind Nash's chair and stalked between Kadar and its owner. Nash immediately ran a hand through the dog's fur, his voice soft and reassuring.

"It's okay, Huntress. Stand down."

The husky did, with a snarky growl, though she stayed at Nash's side.

With the obstacle removed, Kadar stepped right up to his victim. Nash braced his palms against the kitchen table. Taking that as a sign of permission, Kadar lunged forward and clasped Nash's skull between his hands. The husky went berserk, but Kadar paid no attention. In the end, Ryann sat on the floor beside the dog and attempted to hold it steady, in case it tried to attack Kadar mid-unraveling.

Through Kadar's ruby-glazed eyes, I had a front-row seat to the ensuing madness. Kadar hummed. His black smoke responded to the noise, flowing away from him and spiraling in a vortex above the kitchen table. It hovered there, awaiting further instruction.

Deep inside, a rush of energy shivered through our shared veins, crashing along the circulatory network and into our arms, where it careened down to our palms. Red light pulsated against Nash's temples, feeding into his skull and turning his eyes the same ruby shade as Kadar's. I gasped, though nobody heard me, buried within my own body. Nash's pupils swelled, and black tendrils snaked into the red until his eyeballs turned to darkness.

The moment they went completely black, the hovering smoke surged into him, slithering through his mouth, his nose, his ears, and his eyes. I felt sick, watching what could only be described as possession. I wished I could've turned to see the others' reactions, but I had to focus on what held Kadar's attention. And he wasn't about to look away from Nash for anything.

A gurgling sound swished in the back of Nash's open mouth. He slammed his fists on the table, a sheen of sweat glistening across his forehead. His body jerked and jolted as Kadar fed that red light into him. This had to be painful. It hurt us, so I could only imagine what it felt like for Nash. Small stabs of pain struck us in the gut, and our lungs struggled to keep up. Meanwhile, the black of Nash's eyes continued its takeover, snaking out to his skin and spiderwebbing across his features.

"Are you sure this is helping him?" I heard Melody's concerned voice.

"Kadar knows what he's doing," Santana replied. Though she didn't sound entirely convinced.

Nash convulsed violently as the black strands made their way down his neck to the rest of him, prompting Finch and Luke to action. Luke wrapped his arms around Nash's body to stop him from convulsing right off the chair. In retrospect, we should have started with Nash lying down or in restraints to keep him safe. But we had to make do with what we had.

The black strands turned from deadly darkness to a throbbing shade of scarlet. No sooner had the color shifted than the strands receded, gliding back through him in reverse. Eventually, the threads reached his eyes once more, and Nash's whole body shuddered. The inky stain swirled, blending red and black, until red won.

Nash blinked once, and a pulse of searing crimson light exploded outward, hitting everyone in the vicinity with a blast of unadulterated energy that sent them flying. Kadar clung to Nash's head, his palms lodged against his temples, until the light faded.

I looked over and saw that Nash's eyes had returned to normal. He stared up at Kadar, exhausted. The only indication that anything had happened to him lay in the two minuscule specks of red, like freckles, which now sat in his vibrant blue irises.

"Did you… do it?" Nash wheezed.

Kadar smirked, though he'd lost some of his gusto. In his weakened state, this had taken a lot out of him. More than he wanted anyone to realize, though he couldn't hide his pain from me. "I did, and I didn't even need to gouge your eyes out with spoons."

"You could've warned us." Finch picked himself up and dusted himself off.

"What would've been the fun in that?" Kadar replied, delivering his usual sass to keep up appearances. However, I got something very different from my symbiotic partner.

I need to rest, Raffe. It is done, but I have to sleep for some time… That used up more of my energy than I anticipated. I still need to learn my new limits.

Take all the time you need, I replied, changing places with him.

Within me, I sensed Kadar curl up and go to sleep, and my mind felt oddly quiet without him.

As the rest of our group rose to their feet, Ryann crossed over to the couch and picked up a tin box. She brought it to the table and flipped the lid, revealing a syringe and glass vials.

"I brought this from the storage cupboard with the bandages," she explained. "I thought it might save us a trip later."

"I guess you want to stick me like a pincushion now? I suppose it's best to get it out of the way in one go." Nash glanced at me. "You must be itching to separate from that djinn. He's a brutal bastard. My head's going to ring for days."

I forced a smile, grateful Kadar was asleep. "It's what we both want."

"So, who's going to do the honors?" Nash let his gaze move across the group.

"I will," Finch volunteered, sitting next to Nash.

Scraping the tin box along the table, he removed a rubbery tube that lay coiled in the bottom like a yellowish snake. With remarkable precision, he tied the tube above Nash's elbow and pulled it tight. Next, he removed the syringe and slid it seamlessly into the bluish rise of Nash's vein. Unsettlingly, it appeared Finch had done this before. I liked to think I knew everything about my friend, but perhaps he still had old secrets. Tricks and skills he'd learned in his time with the cult that he never used in his new life as one of the good guys.

Deftly, Finch drew eight vials, stoppering each before moving on. That seemed like a lot, but I couldn't question Finch without mentioning the E-word. Besides, Nash didn't seem perturbed by the quantity. He simply sat with his face turned away, not watching the blood spurt out of him and into the vials.

"All done?" Nash asked as Finch stoppered the eighth vial.

He laid them all in the tin box. "Yep, all done. I'd give you a sticker, but I'm fresh out."

"Not even a lollipop?"

"Fresh out of them, too." Finch smiled, but it came off strange. Like guilt was attempting to break through.

"What's the point in having blood taken if you don't get sugar afterward?" Nash seemed jovial enough. "Anyway, now that you've got what you need, do you think you'll do the spell today? I'd like to sit in on that, if you are. I've never seen a djinn separate from a host before."

A bevy of awkward glances drifted around the room.

"I guess you probably have to take it to someone more powerful, right? An old djinn or someone with Voodoo skill? They know blood better than anyone, apart from us Sanguines." Nash waxed thoughtful, oblivious to our discomfort.

"Marie Laveau, actually," Finch blurted out.

Nash's eyes widened. "No way! You're yanking my chain! Well, now I've definitely got to come along. I've wanted to meet her for years. I tried, once, to see if she could help me, but I couldn't get through her door. Guess she didn't want to see me, huh?"

Finch opened his mouth to reply, but whatever he said was drowned out by another voice that blasted through the entire house. It shook the walls, making everyone jump. And we knew that voice all too well.

"Hello there, you little buggers! Did you miss me?"

THIRTY-NINE

Finch

Everyone covered their ears as Davin's voice splintered our ear canals like well-aimed javelins of narcissistic assholery.

"I bet you thought you didn't have to worry about me, in this so-called sanctuary of placated spirits." His voice thundered, shaking the cider bottles off the table and the chintzy porcelain plates from the kitchen shelves. "That little stunt only dazzled me for a moment. Now, I have come to dazzle you with my insight, for briefly stealing my eyesight."

"He can't enter, right?" I sought out Melody, who clung to Luke's side, her eyes wide with panic. "You said the spirits and Kolduny spells protect this house. Tell me he's stuck outside, before my eardrums explode and I can't hear you."

Melody's lip trembled. "There's no way he can enter here."

"Then how is he doing this?" Ryann shouted, covering her ears.

"He can't get in, but that doesn't mean he can't hijack the audio system." Melody talked slowly, as if putting the pieces together as she spoke. "We have a whole setup of speakers for the tourist facility, but some are hooked up in the living quarters, too—an old loudspeaker system for music, which we never use. If he's not inside, the spirits won't interfere."

"Allow me to begin," Davin bellowed. It seemed he couldn't hear us, but that wasn't much comfort. He had the floor, and, if I knew Davin, he was about to put Shakespeare to shame with a well-rehearsed soliloquy. "Nash, I gave you a choice. I asked you nicely to come with me of your own volition. Instead, you decided to go with those miscreants. And it's my pleasure to let you in on a secret—they are no better than I. They are using you. At least I was honest about it, but the same cannot be said for those pernicious weeds."

And things were going so smoothly... Everyone twisted in unison to look at Nash. He still sat in his chair, drenched in sweat, but his eyes focused on the rusty shell of an old speaker.

"What is he talking about?" Nash didn't remove his gaze from the speaker.

Davin answered before any of us could. "Finch Merlin is the worst of them all. He hoodwinked you. If you hadn't buried your head in the sand all these years, you might have heard that he sold himself to Erebus in exchange for murdering my beloved Eris. He wants your blood *for* Erebus, good little slave that he is. He must have told you a charming, touching tale to win you over, but he is in league with the Child of Darkness, and this is all for his benefit."

Ah, dammit! I hated plot twists. And I hated this one more than most.

Nash slowly turned, his eyes narrowing. Two red freckles glinted in his irises—a lasting effect of Kadar's unraveling. We'd put him through hell, and the guilt broiled in my belly. All the excuses and reasons in the world wouldn't sanitize the fact that we'd lied.

"I shall give you a moment to let that sink in, Nash." Davin chuckled through the speakers, the sound stabbing my gut.

"Tell me he's lying," Nash said, his voice low and threatening.

I lowered my gaze.

"Finch. Tell. Me. He's. Lying!" Nash snarled, prompting Huntress's hackles to rise.

What could I say? My shamefaced expression likely gave everything away. He didn't have to be an Empath to sense that Davin told the truth. We'd been caught in our lie, and now that web would untangle.

"Tell me you didn't do this. Tell me you're not the same as everyone else who darkened my door to steal what isn't theirs." Nash stood on shaky legs, Huntress bracing to pounce. "Tell me there's one trustworthy person left in this world."

I lifted my gaze, figuring I owed him that. "There's more to this than meets the eye, Nash. Davin is trying to get under your skin. Let us explain, and it will make sense."

Nash glared. "He's telling the truth, isn't he?"

I looked to the others for backup, but they were all in a similar state of squirmy discomfort. We resembled a bunch of schoolkids who'd been dragged before the principal. Even Santana looked mortified, though she'd been against this entire deception. I supposed, since she hadn't stopped us, she felt as guilty as the rest of us.

"That should be enough time," Davin boomed, his voice reverberating through the old audio network. "Perhaps, had you relinquished Nash, I would have allowed him to believe you were a discerning gentleman, Finch. He would have gone on thinking me the villain. But you sought to defy me, as usual, and now I repay the favor in kind, revealing you for what you truly are. A user and a manipulator, like me. Your mother would be so proud."

My cheeks flamed. *Shut your insipid piehole, you cowardly amoeba!*

"I will leave you with these parting words, Nash," Davin prattled on. "Finch and his minions look after their own. You are not their friend; thus, you do not qualify. You have been had. You should have come with me from the start, for the next time we meet, it will not go pleasantly for you."

I wanted the Winchester mansion to swallow me like a ravenous kraken with a taste for disgraced liars. The worst part was, I couldn't defend myself. Davin had called me out, and he was right to. We *had* tricked Nash. We *had* used him. And he'd trusted us. That stung deep —a massive fishbone of shame, lodged in my throat.

A sharp squeal signaled the end of Davin's *Hamlet* time.

"You piece of crap!" Nash lost it. "Who do you think you are, Finch? You think that because you've got a powerful surname you can treat people like trash and take them for all they're worth?"

Huntress peered up at Nash, appearing confused. She likely wouldn't hesitate to protect her magical if it came to blows.

"I should've known something was off the minute you lied about your name," Nash raged on.

I took a tentative step forward. "Hear me out."

"You've said enough!" He scowled at me with such fury, I thought I might spontaneously combust. "I bet you were terrified I'd say no if you mentioned Erebus, right? All this time, you were working for him! If I had my rifle, I'd blow you sky high."

"Nash, please, let me explain," I sputtered, but he was done listening.

"You plotted all of this so you could run off to him with my blood, tied up in a bow—that evil bastard who hunted me through Davin, all those years ago. *He* stole my life, if we're getting down to the nitty-gritty here. *He* made things unbearable, to the point that I chose to shorten the life I had left. And for what? So he could take my blood anyway and start an open season for the other hunters out there!"

I shook my head. "No, I meant what I said. We'll protect you. Melody will find a way."

"How long have you been working with Erebus, huh? A year? Since Elysium, right?" he spat, and I nodded sheepishly. "Then you've been around him long enough to know that lifting this curse would put me in the line of fire. You think he wants anyone else getting my blood? He ties off his loose ends, Finch."

I gaped at Nash, his words hitting home like a baseball bat to the skull. Erebus had drained the Fountain of Youth and collapsed the whole Jubilee mine to make sure nobody else got their paws on the immortalizing water. Of course he'd get rid of Nash, too, for the same reason. I'd been a colossal idiot not to understand that. But that didn't alter the promise I'd made.

"You're not going to get 'tied off.' I mean it, Nash. We'll do anything to make sure you survive," I told him. "But you have to understand, if I'd told the truth, you'd never have agreed to this. You and Erebus have history. You would've bolted at the first mention of his name. And I needed your help, because there are so many lives on the line."

Nash's face contorted into a mask of bitterness. "Your friends, you mean?"

"Yes, my friends. Their lives and mine. And, I'm sorry, but I had to do what I did. I'm not happy about it. Believe it or not, I like you, Nash. You didn't ask for this, and I didn't want to lie, but I couldn't rely on you to sympathize with the truth." I was desperate now. "But I keep my promises. I won't let anything bad happen to you."

"Shame I can't say the same for you." Nash's hands raised, and a fireball barreled toward me. I ducked away, feeling the heat as it careened past my cheek.

"I don't want to fight you!" I shouted. "That's what Davin wants!"

"I don't care. You fooled me, and you'll regret it." Nash prepared to launch another attack. To my horror, Ryann raced forward, putting herself between me and Nash.

"Stop it, both of you! Let's sit down and talk through this. We don't have to get violent!" she cried, but Nash unleashed a volley of fireballs, aimed straight for Ryann.

I grabbed her around the waist and spun her around, holding her tight as a fireball struck me. A howl tore from my throat as the pain seared my shoulders. It wouldn't leave much of a mark—having Fire in my own arsenal gave me some protection—but it still hurt like hell.

My head whipped around. "You're pissed with me. I get it. You have every right to be. But don't you dare hurt the people I care about!"

"Maybe that's what you need, to teach you a lesson," Nash growled.

A figure darted across the kitchen and launched herself at Nash. Santana tackled him, shoving her knee into his chest to pin him to the ground. Her eyes glowed as her Orishas burst from her.

"Calm down, Nash!" she barked. "Stay down, unless you want my Orishas to keep you there. We're going to talk about this like rational human beings."

Huntress's fur prickled, and she crouched to spring. However, before she could, Raffe sprinted to Santana's side. His skin flashed red, smoke billowing from his shoulders. Kadar had decided to resurface and join the party, and he was ten times the beast Huntress was.

Sure enough, Kadar hunched on all fours and stared Huntress in the eyes. His lips peeled to reveal sharpened teeth. He gnashed them, and an almighty roar thundered into Huntress's face. Her fur flattened under the pressure of the hellish air pouring from Kadar's mouth, a whine squeaking from her throat as she backed away.

"You can let go of me now," Ryann whispered. I realized I still held her in my arms. Awkwardly, I released her.

"Sorry."

"You don't have to apologize for saving me," she said, with a smile. Ryann stepped back, putting a safe distance between herself and Nash. The latter remained on the floor, while Luke ran up to provide some additional muscle to keep him there.

I took my chance, with Nash immobilized. He needed to hear a few truths from me, too, or he'd spend the rest of his hunted life thinking I was the pinnacle of jerk-dom.

I stood over him, holding his furious gaze. "I should have told you that I wanted your blood to free myself. Erebus told me not to mention his name, and now I see why. But I'm not a bad guy. Making a deal with Erebus was the only way to kill Katherine. Since then, I've been in his service, and he won't let me go."

"And that's my problem how?" Nash hissed. "Katherine Shipton was another hunter. Good for you for killing her, but the consequences have nothing to do with me."

"I'm just trying to explain myself." I steeled my resolve. "The thing is, I recently learned that Davin was the only servant of Erebus to ever survive. I don't have his playbook, which means I'm going to die soon. I'm on borrowed time, like you were. But you aren't anymore. You deserve to live without one eye on the clock—and lifting the curse will help you do that. Melody will find a way to ensure you're not a target. Erebus won't make you disappear."

"What does Erebus even want with my blood? I take it you can't use it to free yourself, if you're so sure you're a goner?" Nash's tone softened slightly. Barely perceptible, but enough to give me hope.

I sighed. "Erebus needs your blood to open the Gateway to Atlantis. You're the key, Nash. I'd have told him where to shove it, but that would've meant seeing everyone I care about strung up like puppets and gutted six ways to Sunday. I lied because of my fear. That doesn't make it right, but I hope you can understand my motivation. What would you do, in my position?"

Nash frowned and said nothing, but he cast a small, worried look at Huntress.

"Anyway, I won't survive long past this Atlantis business. All I can look forward to is another mission or death, but I'm pretty sure it'll be death," I went on. "The only way out is using Davin's djinn amulet to resurrect myself. Even then, I've got zero assurances. I'm no Necromancer, after all. But once I have that amulet, I want Davin's head to roll… for good, this time."

Nash relaxed beneath Santana and Luke's grip. "So… you hate Erebus and Davin as much as I do?"

"I'd say I hate them more, but that's a game of one-upmanship I don't want to enter with you." I managed a faint smile and watched him relent.

"I'd win that game. But you should've been honest," he replied tersely. "I want to get back at them for everything they've put me through, and so do you. That should've made us allies from the get-go."

I bit my cheek. "I know, but can you see why I felt I had to lie? I couldn't risk you vamoosing, and you had every reason to fear for your life. Self-preservation makes us do weird things, even give up the chance for revenge."

A smirk twitched at the corner of Nash's mouth. "Well, assuming you stop lying to me, I might consider helping your sorry ass."

FORTY

Finch

Through my little heart-to-heart with the plaid wonder, everyone had been brought up to speed on my progress with Erebus. No stone unturned, no lies lingering in the atmosphere. Well, there was one. Despite Ryann's insistence that I stop resorting to fibs, I kept my encounters with Lux firmly to myself. I was already in deep crap with Erebus. I didn't want to wade through another layer of crap with his friggin' goddess wife by spilling her secrets to people.

"I have to keep at it with this Atlantis ruse, but I'm not rolling over for Erebus," I said.

Nash shrugged, rising to his feet. "You've come this far, might as well see what the hell Erebus wants from Atlantis. It's got me curious, for sure."

Ryann stepped into the now-calmer gathering. "I can get in touch with a couple of magicals I know who've studied ancient Chaos, to see if they can give us any pointers on Erebus's plans."

"Not a chance, Ryann," Santana interjected. "If Harley finds out you're here, cavorting with these deranged lunatics, she'll lock you in the basement for life! You mean well, and kudos for your enthusiasm, but you're coming back to the coven with Raffe and me."

Ryann looked ready to make her case for staying, but Santana had moved on to me, leaving no room for protests. "And you need to tell your sister everything—more than she already knows, especially since it involves Dingleberry Doncaster. Put your Merlin heads together and come up with some kind of contingency plan, in case things with Erebus go south or Davin slithers his way in again."

"Don't you worry about us Merlins," I replied. "I already spoke to Harley. For the time being, she knows everything she needs to so she can prepare for what comes next."

Ryann joined Santana in the "tell all" brigade. "Seriously, Finch? Did you not listen to a word I said before?"

"I did, and I will endeavor to be the picture of honesty going forward, but for now, I've got to keep some of this under wraps a while longer," I said. "You know Harley. She'll start meddling. Usually, that's fine—she's a great meddler—but Erebus will take her out of the equation if he thinks she's trying to stop him. I told her as much."

Raffe put his arm around Santana's waist, Kadar having retreated. "He knows the threat better than anyone. If he thinks this is the way things have to go, then we go with it. Harley does get a bit gung-ho about Finch, and we don't want Erebus getting the wrong idea and putting her in danger."

Santana gazed into his eyes. "As long as he keeps his word, if the worst-case scenario happens, I can live with that."

"*He* is right here," I mumbled. "What happened to the two of you? When you shipped off to the UAE, you could've cut the tension with a knife. And I don't mean the good, sexy kind. Did a djinn put a love spell on you?"

Raffe chuckled. "No, we made our own love spell."

"Could I borrow Huntress to tear out my throat?" I smirked at Nash.

"Careful what you wish for," Nash replied, smirking back.

Santana rolled her eyes at me. "He was speaking metaphorically, dumbass. I realize nuance is hard for your tiny mind to grasp. Anyway, we found out that even if the djinn managed to separate from Erebus, it wouldn't affect the Levi curse. And that got us talking. I made Raffe understand that I want a family with him, even if they're not biologically related to us. And Kadar and Raffe had a chat and concluded that they don't mind being together. So, we're all ready to move forward, accepting that this is our life and our love. And that's worth everything."

"It really is." Raffe kissed Santana tenderly, and I made a well-timed vomiting noise. I didn't want them thinking I'd turned soft, though I was genuinely happy they'd patched up the holes in their relationship. They were one of the most solid couples of the SDC. If they couldn't make it, what chance did the rest of us have?

"Before Finch ruins any more of our romantic reaffirmations of enduring love, we're going home." Santana kissed Raffe again, undoubtedly to make a point. "Ryann, that means you, as well."

Ryann grumbled incoherently.

"What's that?" Santana gave her a stern look.

"I said, whenever you're ready." Ryann smiled sweetly, but I sensed her reluctance.

Santana went to the far wall and drew a chalk door. The lines fizzed, and Raffe opened the door for Santana, ever the chivalrous knight, revealing the Alton Waterhouse Room. The happy couple stepped through first, Ryann bringing up the rear. On the threshold, Ryann turned, her gaze resting on me for a fleeting moment. Her brow furrowed. And then she was gone, the door closing behind them.

What did that mean? Maybe nothing. But why did she stop and look at me? She hadn't glanced at anyone else. Women would never make sense to me, but that momentary look was enough to make me wonder...

I turned to look at Melody. "Melody, Melody, Melody, could you tell me—"

"I'm not telling you what she had going on in her head," she interrupted. "I'm learning to be quieter about people's personal feelings."

I pretended to huff. "Not even a tiny morsel?"

"Nope."

Of all the times to get Empath-shy, why'd it have to be now? I'd have given anything to find out what was in Ryann's mind. I was about to press Melody, putting on my Finch charm, when Mary Foster emerged through the wall and floated toward me.

"This is all exceedingly exciting," she cried. "I did not care for that rude fellow's brusque tone through those bulbous contraptions up there, but it made for a most rousing scene. And if you do happen to die, Finch, you will always be welcome here."

My stomach churned. "Uh... thanks, Miss Foster. Good to know."

"So, what is next on your thrilling agenda?" Mary bobbed eagerly, hands clasped.

I went to the tin box on the table and closed the lid. "I take these to Erebus and see where it leads us."

"And what about ensuring your survival?" Melody leaned against the table. "Davin escaped by allying himself with a djinn, right? Perhaps you can do the same, without the Necromancy aspect."

"You mean, without the key ingredient?" I sighed heavily. "Death is the only end to Erebus's service. And if I can't resurrect myself, then I'd just be... well, dead. But maybe you're right—maybe I can get a different amulet that'll keep me off Erebus's radar. Or I'll go after

Davin and give it the old college try, see if the mojo transfers to us non-Necromancers."

Melody nodded effusively. "You'd only need one resurrection. Perhaps it can grant you that, even if it's not normally one of your skills."

"Sounds like your best chance," Luke chimed in.

I puffed air out of my lips. "Maybe…"

"We'll get it from that devil. You mark my words." Nash grinned, his eyes shining. "And when we've wrung him dry, I look forward to ending him, for everything he's done to me. Let the hunter become the hunted for once. But don't go thinking Davin will give anything away for free. It'll cost us."

"Believe me, I know that much," I replied.

Nash chuckled. "That said, I have no problem helping you torture that scumbag for whatever he's got. In case you were wondering, I *will* be coming with you. I'm not missing this opportunity for anything."

"I wouldn't ask you to." I paused, my determination growing. "We'll find a way to make him squeal like the mucky old pig he is."

While revenge on Davin would have to wait, Erebus couldn't. Wasting no time, I whipped out my phone and sent him a text:

I have the blood.

Short and to the point. Still, I'd never get used to sending a Child of Chaos a text of any kind. It was like sending the Queen of England a quick: *u ok hon?*

My phone pinged almost immediately.

Where?

Huh… That was odd. Gone were the autocorrect nightmares of his usual letter-esque endeavors into the digital world. Just a one-sentence text, no "Dear Flinch" in sight. *San Jose,* I texted back.

Another ping made my heart race, though not in the nice way. *Meet me in the industrial park immediately. Same place as before.*

"What's got you so rattled?" Nash peered at me from across the table. I hadn't realized I *was* rattled, but now that he pointed it out... he was right. Erebus's uncharacteristic texting made me nervous about the mood I might find him in. He should've been jumping for joy. Not that Erebus would ever do that, but figuratively, at least. And those brief responses weren't the hallmark of an ecstatic Child of Chaos.

"Erebus." I nodded to the tin box. "I have to deliver this."

Nash snorted. "He texts now?"

"Oh yeah. He's getting more human by the day. You just wait until he starts Tweeting." I heaved a sigh and tucked the box under my arm.

Melody put her hand on my shoulder. "Do you want someone to come with you?"

I opened my mouth to start the usual diatribe, but she jumped in before I could.

"And before you chatter about the danger, I don't mean one of us actually going and meeting Erebus with you. I just mean one of us coming along for moral support and hanging back while you make the exchange."

I relaxed. "Thanks for the offer, but it's easier if I do this alone. If I'm not back in half an hour, you can assume I'm either dead or shivering on a clifftop somewhere, on a new mission."

"Don't say that!" She looked horrified.

"Bad taste. Sorry." I offered an apologetic grin. "But I should get going."

To my surprise, Melody pulled me into a hug. "I know you hate physical contact, but deal with it for a minute. I'm a hugger."

"Luke is staring," I whispered. Even if I hadn't been able to see his puppy-dog eyes over her shoulder, I'd have sensed his envy a mile off. He might as well have whined like Huntress.

She pulled away sharply and made a show of dusting my arms like a worried mom sending her kid off to college. "You be safe, Finch."

"I will," I replied with a smile.

Nash stood up and extended his hand. "We're going to make this worth it, right? We're going to give that lowlife hell, one of these days?"

"You bet your finest plaid shirt we are." I shook his hand. It felt like a weird goodbye, considering I'd hopefully see them all again within the hour. But Nash probably still had nerves about this, so I didn't mind giving the guy some reassurance.

He smirked. "Nothing wrong with plaid, pal."

I took my bloody goods and headed for the exit. The three of them followed me to the door, looking like a dysfunctional family as they waved me off.

Once I was free of the Winchester House and its spiritual defenses, I opened the tin box and removed the three extra vials, slipping them into my pocket to stow for backup. If my mother had taught me anything, it was to always have a backup for your backup, and even another backup after that, if possible.

With the vials safely hidden, I used my charmed chalk to draw a doorway to the rat-infested alley outside the industrial park where I'd met Erebus before. This time, since I knew exactly where I was going, I didn't have to rely on pricey cabbies charging me an arm and a leg to circle the block a few times. The edges of the doorway crackled as I whispered the *Aperi Si Ostium* spell, then opened onto the grim expanse of massive warehouses and foul-smelling dumpsters. The scent hit me the moment I walked through—that heady aroma of rotting food and chemical waste.

"Erebus?" I called into the gloom. This place was way worse after sunset. The wailing police sirens in the distance did nothing to help my anxiety.

"Over here." Erebus emerged from behind a dumpster, looking— dare I say—a bit disheveled. His sleek shirt had come untucked from his pants, a few buttons undone. His pants showed a few smudges and dark, unsettling stains along the legs.

I approached hesitantly. "Everything peachy, Erebus? I thought you'd dance a jig after hearing I had your blood."

"As if you don't already know." His dark eyes glinted, but it wasn't an angry glint. More of a miffed glitter.

"Know what?" I wanted to see how much he'd found out about the crumbling cookie of his domain.

"You fraternize with djinn. Don't play coy, as I lack the energy for our usual witty repartee. You already know what I am contending with," he replied, his tone cold.

"Hey, the only djinn I know just turned up before I texted you, and he's apparently wiped out. I didn't have much time to chat with him. I have no idea what's going on."

I kept up the ruse, just in case he thought I was somehow responsible. I might've been friggin' euphoric that he'd lost his otherworld to the djinn he'd enslaved, but that didn't mean I wanted to pay for what they'd done. For once, it literally had nothing to do with me.

Erebus paused uncertainly. "You don't know?"

"Know what?"

"That those ungrateful beasts severed themselves from me and stole my otherworld." He stiffened, his hands shaking with quiet rage.

I feigned astonishment. "What?"

"I felt the detachment a short while ago and attempted to return to Tartarus to investigate, only to be rebuffed by my own realm," he hissed, staring at the dumpster as if he wanted to flip it. "Unable to connect to the djinn network, I was left in the dark, and literally left out in the cold. Until a Chaos spirit visited me. That vile witch, the so-called Storyteller. One of my first, now my ultimate betrayer—giving herself to free those cursed wretches. She told me all before she returned to the Chaos stream. A last jab, in utter defiance of every-thing I did for them!"

I gulped. This quiet anger was worse than his usual booming fury. "I didn't even know that was possible."

His lips twisted into a grimace. "You couldn't have. Nobody but her could have. I showed too much to her; I trusted my creations too keenly. And now they have stabbed me in the back."

Phew... I guessed I was off the hook. Although, it felt a little too easy. Maybe I'd gotten lucky this time.

"Can't you make more?" I suggested.

"That is beside the point, Finch!" he snapped. "Of course I can, but that does not lessen the traitorous sting of what they have done. And creating more will mean creating a new Nexus, as the Storyteller destroyed what I had carefully crafted in the undertaking of this mass treachery. But perhaps the djinn were due for an improvement. Had this come at another time, I might have welcomed the challenge of conjuring new entities, far greater and certainly more loyal than before. But I have a veritable mountain of toil to get through, and now those weak specimens have gone and added to it."

I frowned. "Does that mean Atlantis is off the table for now?"

"You would like that, wouldn't you?" He sneered. "But no, that is not the case. I may not be able to undo what they have done, but I will

392 • FINCH MERLIN AND THE DJINN'S CURSE

deal with the djinn and reclaim my otherworld in due time. Atlantis
remains my first priority. Sorry to disappoint you. Now, you said you
had what I require?"

I held out the tin box. "Yep, all here and accounted for." Not exactly
true, but he had the number he'd asked for.

He lifted the lid and checked the vials before closing it again.
"Good work."

Good work? Seriously? That creeped me out even more. Erebus had
become someone I didn't recognize, distant and wrapped up in his
own thoughts, and a little shaken by what had happened with the
djinn. No snark or sass, just a simple "good work" for my efforts. Man,
whatever he wanted in Atlantis truly had to be worth it if he was
paying this price for it. He'd lost his djinn minions, and therefore his
pseudo-omniscience, and he'd lost what was probably the only home
he'd ever had—I didn't know much about his origin story, so I
couldn't say for sure. All for the sake of Atlantis.

"The djinn were meant to be part of my legacy in the mortal world.
How easily such things are lost... and how unexpectedly that which
we create, with painstaking care, can be taken away," he said,
unprompted. "But I might yet regain that chance, that hope, that
dream of a legacy, when I leave my mark on Atlantis. It is all I have
now."

Holy butterballs... is he... emoting? Sincerely? His voice sounded
faraway, underscored by a hint of pain. This usurpation by the djinn
had really hit him hard. And why wouldn't it? They were his children,
in a way, and they'd collectively decided they didn't want him
anymore. I wasn't about to put my arm around the guy and hand him
tissues, or even muster a "there, there" for him, but it made for some
weird spectating. The almighty Prince of Darkness, reduced to a lost,

worried semi-human before my eyes. Honestly, I had no idea what to do with that.

"I must be going. There is much to do, and no djinn to assist me. But at least I have you, Finch." Erebus snapped out of it, casting me a sardonic smile. "This is why making deals with mortals is more efficient than granting life to unworthy beasts. I will call on you again in due course. Expect my summons."

Taking the tin box, he twisted his hand and evaporated in a flash of black smoke and red light, leaving me alone in the darkened alleyway. The scent of decay in my nostrils and the confusion of witnessing a half-broken Erebus bounced around my head. Had he not been a titanic assclown, I might've felt sympathy for him. But, the truth was, he'd hit a losing streak, and that felt damn good. His world was unraveling before him, slipping through his fingers.

As I drew a doorway back to the Winchester House, I patted the spare vials of blood in my pocket—my insurance policy. The prospect of my freedom made it impossible to care for Erebus's suffering, and now that I'd seen him at his lowest point, it made me realize just how weak this road to Atlantis had made him. Nash and I wanted to punish Erebus for his crimes against us, but it looked like the universe had started that ball rolling. If there was any justice, he'd finally find out what it felt like to be brought to a snapping point by circumstances and forces beyond his control, the way he'd done to us.

If I had my way, Erebus wouldn't leave any legacy at all. In any world.

HARLEY MERLIN 13: Finch Merlin and the Locked Gateway

Dear Reader,

Harley Merlin 13: **Finch Merlin and the Locked Gateway** releases **November 7th, 2019**.

Whose head will we get a peek into next? :)

Visit www.bellaforrest.net for details!

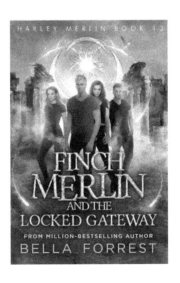

See you there…

Love,

Bella x

P.S. Join my VIP email list and you'll be the first to know when I have a new book out. Visit here to sign up:

www.morebellaforrest.com

(Your email will be kept 100% private and you can unsubscribe at any time.)

P.P.S. Feel free to come say hi on **Twitter** @ashadeofvampire; **Facebook** www.facebook.com/BellaForrestAuthor; or **Instagram** @ashadeofvampire

Read more by Bella Forrest

DARKLIGHT

(BRAND NEW! Fantasy)

Darklight (Book 1)

Darkthirst (Book 2)

HARLEY MERLIN

Harley Merlin and the Secret Coven (Book 1)

Harley Merlin and the Mystery Twins (Book 2)

Harley Merlin and the Stolen Magicals (Book 3)

Harley Merlin and the First Ritual (Book 4)

Harley Merlin and the Broken Spell (Book 5)

Harley Merlin and the Cult of Eris (Book 6)

Harley Merlin and the Detector Fix (Book 7)

Harley Merlin and the Challenge of Chaos (Book 8)

Harley Merlin and the Mortal Pact (Book 9)

Finch Merlin and the Fount of Youth (Book 10)

Finch Merlin and the Lost Map (Book 11)

Finch Merlin and the Djinn's Curse (Book 12)

Finch Merlin and the Locked Gateway (Book 13)

THE GENDER GAME

(Action-adventure/romance. Completed series.)

The Gender Game (Book 1)

The Gender Secret (Book 2)

The Gender Lie (Book 3)

The Gender War (Book 4)

The Gender Fall (Book 5)

The Gender Plan (Book 6)

The Gender End (Book 7)

THE GIRL WHO DARED TO THINK

(Action-adventure/romance. Completed series.)

The Girl Who Dared to Think (Book 1)

The Girl Who Dared to Stand (Book 2)

The Girl Who Dared to Descend (Book 3)

The Girl Who Dared to Rise (Book 4)

The Girl Who Dared to Lead (Book 5)

The Girl Who Dared to Endure (Book 6)

The Girl Who Dared to Fight (Book 7)

THE CHILD THIEF

(Action-adventure/romance. Completed series.)

The Child Thief (Book 1)

Deep Shadows (Book 2)

Thin Lines (Book 3)

Little Lies (Book 4)

Ghost Towns (Book 5)

Zero Hour (Book 6)

HOTBLOODS

(Supernatural adventure/romance. Completed series.)

Hotbloods (Book 1)

Coldbloods (Book 2)

Renegades (Book 3)

Venturers (Book 4)

Traitors (Book 5)

Allies (Book 6)

Invaders (Book 7)

Stargazers (Book 8)

A SHADE OF VAMPIRE SERIES

(Supernatural romance/adventure)

Series 1: Derek & Sofia's story

A Shade of Vampire (Book 1)

A Shade of Blood (Book 2)

A Castle of Sand (Book 3)

A Shadow of Light (Book 4)

A Blaze of Sun (Book 5)

A Gate of Night (Book 6)

A Break of Day (Book 7)

Series 2: Rose & Caleb's story

A Shade of Novak (Book 8)

A Bond of Blood (Book 9)

A Spell of Time (Book 10)

A Chase of Prey (Book 11)

A Shade of Doubt (Book 12)

A Turn of Tides (Book 13)

A Dawn of Strength (Book 14)

A Fall of Secrets (Book 15)

An End of Night (Book 16)

Series 3: The Shade continues with a new hero...

A Wind of Change (Book 17)

A Trail of Echoes (Book 18)

A Soldier of Shadows (Book 19)

A Hero of Realms (Book 20)

A Vial of Life (Book 21)

A Fork of Paths (Book 22)

A Flight of Souls (Book 23)

A Bridge of Stars (Book 24)

Series 4: A Clan of Novaks

A Clan of Novaks (Book 25)

A World of New (Book 26)

A Web of Lies (Book 27)

A Touch of Truth (Book 28)

An Hour of Need (Book 29)

A Game of Risk (Book 30)

A Twist of Fates (Book 31)

A Day of Glory (Book 32)

Series 5: A Dawn of Guardians

A Dawn of Guardians (Book 33)

A Sword of Chance (Book 34)

A Race of Trials (Book 35)

A King of Shadow (Book 36)

An Empire of Stones (Book 37)

A Power of Old (Book 38)

A Rip of Realms (Book 39)

A Throne of Fire (Book 40)

A Tide of War (Book 41)

Series 6: A Gift of Three

A Gift of Three (Book 42)

A House of Mysteries (Book 43)

A Tangle of Hearts (Book 44)

A Meet of Tribes (Book 45)

A Ride of Peril (Book 46)

A Passage of Threats (Book 47)

A Tip of Balance (Book 48)

A Shield of Glass (Book 49)

A Clash of Storms (Book 50)

Series 7: A Call of Vampires

A Call of Vampires (Book 51)

A Valley of Darkness (Book 52)

A Hunt of Fiends (Book 53)

A Den of Tricks (Book 54)

A City of Lies (Book 55)

A League of Exiles (Book 56)

A Charge of Allies (Book 57)

A Snare of Vengeance (Book 58)

A Battle of Souls (Book 59)

Series 8: A Voyage of Founders

A Voyage of Founders (Book 60)

A Land of Perfects (Book 61)

A Citadel of Captives (Book 62)

A Jungle of Rogues (Book 63)

A Camp of Savages (Book 64)

A Plague of Deceit (Book 65)

An Edge of Malice (Book 66)

A Dome of Blood (Book 67)

A Purge of Nature (Book 68)

Season 9: A Birth of Fire

A Birth of Fire (Book 69)

A Breed of Elements (Book 70)

A Sacrifice of Flames (Book 71)

A Conspiracy of Realms (Book 72)

A Search for Death (Book 73)

A Piece of Scythe (Book 74)

A Blade of Thieron (Book 75)

A Phantom of Truth (Book 76)

A Fate of Time (Book 77)

Season 10: An Origin of Vampires

The Test (Book 5)

The Spell (Book 6)

BEAUTIFUL MONSTER DUOLOGY

(Supernatural romance)

Beautiful Monster 1

Beautiful Monster 2

DETECTIVE ERIN BOND

(Adult thriller/mystery)

Lights, Camera, GONE

Write, Edit, KILL

For an updated list of Bella's books, please visit her website: www.bellaforrest.net

Join Bella's VIP email list and you'll be the first to know when new books release. Visit to sign up: www.morebellaforrest.com

CPSIA information can be obtained
at www.ICGtesting.com
Printed in the USA
BVHW071938250122
627125BV00002B/114